THE UNLIKEABLE
DEMON HUNTER

Deborah Wilde

te da media
vancouver

Book Layout ©2015 BookDesignTemplates.com

Cover design by Damonza

Library and Archives Canada Cataloguing in Publication

Wilde, Deborah, 1970-, author
        The unlikeable demon hunter / Deborah Wilde.

(Nava Katz ; 1)
Issued in print and electronic formats.
ISBN   978-0-9920709-8-4   (softcover).--ISBN   978-0-9920709-9-1 (EPUB).--ISBN 978-1-988681-00-9 (Kindle)

        I. Title.

PS8645.I4137U55 2017   C813'.6   C2016-907805-1
                                               C2016-907806-X

Praise for *The Unlikeable Demon Hunter*

"She's like Buffy from the wrong side of the tracks. And that's okay with me." - Heroes and Heartbreakers

"...a fun, funny, and unapologetically raunchy new urban fantasy series... a clever guilty pleasure at its best." - Fine Print

"The action sequences are terrific and the humour will have you smiling. Nava is the underdog you will cheer on..." - Uncaged Book Reviews

"The story is emotional, action packed, and fast-paced... It's an intoxicating and invigorating read." - Angel's Guilty Pleasures

"Nava's like the fun-loving, dirty-talking, drink-tossing best friend you'd want to take to the bar. But you'd also want her around, because, you know, demons." – Lady Smut

"...an original entry into the genre..." - BrizzleLass Books

1

Mornings after sucked.

Walks of shame were a necessary evil, but that didn't mean I enjoyed shimmying back into the same trollop togs twice. I picked glitter out of my hair, then straightened my sequined top. I was officially decommissioning it. Multiple washings never quite managed to remove the lingering aura of bad decisions I made while wearing party clothes. My philosophy? Cross my fingers and hope for the most bang for the bucks spent later on new outfits.

The surly cabbie evil-eyed me to hurry up.

I complied, rooting around in my clutch for some crumpled bills before handing them over and stumbling out of the taxi onto the sidewalk.

Fresh air was a godsend after the stale bitter coffee smell I'd been trapped with during the ride. I pressed a finger to my temple, a persistent dull throb stabbing me behind my eyeballs. My residual feel good haze clashed big-time with the glaring sun screaming at me to wake up, and the buzz of a neighbor's lawnmower cutting through the Sunday morning quiet didn't help matters. Best get inside.

Smoothing out my mini skirt, I readied myself for my tame-my-happy-slut-self-to-boring-PG-rating body check when a wave of dizziness crashed through me. Whoa. I brought my gaze back to horizon level, swallowing hard. That sea-sickness technique was doing dick-all so I rummaged in my bag for my ginger chews.

No puking in the bushes, I chided myself, letting the spicy smooth and sweet candy fight my nausea. My mother would toss my bubble ass out if I defiled her precious rhodos.

Again.

The rise and fall of my chest as I took a few deep breaths spotlit a slight problem. My spangly blouse was missing two buttons. And I was missing a bra. Hook-up Dude had been worth the loss of a pair of socks, maybe a bargain bin thong. But the latest in purple push-up technology? No. I allowed myself a second to mourn. It had been a good and loyal bra.

The sex, on the other hand? Total crap. The girls, who were normally perky C cups, seemed a bit subdued. I couldn't blame them. What's-his-name had started out with all the promise of a wild stallion gallop, but he'd ended up more of a gentle trot. I didn't know if the fault lay with the jockey or the ride, but it had been a long time since I'd seen a finish line.

Since I couldn't keep examining my tits on the front walk with Mrs. Jepson side-eyeing me from behind her living room curtains, I thrust my chin up and clacked a staccato rhythm toward my front door on those mini torture chambers that had seemed *such* a good idea yesterday.

Every step made our precisely manicured lawn undulate. I clamped my lips shut, willing the ginger chews to kick in while fumbling my key into the lock. Dad had screwed up the measurements on our striking cedar and stained glass front door and, being a touch too big for the frame, it needed to be shouldered open.

I crashed into the door like a linebacker. Once I'd extricated myself and my keys from the lock, I brushed myself off, and stepped inside. Our house itself was comfortably upper middle class but not huge, since my parents preferred to spend money on trips and books instead of the overpriced real estate found here in Vancouver. A quick glance to my left showed that the TV room was empty. I crossed my fingers that Mom and Dad were out at their squash game, my main reason for picking this specific time to sneak back in.

Really, a twenty-year-old shouldn't have had to sneak. But then again, a twenty-year-old probably should have kept her last menial job for longer than two weeks, so I wasn't in a position to argue rights.

I kicked off my shoes, sighing in delight at the feel of cool tile under my bare feet as I padded through the house to our homey kitchen. No one was in there either. Someone, probably Mom, had tacked the envelope with my final–and only–pay stub from the call center that I'd left lying around onto our small "miscellaneous" cork board. The gleaming quartz counters were now free of their usual clutter of papers, books, and latest gourmet food find. That meant company. Come to think of it, I did hear someone in the living room.

A study in tasteful shades of white, the large formal room was off-limits unless we had special guests. Mom had set that rule when my twin brother Ari and I were little tornados running around the place and while there was no longer a baby gate barring our way, conditioning and several memorable scoldings kept us out.

Hmmm. Could Ari be entertaining an actual human boy? Le gasp.

I beelined for the back of the house, past the row of identically framed family photos hanging in a neat grid, my head cocked. Listening for more voices, but all was quiet. Maybe I'd been wrong? I hoped not. Both finding my brother with a crush–blackmail dirt—and helping myself to the liquor cabinet were positive prospects. What better way to lose that hangover headache than get drunk again? Oh, the joys of being Canadian with socialized health care and legal drinking age of nineteen. After a year (officially) honing that skill, I imbibed at an Olympic level.

The red wine on the modular coffee table gleamed in a shaft of sunlight like its position had been ordained by the gods. I snatched up the crystal decanter, sloshing the liquid into the glass conveniently placed next to it. Once in a while, a girl could actually catch a break.

I fanned myself with one hand. The myriad of lit candles seemed a bit much for Ari's romantic encounter, but wine drinking trumped curiosity so I chugged the booze back. My entire body cheered as the cloyingly-sweet alcohol hit my system, though I hoped it wasn't Manischewitz because hangovers on that were a bitch. I'd slugged back half the contents when I saw my mom on the far side of the room clutch her throat, eyes wide with horror. Not her usual, "you need an intervention" horror. No, her expression indicated I'd reached a whole new level of fuck-up.

"Nava Liron Katz," she gasped in full name outrage.

My cheeks still bulging with wine, I properly scoped out the room. Mom? Check. Dad? Check. Ari?

Check. Rabbi Abrams, here to perform the ceremony to induct my brother as the latest member in the Brotherhood of David, the chosen demon hunters?

Check.

I spit the wine back into what I now realized was a silver chalice and handed it to the elderly bearded rabbi. "Carry on," I told him. Then I threw up on his shoes.

Forty-five minutes later, I huddled on top of the closed toilet seat in my ensuite bathroom sucking the cheesy coating off Doritos while replaying my actions in grisly Technicolor. Even with all the lights off, the room was as bright and insistent as Martha Stewart's smile. A dusty Costco-sized sanitary pad box lay open on the counter–the hiding place for my secret stash of arterial clogging happiness.

Now, though, the chips were less illicit joy and more bite-sized snacks of self-loathing.

I stuck my hand into the bag for another nacho, careful not to crinkle it and give myself away. Hard to say what had been the highlight of that little disaster: drinking the ceremonial wine, vomiting, or the wardrobe malfunction that had released my left boob into the world and caused my dad to strain his back jumping in front of me to block the view.

Go me.

Someone rapped on the door. Chip in mouth like a pacifier, I froze, listening to the raised voices from downstairs–the rabbi yelling, my mother cajoling, and my father reasoning. That left Ari, and right now I was too chickenshit to face him. How could saying sorry cover wrecking the most important moment of his life?

"I know you're eating Doritos," he called from outside the door. "Let me in."

"Nope." I swallowed down the now-mushy chip and gave a lusty groan. "I'm making a hate crime."

"If that were true, you'd be running the water because you're paranoid people will learn you have an anus." He jiggled the knob. "Let me in."

I glared at the tap, assigning blame to the inanimate object for failing to carry out its part of my brilliant plan. Dumping the bag down on the counter with a sigh, I washed orange nacho residue off my hands before I tightened the belt on the fuzzy housecoat now wrapped around me, and unlocked the door.

"I'm so, so sorry, Ari," I said, hanging my head. My fraternal twin deserved all the success and more. Ari never treated me like I was "less than" in any way, not even once. "I know you have no reason to believe me but–"

"Shut up," he said, brushing past me in his navy fitted suit. Very bespoke, except for the tired slump of his shoulders.

He lowered himself down on to the edge of the bathtub, knocking one of the many bottles of citrusy shampoo into the tub. With one hand braced on the mosaic shower tiles for support, he removed his kippah, tossing it onto the counter where its embroidered, gold Star of David winked among the chaos of make-up and hair pins.

"Damn, that itches." He scratched his blond head with a relieved sigh, then jerked his chin at the Doritos bag still in my hand. "You gonna share?"

I locked the door, returned to my throne seat, and held the chips out between us.

We sat there in companionable silence, munching through the party-sized bag.

"These are so disgusting," Ari said, stuffing about ten of them in his mouth.

I reached over and brushed orange crumbs off his suit. "Careful, bubeleh. Wouldn't want you to get dirty. Oh, if the elders knew that their healthy-eating chosen one was up here taking years off his life."

"Eh," he said, spraying chips. "I'd just blame you, o defiler of innocents."

"Useful having an evil twin, isn't it?" My tone was light; my stomach twisted.

He wiped his mouth. "Don't give yourself that much credit. You're not evil. Just misguided."

I drew myself up to my full height. "That's a terrible thing to say."

We finished the bag, then elbowed each other for first rights of tap water. A quick sip later and I slid onto the brown cork floor, bloated and happy. Well, as happy as I could be.

"I don't know how you're not puking given you were still drunk an hour ago," Ari said.

"These chips have magic properties. Plus, I got it all out of my system on the carpet."

He shuddered. "Don't remind me. I think Mom is angrier about that than your spectacular entrance. She was a fairly impressive mottled red when I left her."

"Merlot or tomato?"

"Nava Red," my brother replied. "A special shade named in honor of you."

"Why were you doing the ritual anyway?" I snapped. "The induction is tomorrow. The sixth."

"Or, today, the sixth."

Shit! I hugged my knees into my chest. "Ari–"

He stood up, one hand raised to cut me off. "No. You really want to apologize? Take a shower and get dressed so that I have one person who wants to be at this ceremony for me. Not for status or whatever the hell I am to those people down there."

"Ace," I gasped, "isn't this what you want?"

He affixed the kippah back on his head, staring at his reflection in the mirror above the sink for a long moment. "I've never had a chance to decide whether I wanted it or not. We were five days old when they determined I was an initiate. I didn't get a vote."

We'd both seen the photo of our parents' stunned faces when a somewhat younger, yet still astonishingly ancient Rabbi Abrams had visited my mother–a descendent of King David–to check Ari out. Since the Brotherhood is top secret, my parents weren't clued in to the true nature of the rabbi's visit until after he'd determined Ari as an initiate: a chosen demon hunter. The photo in question had been taken after a lot of explanations and convincing that yes, this was all real, and yes, their son had a hell of an important destiny.

I went into my bedroom to grab some clean clothes to put on after my shower.

Back in the day, and by day I'm talking Old Testament, this shepherd called David took out the giant Goliath for King Saul. While that landed David his place in history, there was more to him than his crazy rock-slinging skills.

I don't know if David was an adrenaline junkie or a major do-gooder but when King Saul was later possessed by a demon, David was all "leave it to me," and cast the hell spawn out. Guess David figured demon removal was a good public service to keep up, because once *he* became king around 1010 B.C.E., he gathered up his buddies to continue the work. Kick-ass Jews. Awesome.

Though it had never made sense why he called his hunters Rasha–the Hebrew word for "wicked."

I tossed my clothes over the hook affixed to the back of the bathroom door. "Talk to me."

My brother had spent his entire life studying and training in preparation for the day he was formally inducted into the Brotherhood. I cocked an eyebrow at Ari, annoyed when he shrugged off my question. "Don't pretend you aren't excited to see what magic power you'll end up with."

His eyes lit up for a second. "Telekinesis or light bender. Those would be cool." He jerked a thumb at the shower and I obediently ran the tap, waiting for the water to hit blistering temperature.

"Slime generator or asphyxiation via lethal ass gas, more like."

"Ha. Ha." Ari gnawed on his bottom lip.

"You want out?" I cracked my knuckles. "You could totally take all three of them downstairs. I'll help."

He shrugged, the motion bunching the dark fabric around his muscles. "I don't know what else I'd do. What else I'm good for."

I poked his bicep. "Kill the pity party, Mr. Perfect GPA. I'm sure between your chem major and biology minor some giant pharmaceutical company somewhere will have a small fortune and loads of interesting problems for you." I wasn't jealous. He and I didn't roll that way. He may have been chosen and wicked smart but the only thing that bugged me about him was that he had prettier lashes than me. It was always the boys with those camel eyes. So unfair.

I tested the water temperature, shaking droplets off my hand until, satisfied with its magma levels of hot, I pulled the knob up to send the water cascading full blast through the shower head.

Ari mussed my hair. "You're gonna do something great some day too," he said. I smacked his hand off of my head. "You just need to find your thing." He rushed that second sentence as if hoping I wouldn't remember that I'd found my thing a long time ago and the chances of finding something else I loved as much were pretty slim.

"Yeah, yeah, whatever." I pushed him toward the door. "Go keep them from cutting me out of the will. I'll be there in ten. The picture of respectability."

Ari snorted. "Don't strain yourself. I'll settle for clean." He sniffed me, fanning in front of his face with a grimace. "Screwing hobos again?"

"College boys. Same, same." I reached for the belt of my housecoat.

He unlocked the door, half-twisting back to me. "Would you care? If I didn't do it?"

I paused, belt still tied. "God, no. The few Rasha I ever met were dick-swinging balls of testosterone. Though I'd hoped for your sake some of them were also dick-sucking. Like that smexy Brazilian they brought in last year to train you in Capoeira."

He failed to appreciate my eyebrow waggle. "Why do I bother?"

King David had realized pretty early on that even if he rid Israel of demons, there was a reason they were part of every culture's mythology. Demons were an international problem. Since Jerusalem was close to this trade route called the King's Highway, David sent his band far and wide to find all the best specimens of manhood from various races and religions including Muslims, Egyptians, Phoenicians, Celts, and Thracians to fight the good fight. The Brotherhood was formed.

It was kind of cool to see how far ranging those original bloodlines had traveled into present day. But what wasn't cool was how serious and stressed my brother was, so I smacked my lips, hell-bent on getting a smile. "Mmm. High quality Brazilian meat."

Ari made a sound of disgust and whipped my loofah glove at me. I ducked, laughing, and it sailed into my shower. "What? You don't want a boyfriend? All those butchy men?" I leered at him. "Odds are good there'd be some friends of Dorothy in that crew."

His lips quirked, despite his best efforts to look stern. "I have no time for dating."

"Me neither. But *I* have a whole bunch of sex instead. Something you, my dear older brother, could use. Regular doing of the nasty might loosen you up."

"I'm loose," he said, tightening his tie.

"Yeah." I shoved him out the door. "A regular whore of Babylon. Now get outta here. I've got to pretty up."

One thing I'd say in my favor, I was not one of those girls who took forever to get ready. I was showered and dressed in something practically Amish in the allotted ten minutes. I twisted my hair into a sleek chignon, and fresh faced, headed downstairs.

Time for my close up, Mr. Demille. Bowing my head, I shuffled into the living room.

"Forgive me, Rabbi." I prostrated myself like a wedding guest begging the Godfather for a favor. "I was involved in a car accident on my way home," I lied. I stood up again. "It's why I needed a drink. I was so rattled." I infused as much pathos into my voice as possible while blinking up at him. Tricky, since I was four inches taller, but not impossible. "I'm sure you've never had that problem."

Men, whether straight, gay, holy, or otherwise, could be such suckers. The rabbi patted my hand in forgiveness, his touch papery dry. "You need to show more respect, Navela," he said, using the Yiddish diminutive of my name.

I nodded, side-stepping around the wet-yet-once-more-spotlessly-clean former puke site on the white, short-velvet-pile carpet. "You're so right. I should come to schul. Isn't your son the Cantor at Park

West Synagogue? Such a beautiful voice when he prays."

A look of abject horror contorted the rabbi's features at the terrifying prospect of me getting my hands on his precious son. Trust me, the guy was a middle-aged balding chub. I had zero designs on his person.

"Start small," Rabbi Abrams said.

While the rabbi had mentored Ari his entire life, having served as a head demon-hunter coach, my contact with him had been limited. In addition to coordinating training and fight instructors, he also taught my brother everything from demon types to creating wards and learning the various aspects of the Brotherhood itself. Ari tended to get pretty vague on those details.

"Shana," the rabbi called out to my mother. "Now that the entire family is here, we can start the ceremony again."

My mother handed him the newly washed chalice. "Of course, Rabbi." Mom watched him shuffle off to prepare something, trailing a faint smell of mothballs in his wake, then, patting her sleek honey-colored bob, stepped past me with a murmured, "Carnage *and* lies? A busy morning."

Mom was a lot harder to fool. A whip-smart, tenured history professor at the University of British Columbia with an annoying tendency to recall events best forgotten, she was also a best-selling author of, big surprise, a tome on King David.

My dad, Dov, dark-haired like me, was a prof, too. Law. Oy vey. Everything was fact-gathering to build a case with him. Case in point, he walked stiffly into the room, courtesy of his recent back injury, all pleated pants and sweater vest, the usual mug of coffee welded to his hand.

I gagged at the smell.

"What's this about a car accident? Was this in the taxi? Did you get the information from him and the other driver?" His questions were gunfire fast. "You'll need it for the claim."

Shit. I hadn't prepared for questioning.

Ace to the rescue. My brother tugged on Dad's sleeve, leading him to his recliner. "Sit. Rabbi wants to start the ceremony." Out of the corner of his mouth he muttered, "You owe me big time."

I gave him a sheepish grin and sat in the brushed twill armchair at the far end like a good little girl, stuffing my hands under my butt.

Rabbi Abrams motioned for Ari to come stand beside him. While the rabbi was the picture of reverence as he lit the first candle, my brother's hand jiggled madly in his pocket.

I threw him a thumbs up. Ari was going to be great.

The rabbi lit the last of the dozen or so large pillar candles on thick glass bases placed in a circle around the living room. The soulless space with its white carpet, white furniture and, wait for it, black and white brocade wallpaper was softened by their glow.

The ceremony involved a lot of singing prayer or chanting or something in Hebrew. I'd pretty much spent my Hebrew school classes reading *Sweet Valley High* so I didn't understand it, but I'd been to synagogue enough that the singing and ritualistic gestures were familiar. The rhythms and cadence of the language lulled me, even soothing my grating headache a bit.

The old guy didn't have a bad voice, probably where his son got his talent, and the ceremony itself was kind of lovely. Even my cold, dead heart couldn't fail to be moved by the reverence and history of this ceremony.

All male descendants of King David–or of any hunter–were tracked as potentials. The first ritual, performed when they were a baby, determined if they could be bumped up to initiate–one who carried the Rasha make-up, versus the regular Muggle descendants. It weeded out about 98% of the potentials. If level two status was unlocked, they were labeled initiates and slated for training. Their second and final ceremony, the official induction to the Brotherhood where they became Rasha, happened at age twenty.

There were a couple of reasons for the wait. First off, it took initiates their entire childhood and adolescence to master the training and studying necessary to take on the gig. And, for more practical reasons, they needed to be inducted once they'd physically stopped growing and were in the prime of health for their body to accept the magic powers that this final ceremony would confer on them. After much trial, error, and loss of life, twenty had been hit on as the magic age.

Rabbi Abrams blessed the wine then handed the chalice to Ari. Once my brother had taken a sip, he dipped his finger in the wine and dripped three fat red drops back into the chalice. A reminder of the precious human blood that would be spilled if they lost their fight against evil.

I discreetly waved off some smudgy smoke, suppressing a tiny smile at my mom doing the exact same thing. If it had been up to my parents, they'd have rented a ballroom and invited every person they'd ever known to watch their little boy become a badass mensch. Let's face it, a demon hunter induction had way more bragging rights than a Bar Mitzvah. But alas, the general populace was not to know the Brotherhood existed, so my parents had to keep quiet about Ari's abilities and his big day today.

I'd always wished Ari's induction would happen in a stone cavern with chanting, hooded members, but old David had mandated humility into Demon Club's mission statement. The chosen one was supposed to selflessly devote his life to demon hunting for the greater good, not personal glory. So it was always just a small ceremony with immediate family, if that, performed in the home.

The rabbi wrapped a small handkerchief around Ari's wrist—white to symbolize piety. Yeah, right. Based on the very few Rasha I'd met, it would take more than a hankie to tamp down their enormous arrogance. Try a textile factory's yearly output.

Rabbi Abrams held fast to the other end of the cloth as he lay his free hand on my brother's head. More Hebrew.

I snuck a look at my parents. To their credit, they didn't look disappointed. In fact, seated there, watching the ceremony with rapt looks, they pretty much glowed with delight.

My own chest warmed in tight mushiness and a tear leaked from my eye, streaking its way down my cheek.

Ouch.

I blinked against the sudden stinging. Everything took on a drugged, underwater quality as the room swam around me. I clasped my hands together, pressing them between my knees. Breathing through my nose. Determined not to mess up the ceremony.

Again.

Ari repeated some Hebrew phrases the rabbi gave him. Aww, look at that twin of mine, embracing his destiny. I focused on my excitement to be here with him as he stepped into his future.

Better him than me.

The edges of my vision flickered. The rabbi's voice, harsh and far too loud, scraped over my skin. Clapping my hands over my ears didn't help. My flesh broke out in goosebumps as whispers sounded around me. A million voices, a million Rasha spirits brought together to welcome the newly chosen.

Carpet fibers pricked the soles of my feet as I stood up. The room spun. Sweat dotted my brow, slid between my shoulder blades.

The rabbi had his back to me but Ari glanced over, a flash of concern rippling through his serious expression.

Did I have delayed alcohol poisoning? I pulled at the neck of my shirt, fighting for air. Was that even a thing?

Rabbi Abrams opened a small, intricately carved box, revealing the fat gold ring that would mark Ari as one of the chosen. Gold from the ancient Judaic symbol for divine or celestial light, a holy blessing sought since David's time.

Propelled by a force beyond my control, I opened my hand, reaching for the ring. Every atom inside me screamed out for that band.

"Sheli." Huh? How did I suddenly know the Hebrew word for "mine?"

The ring floated free to hover in mid-air.

Every head in the room whipped my way. Mom tensed, her body straining forward to look at me. Dad's eyes widened, his coffee mug falling to the floor, brown liquid pooling in a sludge.

Ari and Rabbi Abrams gaped slack-jawed at me.

"Sheli," I repeated, trance-like. My voice was a deep, rich, resonating command. Even though I was freaking out at my total lack of ability to control my actions, I also felt a deep sense of rightness in my gut as I spoke.

That freaked me out more.

The ring launched across the room to fit itself on my right index finger with the mother of all electric shocks. My hair blew back off my face. I snapped out of the trance, once more in full-control of my faculties.

"Fucking hell!" I cursed, shaking out my hand while jumping up and down.

The candles snuffed out, leaving everyone in stunned silence.

Ari was the first to move. He reached over and snapped the ring box in Rabbi Abrams' hand shut with a thud that cracked like gunfire. "It appears you had the wrong twin," he said. He hefted the silver chalice. "L'chaim," he toasted and slugged the whole thing back.

2

"I don't want it," I protested for about the hundredth time, yanking on the ring.

"It won't come off." Rabbi Abrams' face was so wrinkled up in horrified anxiety that he resembled a Shar Pei with a Dumbledore beard.

"It's water weight. Bloating." I ran for the kitchen, dumping half a bottle of dish soap over both my finger and the stainless steel sink. "Move, you motherfucker," I muttered, pulling on it with all my might.

The ring spun round and round in the thick yellow goo, but wouldn't move even a millimeter closer to my knuckle. A hamsa, a palm-shaped design with two symmetrical thumbs meant to ward off the evil eye, was engraved in the center of the band. The single open eye etched into the middle of the palm stared up at me with its tiny blue sapphire iris.

I swear it smirked.

Ari swaggered in. He'd abandoned the chalice and was now swigging directly from the bottle.

"Take it," I hissed, grabbing his wrist.

"Fingers keepers." He flicked my hand away with a painful snap. Soap splattered on to my shirt.

"That is enough of that." My mother marched into the kitchen and snatched the bottle out of his hand, slamming it down on the counter with such force that a chip of white quartz flew off. "You, stop drinking. And you," she whirled on me, finger wagging, "take that ring off right now."

"Have at it." I thrust out my hand at her.

Mom couldn't get the ring off either. "Dov." She smacked her hand on the dented countertop to get Dad's attention. He hovered in the doorway with his mouth half open, in full brain short-circuit mode. Even my boob flying free hadn't upset him this much.

Her second smack shook him out of his Medusa-victim impression.

"Right." Dad hurried over and reached for the ring, but hesitated, his hand hovering just over mine.

I shoved my hand into his. "Get it off me, Daddy," I said in a voice two-octaves too high.

He tried. God knows he tried.

As did Rabbi Abrams, who insisted on running the ceremony again. Of course, he had to do it with Ari sprawled in the recliner because he was now hammered. My brother, the light-weight.

I spent the ceremony holding my breath, my gut knotted into a pretzel as I awaited the outcome.

The rabbi got to the end and tugged on the ring. Nada.

"How could you?" Mom asked, back in the kitchen where we'd reconvened in a glum silence. She twisted her hands together so forcefully, I worried she might break something.

"What part of 'chosen' implies I had any say in the matter?" I bit down on the band, trying to budge it with my teeth.

It was cold and tasted of metal and imprisonment.

Ari belched. "Told you, you'd find your thing." Having reclaimed the wine bottle, he now shook the last few drops into his mouth. "'Course, I didn't expect it to be my thing."

That hurt. I hadn't done this deliberately and I certainly didn't want to be part of a *Brotherhood*. I scrubbed a hand over my face, way too sober to handle taking the blame for this. "You didn't even know if you wanted it, asshole."

My brother wasn't phased. "Too true. But," he said, looking off thoughtfully, "I think that was pre-wedding jitters." He met my eyes; those distinct blue-gray twins of my own that always let me know what he was thinking. Right now the sorrow in them broke my heart. "I think that in fact, I did. Want it," he said.

I dropped my head on the counter.

"Fix this," Mom demanded of the rabbi. "Nava isn't a boy. She can't be Rasha."

My head jerked up. Ari's sorrow and my parents' incredulity were understandable. It just would have been nice if for one second, any of them had stopped to ask me how *I* was doing with all this. Because I wanted to run. Hide away until Demon Club proclaimed that this terrible joke had gone on long enough and we could all return to our regularly scheduled programming, where Ari was the bright shiny twin with a destiny and I most decidedly was not.

"Way to set women's rights back two hundred years, Mom," I snapped. For once, I was innocent of any wrong-doing, but no one could see that. No one cared.

"She didn't mean all women. Just you, honey," Dad said to me in his infuriating, even-handed way. He extended an arm to the rabbi, leading him to the heavily-nicked kitchen table. Twins were a bitch on furniture.

"Let's be logical here," my father said. "Does it matter if some ritual picked Nava? Ari is the one who is trained and competent. He's devoted his life toward this goal. What if we simply ignored this as an odd blip and proceeded with the plan as is?"

Most of me cheered this sentiment. Was completely on-board. A tiny part of me desperately wished that one person had my back.

"Nava is the chosen," Rabbi Abrams said. "She can do this." Wow. Of all the people to champion me. The rabbi stroked his beard. "If Ari takes on demons without a Rasha's power, he will die. Better to let Nava handle them, trained or not."

That sounded suspiciously like "send out the expendable." I snatched the dish towel off its hook and savagely dried my saliva off of my hand.

The rabbi was right. It was the magic that killed demons. Pumping one full of lead might slow it down, but then again, it might simply piss it off enough to rip your head off faster.

Obviously, Ari couldn't go after a demon without having magic power. That was tantamount to a suicide mission, but I refused to believe that he was definitively out of the picture. This destiny fit him with a snug certainty.

"There has to be a loophole," I said.

Dad touched his index finger to his nose then pointed at me like I'd brought up a valid idea. "You can't expect the fate of the world to be in my daughter's hands," he said. "Might as well invite Satan to move on in and throw him a housewarming party."

"Really?" I asked, tossing the towel on the counter.

Dad shrugged. "Do you think you're capable of battling demons?"

I refused to confirm or deny, leaning forward to address Rabbi Abrams directly. "Do I have a say in this?"

The rabbi struggled up out of the chair, came over to me, and laid a gnarled arthritic hand on my shoulder. His knuckles were old-people-XL sized. I tried not to flinch–or think of demon claws. Good luck. A mélange of weirdo animal parts and other unholy bits fused into demony shape assaulted me in image form, courtesy of every nightmare bedtime story Ari had ever foisted on me. I shuddered.

"This situation is..." Rabbi Abrams frowned.

"Unfortunate? Unfair?" I supplied.

"A tragedy," he said.

"Excuse me?!"

He dropped his hand, giving a sharp tug to his black suit jacket. "I need to inform the Executive. We must figure out how best to proceed." He sounded like I'd murdered his favorite puppy and was asking him to shake my blood-drenched hand. Symbolically, that may have been true.

My hands tightened on the hem of my shirt. "Again, I ask if I have a say in the matter?"

Rabbi Abrams frowned, his expression stern. "You cannot ignore your power. Your destiny."

I threw him a grim smile. Challenge accepted.

My first order of business was sneaking out of the house. Mom and Dad rehashing the impossibility of it, the *tragedy* of it, was bad enough. But Ari refusing to speak to me? He'd sent me a final look of absolute betrayal, staggered into his room, and locked the door.

He'd never locked his door against me before. Our twin connection was as necessary as oxygen. Ari had been my shoulder to cry on when my life had fallen apart, supporting me against the folks when I'd taken a time-out from university, while I'd spent my childhood making my brother laugh whenever I saw that his Rasha studies were getting to him. He protected and anchored me, while I lightened up his world. There was no place for locked doors between us.

The fact that there was now cracked my chest open for the black pain to slither in. If anything could turn me even more firmly against being a demon hunter than I already was, it was that damn door. I'd knocked until my knuckles bled. Begged and pleaded, but I was met with silence. I was dead to him.

It was worse than actually being dead.

Taking shallow breaths, I ran through one of my old exercises to get through pre-show performance jitters. Who knew being on stage and learning how to act happy would come in handy so many times in my almost-adult life?

I rummaged among the clean laundry piled on my desk chair for jeans and my favorite hoodie and got changed. Knocking aside the box in my closet filled with my most prized tap dance competition medals,

I pulled my worn leather backpack out, haphazardly throwing in clothes and toiletries.

I allowed myself one last look around my raspberry bedroom: from the random photos of fun times hanging by now-limp tape, to the collage of speeding tickets spelling out *vroom*, to my unmade bed with exactly three pillows–two to sleep on and one to cuddle–and the clothes and books exploding over every surface.

My lucky sunglasses, the ones "liberated" from Ryan Tedder after I'd sweet-talked my way backstage at a OneRepublic concert, lay on my dresser, under my black and white poster of Gregory Hines. He wore an expression of sheer delight as the camera caught him mid-tap step. Somewhere deep inside me still lived the ghost of a memory where no matter what was wrong in my life, I could dance my troubles away. *A one, a two, you know what to do.* My mantra for dance and life.

Yeah, well. That was then.

I grabbed the glasses, stuffing them on my head. Then I hefted my backpack over one shoulder, and pushed up the window. Tap had been the one place I'd shone. My realm. Yeah, I'd readjusted my life around the void when the dream was taken from me, but why should Ari have to experience crushing disappointment and heartache? At my hands? Fuck that.

Maybe if I ran away, did something selfish, or act-ed unworthy of the power, the ring would decide I wasn't the right twin after all and Ari could resume his path to destiny. The Brotherhood had invested twenty years in him, after all. Hopefully they'd work a little harder to bring him back into the fold.

Taking a deep breath, I swung my leg over the sill and reached for the gnarled tree branch outside my window. My stomach surged in that split second before my fingers connected with the rough bark but once they did, it was an easy climb down. I dropped the final few feet to the ground in a hard crouch, then commenced running away from home, trotting past well-kept family homes toward the main street.

Much as I hated to admit it, my dad was right. Demon Club and I were a terrible fit. First off, it had always been kept secret through the centuries, both to preserve its existence under the official "no de-mons here" stance of organized Judaism, and, since very few knew that demons existed, to keep mass panic from breaking out.

Sure, I'd kept mum about all of it, but let's be serious. If magic powers could score me free clothes or booze, #MoveOverBuffy would be trending by dinner.

I slowed down when I hit the corner house two blocks over, just long enough to stop inches from the fence and do a little dance for the old Golden Retriever, sending her into a yappy frenzy of joy.

Still barking, she jumped onto her hind legs, resting her front paws on the fence so I could scratch her between the ears.

The uptight gay couple that owned her twitched their curtain aside to move me along with a dismissive point of their fingers. I wiggled my ass one last time, snickering at their twin expressions of thin-lipped displeasure. Knowing Goldie would keep barking for another twenty minutes was just an added bonus.

Then I took off.

It might seem amazing that in this age of CCTV and camera phones, where every little transgression was posted to social media, that the Brotherhood and demons managed to remain a secret from both the Jewish community and wider world. As Ari had taught me, the explanation was simple: never underestimate humans' desire to stay within our comfort zones.

Case in point, the yoga-clad mommy mafia clogging up the tree-lined sidewalk, venti lattes in hand. I swerved to avoid their race car pricey strollers and the judgmental stank wafting off them as they eyed me. We all sought affirmation. That's why, as a species, we were such hypercritical assholes. We wanted proof we'd picked the right career or married the right person, even if said proof was of the *at least we're not them variety*. We wanted our lives to tally in the positives column.

Only the whackjob paranormal bloggers some-times got closer to the truth than everyone gave them credit for. Ari and I had spent a bunch of late nights being highly entertained by their theories.

While membership had grown since David's time, the formal structure of the Brotherhood wasn't put into place until October 10, 1871 with the great fire of Chicago. With the city destroyed, hundreds dead, and the entire thing being blamed on a *cow*, the Brotherhood had stepped up and gotten globally organized to make, well, order of the chaos. No more pockets of hunters fighting demons under a loosely affiliated umbrella. They were now ruthlessly effi-cient in the war on evil with chapters all over the world.

Which was the second reason I wanted no part of this. "Ruthless" and "efficient" were not words to describe me. If humanity was depending on me to be part of some protector squad, they were screwed. I'd be dead within minutes of my first demon encounter, destiny notwithstanding.

A horn blared at me, jarring me out of my reverie.

I scrambled across the busy retail street, narrowly avoiding getting pancaked, and stepped onto the far curb in front of the dry cleaners, my heart pounding. "A little respect for the jay-walker here!"

Where was this magic I was supposed to have received? Had there been a glitch because I was female? Because *I* was glitch? If I really had some cool new superpower, wouldn't I have sped after the Mazda and flipped it on its side, mashing it to a pulp with angry pounds of my fists instead of standing here shaking? And if my magic did show up, would I have some stupid or embarrassing power like I'd teased Ari about?

I made my way to the bank machine, opening my wallet to sort through my credit cards. The Visa was bunk. I was scared to even stick it in an ATM for fear some collection agency bruiser would appear to hustle me off. But the AMEX? I tapped it against my chin. This baby was my emergency card, paid in full each month by Daddy Dearest.

Sliding the card into the cash machine, I punched in the ten thousand dollar limit. It made a beeping noise that sounded suspiciously like laughter, informing me in neat print that my cash advance limit was $500. Bah.

The money got tucked deep in an inside pocket in the backpack. Then I boarded the downtown bus, unsure of my destination. What I needed right now was a best friend I could crash with. What I had were tons of fellow partygoers and acquaintances.

The bus driver slammed on his brakes. I stumbled forward, whacking my head on the guitar case of the dude next to me. I'd had an awesome best friend in high school. Leonie Hendricks. It wasn't as if we'd had a fight or anything after grad. We'd still hung out. But Leo had jumped headlong into university while I'd bounced around for a few semesters before withdrawing.

My hand went for my phone. Maybe I could call Leo. I snorted. Yeah, right. We could catch up. Leo could tell me about her criminology classes and I could tell her that in an impossible twist, I was the first lady Rasha and newest member of Demon Club. Oh yeah, and that demons existed. Then she'd roll her eyes sadly at me making a joke of everything, finish our social call with polite small talk, and that would be that.

Well, that decided where I should go. A drink was in order. I headed over to my favorite business district pub for their pint and burger lunch special. A girl had to have a decent last meal, and the football-sized patties this place served would keep me full for a good twenty-four hours. Plus, the barkeep was adorable and amenable to flirting for free refills.

I sailed into the dimly lit interior with its multiple screens offering various sports replays set to classic rock blasting from the speakers, and seated myself at the scarred wood bar.

Josh, my barboy, grinned his hello. "Hey, beautiful," he said, all white teeth, platinum hair, and that unnatural level of pretty attained by certain actors. It was enough to give a girl an inferiority complex. "Haven't seen you around in a while. What can I get you and whatcha been up to?"

"Burger special and becoming the chosen one," I replied with a breezy flip of my curls.

"Sweet."

His attention reaffirmed my determination to stay far away from all things demon and huntery. I was young. I had my looks. Why would I want to mess that up fighting nasty creatures from the bowels of Hell? Or wherever they came from, since they didn't exactly leave a home address and weren't just a Christian concept.

I know Buffy looked good killing vamps, but come on, even I could separate fiction from fact enough to know that a team of hair, make-up, and wardrobe experts were not going to be a perk of my gig. Besides, hunting would cut in to my important to-dos like be adored and get free refills.

I waggled my pint glass at Josh as he placed my burger in front of me, noticing he hadn't skimped on the fries. Salt and grease good. "Thanks, barkeep. What's new with you?"

Turns out he'd landed a small but pivotal role in *Hard Knock Strife*, some big-budget picture shooting here in Vancouver. Something about childhood buddies caught up in the lure of easy money. "That's worth celebrating," I said, raising my new full glass in cheers.

"Stick around till I get off?" He nodded at my backpack, stuffed on the seat beside me, which was ringing for the umpteenth time. "Or do you have plans?"

"Nope." I pulled out my phone and turned it off. But not before glancing at the screen. Seventeen messages all from my home number. My parents, not Ari. With a sigh, I shoved it into my hoodie pocket and threw him a coy look from under my lashes. "I'm all yours."

"I'm counting on it," he replied with a wicked grin.

Ladytown flooded like it was time to start collecting two of every animal. Whoa, baby. Praying that Josh was my golden O ticket, I found myself back at his place hours later, half-drunk, partially naked, and totally giving him the hand job of his life. Doing it for him, in hopes that he'd be able to do it for me. Honestly though, my thoughts pre-occupied me more than his cock. That I could work on autopilot.

"Maybe they chose me because of my attitude issues." I lay on my side facing Josh, my head propped in my free hand. "Though technically, the choosing happened when I was born so they didn't have any way of knowing how I'd turn out." I kept the details vague since there was no knowing if Demon Club would kill Josh for hearing top secret intel.

"Mmmm, yeah," Josh moaned, kicking his jeans off. His movement made the thin mattress bounce. His sculpted abs jiggled not at all.

"But what if that's why I'm such a dick? Such an epic failure. Because I was destined for something amazing and denied it." *You talking dance or demon hunting, Nava?* "You think I could sue them for existential pain and suffering?"

"Full-on." Josh thrust his hips in a rhythmic motion.

I rolled onto my back, my hand still working away. I'd always been a good multitasker. "I didn't ask for it. It's not fair for my brother to be so pissed off."

"Uh, babe?" Josh poked me in my side. "Discussions of brothers while your hand's on my junk? Kinda killing the buzz."

"Sorry."

He leaned over me, his eyes glazed with lust. "Think you could...?" He motioned for me to go down on him.

"Yeah, sure." My hand was getting tired anyway. I slid down his body. "Thing is," I began. With my mouth full, the words came out garbled and I guess I caught some skin because Josh flinched.

"Go back to the hand job," he sighed.

Geez, make up your mind. I shimmied back to my starting position. "I don't even want this. It isn't some lady-doth-protest-too-much shit either. The pressure would be insane. Everyone would be watching me, waiting for me to screw up. Plus the possible death of it all. I'm not big on that either."

A niggle of guilt prodded at me for dumping my problems on Josh, so I gave him a flirty smile. He shot me a heated look in response. Lust tumbled hot and furious down from my now-dry throat to much, much lower. I crossed my legs, squirming, as I stole another glance at him.

His face seemed to... *flicker?* for a second. The line of his jaw blurring, his skin suddenly much furrier than his five o'clock shadow warranted.

I blinked and the room snapped into a sharp clarity. Just me and a gorgeous guy. But his serious sex appeal had me so lightheaded that all the color in the room bleached out briefly. In fact, I felt like I'd bleached out briefly.

"As I was saying... ouch!" My hand seized up. I shook it out and switched to my right.

My fingertips tingled. I amped up the speed, hoping he'd finish already. More than ready for my turn. I'd give up a kidney for an orgasm after the day I'd had.

Josh's eyes were closed, his breathing ragged. All positive signs for his happy ending.

Thank God, because my hand hurt. Had I pinched a nerve? I grit my teeth. Cramp or no cramp, I wasn't about to break my personal record of every man left satisfied. A girl had to have some skill she could be proud of, even if she couldn't put it on a résumé.

Josh let out a guttural moan.

Being well-versed in the nuances of guttural, I translated this one as "gold star, Nava." But my smugness fell away at the tugging pull starting low in my gut. Not a virulent food poisoning, all-out cramping, but more like my soul was being manhandled. I slowed down my strokes, rubbing my belly with my free hand.

Josh's eyes sparked like he was getting off more on my discomfort than on my expert dexterity. A prickle of unease danced across the back of my neck.

"Let yourself go, baby," he growled.

Please. He was hot but coming by osmosis wasn't a thing. I was overreacting. Josh wasn't a threat, just a douche.

Sweat trickled down my scalp and a sharp pressure rose through the fingers of my right hand, now cramped tight around his knob. I hadn't been jerking him off long enough to be this tired. Pain pulsed outward from the middle of my palm as if my synapses had starting shooting electric bullets.

"Almost there," he mumbled. His hips were practically levitating they were lifting off the bed so high.

My belly twisted and I drew my knees into my chest for some relief, yet I couldn't stop touching Josh. The more I tugged, the more he moaned lustily, and the more I grit my teeth. My abdomen felt like it was a leaking tire, but I wasn't injured. More like with each stroke I was losing something essential, growing wearier, and I wasn't able to explain why.

Sparks flew off my hand.

Holy. Shit.

Josh's body flickered like a stuttering screen, revealing a ram's head.

Oh, hell no!

I spasmed, engulfed by a snapping blue electrical arc that traveled through my hand to envelop Josh's dick, momentarily gluing us together with a disturbing sizzle and a whiff of burning flesh.

His eyes snapped open in alarm.

Given how every blink caused sparks to dance in front of me, I figured I was lit up from head to foot, but before I could check, Josh convulsed with a hot spurt. Then his body exploded into gold dust.

Both the pain in my hand and the pyrotechnics immediately ceased.

I wiped my fingers off on the rumpled sheet with a grimace. The downside was that I'd just met my first demon. The upside? Not only was he not naturally better-looking than me, my record was intact. Another satisfied guy. Dispatched to oblivion, but not every date was a winner.

3

The shock kicked in about thirty seconds later. I clutched Josh's pillow, rocking back and forth emitting weird "guh" noises until I got my throat working again. Sure, I could step on a very small spider like the manliest of men, but that smattering of gold powder on the sheets had been Josh. My intermittent flirt buddy for the past six months.

An icy slither ran up my core as I stared at my right hand, its tremors Richter scale violent. Was this my demon-killing ability? Destined to be some supernatural whore luring hell spawn into back alleys for deadly rub and tugs?

Leaping from the bed, a hand clapped over my mouth, I sprinted over the cheap beige carpet to the bathroom. I barely made it to the toilet, throwing up all the contents of my stomach until the dry heaves kicked in. Beer and grease did not taste better coming back up.

I cleaned up as best I could, blowing my nose and using an entire travel bottle of mouthwash that I found in Josh's cluttered medicine cabinet to rinse out my mouth. I considered using his toothbrush but that seemed too intimate for a guy I hardly knew.

I hiccuped in a half-sob, half-laugh. Orgasming to death okay, shared oral hygiene a line too far.

I gripped the sink so hard my fingertips turned white, forcing myself to take deep, calming breaths. Getting myself down to the functioning side of hysterical. I ran my fingers through my sweat-matted hair, taking in my reflection in the mirror of his bathroom cabinet. Pale, crazed, I couldn't stare too long at myself so I yanked on the tap, washing my hands vigorously enough to rub them raw.

Taking a layer or six of epidermis off myself helped. The color had returned to my cheeks. Somewhat. But with my shocky adrenaline high wearing off came the painful realization that my boobs burned like crazy.

With the utmost care, I peeled my shirt and bra off to find a scorched, puckered burn line matching the now-melted underwire. As a natural disaster show connoisseur, I knew that metal conducted electricity but, come on! My girls demanded underwire.

I pressed a fingertip to the red angry skin with a hiss. Seems right now they demanded burn lotion. I rummaged through Josh's cupboard but he was light on first aid products, so I tossed the bra in the trash and eased back into my shirt, flinching as the soft material made contact.

It was too much.

Wobbly from a cocktail of exhaustion and pain, I pressed my head to the cool glass of the mirror. Giving myself a moment to get my jumpy pulse under control and let the throbbing in my tits subside enough to be able to walk because that basic motor function seemed an impossible dream.

I had no idea how much time passed before I was able to move, though moonlight now streamed in through Josh's bedroom window as I dressed. No drunken ramblings were heard from homeward-bound revelers, the city deep in slumber.

I shrugged on my jeans, unable to shake my sense of unease. Sidling over to the window, I peered outside through the slats of the bent plastic blinds.

Some guy stood in the alley framed in a pool of light cast by a poster-plastered streetlamp. Hands in the pockets of his leather jacket, he seemed every bit a relaxed bystander, but I wasn't deceived.

The question was, was he here hunting Josh? Or me?

I widened the blinds a touch.

Startlingly gold eyes bored straight into my soul, rooting me to the spot. His hair, several shades darker than his light brown skin, was kind of shaggy, curling thick and sexy around his ear lobes. He had to be a demon. My hand didn't tingle or anything in recognition but ordinary mortals were not created this ridiculously gorgeous. I'd know. I trolled the internet plenty looking at hot dude Pinterest boards.

Plus, perched above him on the telephone wire was a white crow, albeit a weirdly stocky one. Contrary to popular opinion, white crows were not an albino rarity but demons who, once fixated on their prey like this one was on me, dive-bombed a person feeding off their blood and flesh. I had never been so glad for a pane of glass. And when Alley Dude trained his sights on the bird, the white crow exploded off the line with a panicked "caw," flying away so fast that it trailed feathers.

Some primal survival sense screamed at me that whoever or whatever this guy was, he was a million times more dangerous than Josh. But it also kicked me into gear.

I jerked away from the window, pressing myself flat against the wall. My heart threatened to explode out of my chest. Had Josh's death set some demon phone tree into motion and now they were all after me? Keeping low so the guy couldn't see me, I gathered up my backpack, smelling the lingering scent of Josh's cologne from when he'd carried it home for me.

He'd never carry anything again.

I pressed my fist to my mouth. I'd killed a man. Demon. Barkeep. Panic flared hot and bright. I jammed my feet into my shoes then raced for the front door. Fleeing the scene of the crime while cradling one arm against my chest to keep my poor burned babies from jiggling.

As I reached for the lock, my hip bumped the small white plastic table next to the door. The green sides from yesterday's shoot–the small, color-coded script pages for that day–fell to the ground and I bent to pick them up, not wanting to leave his place in worse shape than I found it. Other than its loss of occupant.

Josh had been cast as the happy-go-lucky play-boy of the group. In this scene at least, no woman could resist his charm. That was one word for it. I shivered, remembering the unsettling tugging right before Josh had orgasmed. In retrospect, his "let go" was probably a command, not a suggestion. Had I not been Rasha, they would have been last words I ever heard.

I dropped the paper like it was a hot coal, fumbling in my pocket for my phone and punching in Ari's speed dial number. The call went straight to voice mail.

"Ari," I mewled. I slid down the wall, hugging my arms to my chest, paralyzed between fright and flight.

Shortly after, there was a frantic pounding on the door. "Nava!" The cavalry had come. I scrambled to my feet, unlocked the bolt, and flung open the door, launching myself into my brother's arms.

He patted me awkwardly. "Nee, what's wrong?"

The story poured out of me. Ari let me ramble, leading me to the sofa in Josh's cramped

IKEA-themed living room and listening in silence as I described killing my hook-up.

"Say something," I begged, clutching the leg of his blue plaid pajama pants.

Ari hadn't even gotten dressed. Just stuffed his feet into slippers and thrown on a sweatshirt in his haste to save me.

"You washed your hands, right?" he asked.

I punched him in the arm. "That's the sum total of what you have to say?"

He punched me back. His was harder than mine and I pouted as I rubbed the sore spot. "You," he mimed giving a hand job, "a demon to death. I think I need therapy." He shuddered.

"You think you need therapy?" I screeched. "How do you think I feel? You know what my big plan for today was? A nap! Instead I've made you hate me and my hand is a red light district instrument of destruction."

I paused for him to interject that of course he didn't hate me, but he didn't. So I babbled the rest of my story, punctuating my words with flailing gestures. That just sent a fresh shaft of pain through my boobs.

"I mean, what happens when I meet a nice guy that I like and things start to get intimate?" I said. "Will my hand know the difference? Because I'm not sure there is an appropriate greeting card to apologize for penile third degree burns!"

"I'd say it with flowers," he pronounced.

The clock on the wall ticked once. Twice.

We burst out laughing. A brittle manic laughter that morphed into way-over-the-top snorting guffaws complete with shaking body and streaming tears. Cathartically spent, I sagged back against the couch.

Ari stood up, rolling out his shoulders. "You ready to quit running away from home now and go deal with this?"

I scrunched up my face. "How'd you know I'd run away?"

"I always know."

A wistful pang hit me square in the chest. I rubbed my hand over the back of my neck. "Right."

"Dumbass." He boffed me across the head. "I don't hate you."

My relief swam clear down to my toes. "That's because I'm Twin Amazing and I brighten up your life," I said.

He shot me a look of fond exasperation.

I could have kissed him in a sister-appropriate way for it–e.g. raspberried his cheek. "Think you can help me not get killed?" I asked.

"Up to a point. But we're going to have to call Rabbi Abrams."

"And get our heavily edited stories straight," I added.

Ari pulled me up. "That's your area of expertise."

My right hand gave an aftershocky jerk. I placed my other one on top of it to stop the shaking. "You may need to carry me."

"You need electrolytes." Ari went into the kitchen, opening and closing cupboards. "He doesn't have any salt," he said, coming back and finding me slumped over the top of the sofa. "Come on, I'll buy you a Gatorade."

I threw my arm over my brother's shoulder, letting him support me. He grabbed my backpack and helped me out the door. Any comfort I took in having Ari's forgiveness disappeared when we hit the front sidewalk outside Josh's three-story stucco apartment building and saw the hot platinum blonde leaning against the glass front door, all long limbs and porn star mouth in this slinky gold halter dress I coveted.

"Hey, lover," she said to Ari, ignoring my existence.

I was so not in the mood to deal with some west side chick on the pointless make for my brother.

He gave her a polite smile, maneuvering us past both her and the broken furniture someone had left out for garbage pick up.

"You think you could help me?" she asked, catching up to us and waving her cell. "My friend stood me up and my phone is dead."

I stopped, forcing Ari to stop with me. I couldn't in good conscience leave this woman stranded in the middle of the night. Especially outside this dump with its sketchy lighting. I dug out my phone, shuffled a few steps closer, and handed it to her. "Here. Use mine."

"Thanks," she said, latching onto my wrist with a talon. My phone tumbled to the concrete as her mouth elongated into a distorted sneer. "Have fun with my brother tonight?"

I tried to scramble back, terrified her jaw was about to unhinge and swallow me whole, but she held me fast. Good thing because I still hadn't re-charged and lack of energy plus fear equaled my knees buckling.

I batted at her with my right hand, which was totally failing to shock her.

"Bitch," she snarled, her stilettos morphing to crow's feet, "I liked him. He was the only one of my siblings I hadn't eaten."

Ew. Phrasing.

A surge of adrenaline raced through me and I snapped my knee up into her crotch.

She gasped, doubling over.

That's when I head-butted her, a technique learned while hanging with this hockey player I'd wanted to bang. The demon's nose made a satisfying crunch as the cartilage shattered. I snatched my arm loose with a laugh. "Booyah, mother–"

With a roar she puffed up into an ogre. A solid muscle demon ogre with a now-tattered dress hang-ing off her body. Her shiny mane of hair erupted into white feathers and her nose transformed into a pointed beak. The crow/ogre hybrid grabbed me by the throat.

My powers were still in absentia and all thoughts of *electrocute the bitch*, were supplanted by *get air to brain* as she continued to squeeze. Spots danced in front of my watering eyes, my vision tunneling down to the narrow pinprick of her bumpy chin. I flailed my limbs.

"Get your own sibling," Ari said, "I spent years training this one."

SPLOOSH! Murky goo splattered all over my face. She dropped me like a hot potato.

I stood there wheezing, staring in incredulity at my brother. Not only had he jammed a standing lamp through the demon's neck, he'd taken advantage of her clawing at the thing to whip out a knife from an ankle sheath, firing it into her just below her navel.

A scream ripped from the demon's throat, her skin blistering in a way that made me think of crackling. I might never eat bacon again. Yeah, who was I kidding? Tendrils of smoke wafted off her bubbling flesh. She screeched a high-pitched, inhuman cry of pain and rage.

"Nee, finish her!"

I stared at him blankly. Ari grabbed my hand and, hauling me over to the demon, placed my fingers around the knife so they touched her rubbery skin.

A tingle deep inside me rippled into a concentrated bolt of lightning, firing straight into the demon.

She exploded. The lamp and the knife clattered to the ground.

Shimmery gold dust floated down from the star-filled night sky. It coated Ari, turning him into a sparkling hero.

"How?" It was all I managed to stutter out.

He shrugged and picked up his knife. "Training."

"But..." I pointed at the weapon.

"Iron blade coated in salt. Two things demons hate."

"And..." I made a thrusting motion with my hand.

Ari stared at me for a second before he clued in. "Ohhh. The lamp. Again, training." He ran his fingers through his hair, shaking out the dust as he walked along the sidewalk. His slippers made soft padding sounds with each step.

Avoiding the trail of demon dust on the sidewalk, I scooped up my phone with my thumb and index finger, not touching any more of it than I had to, then hurried after him. I punched his shoulder. "Don't fight demons without magic."

"I didn't. You were right there."

I growled at him. "Your own magic."

Ari turned the corner, pulled his key fob out, and beeped it at our father's blue Prius parked at the curb.

"I know you, Ace. Magic or no, you come across someone in need of saving from a demon, you'll rush in. You can't."

He shrugged as he opened the passenger door and helped me inside.

"Unlike me," I said, "you possess that stupid selfless gene that Rasha are supposed to have. Tonight proves there's been a colossal mistake."

"You killed the demon," he said. "No mistake."

"*You* killed that demon. I was merely a tool." I forgave him the small smirk at my word choice as he shut my door. Didn't lessen my desire to throttle him, though.

Ari got in the driver's side, tossing the blade into the pocket on the door.

Pushing him about staying safe would only spur him in the other direction. "Why are you not more excited about this? Or upset about it? Or something resembling anything?" I asked.

My brother placed the key in the ignition and started the engine with the press of the power button. He pulled out into the street to the strains of shitty soft rock. Dad must have been the last one to drive the car. "Big deal. Another assist. Not like I got to score on goal directly."

I rested my feet on the dashboard, slouched in my seat. "Not enough excitement for you, brother dear?"

He shrugged. "Eh."

I stuffed my fists under my butt, the sight of my hands still troubling. "That disturbs me about you." As did the fact that the idiot was *going to get himself killed.*

"Sucks a bit less since it was only a PD." He flicked on his blinker, pissing off the chick behind us who honked multiple times.

I lowered my window to shoot her the finger. The cool night air streaming over me was invigorating enough to keep me upright so I kept it unrolled. "What kind of a demon is a PD?"

"Old Rasha joke. What do you call a half-demon?"

I shook my head.

"Practice. Practice demon."

"PD. Ooh, bitchy. But she was a hybrid."

"Yeah. Probably some genetic throwback on the demon side. Still just half-demonic. Half-human."

"How do you know?"

"Dust 'em and you're gold. Literally. PDs explode into gold dust. Josh was a halfie as well." Ari made a sharp left, pulling into a convenience store parking lot. "Back in a sec," he said, leaving me in the car with the motor running.

I fiddled with the stereo knob, unable to take any more musical torture.

Moments later he was back with a plastic bag. He pulled out a blue sports drink, cracked the cap, and handed it to me. "Drink. You need the electrolytes."

I wasn't a fan of these things so my first sip was tentative, but the liquid hit my system like a rush of cocaine. I chugged the rest down in one go. "More," I breathed.

He handed me the other drink that he'd purchased, this one a yummy orange-esque flavor. Once I'd downed that too, I sighed in satisfaction. "That was amazing."

Ari backed out of the spot, shaking his head. "Don't ever make that sound in my presence again."

I twisted the cap shut, jamming it back into the bag with the other empty bottle. "If I could give the power back, I would. It should be you joining Demon Club."

My brother merged back into the light traffic, homeward bound. "I know." He ran a hand though his bedhead, spiking his blond tufts. "But it doesn't seem like either of us are going to get what we want."

There was nothing I could say to that, so I channel-surfed, looking for a song to reflect my mood. The only thing that came close was "Bound," an angsty charged hit from a few years ago by Fugue State Five. I sang along to the last verse.

"You know the words?" Ari didn't sound impressed.

I shrugged, betting he did too since we would have had to been living in a cave during our teen years not to know the emo boy band that had taken the world by storm. Also, Leonie had been obsessed with them, playing their music incessantly.

The next song was some crap rock ballad so I punched the radio button off. The silence was deafening.

Ari shot me a sideways glance. "Gotta say I'm surprised you're not celebrating. Finally having a tangible way of keeping people at bay and all."

I slapped my feet onto the car mat. "I don't do that."

My brother snorted. "Right. You welcome them in with open arms." He pursed his lips. "These last few years? It's like you decided to make yourself this prickly ball of chaos."

"The PC among us call it 'hot mess,'" I quipped.

"Kinda ironic that your power is a physical manifestation of that."

The vein at my temple throbbed. "You're wrong. My sucky superpower is just that. Sucky. Not some kind of subconscious desire made real."

One hand on the wheel, he waved the other around, speaking in a mock scary voice. "Whooo, don't get too close to me, I might shock you." He dropped his voice an octave into horror movie voice over. "And this time, it's deadly."

"I'm not the only deadly one," I said waspishly. "Got any other weapons strapped to your body?"

"Nah. The knives were something I started playing around with a while ago. Doctoring up the best high salt concentration, finding the most effective method of coating the blade." He flashed me the thick silver ring on his middle finger with a ruby or red garnet in the middle. "See this? Iron poison ring. Literally." He spared another glance at the ring before his hands tightened on the wheel. "I was playing around with stuff for when I took my rightful place and all that."

My anger deflated at the reminder of what he'd lost. "You, Ari Katz, are my hero."

My brother took his eyes off the road long enough to give me a crooked grin. "And you, Nava Katz, are a really shitty demon hunter."

4

The lights were blazing in every room in our house when we pulled into the car port out back. It kind of kiboshed my plan to sneak in and then hide out in my room until my parents cooled down. Ari, the keener, bounded off ahead of me. My walk had more of a "headed to the guillotine" vibe to it.

I veered into the backyard to snap a few stalks off Mom's aloe plant to apply to my still-throbbing chest. It was a gorgeous night, made more so by the fact that I was still alive. I raised my face up to the stars, calmed by their distant pulsing. All was peaceful and still until my shoulder blades tensed like someone was behind me.

The maybe-demon from Josh's alleyway was back, having stopped about five feet away, triggering the motion sensor. What with Josh's sister trying to kill me and all, he'd fallen off my radar.

Aloe gooped over my fingers, having clutched the frond hard enough to break it, and my terror and an intense curiosity resurfaced. There was no denying his compelling presence. Plus, he had those long lashes that were my Kryptonite. I opened my mouth to scream. Or drool.

He held a finger up to his delectable lips to keep me quiet, circling me with lazy strides, checking me out.

I'd have been offended by the blatant appraisal except under his intense scrutiny, my clit, Cuntessa de Spluge lit up with an electric zing. I found myself stroking the aloe stalks in an obscene manner. Even knowing he couldn't see my blush since I was in the shadows didn't kill my utter mortification at jerking off plant life in not-so-subtextual yearning.

He stalked toward me, his leather jacket rustling with each step.

I held up a hand to stop him, the faintest electric crackle pulsing off my skin.

He didn't stop, didn't slow. In fact, he kept up his steady approach until his hand covered mine. My magic shocked us both at his touch. I gasped and shivered as pleasure, not pain, rumbled through me.

Hand still clasped in his, he stared at me suspiciously, instead of in fear, but had I wanted, I could have broken his hold. Not a demon, then? He fingered the thin silver necklace I wore with surprising gentleness, toying with the cute floral pendant dangling off it that read "I will kick you in the balls if I have to."

"Should I be scared?" Given how he sounded like sex, sin, and salaciousness–the true definition of a triple threat–I decided that yes, he was most definitely a demon.

I met his mocking gaze, my rooted stance and beating heart placing me somewhere between morbid fascination and noping the fuck out at warp speed.

"Nava," Ari called from the top of the stairs.

I jerked toward his voice. "Here."

My intruder backed away, melting into the night. I might have followed had Ari not called for me again. Instead, I hurried into the kitchen to find Mom, Dad, Rabbi Abrams, and a tree trunk of a man, about ten years older than me, with shoulder-length black hair and sharp blue eyes sitting at the kitchen table. His hair, combined with the hemp bracelets around his wrist, made him look like a Special Ops surfer dude. The floral yellow espresso cup that my parents had picked up at some overpriced ceramics studio in Italy was like a toy in his huge hand.

A platter of mostly untouched Danish pastry sat in the middle of the table, though given the three on his plate, Rabbi Abrams was doing his best to plough through them. I sent the dessert a longing glance, but before I could reach for a pastry, Tree Trunk rose to his almost six and a half feet, cracked his neck that was bigger than my thigh, and lumbered toward me.

"Baruch Ya'ari," Ari said in the most awestruck voice I'd ever heard him use.

I didn't care if this Baruch guy was the second coming, I hid behind my brother. Ari tugged me out to face the scary stranger, pushing me forward into his path.

"Baruch is usually based at HQ in Jerusalem," Rabbi Abrams piped up, chewing. "He—"

"Invented the Stinger," Ari said. Wow. Fanboy a little more, bro.

"Ari is the chemistry student I told you about," the rabbi said to Baruch.

My unflappable brother actually squeaked when he said that.

"But due to the... situation," Rabbi Abrams continued, "it is Nava you will be training in fighting and weapons skills."

How about showing some tact, old man? Couldn't he see Ari's shoulders slump? Though I perked up at hearing there were weapons. I looked down at the aloe in my hand. I could do weapons.

Baruch let his gaze roam slowly up my body like he was cataloging my every weakness and maybe taking my blood pressure.

I jutted my chin out.

Mom tapped her finger against her cup, her wedding ring clinking against the ceramic.

"No," Tree Trunk barked when he'd finished his inspection. He spoke with that gravelly abruptness of many Israeli men.

I dropped the aloe on the counter. "No, what?" I didn't recall hearing a question.

Baruch made a dismissive raspberry noise. "She is not Rasha material."

Mom deflated. Dad put his arm around her and she leaned into him. WTF?

I didn't have time to process them being upset on my behalf, because this was my shot. "You're right. I'm not." I shoved Ari at him. "But he is. He killed a demon tonight. Saved my life."

Tree Trunk stilled. He zeroed in on my brother who scowled at me. I nodded virtuously. There was only room for one demon hunter in our family and it was going to be Ari.

"How?" Baruch asked.

Ari launched into an explanation.

Tree Trunk's stoic demeanor loosened up enough to blink approvingly during Ari's recounting of the lamp post and ankle sheath. I took it as him being impressed with my twin.

Even the rabbi beamed with pride. My parents were certainly happy. When Ari finished, my mother prodded the still silent Baruch. "Well?"

I crossed my fingers.

Baruch gave another infuriating raspberry. "He took down some bastard of Asmodeus."

"*The* demon of lust," Ari murmured at my questioning glance. "Major player in the demon hierarchy."

"...And the other one did the killing," Baruch said.

"Big deal. Get him a magic hand," I said through gritted teeth. "I'm alive thanks to Ari and his training. I refuse to believe he isn't supposed to be Rasha." Rabbi Abrams opened his mouth but I cut him off, knowing what he was going to say. "I don't care if you ran the ceremony again. Ari is the chosen one, not me."

Baruch swung his gaze to me.

Uh-oh. I'd put myself back on his radar. "Yes?"

"What did you do to her brother?" he asked. "What was the demon referring to?"

Picked up on that part of the story, had he? Mostly I'd done *with* her brother. Just a little bit of *to* at the end of our time together. "Nothing worth recounting." In front of my parents. "She was an evil fiend," I continued. "Talking crazy. Back to Ari."

"Nava killed him as well," Ari piped up.

I slapped my hand over his mouth. "As I was saying, back to Ari who is humble, which I believe is the first rule of Demon Club. He's so humble, in fact, that he's willing to lie like a rug to throw the spotlight off of him."

"There is no Demon Club," Baruch pronounced.

Ari yanked my hand off him at the same time that I said, "Fine. Sorry. Not Demon Club." Seems they were touchy about their nickname. "The Brotherhood of David."

"No," Baruch corrected me, "The first rule of Demon Club. It's 'there is no Demon Club.'"

I crossed my arms. "Really? You're going to get a sense of humor now?"

He mirrored my stance. "Really? You're going to keep avoiding my question?"

I mimed zipping my lips and throwing away the key.

Tree Trunk turned to Ari. "How?" Such a popular question this evening.

My brother opened his mouth, blanched at the realization that we'd neglected to create a parent-friendly version of events, then pointed at me. "Ask her."

I tugged on my lips to show they were still zipped.

The rabbi said a few words in Hebrew.

This time Baruch's blink conveyed such disapproval that everyone leaned away from him. Who was this guy? Some kind of Zen eye master?

Rabbi Abrams said a few more things. None of them the ten words of Hebrew still imprinted on my brain from summer camp.

Baruch's hand shot out and grabbed my right hand. He pulled on the ring so hard I howled in pain, attempting to jerk away. Emphasis on attempt. Vises were easier to escape. He leaned in close, his fingers tightening. "Give. It. Back." His blue eyes darkened in menace.

That was it. My limit on bullying for today. I was exhausted and I'd kill for a shower because the demon dust on my skin was starting to itch. I leaned in until our noses practically touched. "Bite. Me."

The room fell into shocked silence. Then Baruch laughed. A rusty bark of surprise. "Beseder," he said using the Hebrew word for okay. He patted my head. "Sleep. Tomorrow you start."

"Uh, no. Tomorrow you figure out how to fix this." I pointed at my brother. "He's the one you want, not me."

"True," Baruch said with a smile Ari's way that made him preen. I gagged. "But you are who we have," Baruch said to me, his smile gone. "So we will keep you alive and you will kill many demons." Before I could present any further arguments, he strode out the back door and into the night without a look back.

Rabbi Abrams gave us a kind of half bow and shuffled after him. "Baruch, wait! You drove."

Dad closed the back door after making sure the rabbi had made it down the stairs unharmed.

"I think that went very well," Mom said, rising. She grabbed a rag from the sink and started vigorously wiping down the counter.

I slumped into a chair. "In what way?" When I'd left the house this afternoon, my parents had not been onboard with this new reality.

"You made a positive impression on Baruch. Today was a bit of a shock. For all of us. But now we'll readjust. This could be the new start you've been looking for." Interesting that she was spouting all this positive affirmation crap yet hadn't once met my eyes.

Plus, I hadn't been looking for a new start. My present stagnation was warm and cozy.

My father gathered up the espresso cups. "Your mother is right."

I side-eyed Ari. He sat at the table, toying with a linen placemat. My rock of a brother looked deflated. Like sorrow was the only thing holding him together. "What about Ari?" I asked. "What's he supposed to do now?"

Mom stopped wiping. Her voice wavered as she said, "Ari will be… The world is still his for the taking."

Ari flinched.

I slid off the stool, and snatched up my aloe, bound for hot water and then bed. "I haven't agreed to this."

"You don't have a choice," Dad said. There it was again. Not, "You'll be great." Not even, "You can do this." Just, "You have no option." Everyone had made it very clear they were stuck with me. Maybe it was time for me to make it clear that I may have been chosen, but I still very much had a choice.

I shrugged. "There's not any way you can force me, is there?"

My parents froze. That fact hadn't occurred to them.

I lay my hand on Ari's shoulder. "Hey, Ace?" I murmured. "Thanks for the rescue. But the next time I run away, ignore my calls, stay out of the Find My iPhone, and let me stay gone."

Minutes later, I stood with my head bowed while scalding water pounded down the back of my neck. Hot showers might be evidence of the existence of angels and if they were, then the glowy buggers could show up any time and corral their wayward relations.

The combination of the steam and the sugar scrub smeared all over my body was softening my stiff muscles, washing away fears and tensions. All right, washing away sweat and demon goo but they tamped the fears and tensions down a tad. I washed my death hand about sixty-seven times before I pronounced it free of demon and karma.

Bad things really did come in threes. I'd been lucky tonight. No previous female Rasha meant that Josh had been unaware of the danger he'd been in from me, allowing my first show of magic to dust him. With his sister, Ari had been there. And with that last encounter in my backyard? I didn't know what to make of that whole meeting and that bothered me more than the other two combined. Loath as I was to admit it, tomorrow I was going to march myself over to the Vancouver chapter and let them take me in hand.

I shuddered, remembering Josh. Phrasing.

I dumped some argon oil shampoo in my palm, lathering up. I'd tried running away and that had gotten me nowhere. Since I didn't want to find myself in a repeat of tonight or, you know, actually dead the next time I met a demon, I'd play nice with Demon Club.

More importantly, I had to help Ari. I wasn't going to let my brother wither away. Much as Brotherhood history and tradition were screwing me hard and dry with no money on the bedside table afterwards, they worked in Ari's favor. Whenever the Brotherhood determined Rasha initiate status, they committed to that (male) person without hesitation. Right now, they thought that they'd made a mistake with Ari, so their conviction that Ari was no longer an initiate was the biggest hurdle. Get the proof to correct that and his induction would swiftly follow. He'd be back on his rightful path.

I rinsed out my hair, finger combing conditioner through it.

My plan for tomorrow had two-parts: A) master my power since it appeared demons were actively targeting me now and, B) get the Brotherhood to confirm Ari's initiate status. Me being Rasha was a weird glitch that didn't negate my brother's destiny.

Oh, and try not to be freaked by all this. Okay, three parts. But that's where I capped it.

Clean of body and soul, I shut off the tap, giving myself a small electric shock in the process. Damn faulty piece of shit hand. I stepped out of the shower, wrapping the towel around my head like a giant turban before breaking open the fronds to smear aloe on my tender boobs.

I slathered body lotion on the rest of me, slipping nice and moisturized into my pink baby doll tee reading "I know guacamole is extra" and matching pink pajama shorts with small avocados printed on them. Finally, I brushed my teeth and towel dried my hair. The normalcy of following my nighttime routine was comforting.

Dumping the damp towel on the floor, I picked up the Doritos bag to throw in to my bedroom trash, since my bathroom's was full. I opened the door with a cloud of steam, and wandered into my comparatively cooler bedroom.

Where I collided with a hard chest.

I screamed. Or tried to. A strong hand slammed down over my mouth to smoother my cries. I attempted my knee smash, but was blocked before I could even finish the thought, much less execute the move. The intruder picked me up and tossed me on my bed. My memory foam mattress contoured itself around the shape of my ass.

"You telegraph way too much," a smooth voice said to me. Backyard guy was back.

Ignoring the decadent images that his voice conjured up, I shoved my hand into the Doritos bag which contained about 237% salt, crawled to the edge of the bed, and threw the crumbs in the demon's face. "Burn, fucker!"

The demon glared at me as he wiped orange dust off his cheeks and sweater. "This is cashmere," he said, frowning at the deep blue fabric.

I scrambled to my feet, holding the bag out in front of me like a cross. Which, incidentally, did nothing against demons. And since vampires didn't exist, did nothing against them either. Some demon happened to get its kicks feeding from the neck and suddenly everyone was rushing in with garlic and stakes looking to take down Count Dracula. Those who weren't romanticizing them as life partners, that is.

"There is enough salt in this bag to blister you back to your evil dimension." Smirking, I batted my lashes at him. "Feel free to be scared."

He swiped the bag out of my hands, tossing it into the trash behind him. "A, if you're gonna eat chips, at least eat decent ones. B, not a demon. And C," he said, reading my baby doll tee, "love the outfit, Nava."

I scowled at him. "You are absolutely a demon."

He pulled out my desk chair, turned it around with a snap of his wrists, and straddled it. "Why?"

"For starters, I never told you my name. Probably got it from the demon phone tree that went out about me."

He grinned at me, flashing toothpaste-ad-perfect, even, white teeth. "I'm not on the list."

I crossed my arms over my nipples which were now so hard from that grin he'd leveled at me that one good operatic scream could shatter them. I shut down all possibilities of how said scream could be achieved, locking them inside a box deep in my psyche.

"Any other proof you want to dazzle me with?" he asked.

How about the fact that his grin made Josh's seem like a neutered puppy's and Josh was a lust demon. Half-demon. Which made this guy full-evil status. "You broke into my bedroom and are holding me hostage." With your incredible looks.

Damn. Why not roll over already, idiot girl?

I hadn't been able to scope out his body in detail on our previous two encounters, but now, under proper lighting, I could tell he'd be nicely cut under that sweater that molded to him like a second skin. Underwear model nice and not the low rent, flyer-insert kind either. One of those glorious torsos caught in haunting black and white by Herb Ritts, the stark white of his briefs throwing his generous package into sharp relief.

Then there was his face. If it hadn't been for the slight bent of his nose, indicating it had been broken, his South Asian beauty would have been too painful and/or depressing to look at. Killer cheekbones, firm chin, gorgeous brown skin and lips that were created to do bad, bad, wonderful things. It was going to be a crime against humanity to kill him.

I leaned in toward the slight breeze drifting in through my open window, refusing to fan myself in front of him.

He sat there under my scrutiny, totally comfortable. A sign of excess confidence and further proof of evil. Though the more I stared at him, the more I got a niggling feeling that I knew him.

"Did we ever..." I made a fist and pumped away in a back and forth motion.

Amusement lit his amber eyes. "I was the lead singer of Fugue State Five." He smirked, saying the words as if obviously I'd heard of them. Fair enough.

Rohan Mitra had been the broody frontman whose so sensitive lyrics and rough growl singing voice induced mass hysteria at concerts world-wide. It was rumored he'd averted an oil crisis with a personal visit to a Sheik's daughter. Watching the beautiful bastard now, I believed it.

"Oh my God!" I squealed. "Your mom is Maya Mitra. I love her!"

"My mom." The smirk vanished.

The words tripped out of my mouth, I was so psyched to be one degree of separation away from this woman. "Punk rock Indian Jewish chick who blew every stereotype out of the water in her rise to hottest music producer in the biz? You get to be related to her?!" I bounced on the bed in sheer excitement, clapping a hand over my protesting boobs.

"And she to me," he said dryly.

"Whatever." I studied him. When Rohan had first gotten famous, he'd been an extremely pretty sixteen-year-old, all long limbs, smoldering doe eyes, and his trademark platinum blond hair falling into his face, but from his tightly muscled body to his five o'clock shadow, that boy was long gone. He seemed... harder. *Don't go there, honey.* Thankfully his standard issue wear of Vans, black skinny jeans, and vintage-looking weird graphic T-shirts were no longer a part of his repertoire.

Even Leo, his super fan, might have needed time to make the connection between his past and present selves.

I raked an approving glance over his vastly improved fashion sense, enjoying the view from the top of his fitted sweater, along his tailored black dress pants, and down to the tips of his Italian footwear. His leather jacket was tossed on my windowsill. "I didn't recognize you without the eyeliner and glaring dye job, Rohan."

He tipped his head. "Yeah. Thrilled that look is immortalized for all time. Now, come on."

"Come on and what?"

"Show me your power." His hand snaked out and caught my wrist, pressing his palm against mine. Holding me in a barely contained show of strength.

"Death wish, much? I showed you in the backyard."

"Barely even a tease." He drawled the words.

I meant to pull away but I got my directions mixed up and pushed back against the warmth of his skin. "I *will* fire up. I'm warning you."

Rohan leaned in. "Do it." His eyes flared and I caught my bottom lip between my teeth.

Then some last iota of common sense–and self-preservation–raised its hand. I jerked away from him. If he was a demon, I should have killed him six times over by now. What the hell was I doing? "You still haven't convinced me that you're not a demon," I said, giving the evil spawn another chance for reasons I didn't want to examine too closely. "Fame doesn't preclude that. Nor does having a super cool mom."

"That doesn't, but this does." He held up his pinky finger, showing me the same gold ring as mine, with the same engraved hamsa and blue sapphire iris, which it turns out, was standard issue. And here

I'd been hoping for a succession of property-stamping jewelry as I rose through the hunter ranks.

I fell back against my headboard. "You're part of Demon Club. Fuck. Me."

Rohan oogled me. "I won't take that off the table yet." He propped his chin on his hands on the top of the chair.

I cocked an eyebrow at him. "Did you just put me on a table?"

"More invoked a proverbial table and a conditional 'yet.' The 'yet' is an important component of this potential event," he said.

You know what else was an important component? The presumptuous jerk still having attached balls for our proverbial fuck.

"I used to write fanfic about Fugue State Five," I said in a conversational tone.

Lookie lookie. Return of the amused smirk. "How was I?" he asked.

I shrugged, examining my chipped nail polish. "No clue. I wrote self-insert fanfic about the *rest* of your band. Zack, your keyboardist was astounding." I drawled that last word so he'd get the full implication.

"My keyboardist?" Rohan's smugness was R.I.P. "But he's gay."

"I assure you that didn't matter." I gave a self-satisfied sigh. "He succumbed to my fifteen-year-old self's wiles."

Rohan straightened. "Which of my much older bandmates also succumbed, Lolita?"

"Please. You guys were only three years older." I twisted a dark curl around my finger. "But pretty much all of them." I raked a pointed look over him. "The ones worth writing about." He didn't react. "Though succumbing is far more innocent than you're imagining," I admitted.

"I doubt you were ever innocent."

That was highly insulting. Did he think I'd been born this way? Please. I'd worked hard to cultivate this level of sexual awesomeness. Totally offended here. And equally turned on because he'd said it in that low rumbly voice that made me want to roll onto my back, knees falling open. If he rubbed my belly or lower, all good.

I tossed my hair. "Excellent. Assume the worst." Straightening my legs, I crossed one over the other. Forcing them to stay closed. Then I leaned back on my elbows and gave him my best smirk. "Now, what are you doing in my bedroom?"

I prayed he couldn't hear how hard my heart was thumping.

"I'm your new CO."

"My what?"

"Commanding Officer." He picked up a porcelain Fred Astaire and Ginger Rogers dancing together in their finery, from my shelf. "That means you have to do as I say."

I leapt off the bed and snatched Fred and Ginger back. "Oh, hell no."

Rohan raised an eyebrow. I petted my dancers' ceramic heads and carefully put them back as I scrambled for a somewhat less mutinous excuse. "You're full of shit. CO's are only appointed on missions. Otherwise, Rabbi Abrams runs the local chapter."

Even though not all Rasha were Jewish, when it came to running Demon Club, tracking and training the descendants, and performing rituals, David had only trusted a select group of Sanhedrin, the highest of High Rabbis. Rabbis still performed those duties today, despite the fact that the Brotherhood wasn't technically a religious organization. Something about trade secrets and the magic involved. I suspected the Brotherhood just didn't like change.

"Your brother talks too much." Rohan's voice was a silky threat.

I stormed over to him. "Leave Ari out of this."

"Or what?" He didn't bother to hide his amusement.

I leaned in, letting my sideboob brush against his arm. "A girl can't give away all her secrets," I purred. My hair teased his shoulder blades. Bad idea. This close, I could smell him, a blend of musky cologne with an underbite of iron that had skyrocketed to being the sexiest scent I'd ever inhaled.

"That a challenge?" He tucked a strand behind my ear, his face tilted up to mine.

I refused to back down, no matter how I longed to brush my tingling skin and capture the sensation for a moment longer. This was all an act, albeit one that got results. Rohan's player ways were the stuff of well-documented legend.

Maybe that's how he killed demons. He hit them with the look and the grin and then, when they fell to their knees in a puddle of feels, ripped their hearts out.

I wasn't going to fall quite so easily. "Nope. Wouldn't want you to tax yourself, Rock Boy."

His jaw tightened. Swinging his leg off the chair, he stood up abruptly, forcing me to scramble back to avoid being clipped on the underside of my chin.

I stared up at his good six inches on my five-foot-eight self.

"Tomorrow. 9AM at the chapter house," he ordered. "Get Ari to drive you if you don't know where it is." Rohan sauntered over to the open window, all lethal elegance. "And Lolita? Don't even think about blowing me off." His smile was ruthless. "Remember, I know where you live."

With that he jumped out the window and into the night.

5

Monday morning, I slammed back two chilled Diet Cokes, my surefire technique for bright-eyed, bushytailedness after a sleepless night. I'd applied a generous smear of fresh aloe under my cloth sports bra, and popped a couple of painkillers in preparation for the day to come. I'd even prepared a demon hunter kit: water bottle, trail mix, aloe fronds, a box of salt, a pen, and an unused Moleskine journal, all thrown into my messenger bag.

Dad drove me. He'd pulled chauffeur duty since I hadn't had the heart to ask Ari. "Nervous?" he asked.

"Nope." I adjusted the A/C vent. Events of the past twenty-four hours had coalesced into a hard ball of pissed off in my chest. "I am going to kick ass and take names."

I adjusted the vent again because I couldn't find the sweet spot of cool air. A stoplight turned yellow, then red in front of us, and I kept fumbling with the A/C. Take three's the charm.

Dad reached over and stilled my hand. "Nava."

"Okay, maybe I'm a bit nervous."

"I think that's a good sign. It means this matters."

No, it means this might be my last day on earth. I gave my dad a weak smile.

The rest of the ride was silent except for his execrable musical choices. Every now and again, I wiped my sweaty palms, hoping Dad wouldn't comment.

My imagination ran riot on what our local Demon Club chapter might look like. I'd gotten as far as a stone fortress with archers on the ramparts and boiling pitch down the walls, all of which would be unleashed at the sight of my estrogen-laden fineness, before I shut that shit down. It was just a house, right?

One of three chapters in Canada, along with Toronto and Montreal, the one here in Vancouver provided training to any initiates and support to any Rasha living or working on a mission in western Canada.

All too soon, we hit Southwest Marine Drive, a street of wide-spaced mansions hidden behind tall hedges and fencing. A few more winding turns later, and Dad pulled up to a half-open, wrought-iron gate set into a high stone fence. A dense press of Evergreens swayed in the distance.

My nerves flared back up into overdrive.

Putting the car in park, he leaned over to press a kiss to my cheek. "Go get 'em, honey."

My hand stilled on the seatbelt release. "How about we grab a mocha first?" Not that I needed any more caffeine.

"Sorry, kiddo. They're waiting."

He pointed out the window at Rohan, now slouching against the fence, his hands jammed into the pockets of his worn yet no doubt expensive jeans. He probably practiced that pose in the mirror, aiming for maximum bicep bulge under his fitted charcoal gray T-shirt.

Rohan raised his eyebrows at me like I was late and needed to hurry up. That tiniest of gestures packed with maximum arrogance. My heart relaxed back down out of my throat, my hands balling into fists as I got out of the car. Bite me, rock star.

I said good-bye to Dad, waving until he'd turned the corner.

Baruch jogged down the driveway to us. His hair floated loose in black waves around his shoulders. It matched his all-black attire of board shorts and a long sleeved tee with DSI printed in small white block letters over his heart.

David Security International was the Brotherhood's public persona. Having an actual company provided a cover for everything from liaising with suppliers to allowing Rasha to answer the question of what they did for a living. Most importantly, it gave them access to high-level places and people that might provide valuable intel for their real business of demon hunting. They'd always had proxies like this. Back in the middle ages it was a knight's order–not the Templars. In Victorian times, they owned gentlemen's clubs. Nowadays, it was an elite security organization.

Eying Baruch, I totally bought him as a top level security expert. Aside from the bare feet. Nice calves, dude.

"Boker tov," I said, punctuating my good morning wishes with a salute. I glanced down at a skittering sound by my feet to find two kitten-sized, fanged spiders with glowing red eyes charging at me.

I bolted past Rohan onto the property, screaming.

Baruch caught me, turning me around. "Look." Despite throwing themselves at the open gate, the spider demons were being repelled, as if bouncing off an invisible rubber shield. "Wards," he explained. "Keeps out anything with even a drop of demon blood."

Feeling braver, but no less disturbed because *big-ass spider demons*, I inched closer. "Kind of stupid to attack Demon Club, especially when they can't get in."

"Araculum aren't known for their brains." Rohan grabbed one of the hairy leggy fuckers in mid-repel, handing it over to Baruch, who pinned it, immobile, in one hand.

I jumped back. "What happened to them not getting through?"

"Of their own accord. We can bring them in just fine." Rohan's lips curled in a small smirk. "They don't like that much."

I pressed in closer to Baruch, who despite holding a demon, seemed like the safer of the two Rasha to hang with right now.

Baruch pointed to the araculum's rows of eyes, currently trained with laser focus on me. "See that?"

"Creepy show and tell time?" I asked.

The araculum growled. A million nails raking down a chalkboard fed through a broken, scratchy windpipe filter, the noise hooked into the base of my spine.

Its friend ramped up its pointless attempt to get through the wards.

Baruch shook the fiend that he held. "Sheket!"

"Bevakasha. Hey!" I sang, finishing off Baruch's "quiet" with a "please." He shook his head at me. "What?" I said. "I went to Jewish camp."

"Araculum store images for later replaying," Baruch said. "Bottom feeders farmed out to gather intel. But what exactly?" he added in a murmur, jamming his thumb into the underside of the demon's neck.

It spasmed, keening.

Expression grim, Baruch jerked the still convulsing creature toward us. A series of images flashed across its rows of eyes as if from a stuttering projector.

They were playing too fast for me to make sense of them but Rohan glared at me.

"It met with Asmodeus," he said.

"That's not my fault."

"No, but Asmodeus probably sent them here, scouting for information on who killed his children," Baruch explained.

Rohan shot me a pointed look. "That would be you."

My stomach twisted into knots worthy of any BDSM Dom. I let out a squeaky "eep."

"Ro." Baruch's chastisement was no less effective for his calm tone.

Rohan gave an annoyed sigh.

Baruch punched the demon in the left side of its head. Its eyes widened, briefly, comically, then all light and life faded as the demon disappeared with a pop and a puff of wiry hairs. Baruch brushed his hands off.

I gave him a shaky smile. "Tree Trunk, you're my hero."

Behind me, someone gave a snorting laugh. "Oh my God! I've been trying to place him for three years now. It was less celebrity, more Ent. My bad."

My mouth fell open. The voice belonged to a Japanese guy, probably in his mid-twenties, with spiky hair and a sculpted body. How could I tell? He was only clad in tight black shorts, black combat boots, and a smattering of silver dust across his bare chest. Accessorized with cool nipple rings and a giant coffee cup in one hand that he sipped at. He stepped on the remaining araculum's head without pause as he swaggered onto the property, not even bothering to confirm that he'd killed the demon. Which he had.

"Mtsots li ta-zain," Baruch replied. He pressed his hand to a scanner on the inside of the fence and the gate swung shut.

The new guy made a kissy face at him. "Promises, promises."

"What'd he say?" I asked.

In response he jammed his tongue in his cheek, miming a blow job. Then he mouthed the words "suck my cock."

Ooh. I clapped my hands. "Say it again, slowly so I can learn," I told Baruch.

"Rohan," Baruch said, "kill him and bring her to the Vault."

"That sounds suspiciously like the same thing," I said, watching with dismay as Baruch stalked up the drive.

New guy shrugged. "In your case, they'll still leave a body for the family to claim." He didn't seem particularly upset about his fate. I liked him.

Rohan took my elbow to steer me to this Vault, but I tugged free. "Don't be rude. Introduce me to my new best friend." I turned my back on Rohan in anticipation of the intro, resisting a giggle as I felt him bristle behind me.

"Nava Katz, Kane Hashimoto. Kane, Nava. Our newest Rasha."

While Rohan delivered my credentials in a disgruntled voice, Kane eyed me up and down, took another sip of coffee, and then apparently finding me worthy, held out his hand to be kissed. "Charmed, I'm sure."

I complied with the obligatory respectful pressing of lips to skin then pressed Kane's hand to my heart. "Please tell me you don't have a boyfriend."

Kane ran a hand along his body in show model form. "Like I could limit this prize to one lucky winner."

Oooh. How much would Ari adore me if I set them up? Probably not at all but Kane looked like serious fun. I grinned at him.

"You're nowhere near as uptight as the other twin," Kane said.

I flung an errant strand of hair out of my face, planting my hands on my hips. "You better not be dissing my brother."

"As if I'd waste my time."

"Ari should be the one here," I said, starting my plug to put the rightful Katz child in his chosen place.

A flash of... *guilt? agreement?* crossed Kane's face. "The power has spoken."

I let out a frustrated breath. Stonewalled again.

Rohan tugged on my arm, having reached the end of his limited patience. "Come on, Lolita."

I blew Kane a kiss and skedaddled after broody.

We headed deeper onto the property, walking–or in my case, jogging–past towering Cypress and Arbutus trees dotting a perfectly manicured lawn. I gave a low whistle at the amount of land the Brotherhood owned. "This is like a whole city block."

"Deep pockets." Rohan rounded a corner and a massive 1920's brick manor, flanked by two long, raised beds, their flowers in bud, came into view. It wasn't Windsor castle but it still qualified for mansion status.

Messenger bag pressed to my chest, I craned my neck up to take in the arched doors, beveled bay window in the turret, and multiple chimneys. Impressive, but with nary an archer or vat of boiling pitch in sight. My shoulders relaxed out of my ears. "Gatsby throw a party or two here?"

"Close." Rohan picked up the pace, forcing me to run up the front walk. "The estate was originally built with bootlegger money."

"Where's Rabbi Abrams?" The sooner I could make a strong case for getting Ari *re*-confirmed as an initiate, the better.

"Away for a couple days," Rohan said.

Hmm. Perhaps I could speak with someone at Brotherhood HQ in Jerusalem. I eyed the offices on the ground floor, sussing out if there was a lowly admin assistant I could charm contact info out of, but Rohan twirled his hand at me to move me along.

I marched up the wide front stairs, my determination to put Ari back on his rightful path the only thing keeping me from punching Rohan in the head. Though I knocked into him as I shouldered past into the cathedral ceilinged foyer. I glanced up the wide curving staircase to the second floor but no help appeared from those quarters. Fine. I'd be the perfect newbie Rasha so my new mentors would be more inclined to listen to me.

I hung my bag on the knob of the coat closet door, along with my hoodie, leaving me in my red *Good Morning, I see the assassins have failed* T-shirt.

"Nice to see you dressed for the occasion," Rohan said, tilting his head to check out my ass. "Tap," he read. The word written across my butt on my black sweats. "I don't get it. Is it some kinky promise of backdoor spirits?"

I forced my teeth to unclench. "Tap as in dance, you perv."

His face lit up in unholy glee. "Like Shirley Temple? Please tell me there's video."

There was and I was hot shit in it. I gestured to my outfit. "These are my workout clothes. Since I'm guessing there will be working out involved."

As Rohan marched me through the house, I caught glimpses of bright rooms with wide arched doorways, dazzling crown molding, and intricate inlaid wood flooring "Are all Rasha as crazy good-looking as Kane?" I asked, rubbernecking at the rooms like a tourist. From the decidedly masculine furniture, there was no doubt this was an all-male lair.

"There's a reason we're called the Fallen Angels," Rohan replied.

"Yeah, delusions of grandeur." I scooted past a massive painting of a malevolent demon hurtling toward the fires of Hell. On the table next to it was a small, painted demon statue with an exaggerated grimace and tusks who I'd guess to be of Thai or Indonesian origin. "You named yourselves."

He flashed me a grin. "If the label fits."

"Don't be cocky. It's insufferable."

"Only if you can't pull it off."

Wow.

"Question," I said, curious about how clean and clutter-free the place was. Very weird given the all-alpha atmosphere. "Who takes care of things? 'Cause I'm not doing some Snow White gig where I keep house. I am Rasha. Hear me roar." I thought about it. "Well, crackle."

"We have Ms. Clara for that." Kane had joined us, minus the coffee cup, but not plus any more clothing yet. An elaborate set of black wings was tattooed on his back, their tips licked by flame. A few feathers had fallen, scorched, to the base of his spine. Had he not been gay and already assigned in my mind to my brother, I'd have enjoyed exploring that tattoo. With my tongue.

The heavenly scent of fresh baked chocolate chip cookies broke into my lustful imaginings. "Does she make cookies on a regular basis?" I crossed my fingers behind my back.

"The best," Kane said. "Come on, I'll introduce you."

Yes please. Happy to meet the kindly housekeeper who baked. Ignoring Rohan's growled, "Downstairs in two, or else," I skipped off to the kitchen, envisioning the plump, good-natured granny wearing her white ruffled apron, a tray of cookies in hand, fresh from the oven.

I got the tray part right.

"Ms. Clara, meet Nava."

I put out my hand, my smile freezing in place as the five-foot-nothing woman at the stove faced me. Yes, with the envisioned tray of cookies but could I have been more wrong about the rest? For starters, the only plump thing about this chick were her boobs, which strained against her buttery yellow wrap dress.

She plunked the tray on top of the stove.

I dropped my hand along with the lower half of my jaw. Ms. Clara was stunning. Late-twenties, tops, she was also like a giant–*sorry*–mini ball of sunshine from her golden sun-kissed skin to her blonde curls and blue eyes.

"Another girl." She beamed at me, her voice breathy, as she tossed the oven mitt on the counter. "Finally."

"Nice to meet you, Clara," I said.

"Ms. Clara," she snapped in a voice so stern that I flinched, standing at attention.

She giggled. "Oops."

"Ms. Clara secretly moonlights as one of Vancouver's top dominatrixes," Kane informed me. He stared at her in open adoration. "She's so badass."

I was supposed to be the lone badass girl in this place. It was the one thing I had going for me here. She was supposed to be the old caretaker they adored like a nanny. "Sorry," I said, smoothing out my T-shirt. "Nice to meet you, Ms. Clara."

"Have a cookie, doll." She held out a plate of perfectly formed, perfectly warm, and perfectly melty chocolate chip cookies. Perfect seemed to be a theme with her.

"Thanks." I bit into it and moaned. "Oh. My. God."

"A sound many a man and woman has made in Ms. Clara's presence," Rohan said, coming into the kitchen. He rounded on me with a mouthed "Or else."

I took another bite.

"Rohan!" Ms. Clara was at least a foot shorter than Rohan, but when she caught him up in a hug, it was he who stumbled, her lean but toned arms pulling him down to her height. "I'd heard you were coming. How long are you back for?"

"Who knows? With this one?" He jerked his thumb at me. "You may be stuck with me forever."

"He's terrible," Ms. Clara said to me, with an affectionate shake of the head.

"With worse depths revealed every moment," I agreed, savagely taking another bite.

He shot me a wolfish grin. "Duty calls." He gripped the back of my T-shirt and gave a sharp tug to get me moving.

I stood there, finishing my cookie.

"Don't let them bully you," she said. "And make sure they let you come up for lunch. I make a great iced tea with plenty of electrolytes." She winked at me. "Plus, I'd be happy to give you some whip usage tips."

"Damn. I'm going to like you, aren't I?" I felt retroactively bad for feeling like I had to compete against her. I popped the rest of the cookie in my mouth, taking a moment to savor the joy dissolving on my tongue. "If only for more mouthgasms on a regular basis."

"Aww, smutty." She patted my cheek. "We're going to get along just fine."

Rohan groaned. "That's all we need." He led me from the room.

I tried to wriggle away from him but he kept his hand hot and steady on my coccyx. Fuck, he was turning my innocent body part into a dirty erogenous zone. "I can walk without assistance," I said. "Upright and everything."

"I'm checking to see if you go where I put you."

"First into the line of fire?"

"You're smarter than the average bear, aren't you?" He poked me in the back to steer me down two flights of narrow stairs, past the ground floor offices, and into a basement. Even though the basement walls consisted of solid concrete blocks painted a bright white, the ceilings were still a good nine feet high, with wide, well-lit hallways. It wouldn't surprise me if there were secret tunnels that they'd carted booze through back during Prohibition.

"Why'd someone choose the name the Fallen Angels? You're not something that goes bump in the night."

"We're powerful beings fighting for good in the shadows." Rohan stopped so abruptly before a thick iron door that I whacked into him. I stepped back, rubbing my nose while he placed his hand on a pad mounted beside the door to be scanned.

"Again, that's my point. Fighting for good. Not fallen."

"Everything falls eventually, Lolita, it's all just a matter of when gravity kicks in. Either way, we're the badass chosen ones wrapped in a really hot package." He tugged on one of my curls. "Time to prove you're one of us."

"One of us" as in chosen? Or did I get badass and hot status, too?

The door unlatched with a click.

"Welcome to the Vault." Rohan's eyes lit up with an evil glint, then he pushed me inside the all-consuming darkness and slammed the door.

6

I froze, straining my eyes seeking out the demons that I was positive they had stashed in here with me.

After a moment, Rohan opened the door again. "Kidding."

He flicked on the light to reveal a vast, well-lit studio. The ceilings and walls were the same concrete blocks as the hallway, but the floor was wall-to-wall blue padding. There were no windows.

"You're a dick," I told him.

He glanced down at his crotch. "It *is* legendary, but it doesn't fully define me."

"My God," I muttered. Noting Rohan's bare feet on the pads, I toed out of my shoes, stacking them beside the door. "Why is this called the Vault?" If there were valuables they were well hidden because there was nothing to see. Not even a punching bag.

"It's the most secure room."

I rolled out my shoulders. "Now what?"

"Training," Baruch said, entering.

"Shalom, Sensei Tree Trunk," I said, bowing with my hands together in Namaste position. "What's first? Weapons?" I could totally rock a weapon.

Baruch and Rohan exchanged glances. "Absolutely not," they said in unison.

Baruch's fist whipped out and bopped me on the nose.

"What the hell, dude?" I prodded for broken cartilage and blood but it had been more of a tap for shock effect than to do any damage. I was surprised, but otherwise fine.

"Demon tag. Now you're dead," Rohan said.

Baruch kicked out, swiping my legs out from underneath me.

I landed hard on my back. My hands flew up to cover my face as Baruch dove down, grabbing me lightly by the throat.

"Dead." Rohan yawned.

Baruch helped me up.

"I wasn't ready–"

Baruch mimed ripping out my heart.

Rohan smirked. "And dead. Getting the idea?"

I turned my back to him, refusing to let him taunt me. "Baruch, please tell me what I did wrong so that I do not repeat the experience. Since I refuse to give Emo Snowflake the satisfaction of dying."

The nickname earned me a sharp jab in my back.

The side of Baruch's mouth kicked up in the tiniest of grins but his voice was serious when he spoke to me. "You did not access your power. Your first instinct right now is to scream and run, like you did with the araculum." He pinned me with the weight of his shrewd blue gaze. "You'll be dead by nightfall unless you access your power at the first prickling of trouble."

"Got it. But the power seems to show up on its own."

"Your magic wants to be used," Baruch explained. "If it's not the first thing you fire up, you won't live long enough to use it. Activate it. Get in, kill, and get out with as little physical contact as possible. Run if you have to."

I shook out my arms and legs. "How do I access it?"

"How do you spit?" He waved off my grimace. "I'm serious. You spit saliva. You spit electricity. Both come from inside you. What do you do when you want to spit?"

I braced for some snarky comment from Rohan but he watched Baruch with a fascinated expression. "Okay, well." I took myself through the motions. "First, I tense up my jaw. To activate the saliva."

"Good. Then what's the power equivalent of that action? Close your eyes. Visualize. Where is your power?"

I did as I was told, eyes closed. "It's like there's a switch."

"Touch the spot." That was Rohan in a silky rumble, who now stood beside me. "Where do you envision it?"

Oh, Lordy. What I was actually envisioning right now? Very different from what Rohan intended. My eyes snapped open and I pushed him back. He didn't go anywhere so I stepped away from him. "Begone, irritant."

The look he shot me from under his eyelashes, full of wicked heat, made my mouth flood with saliva. I swallowed hard.

Baruch tsked at him. "Stop toying with her."

"I'm not toying. I'm deliberately distracting. Seeing if she can multitask." He smiled innocently at me. "I can't help it if she finds me irresistible."

"Oh, I find you something, all right," I growled, my hands out to throttle him. My fingertips sparked.

"Freeze," Rohan commanded in a steely voice.

"Anger," Baruch said. "Not fear. That's what turns you on."

Rohan barked a laugh, smoothing out his expression at Baruch's pointed stare.

I twisted my hands one way then the other, now glowing and crackling away. "So I just need to internalize you as my trigger?" I asked Rohan.

He batted his lashes at me. "Do what you need to, baby."

"Baruch?" I pleaded.

Baruch pointed to the door. "Go."

Rohan was undeterred. "You can't send me away."

Baruch quirked an eyebrow.

"Fine. I'm leaving. You're welcome," Rohan called out to me over his shoulder.

"Can you turn it off?" Baruch grasped my wrist, twisting my hand from side-to-side.

I closed my eyes, thinking about the switch inside me. I located it slightly down and to the back of my belly button, imagining it rooted there, with invisible cables snaking out to all parts of my body and the bright white switch set to on. Mentally, I flicked it the other way. Off.

I opened my eyes. My hands still crackled.

"They dimmed for a second," Baruch said. "Tell me what you know about demons."

"Nothing. Ari told me nothing." My words came out in a rush.

His expression gentled. "He won't be in trouble. I just want to know what information you already have."

I lowered my hands. "Okay, well–"

"Did I say stop your visualization?" he barked. "Do you think you'll be encountering demons with no distractions? Nothing else demanding your attention? Talk and train."

I made a snarky face–okay, imagined it–but in my head, man, did I put Tree Trunk in his place. I closed my eyes, picturing my power switch. "There are different levels of demons. Some work on a more global scale either in the shadows or more overtly to bring about civil unrest or world wars."

I tugged on my mental switch. I got the barest hold on it and it vibrated but didn't flick off. My magic continued to thrum through me. "Hey, how did Vancouver land a spot?"

"This chapter is the Canadian HQ. The fault lines along the west coast draws demons because they like the seismic activity. A naturally occurring instability."

"That's the heart of it, isn't it?" I asked, opening my eyes. "Instability. Natural, political, or emotional, demons thrive in those environments."

Baruch blinked proudly at me for making the connection. For half a second. "Again."

I threw all my mental power against the switch. "Some create more localized disasters, collapsing bridges or making sure levees fail." I had my suspicions about New Orleans. "Then they rush in to exploit an already vulnerable population. Same with areas hit by earthquakes or famine or flood. They feed off the chaos and pain."

My switch bucked to the halfway point, then crashed back to the "on" position. A sharp crack resounded through my hands. I shook them out.

"Again."

"Demons are also drawn to big cities. Tons of humans easily tempted. The New York chapter house has at least a dozen hunters stationed there at any given time."

I kept at my envisioned on/off switch. It took a while. A long while, but eventually, through sheer mind power, I made the electricity in my hands turn on and off at will.

"Mazel tov," Baruch congratulated me.

I jumped over to him like a little kid and hugged him. "That. Was. So. Cool!" It reminded me of when my balance and movement had come together and I'd done my first perfect shuffle in tap, instead of the clunky, wobbly steps up to that point. The moment when it all just clicked.

I was super proud of myself. Sweaty, metallic-smelling, and tomorrow I'd probably hurt like crazy, but proud. I'd done it. I could access my power at will. Even if this was a baby step, I'd mastered it. I wasn't sure anyone had thought I'd even get this far.

I wasn't sure I had.

Staying alive and being an asset. Yay me.

Baruch disengaged. "Now we work on firing up the rest. It might require a kick or even a head-butt to hit the kill spot and you want your power coming out of all of you."

Rohan popped back in. "How's she doing?"

I held up a fist. "The sisterhood for the win."

A paragon of blond-haired, green-eyed perfection stepped into the doorway. His loose, light brown linen pants and shirt really complimented his dark scowl. "As if a girl could become one of us," he spat in a super sexy Italian accent.

"One did, so suck it up, honey." I managed to give him the finger and waggle my Rasha ring at him, which was very talented of me, if I did say so myself.

Out in the hallway, Kane snickered.

Hot Angry Dude stalked toward me.

"Drio–" Rohan was cut off as Drio shouldered past him.

Baruch sighed and stepped into his path. Drio was a beautiful racehorse. Baruch was a bull.

"You said no one knew what to do with her. That that was why we got abruptly reassigned, with me and Ro on guard duty at the expense of our own mission. Remember?" Drio didn't back down, even with Baruch blocking his way. It was quite the commitment to hating me. "Can you say you're happy about it?" he asked Baruch.

"They reassigned people to me?"

"What did you think would happen, principessa?" he sneered. "That we wouldn't give you extra special treatment?"

I shoved myself between Tree Trunk and him. I could fight my own damn battles, thank you very much. "Newsflash, jerkwad, no one has told me jack. Believe it or not, I want to be part of your 'no girls allowed' club even less than you want me here. But you can't keep me in the dark." I whirled to Rohan. "You have to tell me important stuff."

"The Executive hasn't decided how they feel about you," Rohan answered, not bothering to soften that information. "As the first female Rasha, you're either a dream secret weapon or–"

"A walking nightmare," Drio cut in.

Rohan raised his eyebrows at him like "really?"

"With the deciding factor being what?" I asked.

Drio clicked his tongue. "Your performance. Supposedly your early death would be a bad thing."

"Wow," I said, "don't I feel precious?"

"You," Rohan said to Drio, "stop antagonizing. And you," he turned to me, "don't think I'm thrilled to babysit your ass."

"Why you?" I demanded.

"Because I'm such a people person."

"Or because you're a screw up?" I scratched my chin with the edge of my thumbnail. "Is that it? Did I get exiled to the island of misfit toys?"

Drio's hands balled into fists.

"Enough." Kane's voice cut smoothly through the tension. He pushed me back a few steps. "A little gratitude here," he said, with a tap to the end of my nose. "You've been given the best of the best. Baruch has put his brilliant military mind to use creating weapons and training Rasha to become even more effective. Rohan and Drio," Kane placed a hand on Angry's shoulder, "are two of our top intelligence officers and analysts on demon behavior. Thanks to them, we've unearthed and taken down a lot of demons living among us in positions of enormous power."

I cocked my head. "And you?"

He shrugged. "I'm just the lone Vancouver member who wasn't re-assigned."

Drio laughed. "Kane's nickname is the Kiss of the Death. He's one of the top Rasha in demon kills." His fond amusement morphed into an ugly leer. "We are the best. And you're the bright shiny trophy the entire demon world will want to bag. Be grateful or we won't keep you alive."

I rubbed my skin as if to wash his disgusting look off. "Never in a million years."

Drio shrugged, exiting with a tossed-out, "If the demons do get you, you won't be missed."

I flinched.

White spots of rage appeared on Rohan's cheeks. His eyes darkened to volcanic fire. He didn't say a word. Just sped from the room.

"Oh no," Kane said. He and Baruch raced after him, with me bringing up the rear.

We caught up in time to see Rohan leap from midway up the second flight of stairs onto Drio, tackling him. They crashed onto the main floor landing.

Drio managed to flip onto his back, but that merely allowed Rohan to pin him between his thighs.

Rohan pulled his left arm back. I tensed, waiting for his hand to curl into a fist and Drio's nose to be shattered. Instead, five short, wickedly sharp looking blades snicked out of Rohan's fingertips, with one long blade running up the entire outer edge of his arm. Like an outline. That longer blade slashed right through the center of the heart tattoo on his bicep.

Holy. Fuck.

"Finally decide to kill me?" I couldn't tell if Drio sounded anxious or hopeful.

I stared wide-eyed at the two of them. Not even daring to breathe. There was a powder keg of unspoken issues between them, and I was scared I was the fuse that could blow it all sky high. I didn't like Drio but I didn't want his death on my conscious.

Necessarily.

With a blur of motion, Rohan swiped.

Drio flinched, eyes closed, but Rohan jammed the blades into the ground beside his head.

"The demons will be after her," Rohan said, in a low rumble. "Which means we stick close and protect her. With. Our. Lives." He sounded oddly bleak about the concept. "Got it?"

Drio pushed Rohan off him. He gave a mocking salute. "Got it." With one last baleful look my way, he jumped to his feet and blazed off.

Rohan yanked his finger blades from the floor, leaving two inch gauges in the pretty planking. He shot an unreadable look after Drio before storming off in the opposite direction.

That left Baruch, Kane, and me standing there. "What was that about?" I asked.

Baruch was Mr. Impassive, which was no great surprise, but based on my short acquaintance with Kane, I was sure he'd give up the goods. Nope. He remained infuriatingly tight-lipped as well, simply saying, "I'll check on Drio."

Baruch shook his head when I glanced in the direction Rohan had taken. "Let him cool down," he said, before following Kane.

I never was any good at doing what I was told.

7

I found Rohan in the library, one of those massive floor-to-ceiling, wall-to-wall, book-filled rooms found only in Victorian mansions and Hollywood movies. It even had rolling ladders to reach high shelves, Persian carpets on the floor, and comfortable seating to curl up in. A long wood table with sturdy chairs ran along the bank of windows on the far side of the room.

I sank onto the leather club chair, a match to Rohan's that was grouped next to a large unlit fireplace, sneaking glances to gauge his mood. Tough to do since he was slumped on the sofa next to me, head bowed.

Neither of us said anything for a good long while.

I sniffed my T-shirt to make sure I didn't smell too disgusting. Not bad. Casting around for something else to do, I studied the pile of history texts left on the low mahogany coffee table, then got bored and just watched Rohan, waiting for his hands to unclench from the padded arm rest before I spoke.

"Why'd you quit singing?"

His head jerked up. "What?"

"It was around the time when you became Rasha, and maybe touring or being in the band might have been tough, but you could have kept singing. Writing music. You left the biz entirely."

"Yup," he replied in a "leave it alone" voice.

I'd only raised the topic trying to forge some kind of connection between us. I'd had my dancing, he'd had his singing, and I'd thought maybe there'd be some common ground we could bond over. After meeting Drio, having Rohan on my side was imperative. But his reticence made me actively curious.

"Was it a vocal chord thing? Did potential permanent damage end it?" In about three seconds, I wove an entire tale of the doors closing on Rohan's musical dreams, finishing up with him staring up at his doctor with impossibly sad eyes and asking à la Oliver Twist, "Please sir, may I sing another?"

Rohan glared at me.

"All right. Sheesh." I slouched back against my chair. "I'm sorry you got stuck with me," I said in a sincere voice. "I'll try not to die on your watch."

"Drio was right. You're the shiny prize. The demons are going to want bragging rights of killing the first female Rasha. And your head. They'll want that too."

"So they re-assigned you boys here to keep it attached to my body. Was this a demotion for you?"

"You'd think so."

I stopped fidgeting and met his eyes. Unimpressed. "Gee, thanks."

Rohan nudged my knee with his. "No. Until consensus among the Executive is reached on your status, they want the best around you."

I tried to ignore my queasiness at what would happen if consensus wasn't reached in my favor. Also, the tingle running up my leg from his touch.

"I appreciate it." I hoped I sounded suitably grateful. These guys were right about needing them to keep me safe and help me find my footing, especially if Asmodeus figured out it was me who'd offed his spawn. Much as I wished this would go away, I was a Rasha until death do us part.

"What happens if the Brotherhood decides they don't want a sister after all?"

Rohan took his sweet time answering. "I think if push came to shove, they'd decommission you."

My stomach squicked. "Is that a euphemism for 'bullet to the head?'"

Another long pause. Seriously? I drowned my apprehension in a tidal wave of positive sentiment but my apprehension broke free and bobbed to the surface, shooting me the finger for my efforts.

"Not murder," he finally said. "You already have too public a profile within the Brotherhood."

"Knowing I'm only going to stay alive because they might get caught is hardly reassuring." I grimaced.

"What about a timely unfortunate accident? I mean, Rasha die."

"They'd try to quietly retire you. Alive," he reassured me.

"Would that be so bad?" I sat up, intrigued. "Hey, could we transfer my powers to Ari?"

Exasperation on his face, Rohan got up.

I grabbed the side of his jeans, his quad muscle tensing under my palm as I pushed him back onto the couch. "Fine. Maybe it doesn't work that way. But I refuse to believe that simply re-running the ceremony was the final proof that I'm the sole Rasha twin. Ari is still an initiate and I'm going to prove it."

"Good luck with that."

"I'll train hard. In return," I continued, "you help me petition the Executive on Ari's behalf."

"Me? No. Not interested in getting involved."

Why were all of them so block-headed about helping me with this? "You don't want to be here. The faster I get up to speed, the faster you get to go home."

"I have a mission here other than you, you know."

"Yeah, but if you're as good as Kane says you are, then I bet you'll wrap that up soon. Come on, what could it hurt to try? At best, Demon Club gets the Rasha it wanted. At worst, my training schedule is accelerated and you go on your merry way. Deal?" I held out my hand to shake.

"No deal. I wrap up the primary mission, and I'll be on my merry way regardless. There's enough other people to watch you."

I leaned back, arms crossed. "Then let's negotiate." I'd spent a lifetime listening to my lawyer father.

"You've got nothing of value to offer me," Rohan said.

"What's the mission?" What if I could help Rohan complete this mission his way?

"Look, the gig that brought me to Vancouver is..." Rohan rubbed his hand roughly through his hair, sending it into spiky disarray. "I'm getting a lot of pressure to take it in a direction I don't agree with. Got enough of my own shit to deal with as far as the Executive is concerned. You're on your own."

"Now you've got me curious. What's up?"

Rohan hesitated.

I raised my hands. "If I haven't earned need-to-know clearance yet, I get it."

"It's not that. You'll freak out."

I picked up a pen left on top of the book pile and chucked it at him.

He caught it one-handed, studying me a moment, tapping the pen against his thigh.

I tried not to stare, my fingers twitching at the memory of his steely hard muscles. Or replace the pen with my tongue.

"First off, you understand now that you're bound by all Rasha oaths of secrecy not to discuss what you've heard." He shot me a wry look. "That includes not telling your brother."

I totally met his eyes when I agreed but he stared me down until I squirmed. "All right, already," I groused. "I won't dish."

"We suspect Samson King is a demon."

Rohan winced as I smacked his arm.

"No way! He's a celeb A-lister. I mean, yeah, he's got that smug rich kid vibe, even though he's got to be pushing thirty, but I figured someone that famous was just another overcompensating," I wagged my pinky meaningfully, "asshole celeb."

Rohan leaned in, his elbows braced on his knees, and a serious expression on his face. "I'm concerned about your fetish for the peen, Lolita. Do we need to have a talk?"

"Curiosity about celebrity genitalia is hardly fetish. It's practically hardwired into Western society's DNA."

"Hence, the race to the bottom," he muttered.

"Besides, I bet you fifty bucks there's more than a few sites devoted to your particular width and girth, Mr. Mitra."

"All of which would be staggeringly wrong."

The twin desires to both smack the smug off his face and rip off his pants to see for myself should have negated each other and yet, there they were. "Seriously, his stupid reality show *Live like a King* hits douchebag territory, but a demon?"

Rohan spread his fingers three inches apart. "Our dossier on him is already that thick." His hand clenched into a fist. "Trouble is, everything is circumstantial. Rumors and speculation. We don't have the hard proof such as his name or true form that would allow me to sanction the kill."

"Yet."

His eyes crinkled at the corners. "Yet. The seven deadly sins are mother's milk to demons and that show? It's the ultimate in envy with those humiliating challenges contestants do to be part of King's entourage."

"It's almost worse that he's not around to witness most of it," I said. "He just drops in with the occasional visit, a cocky smile, and a joke, and contestants redouble their efforts take each other out and get near him."

"He incites jealousy, even though on the surface it seems like he's inviting people along for the ride. In fact, if you deconstruct it, most of his brand is devoted to making people feel bad about themselves."

"By reminding them they're not him." I nodded. "He has that other reality show too, all about his limitless wealth and partying and he's always living large in his movies. The ultimate good-time dude and people love it. Love *him*."

"That's the problem." Rohan braced one foot on the coffee table. "His public persona is funny and charming. He's smart. Comes off as the guy most likely to buy a round, fly everyone to Vegas for a night out. No scandals, no rumors of deviant behavior. He's a huge star with a huge social media presence—a huge reach—and that makes him very dangerous." He stretched an arm out along the top of the sofa. "His brand has an adverse affect on people that's way out of line with other celebs. More than people jealous or bummed out that they don't get to live his lifestyle."

"Like what? People quitting this cruel world because they don't get to be him?" Had I known being Rasha meant getting all up in stars' dirty business, I'd have signed up years ago.

"Yeah. After *Live like a King* aired, Drio and I started tracking down everyone affiliated with the show. A lot of contestants and crew had died." He danced the pen over his knuckles as he spoke. "They all seemed like accidents: motorcycle crash, OD, that kind of thing, but given the mental state of the people, we believe they were suicides." He white-knuckled the pen. "Then there was the disaster at *Kingdom Come*."

Talk about a nightmare. Samson had invited a bunch of his rock star and hip hop friends to a concert in the desert. A couple hundred thousand people packed in all day with insufficient water and for the grand finale, when King himself took the stage for his singing debut, some scaffolding collapsed. Between that carnage and sunstroked dehydration, hundreds were left dead and wounded. And still people fell all over themselves to defend him and his shitty concert.

"Was the collapse deliberate?" I tugged the pen out of his hand because he was about to pulverize the poor thing. Had Rohan known any of the performers that had died?

He looked down in surprise, as if he'd forgotten he'd had the writing utensil in the first place. "We have questions about the mindset of the rigger in charge. He'd been tight with Samson. If King is feeding off the pain and misery he causes, he's gaining incredible power, but to what end?"

I made a *pffft* noise. "World domination. You're welcome."

He failed to look impressed. "No shit. But how? What's his final move and is there a specific trigger for it? Another disaster like *Kingdom Come* but on a bigger scale? Something else entirely? What's the timeline?" Rohan blew out his cheeks in frustration. "That's what we have yet to determine. It would help if we could figure out what type of demon he is. We need to crack someone in his inner circle, get in close to monitor him, but we've had no luck gaining entry."

"So what's causing the dissenting plans of attack?"

"Doesn't matter," Rohan said.

Nice blow off but I wasn't that easily dissuaded. "You ended up here in Vancouver why?" I asked.

"King is shooting a movie and—"

"*Hard Knock Strife*!" I bolted upright in my seat.

Rohan ducked as the pen shattered in *my* grip, sending plastic shards flying.

"Josh, the lust demon that I–" I shot Rohan a warning look as I tossed pen remnants on the table. "Anyway, he'd been cast in that movie. I didn't realize it was King's." I gnawed on my bottom lip. "How many of the other actors in the gang are demons? Samson is smart enough to cover his tracks. But what about the others? Josh didn't strike me as the sharpest tool in the shed. Has King worked with other demons before?"

Rohan studied me with a coolly assessing look. "That's a good idea."

"Yeah, I get them when the moon lines up with Uranus."

He didn't appreciate my wit. "Except we already checked that avenue out. There was one demon that King worked with on a regular basis but my buddy Eyal took him out in Boston a couple of months ago. Probably how your boy Josh got the part."

Rohan must have seen how bummed I was that I hadn't provided the golden nugget needed to get close to Samson, because he added, "You're off to a good start. Eventually, you'll become a good fighter, too."

"I have no idea how I specifically killed either Josh or his sister and I'm not thrilled about having to trial and error my way to survive every demon encounter."

"Then learn about as many demons as possible and where their weak spot is located. That will keep you alive as much as your magic." Rohan got up and walked over to one of the neatly arranged shelves where he extracted a thin, red, leather-bound book. He flipped through it. "All demons of the same type, say, all araculum, have the same weak spot," he explained. "It gets trickier with the Uniques, the one-off demons like Lady Midday. In those cases we don't have the multiple kills that have taught us where to aim for. Though if we've had a few encounters, then sometimes we've figured out the location for when we finally get close enough to make the kill."

Rohan brought the open book over to me. He nudged my elbow away to perch on the arm of my chair, shoving the book under my nose.

I read the passage he pointed to. "Okay, this weak spot can be located anywhere in a demon's body, ranging from the bottom of their foot to behind their eyes." I scanned the rest of the page. "You know, I always thought that the way to kill a demon was through its heart."

Rohan snorted. "What do you think a heart is?"

I twisted about half an inch to better face him. My arm skimmed his thigh, his muscles clenching in response. I could do this call and answer with his body part all day. "Does this weak spot have a name?" I asked.

He shifted his weight, his hip resting against my shoulder. "I told you, the heart."

The words blurred meaninglessly on the page. I felt like I was back in ninth grade at the movie theater with Adam Kim, so focused on the minutiae of movements between our bodies that the entire screen had been a giant white blob.

My chest brushed his forearm. I was more than a bit curious if all this touching was a coincidence on his part or more of some endless game we seemed to be playing. "You aren't being metaphoric, then."

"It's true on many levels."

I ran my finger over the heart tattoo on his left bicep. "What baggage-laden break up led to this visual reminder, hmmm?"

"Focus." His breath tickled the back of my neck as he leaned over me.

Dilemma. I was torn between prolonging any part of Rohan touching any part of me and giving in to being a curious kitten. I raised my eyes to his, unable to resist asking. "Come on, who was she?"

Rohan stood up abruptly, snapping the book shut.

Stupid curiosity.

"You can't be buried in a Jewish cemetery," I said, trying a different tack. "Not with tattoos."

That got me a wry smile. "What gives you the impression I think there will be anything left of me to bury?"

Wow. These dudes were grim.

"How am I supposed to know which demon has which weak spot?"

Rohan replaced the book, waving a hand around the library. "You learn."

Sure, Ari had shared some details of demons and hunting with me, but taking in the plethora of books now, I had a long way to go to even learn the basics. I sighed in resignation. "Where's my Giles?"

Rohan stared blankly at me.

"You know," I said, "the stuffy-yet-caring resident librarian mentor who provides helpful and timely info on a demon-by-demon basis?"

"There's no librarian." Rohan tapped his head. "You are your own librarian."

Great. Initiates got a lifetime of mentoring in demonology but I was told to independent study my way through. "Right."

I trolled the shelves, running my finger along the spines. Most of the books featured the same publisher's imprint on their spine: the letters BD in white against a black square background. Made sense that the Brotherhood printed their material in-house. "How about a podcast?"

"No."

"Cheat sheet?"

Rohan gave a slow, disbelieving shake of his head. "It's called reading. Your commitment to apathy is impressive."

I moved to the next bookshelf, tossing him a smile over my shoulder. "Why, Mr. Mitra, you say the sweetest things."

In the window's reflection, I caught Rohan massaging his temples. Taunting him was fun, however... "You're wrong about my impressive commitment," I said, turning to face him. "It's not to apathy. You've had your entire life to learn this stuff. I'm not against reading. I'm against the amount of time I'd need to get up to speed. Time which, if demons are gunning for me? I don't have."

"Cheat sheets." He looked glum.

"Twelve point Helvetica is fine. Start with the main bad guys, ranking from domain down through species. Or a *Demons for Dummies* book. With lots of pictures. That works too."

He brightened. "We have that." He jogged over to a far corner of the library.

I stared in amazement as he pulled out a fat primer entitled *Most Common Demons* and presented it to me. "That's a kids' book," I said, frowning at the bright cover.

"Yup." Rohan shoved it into my chest. I caught it with an unhappy thump. "None of our initiates are dummies," he said, "but I'm guessing even you can keep up with a seven-year-old's reading comprehension." He patted my head.

Did people have weak spots? Or could I just aim for the actual heart with humans? I eyed Rohan, sizing him up.

Kane strolled into the library with a pile of books, whistling when he saw what I held. Seriously, did this guy ever wear proper clothes? "*Hel-lo* nightmares for days." He dumped his books on a table, snatched mine out of my hands, and flipped through it. "This sucker frightened me out of my wits."

I peered at the illustration. "It looks like an evil Teenage Mutant Ninja Turtle."

His eyes lit up. "Exactly! It's a kappa demon from Japan. I lived in terror of it coming after me."

"Why? Some kind of connection to your heritage?"

He stared at me like I was stupid. "It sucks your entrails out through the ass. Do you know how scary that was to a chubby gay kid?" He gave an exaggerated shudder, handing the book back to me.

"I look forward to finding my own personal nightmare," I said.

Speaking of Rohan, he rolled his eyes but before he could say anything, there was an unsettling high-pitched whistle from the woods out back.

Kane peered out the window. "Demon."

I hugged the book to my chest. "Asmodeus?"

"Nope. That was the cry of the curupira." Kane shot me an odd look. "Why would you think that?"

I sank into a chair, weak-kneed in relief. "You better go kill it."

"Wrong pronoun, Lolita." Rohan tugged me to my feet. "Show time."

8

When my protests of "I've only been training for a couple of hours," and "you should
never meet a demon on an empty stomach," failed to
work, I went for Plan B and dug my heels into the
grass in the backyard like a little kid.

Rohan hauled me over his shoulder in a fireman's
carry, ignoring all my pummeling until he'd stepped
through a heavy iron door set into the back fence, at
which point he dumped me on the ground.

Outside the wards.

I scrambled to my feet.

Rohan whistled some bird call and a moment later Baruch jogged out of the trees, a bruise blossom-
ing on his cheekbone. He nodded when he saw me.
"Good. Now you can show us what you did with the
brother."

"Huh?"

As if choreographed, he and Rohan stepped in
sync to one side, right as a demon charged me with a
chilling growl. Unlike the araculum, this demon was
humanoid. Ish. About the height of your standard

NBA player, his red eyes burned like glowing coals. Jagged fangs protruded from his fleshy lips and a matted black pelt covered his torso, but the most terrifying thing about him was his enormous cock. It jutted out erect, a non-bobbing zucchini of such knobby rigidity that I wouldn't have been surprised if he swatted Mack trucks out of his path with it.

This time when I ran screaming, hopping tree roots, and stirring up piles of damp, decomposing leaves, I shot off wild blasts of electricity. My training had really taken.

"I wouldn't," Rohan called out. "He'll just see you as prey."

"Do what you did to the brother," Baruch ordered.

I glanced over my shoulder at Penisaurus Rex. Hell, no. Having run in a wide circle back to my starting point, I beelined for Tree Trunk, determined to hide behind him. Yeah, right. As soon as I got within arm's range, Baruch pushed me back into the demon's path.

The evil spawn scooped me up from behind and squeezed. Not the boobs! I gritted my teeth against the pain flaring in my sensitive flesh and yanked my knees up to my chest, grateful for my years of tap training and core strength because no way were my parents going to identify my body while impaled on his member.

Pain quickly became my secondary concern. The pressure on my rib cage soon hurtled toward total pulverization. I couldn't access my magic, couldn't do anything except be crushed to death. At least I'd have a lovely soundtrack of gaily twittering birds to accompany my death throes.

Keeping me imprisoned with one arm, the curupira scrabbled the fingers of his other hand against my skull, as if trying to pierce the skin.

"He's going to suck your brains out like a lobster claw," Rohan said in a conversational tone.

I jerked my head sideways, trying to escape the demon's sharp fingernail now seeking the right spot to drill down into my head, and was rewarded with a sapling thwack to the cheek.

"Show me how you killed Asmodeus' bastard," Baruch said. "When it was just you and him. You've got the power. Use it."

Any second now, I'd black out and become lunch. I clawed at the demon's arms, desperate to loosen his hold so I could inhale, but there was no shaking him loose.

Assholes one and two did nothing.

My body burned. With rage. A scream tore from my throat as I fired up. The current arcing off my fingertips was a sharp agony. The air stank of burning hair. The demon's chest, my head.

Visualizing, I slammed my switch on, letting it pulsate with electricity. I imagined it racing through my veins, my very blood alight. My entire body glowed blue, a violent crackle filling my ears.

I slammed my hand onto the demon's thigh. Hang on. His thigh should have been too big for my hand to curve around.

Damnation, not again! I ripped my hand off his dick and planted it on his hip.

The demon flinched enough to drop me but he didn't die. I hit the ground in a sprawl, brushing dirt from my eyes, my shin cracking against the edge of a small boulder. "Fuck," I gasped, gulping down blessed lungfuls of air.

Sparks flew off me, one catching fire on the edge of a dry, rotting log. Out of the corner of my eye, I saw Rohan spring into action, smothering the wood with wet leaves.

I was more pre-occupied by the fact that even though the demon stood in front of me, I was looking at his heels and not his toes. I didn't have time to ponder the mystery because he grabbed my hair, yanking a good handful out in my subsequent roll away.

I jumped up. Tiny sparks crunched between the soles of my feet and the dirt, tickling in an itchy sensation.

The demon lunged for me on what I now saw were his backwards feet.

Dancing and bobbing, careful not to trip on the uneven ground, I focused on not being grabbed, because I had no clue how to fight this thing. The only thing that came to mind was Sandra Bullock's self-defense demo in one of my favorite movies *Miss Congeniality*. S.I.N.G.

I didn't think I could get in close enough to do any damage to his solar plexus but maybe his instep was a possibility. Take him down via his freaky toot-sies. I dove onto the ground, rolling to grab his ankle. Once I had a firm grasp, I fired my current into him.

A furious howl tore from his throat and he kicked out, trying to buck me off, but I held strong, so he picked me up by my ankles, facing outward. The for-est swung upside down with a sickening blur.

I slid my zapping hands up his sandpapery calves, trying to get a hold on him to break free. Sadly, my attack provoked more than pained him. Still holding me by my ankles, he shook me violently, his bulbous knob poking me in the small of my back. Beyond gross. Trying not to touch it, I shot my magic behind me in what I hoped was the right direction. There was a sizzling sound, like franks on a grill. Though given that his dick fell to the ground wizened and black, his wiener did not plump when you cooked it.

The demon roared, shaking me hard enough to rattle my teeth.

Using what little stamina I had left, I rocked my-self backward, getting a firmer grip on his legs. I pretty much pawed him all over, and while my magic had to hurt, my situation seemed pointless until I grabbed and squeezed the demon's kneecap.

The sweet spot.

The creature was engulfed in current. He dropped me on my back with a hard *thunk*, as he exploded into red dust. White and blue spots danced before my eyes.

I lay there a moment, letting the tree canopy come into focus before sitting up, rubbing my shoulder, and spitting demony powder out of my mouth. As glad as I was to be alive, I was livid at having been pushed into that little demonstration that way. How about a gentle guiding on day one for the new girl? I glowered at Rohan and Baruch.

They stared back at me gobsmacked, all color drained from their faces. Rohan's hand snaked protectively in front of his crotch as my eyes met his.

That's what he took away from this?

I pushed to my feet. There were a million snarky remarks I could have made except I didn't trust my voice right now. I couldn't get my ribcage to unconstrict and I was shaking so hard, I'm amazed my brain didn't plop out.

Ignoring the tiny abrasions on my soles, I strode off without a look back, my breath coming in furious gasps. I entered the house via the back door in the kitchen, searching for a woman's washroom until I realized there wasn't one because *they all sucked* and then barricaded myself in the one bathroom I was able to find. For something used by all men, it was a clean enough room with the dark wood vanity/white counter combo all in vogue.

Expression stuck in a snarl, I pumped soap onto my hand, wincing as it hit my cracked bleeding skin from my demon-inspired obsessive hand washing. Kicking the vanity door didn't help. It hurt my toes and did nothing to make me feel better.

What kind of sick sadists threw a total newbie into proving herself like that? Those two would have let me die and chalked it up to *my* incompetence. I grabbed some toilet paper and blew my nose.

Forget the demons, these people were the monsters.

There was a soft rap at the door. "Nava?" It sounded like Kane but I wasn't sure so I didn't answer. "Babyslay, let me in."

I debated ignoring him some more, but I was going to need an escort to get out of this place unharmed and Kane seemed like my sole ally. I tossed the toilet paper into the bowl and unlocked the door.

The first thing I noticed was his terrible taste in shirts. A paisley pattern in lurid purples, it was a bold look. A look that slapped itself on the crotch and said, "Here I am." I respected that about it.

The second thing I noticed was the compassion in his eyes.

The third was the Gatorade he held out to me.

I chugged half the bottle in one go, before pressing it in sweet relief against my forehead. "I don't even like this shit."

"Doesn't matter. Your body craves the electrolytes to recharge after using your power. You'll learn to keep stashes handy." Kane leaned back against the closed door. "Our powers don't manifest the second they do the induction ceremony. I don't know if anyone told you that."

"I've been told very little about this process."

"It means that a lot of us find ourselves in extremely embarrassing situations when it shows up."

"Was yours bad?" I asked.

He laughed mirthlessly, his hip braced against the door. "Dad had this vintage Ferrari convertible. She was the most beautiful thing I'd ever seen in my life. He'd take me out for rides." Kane's expression grew dreamy. "We wouldn't even talk. It was all about feeling the curve of the road. The sun on our faces and the wind in our hair."

The past tense of this didn't sound good. "What happened?"

"After I became Rasha, my parents were so thrilled that Dad said I could take her for a spin. So long as I washed her first, she was mine for the rest of the day." A wistful look came over his face, as he leaned back against the door. "I think I was more excited about that then fighting demons. Picture it. This perfect summer day. This perfect specimen of a man washing this perfect car."

I gave the requisite smile.

"Do you know the effects of water and salt on iron?" he asked.

"Rust," I replied, confused at the change in topic.

He nodded and held out his arm. "Look, but don't touch." His flesh broke out in an oily sheen. An iridescent purple flecked with tiny white crystals. "It's a salt-based poison."

I would have guessed that from the smell alone. My mouth watered bitterly. I raised my eyes to his and gasped. Even his face was coated with it.

"One bad touch and the demons die," he said.

I peered at his flesh, fascinated. "What about if a person touches it?"

"Trust me. You don't want to know." The sheen disappeared from his body.

I reached out to touch him but he flinched away, shaking his head. "Wait." He turned on the tap and dispensing a good handful of liquid soap with his clean hand, washed where the poison had been. "Until I clean off, I can still burn you."

"I'm sorry." That seemed like it might be a lonely existence.

"It's always the pretty ones you have to look out for." He shrugged. "I can control it. Now. But the poor, wet car? When my powers showed up?"

"Rusted," I gasped.

"Instantly."

"What did your dad do?"

An unreadable expression flashed across his face. "That, dear girl, is a story for another day. All this to say: your. Power. Is. Fabulous!" His face brightened.

"Do you know how many asshole dates I could have cut short with it?"

"I am not giving demon hand jobs."

Kane pulled the hand towel off the rack and wiped his dripping face and arm dry. "While I can't wait to hear the story of your first kill, Baruch and Rohan just did what they'd do to any new member." His eyes widened theatrically. "Oops. Phrasing."

I prodded the side of my head, wincing at the bright burst of pain. "Except I wasn't trained my whole life for this. It was horrible. A super unfair trial by fire."

He placed his hand on my shoulder with a sympathetic smile. "It's your life now, babyslay. But it doesn't mean you have to go it alone."

No, it just meant that Ari had to. Still, I smiled back. "Thanks, Kane."

"Anytime." With a wink, he took my empty sports drink bottle.

Baruch was waiting for me outside the door. "I made you a sandwich." Guilt food. Good. Those usually came with extra side dishes.

He led me into the kitchen, my stomach gurgling. On the large table by the sunny window, Baruch had laid out two plates along with big glasses of very cold iced tea from a blue glass pitcher.

There was a distinct lack of sides, but I accepted the peace offering of shaved meat, sliced bocconcini, and tomato on a crusty Portuguese bun. I sank into a chair, eager to dig in.

Baruch sat beside me. Even though his ass extended past the seat, it was so rock hard that it didn't droop over the sides. I checked twice to make sure.

"So you were in Jerusalem before now?" I asked.

"No, Cairo. They needed extra hands with all the civil unrest. But I was in Chicago when I got the heads up about you."

I bit into the pickle that Baruch had laid as garnish on the side of my plate. He'd given me the perfect segue. "If Rasha are needed," I said, "all the more reason to make sure about Ari's status. What if the ritual when we were babies determined that we were *both* initiates?"

Baruch picked up the other half of his sandwich. "And what if as your twin, Ari carried an echo of your potential, your magic, from sharing the womb, and that's what Rabbi Abrams picked up?"

"How is that possible? Ari and I are fraternal twins. We don't share DNA, we didn't share a placenta or amniotic fluid, so why would sharing the womb matter?" Mom had versed Ari and I in all sorts of twin facts.

"If your brother did not carry the magic passed down through the bloodlines to the descendants of the original Rasha, then the reason Rabbi Abrams would have thought Ari did is because he felt the residue of your power on your twin."

"Is that what the Brotherhood believes?" I squirted another dollop of spicy mustard on my sandwich.

He nodded. "If Ari was an initiate, re-running the ceremony should have worked. He would have become Rasha."

The mustard lid snapped shut with a hard click. "But I'm a complicating factor. Hasn't anyone thought of that? My existence could have screwed everything up that would normally work. You don't just give up on someone you've invested in."

Baruch bit into his roast beef, chewing slowly and methodically before swallowing. "There is a way of things."

I didn't get a chance to further refute his argument because Rohan entered the kitchen and slapped a piece of paper down on the table beside me. "Your schedule."

It was color coded to within an inch of its life. "Three entire meals a day? Wow. You really follow minimum prison standards around here." I tapped the paper. "Where are my snack breaks?"

Rohan pulled a chair out, doing his straddle backwards thing again. "What are you, five?"

"I have a very fast metabolism." I grumbled at the only eight hours of sleep he'd allotted. "You've accounted for every second of my day."

"Yeah, and?"

Baruch pushed his chair back, carrying his plate and glass to the sink. "Five minutes then back to the Vault. I want to go over what you could have done differently in the fight."

I nodded to show I'd heard. "What about free time?"

"For all your scintillating hobbies?" Rohan plucked an apple out of the fruit bowl on the table and bit into it.

"Yes. As well as the many good works I do."

He arched his eyebrow, miming giving a hand job.

"Are you ever going to let that go?"

He took another bite. "Not when there are still hours of fun to be had from it. You know you don't have to jerk the demons off to kill them, right?"

"It was one time."

He slapped the table. "Knew it! Baruch owes me twenty."

I groaned at the fact that I'd just confirmed his suspicions.

"Don't feel bad," he said with a smirk, "I puzzled it out when reaching for the curupira's dick was your first move."

"I couldn't not reach for Mount Phallus. He was hung like a horse."

He held up his hands. "If that's your kink, then hey, no judgment."

Here we go. "No judgment, huh?"

"No way, Shaft." Rohan's composure cracked, his shoulders shaking as he hummed the *Shaft* theme music. "Though I wouldn't rely on it as a kill tactic," he said, now howling with laughter.

Bastard. "How about my thanks for taking me in hand, then?" I purred, leaning over to run my fingertips up his leg. "So to speak." I was bluffing, but he'd already unsettled me so many times that I wanted to rattle him back and my arsenal of weapons was laughably small.

His hand clamped over mine, millimeters from his crotch. "Seems I didn't need to go after Drio for his gratitude crack. Since you're giving it away."

"I'm not offering it to all and sundry, asshole." I yanked my hand away. "That little tussle between you boys had nothing to do with me. And for the record, what I did to Josh was not intended as a fighting maneuver. It was grown-up time."

"I'm a grown-up."

"You're more of a growth," I said. "There's a difference. And with that thing? Trust me, his dick was the last thing I wanted to touch."

"Curupira," Rohan repeated. "From Brazil."

"It should have stayed there."

"Next objection?" Rohan took the last bite of fruit then pitched the core across the room into the trash. Nice shot.

"Do we get paid for this?" I asked.

"Yes. You start at minimum wage."

"What about danger pay?"

Rohan cocked his fingers at me like a gun. "That's a good idea. I'll talk to Ms. Clara about adding it while we're stuck with you."

I stood, snatching up my dirty dishes. "I may not want to be here any more than you want me here, but that doesn't give you the right to treat me with a lack of respect." I dumped them into the sink then whirled to face him. "Now," I continued, "we're going to set some ground rules. The first is, you're going to remember that unlike the rest of you, I didn't get to spend my entire life training and studying because Demon Club was so short-sighted, they couldn't see that a girl was the chosen one."

Rohan pushed to his feet in one fluid move. I was going to have to learn that trick. My standing up always involved weirdly jutting out body parts.

"Fine," he said, getting in my face. "Then the second has to be that you shut up and listen. Yeah, we threw you in the deep end. There's no time to pussyfoot around with you. Your magic is active. That means you need to know how to use it because I guarantee that demons are gonna be a regular part of your life now."

"You still played dirty," I said. "I get that I'm a huge target, but I thought you guys were supposed to have my back." He opened his mouth but I held up a hand, cutting him off. "How far would you have let it go with the curupira before you stepped in to help?"

His hesitation told me everything I needed to know.

I slammed on the tap to rinse off my plate, my back to him.

"We would never have let it kill you," he said in a low voice.

I blinked rapidly, my eyes hot and itchy. I gave myself to the count of five to compose myself and face him. "I'm still the special unicorn Demon Club wants protected. I can make your life very hard if I want to."

"Back at you, Lolita."

I bit back my retort for the sake of my Ari plan. "I better return to my training, then." I'd almost made it to the doorway when something pointy hit my back. I turned around to see my schedule, now in paper airplane form flutter to the ground.

Rohan smirked at me, but I gave him a sweet smile, picked up the damn schedule, and left. I saved my outburst for my bedroom later that night, flinging my bag at the wall. The thunk that the demon primer made as the bag connected wasn't nearly satisfying enough.

Ari poked his head in. "What happened?"

"They threw a demon at me."

Ari's eye bulge was gratifying. "On your first day? It took me years to get up close to one. Under major supervision."

"Yeah, well." I snatched up my bag, dumping the contents out on my bed. Perhaps a tad viciously.

Ari picked up the book, glancing at the cover with a soft laugh before turning back to me. "That was kind of shitty but they made sure it was a relatively harmless one, right? An imp or a—"

"Curupira."

Ari stilled, turning an interesting shade of red. "A what?" His voice chilled me.

I tugged the book from his hands. "Ace."

"No. You could have died."

"I killed it. In the end." He gave a choking cough like he didn't believe me. I slammed the book down on my mattress. "Thanks for the vote of confidence, bro."

Ari crossed his arms. "On your first day? You killed a curupira?"

I crossed my arms right back. "Technically, it was my second day. And my third kill." You know, put that way, I had a pretty sweet success rate.

His eyes narrowed. "No one helped you?"

"Screw you. Is it so tough to believe I did it?"

"Yeah, all right? It is." He slammed the door on the way out and I flopped down on my bed.

Even when I beat the odds and did well, somehow things overwhelmingly sucked. Thanks for nothing, universe.

9

The next few days were a blur of training, training, and more training. I'd gotten to the point where no matter how Baruch lunged at me or otherwise tried to surprise me, I could turn my power on, going all shocktastic on him. With no more screaming and running. My defense was awesome, too. I was queen of blocking and could break most holds.

The first time I earned a "tov meod" or "very good" from Baruch for my efforts, I swear, cartoon birds danced around my head. I even had a new self-anointed superhero name–Lady Shock and Awe. Ari and his pop psychology could suck it.

On this drizzly Thursday morning, or as I called it, *Nava's Origin Story, Day Five: In Which Her Last Bit of Skin Gets Pummeled by Tree Trunk,* I found my brother in the kitchen, still dressed in yesterday's clothes, asleep on his homework. Our paths had barely crossed since our fight the other night, but even our brief encounters were enough to note his descent into depression. Careful not to wake him, I moved the binder out from under his cheek, finding a scrawled "I hate my life" at the top of his chem equations page.

I bowed my head, exhausted and frustrated at being no further along with my Ari plan. Rabbi Abrams had been detained on business and Ms. Clara, though sympathetic, was unwilling to put me in touch with the Executive. The one bright spot was my brother was too bummed to go out and fight demons himself.

I couldn't let him keep spiraling downward. Dad always said to take emotion out of the equation and see what things boiled down to. The Brotherhood already owned my ass. Still, a hot start up garnered more attention and resources than a dud subsidiary. I needed a win. A big one. And the biggest potential win I could think of was already sending spider demons after me.

It was time to take my training to a new level.

Baruch showed up at my house moments later in a warded-up, reinforced Hummer. Not that you could tell from looking at it. Another benefit of the Brotherhood having a fuckton of cash.

I slumped on the leather passenger seat, stifling a yawn. "Why are you pulling chauffeur duty?"

"Asmodeus is intensifying his efforts to find out who killed his kids." He shrugged out of his sweater, tossing it into the backseat. Ragged gashes peeped above the neckline of his shirt.

I stuttered out a harsh breath. "Are you okay?"

"Yes." Baruch patted my head. Oddly, coming from him, this gesture felt sweet and did not inspire me to rip his condescending hand off. "I won't let the demon get you. You're my sister now."

Aww. My jacked-up insides went gooey. The lack of any demons waiting to ambush us when we pulled up to the gate helped too.

Rohan bounded down the stairs as I dumped my jacket and shoes in the foyer. Our few encounters had been decidedly tense since our spat in the kitchen. One look at me and he sighed. "Baruch told you."

"Yup."

He placed a hand on my shoulder. "He'll have to get through me first." Sure, because he didn't want to hear the Executive bitch about it if I died before they'd decided on my fate.

I shook him off. "Thanks. Better find Tree Trunk."

Rohan searched my face, then with a nod, stepped aside to let me go.

Ms. Clara ambushed me the moment I hit the ground floor, beckoning me over. "Well, don't just stand there."

"Better go," Baruch said from behind me. "Clara gets a hard-on for signatures."

She narrowed her baby blues on him. "I heard that, Mr. Ya'ari." She clapped her hands. "Chop. Chop." Tiny, breathy, and steel-spined. No way was I disobeying her.

I scurried down the hall past the conference room and a couple smaller meeting rooms/floating offices for Rasha or Executive in town, dragging Baruch with me. Rather, he let himself be dragged. "Since when are you given permission to call her Clara?" I asked in a low voice, as Ms. Clara turned into her office. "Are you and her...?" I was about to make a lewd motion but the look on his face had me rethink that. "Are you a thing?"

He didn't answer me. One more item to add to my list of mysteries about these guys.

Her office was meticulous. Tasteful photographic prints of the city, from towering Douglas fir in Pacific Spirit Park to neon signs in Chinatown framed her white walls. Three normal humans would have been comfortable in the small space. With Tree Trunk in there, our fit was positively snug.

Ms. Clara sat down in her black and brushed steel Aeron chair that matched her desk. She twisted the large monitor out of the way, pushing a thick file with my name typed on the tab toward me. "This covers the basics of your employment."

Like my severance pay body bag?

I flipped the file open. "Hang on. I've been here since Monday. It's Thursday and you're just getting around to having me fill out the paperwork now?" That seemed oddly lax for her. "Was the Brotherhood hoping I wouldn't last the week so they wouldn't have to bother processing me?"

Ms. Clara selected a pen from the cup on her desk with intense concentration while Baruch just sat there, arms crossed, poker faced.

"*Are you fucking kidding me?*" I didn't even apologize at Ms. Clara's admonishing glance.

"I'll need your phone and laptop," she said, handing me the pen. "Your data will be transferred over to encrypted models." Ari had been given his first encrypted phone from Demon Club when he was fifteen. I knew how this worked.

I signed about ten times, my writing furious scrawls before I was calm enough to speak. "You mean you're going to track me. Glad to know I've earned that minimal protection."

"Enough." Baruch's quiet command defused the temper tantrum I wanted to throw.

Ari. Ari. Ari. I set the mantra to loop in my head. "The phone is upstairs in my bag. I'll bring in the laptop tomorrow."

Ms. Clara leaned across the desk to tap a signature I'd missed. "Good. Our tracking program ups the odds of finding you should you run into trouble. Twenty-four hours of inactivity and the Brotherhood is alerted to its last known location. Same if it gets destroyed."

Much as I loathed the idea of Big Brotherhood keeping tabs on my every move, I wasn't about to argue with something that could save my skin.

Ms. Clara wasn't kidding about the paperwork. Forget chosen one crap. I'd joined the mother of all corporations. My hand started cramping up from the sheer number of signatures and forms to fill out, like the swearing to secrecy shit. Damn, I hadn't been bound by any oaths yet when I'd talked to Rohan in the library. "I don't get it. You're the housekeeper *and* clerical worker?"

Baruch guffawed.

Ms. Clara stilled, looking up from where she was initialing a form. "Housekeeper? Wherever did you get that idea?"

I edged back on the seat. Her tone was kind of scary and she knew how to use a whip. "I asked who cleaned the house." Leaving *who* I asked purposefully vague since I wasn't about to sell Kane out to a woman who could inflict thirty lashes. "And was told you took care of it. Plus, you made cookies."

Yeah, that sounded like reaching, even to me.

Any hope of support from Baruch was pointless. He sat there, his eye blinks conveying his hilarity.

"I take care of it because I take care of everything in this house of overgrown children," she informed me, her voice less breathy, more steely. "I'm in charge of all Brotherhood administrative business in Canada. Rasha, rabbi, or Executive member living or visiting this country, I'm their go-to."

"How does the Executive work? Do they fly out here often?" With all the training and plotting, I hadn't had a chance to learn much about them yet and every bit of intel helped.

"No. Rabbi Abrams passes on any local concerns that they need to be involved in. The six rabbis chosen to make up the Executive handle big picture organizational issues like establishing new chapter houses." Ms. Clara pointed at a couple of places where I'd missed signing.

"We have them in many major cities across the globe but as global crises change," she said, "so do locations and the number of Rasha stationed there. Hunters are reassigned all the time. The Executive has been busy with field offices in Northern Africa these past few years. And of course the head of the Executive, Rabbi Mandelbaum, also personally interacts with the intelligence department."

"Like hunter Homeland Security?" I glanced at Baruch to see if he'd weigh in but he was checking something on his phone.

Ms. Clara kept up the explanation. "Security on an international level. They monitor crimes across the globe for certain details that could be evidence of demonic activity. Social media activity as well as anything gleaned through work under DSI. All intelligence gathered goes through them before being handed over to Rasha as specific missions."

I shook out my hand. "James Bond epic."

"As for the cookies–"

"Really, really good cookies," I interjected.

Her expression softened. "Thank you, doll. I like making cookies." She picked up a stress ball from her desk, squeezing it. "With this bunch in town, I need all the stress relief I can get." She winged the ball at Baruch's head, nailing him in the temple and killing his amused eye blinks.

Baruch bent to retrieve the ball from the floor and placed it back on her desk. He tucked his hair behind his ears, sliding his phone into his pocket. "Our stress is what makes you the most in-demand dominatrix in the country. You wouldn't be half so good if we didn't push you to your breaking point."

"You wouldn't even begin to know where I break," Ms. Clara replied darkly.

"Perhaps not." Baruch shrugged and I leaned in. This was better than HBO. Oh, to have popcorn.

Sadly, Ms. Clara veered off the juicy stuff to give me a lecture about requisition forms that was so dull, my eyes glazed over. Though I did perk up a bit at the myriad of medical treatments I was entitled to. "Two massage therapy sessions a month, you say?"

"No one uses them," Baruch said with a dismissive wave.

Ms. Clara eyed him with distaste before turning back to me. "I'd be happy to provide you with a list of approved practitioners."

Twisting her monitor back into position, she pressed her palm to a small pad on her desk to be scanned. Once the light turned green, she started typing. "Better than a password," she said, noting my curiosity.

I placed the last of the signed forms in the file. The Brotherhood could proclaim Rabbi Abrams was in charge here, but it was clear to me who really ran the show.

The final item of business was to get my palm scanned so I could access the Vault and stuff on my own. Ms. Clara explained it would take twenty-four hours to process, then pronounced us done.

"Excellent. I promise to behave like a pampered princess and exploit every last thing I'm entitled to."

One side of her mouth quirked up at that. "Provided you have the correct requisition form," she said.

That's when Baruch hit his limit. He engulfed my hand in his and tugged me to my feet. "Yes, Nava will pretend the best of intentions for your forms and you will pretend you don't enjoy filling everything out on our behalf, and natural order will be maintained."

He dragged me to the door.

"Leave the pen," Ms. Clara called out.

Baruch growled.

I tossed it back at her as I cleared the door, being rewarded with a wink.

Oh yeah. Way better than cable.

Baruch warmed up on the punching bag. I watched him in amazement for a few minutes as I stretched.

I'd never seen anyone's fist almost punch through the bag before. The most astounding thing of all was how calm he was. It was pretty sexy the way he pummeled the thing in a total state of Zen. The fact that he'd taken off his shirt and was working out bare-chested didn't hurt the cause any, even if he was more muscular than my tastes generally ran.

One thing Baruch had gotten into my skull was staying in the present during any fighting since letting my thoughts wander led to meatsack tenderization. Even with my accelerated healing, I was tenderized enough. "Doesn't super strength usually come with anger issues?"

He stopped punching.

"I mean, you're pretty mellow. Which is great. I, for one, would not want my baggage infringing on Drio's. Because holy wow, two wounded angry people. That's not even counting Rohan, although Drio would win any diva-off hands down."

Baruch lifted the punching bag off the hook with one hand. "Do you say everything you think?"

"Nope. Amazingly I share merely a fraction of the brilliance in my head." I followed him over to the wall.

He touched a light on a small display panel and part of the wall slid away to reveal another good-sized room, filled top to bottom with weapons and training equipment.

"Cool," I breathed, peering in. "Did you design all these?"

"Some." He pushed me back a few steps. "You haven't unlocked entrance privileges yet," he said, heading inside.

"Nerd," I teased.

He gave me a sheepish grin as he stashed the bag up on a hook.

I eyed the weapons: knives of all shapes and sizes, throwing stars, staffs, iron-based things that I couldn't discern the purpose of but given their scary shape was certain I was better off without the visual, boxing gloves, pads, and whatever was stored in the cabinets running the length of one wall. No guns though.

The Brotherhood required a massive bottom line to run.

"Who funds the Brotherhood? Can we change the name now that I'm here?"

"It funds itself and no. Hundreds of years in investments plus, these days, the income DSI brings in." He smiled. "We don't come cheap. The Brotherhood takes care of us. If we die, our funeral expenses are handled."

My gut twisted at that last sentiment. "You're awfully matter-of-fact about death."

He spread his hands wide. "We do what we do. We try not to die but it happens. Which is why I will train you to have the best shot at walking away."

See, this was a guy who genuinely had my back. "Teach me fight moves." Defense wasn't going to be enough when I came up against Asmodeus.

He assessed me for a long moment. "Most demons will be larger than you. Stronger."

"That's a yes, then?"

"But that also means their balance and speed is compromised as a result."

I eyed him up and down. "Speaking from experience are we, Tree Trunk?"

"You're very annoying," he said.

"It's my birth power," I replied.

"Oh? That's not being delusional?"

"Ladies and gentlemen, Baruch Ya'ari," I said. "He's here all week. Try the shrimp."

He peered at me. "Is English your first language?"

"Vaudeville? The old schtick? Nothing?" I shook my head in dismay before dancing around him, throwing air punches.

He swatted me away. "Build up your side to side movement. Get inside the tip of their punches and kicks. Build an infighting and clinch game. Get comfortable striking and fighting from your back in case you're thrown down."

Baruch showed me some basic moves–a couple of punches and a few kicks–running me through them over and over again, making minute adjustments. Talking me through both my mistakes and what I was doing right.

I stripped down to my sports bra and booty shorts which was great on the heat front but left more exposed skin, and psychologically, made me feel more vulnerable. My muscles quivered as every attack became more of a grinding exertion.

The flooring pads became sticky with sweat, each footstep a pronounced slapping sound, the room turning steamy and dank. Finally, Baruch called a much-desired halt to the training but only to bring Kane down to ensure I didn't get complacent fighting just him.

Kane raised an eyebrow as he handed me a glass of Ms. Clara's electrolyte-filled iced tea. "Well?" he asked Baruch.

I'd gulped back the cold liquid by the time his question was asked.

"Help me attack her on two fronts," Baruch said.

I left the empty glass in a corner, my arms wobbly. "Awesome."

Seeing me swipe at the sweat on my neck, Kane boosted the air conditioning to blessed arctic levels and then the two of them leapt into battle against me. All right, they engaged me in slow motion combat while Baruch barked grips, counter-grips, and attack strategy, showing me how to use my weight against them.

The cool part was making connections on my own about how and where certain moves would come in handy. When my suggestions were wrong, the guys showed me why, then explained the better way of proceeding.

"For someone who hasn't spent years training, you pick things up fast," Kane said, after I'd executed a pretty sweet roundhouse kick.

"Your power isn't there yet and your technique is rough, but balance, even speed?" Baruch's approving eye blink was the sweetest compliment ever.

"I'm not a trained fighter, but I am a trained dancer. I was always good at picking up moves quickly, getting new routines faster than other people. Tap taught me balance, weight placement, being aware of my body. Those skills are transferable," I informed them.

"Those skills are a foundation," Baruch said. "Do the kick again. Don't throw your left hip out so much this time."

Neither of them held back or went easy on me because I was female. I appreciated that up until the point that I collapsed on burning legs with a plea of "Have mercy!" Not even my most rigorous dance session had drained me this much.

Kane prodded my belly with a toe. My tummy jiggled. His bare-chested, rock hard body didn't. "We better feed her. And hose her off."

I think I gave him the finger but I might have just imagined it, distracted as I was by the shiny of his nipple rings. That boy had two modes of dress–barely and horribly. I vowed to do a fashion intervention one day.

"For God's sakes, woman, get up," Kane said, holding a hand out to me.

I lay there, too tired to even reach for him. "Can I have a cookie?" I wheezed.

"Yes, Nava," Baruch said, sounding amused. "You may. They're in the cupboard upstairs."

"Will you get it for me? Pleeeeeeaaaase?"

He nodded, pulling his hair free from his elastic band. Pretty hair.

"Todah rabah," I called out in thanks as he and Kane left. I closed my eyes, my arm thrown over my face. If I played my cards right, maybe I could pull this off. Maybe Ari and I could be real live Wonder Twins soon. But you know, not lame. For the first time since I'd become Rasha, I felt like I could take a deep breath.

Footsteps neared and fabric swished as Baruch knelt down beside me. I opened my eyes, hand out to take the cookie, and then drew back. It wasn't Baruch. It was Drio, squatting down. I burst into full-body Lady Shock mode, my exhaustion trumped by adrenaline.

"Showing off or scared?" he smirked.

"Touch me and find out." I sat up as calmly as I could manage, given I was alone with a man who aggressively hated me and whose powers were a giant question mark. I didn't trust his promise to keep me safe.

Where were my guards? The ones that liked me. Or at least tolerated me.

He pursed his lips. "Just came to see the progress. Checking if you're earning your keep."

"Impressed?" My heart was hammering and I could feel the electricity rising and falling like swells within me.

"I've seen better."

"Sorry to disappoint." I scrambled to my feet, sparking so brightly that residual blue sunspots danced before my eyes.

Drio stood up as well. "Shut it down." He scowled at me.

The electricity flared, cresting off my skin in sharp bursts. I tried to visualize the off-switch but nothing happened.

"Nava." He grabbed me by the shoulders, but after one quick shake was forced to release me, flinching in the wake of my magic.

A hot tight pain speared my chest. I clutched at it, my eyes watering, sensing this was all about to go sideways.

"Porco Dio," Drio swore. "Baruch!" he yelled.

I hyperventilated. Pops and crackles jumped off my skin, a metal burning smell clogging my nostrils.

Footsteps pounded down the stairs.

I fell to my knees, feeling every charged particle in my body as the electricity wrapped around me like a snake with its coily embrace. I wheezed, desperate for air.

A heavy blanket lined with rubber enveloped me, arms holding tight around me. "You're safe," Rohan said. "Turn it off, Nava. You can do it."

My cheek pressed against the blanket resting on his chest, I latched on to the even rise and fall of his breathing like it was my lifeline. He kept murmuring to me that I was safe, cradling me in his arms, and ignoring the small sparks not contained by the blanket that were blackening his skin in tiny dots. His voice was hypnotic, soothing me enough that my magic turned off. But I still couldn't breathe for the pain lancing my chest. I shot him a panicked look.

Rohan lay me down on the floor. The last thing I heard was, "Clear!"

Not more current, I thought, and blacked out.

I came to, still on the padded floor, with four male faces showing varying degrees of concern hovering over me. Baruch crumpled the rubber blanket in one hand. Kane held a defibrillator limply. Rohan's left eyebrow was scorched.

It wasn't until I saw Drio, his hands burned from my magic, watching me like he'd missed some kind of manslaughter opportunity, that I was reassured I was okay. I struggled to sit up, Baruch assisting me.

I squinted at the electrodes placed around my sports bra, hooking me up to the bastard child of a fax and an answering machine. Ticker tape stuck out of one end of it. "What happened?"

I had to clear my throat a couple of times to get the words out.

"Not a heart attack," Ms. Clara said cheerfully. I scrunched up my face in confusion and she tapped the machine. "Portable ECG." She pulled the electrodes off of me.

"You're qualified to read it, how?"

"Two years of med school before I dropped out. Apparently I didn't have the right bedside manner."

"O-kay."

"You got... riled up," Rohan said.

I glared at Drio who bared his teeth at me. "By-product of him wanting me dead," I said.

"He doesn't want–" Kane began.

"I don't?" Drio asked.

"Drio," Rohan warned.

"I was being friendly and she freaked out." Drio cocked his thumb and forefinger like a gun, rocking them from side to side in some kind of Italian hand gesture. "Our new Rasha doesn't play well with others."

I tugged my clammy T-shirt over my head. "If you call your passive-aggressive intimidation 'being friendly' then you've got the social graces of a walnut. Pony up. You wanted my power off so you could hurt me."

"It was becoming unstable." He tapped his forefinger to his temple. "You're unstable. Are you on your period?"

Sparks literally shot from my eyes.

Baruch blocked Drio from me, saving him from being turned into a human tiki torch.

The proverbial straw had hit this camel's back. "I'm out of here."

The guys did that annoying silent communication thing. Seriously could kill the alpha brood right now.

"Home it is," Ms. Clara said, with an undecipherable look at them. I didn't know what I was missing here and frankly, I didn't care.

Ms. Clara helped me up. I didn't have it in me to make polite small talk, so I grabbed my shoes and left the room without saying goodbye. Ms. Clara accompanied me, retrieving my messenger bag, along with my hoodie.

"Thank you." I pulled out my phone as we exited onto the porch, calling home for a ride and determined to keep my shit together until someone from my family came and got me.

The second I hung up, Ms. Clara held out her hand for the phone, giving me a slip of paper from her pocket in return as my receipt. "You'll get another one when you hand in the laptop," she assured me. Because that was such a concern right now.

We sat outside on the top step, waiting. The sun provided a welcome warmth and the sound of a car driving by blasting Top 40 went a long way to making me feel normal.

"Is that going to happen to me every time?" I threaded my hands in my hair, weary beyond belief.

"The instability or the heart problem?" she asked.

"Yes."

"Magic takes a while to master, but you'll get there." Her expression grew distant. "The thing about magic powers is that there's a cost."

"How come you're a part of all this?"

She blinked back to attention. "My dad was Rasha."

Past tense noted. "Sorry."

She shrugged. "Not your fault."

Kane joined us, his footsteps creaking the weathered boards. "Rest easy tonight, babe."

"Thanks," I said, peering up at him, one hand shielding my eyes from the sun.

My dad's Prius fishtailed up the driveway. Ari threw open the driver's side, engine still running. He raced over to me in his frayed T-shirt and jeans. I'd never seen him this upset.

"What did you do to her?" he spat at Kane.

Ms. Clara squeezed my hand and went inside.

"Danger comes with the job," Kane said. He braced a hand on the top of the railing. "She knows this."

Ari led me to the car. He bundled me in, then slammed my door so hard I jumped. "You were supposed to take it easy on her," he said.

Had they discussed me before? I shamelessly eavesdropped through Ari's open door.

"Around here we do what has to be done." Kane sat down on the top step, almost insolent in his indifference. "That's how it works at the adults' table."

Bastard. I put my hand on the door handle ready to lay into Kane but Ari surprised me.

He threw Kane a cool smile. "Keep telling yourself that." On that note, he got into the car and we drove away.

10

I lasted all of ten seconds before I opened my mouth to demand an explanation but Ari cut me off. "Rest. We can talk later." I would have protested, but the next thing I knew, he was shaking me awake. "Rise and shine. We're home."

The sky flamed gold for one brief instance before relaxing into the pink and oranges of sunset. That was pretty. My mother's scream of horror at the sight of me stumbling into the house, not so much. She tried to backpedal but you know, there's no coming back from reacting to your kid like she's something out of a scary movie.

"Bath," she proclaimed and marched me upstairs to my room.

Sitting on the edge of my tub, testing the water, I caught sight of myself in the mirror. Mom's reaction was not unwarranted. My hair snarled in rat's nest fashion. Giant sweat and pit stains graced my T-shirt. All I needed was a Pig Pen cloud of dirt to complete the look. Any confidence, any pride in my accomplishments today disappeared.

First I took a fast shower, then I plugged the tub, shivering and waiting impatiently for it to fill. Finally, inching into the hot water, I slid onto my back, fully submerged except for my nose and lips.

I brushed the underside of the tap with my big toe, catching the final tiny warm drops.

The inset LEDs smudged a soft luminescence like a milky way across the ceiling. I lay there staring up at the world through my watery lens until my overwhelmed panic subsided. The same trick I'd used since I was a kid and hadn't wanted anyone to know that I wasn't tough enough to keep up with my brother, who generally took everything in stride.

Being thrown into Demon Club was like playing the world's craziest game of *Survivor*, except with no defined rules and a funeral service for a consolation prize. And now I was planning on taking on a major big bad. Was I crazy?

Submerged in doubt as much as the water, only the water grew cold before I pulled the plug. Cocooning myself in a massive towel, I gave a curt nod to my reflection then headed into my room to slip into my softest worn cotton pjs. Rehashing today was not on the table.

A while later, I was lost in the study of all the books I'd brought home, alternately fascinated and disgusted by the forms demons took, their various abilities, and the ways in which they could be killed. While none left any physical evidence once killed, some, like ghish demons, died in a whoosh of sulphuric stank so noxious it had been known to induce temporary blindness. It was all important information, but I'd gotten no closer to finding where Asmodeus' sweet spot lay. He was a Unique. Maybe no one knew.

I'd filled the book with color-coded sticky tabs and a growing pile of notes lay on my lap. While I loved technology, when it came to note taking, longhand was my preference. Something about the act of writing the information down instead of typing it helped me remember it better.

Ari poked his head in, a bowl of steaming chicken soup in one hand.

I inhaled deeply. "There better be matzoh balls in that." The fluffy Jewish dumplings were, in my opinion, the best thing to come out of my religion. Except maybe that naked photo of Adam Levine in his all his tatted-up glory.

"Like you even have to ask." He placed the bowl on my bedside table.

I eyed it, noting Mom had stuffed four giant matzoh balls in it plus put in extra carrot slivers. She must really have been freaked out by my appearance to give me the deluxe soup treatment.

Not wanting my demon book or notes to get accidentally soupified, I moved everything over to one side of my bed. The pillows behind me were rearranged to optimize my eating position, then I picked up the warm bowl and dug in. I know the soup wasn't literally magic, but it was soul-soothing. I sighed happily, the hot broth filling my belly. There was an art to matzoh ball making. With some people, it was like eating cannonballs, but Mom's melted in my mouth.

"I like big balls and I cannot lie," I sang around a mouthful.

"What set you off?" Ari regarded me from his usual spot at the foot of my bed, where he sat cross legged.

"What do you know about a Rasha called Drio?"

Ari shrugged. "Don't know him. Why?"

"He has it in for me. Things were said and he got me alone and..." I shivered remembering the aggressive dislike pouring off him. I chopped my remaining balls into bits. "I freaked out. The curupira was scary too, but when you're female, a threatening human male taps into an entirely different kind of fear." I met Ari's eyes and he nodded in understanding. "My power went haywire. Then the chest pains kicked in and bam! Defibrillation."

He bunched up my comforter in his fists.

The remaining soup was gone before I knew it, my spoon hitting the bottom with a clang. I peered into the bowl, as if staring might make a second helping appear. Sadly, no. Placing it on the night table beside me, I stroked my finger over my heart. "Ms. Clara said something about the cost of magic. Is this mine? Do I run the risk of dying every time I access my power?"

"You're not going to die," he said.

"You're avoiding my question. Tell me, because I don't have time to read my way through that library."

Ari toyed with the edge of my stack of notes. "She's right about the cost. But ninety-nine percent of the time, the only thing you'll feel is tired. Craving those electrolytes."

"And the one percent?" I asked.

Ari hesitated.

"Don't sugarcoat it." I grabbed my pen, on the verge of rolling off my mattress.

He nodded reluctantly. "If you draw on the power for too long, or become agitated to the point where it controls you instead of the other way around? Yeah. It could kill you. In your case, via heart attack it seems."

I absorbed that, re-arranging my pillows to face Ari. "Then I have to control it. Now that I know it can happen and why, I won't let the situation get away from me again."

"Just like that? Sheer will power?"

"Do you doubt me?"

My brother regarded me steadily before shaking his head. "What was it like training with Baruch?" he asked.

"You looooove him." I made a kissy noise.

Ari raised his hands in tickle formation. "Keep talking, Katz. It'll end in tears and pee."

I threw a pillow at him that he caught one-handed. "He's amazing," I said. "He knows how to both motivate me and push me."

"He breaks down battles looking for ways to improve our–their–odds." Ari stumbled over the pronoun but caught himself. I kept my mouth shut. "Not to mention his inventions," he said.

"Yeah, what was that thing you mentioned the first night?"

"The Stinger." Ari's face lit up. "Baruch found a way to stabilize demon secretions in a chemical compound that worked on the neural system of most demons to temporarily paralyze them. He dipped needle tips in the liquid then he designed a wrist holder that let the wearer flick the weapon at the target."

My eyebrows rose. "Why don't all Rasha wear them then?"

"Once you take the secretion from this particular demon, it dies. Kind of like a bee with its stinger. Which would be fine since the only good demon is a dead demon, but there aren't a lot of this breed so Stingers are pretty rare."

"Wow. Tell me about Kane." My sneaky segue failed to catch him off-guard.

Ari spread his hands wide. Totally nonplussed. "What do you want to know?"

"All that delightful antagonism back there? Did you screw him?"

"He trained me for a while."

"Knowing you, that's not even a euphemism," I said.

"I don't think it's appropriate to discuss your colleagues' sex lives."

I shot him an incredulous look. "Of course it's not appropriate. Why do you think everyone does it?"

"You need new hobbies."

"You know I can sit here all night saying–" I adopted the whiniest voice I could– "did you sleep with Kane? Did you sleep with Kane? Did you–"

He flung the pillow back at me. "No. Geez. Shut up already. I didn't."

"But you wanted to."

Full credit to my brother, he nailed his poker face. The red flush on his neck, however, told a different story.

"You like him," I teased.

"I really don't. I may have at one time. Long ago in a galaxy far, far away."

I snorted.

"But he's toxic."

I gathered my notes up, tapping them into a neat pile. "That's not fair. He can't help having that poison power."

"I meant in his relationships. I wasn't kidding about your power reflecting who you are. The magic reflects an aspect of the user's personality. You shock. Kane poisons."

I sat up straight. This was fascinating. Wrong about me but amazing insight to have about everyone else. "What about Baruch? He's so Zen and strong. How does that fit?"

Ari worried at a hole in his jeans. "Baruch is a good guy."

"Relax, president of his fan club. This isn't gossip." Ari raised a single eyebrow. "Isn't just gossip," I clarified. "Pay attention. These guys are the ones sent to protect me. After today, I'm thinking that having the cheat sheet on them may help keep me alive as much as any fighting skills."

"Oh," he conceded. "Smart thinking."

"No shit."

Ari rolled onto his side, laying his head on his bent arm. He rubbed a hand over his bleary eyes. At this angle, I saw the purple bags under them.

"How you doing there?" I asked.

"Neither homicidal nor suicidal so quit looking at me like that," he said.

He lay his fist under his cheek, a lock of blond hair falling across his brow. It was so reminiscent of his little kid self, but without his even-tempered, good natured air, that it took all my will power not to hug him. He despised pity. Or sympathy, which he always took as pity. Stupid boy.

"My take on Baruch?" He scratched his jaw. "From what I've heard, he's taken some bad hits fighting."

I waited out his pause.

"He fights past the pain," Ari said. "Not always in a good way. Like he's denying its existence."

"So my guard consists of the poison prince, the man who refuses to admit he's human, angry Italian whose powers are still unknown to me, and the human blade. What do you know about him? Rohan?"

"Sorry, don't know much about him either. As an initiate I was only in contact with Rasha who stayed at the chapter house." Had Ari become Rasha that would have changed. He'd have been traveling the world, having adventures, and meeting his fellow brethren.

I sighed, motioning for my brother to hand over his phone. "You got a new one?"

"No longer an initiate. No longer worth tracking."

My hand closed tight around his phone. "Bastards." I calmed myself remembering that I was going to make this right for him. Since I couldn't do anything about that at this moment, I typed Rohan's name in to Google. Ms. Clara still had mine but hey, this way no one could track my search history on Snowflake. Millions of hits. I started scrolling.

"You're not going to find Rasha intel online," Ari pointed out. But he scooted closer to peer over my shoulder.

"Not Rasha. Break up. Dude has a fuckton of baggage. There's something going on with him and Drio. Love triangle maybe? Though I can't tell which of them was the loser in the scenario because neither strikes me as the girlfriend type." Saying the word "girlfriend" in conjunction with Rohan left a bad taste in my mouth.

I gave up after about forty pages of search results, tossing him back his phone in disgust. "Nothing."

"Maybe neither was the winner." Ari checked his email. "Demons, remember? People die."

I rubbed the back of my neck. If that were true, if they'd been in love with the same girl and somehow she died? It would explain a lot of the weirdness today. I turned bleak eyes on Ari. "If demons come after Rasha's loved ones, what does that mean for our family? I mean, what if one of them follows me home somehow?"

My brother stuffed the phone in his back pocket. "The Rasha laid wards around the house earlier. It'll keep us safe."

"That's good." Why was he staring at the corner of my wall like it fascinated him?

"Spill." I caught him in mid-rise, tumbling both of us on our asses on the bed.

"Why do I have to be the bearer of bad news?" he snapped, jumping up again. "I'm not even one of them and I have to do their dirty work? Screw that." He stormed from my room.

I pursed my lips, reviewing everything we'd said in the last couple of minutes but try as I might, I couldn't figure out what had set Ari off. I rewound further. Back to conversations at the Brotherhood's mansion.

I slipped on a pair of sneakers, threw a hoodie over my pajamas and pushed up my window. I couldn't see anyone out in the dark yard, but that didn't mean they weren't there. No way would Demon Club have left me unsupervised. It didn't account for Ari's freak out, but it did give me someone else to question.

Taking my tree escape route, I dropped onto the ground with no attempt to be stealthy, since I wanted to be seen by whoever was on guard duty.

The operative word being "seen." Not tackled to the ground, hitting it with a hard whoosh as all my breath left me. Though that may have been for another reason as my body instinctively recognized the scent of iron and musk.

"What have we here?" Rohan's voice vibrated against me.

I had to turn my head to answer or risk eating dirt. "Do you mean 'we' in the royal sense or are the voices in your head clamoring in unison?"

He stretched out on top of me, pinning me more firmly between him and the ground. "You didn't give the code word," he said, lazy amusement threading his voice.

"Eyeliner?" Grass tickled my cheek.

"Nope. Two more wrong guesses and I'll have to deal with you."

He was sick. Which made me doubly so because I shivered in pleasure at that so-called threat, my entire body yelling "throw the guesses!"

"Hamsa?" I asked.

"You Googled the engraving, huh?"

I was many things. Stupid was not one of them. I slammed my crackling left hand into him, being careful to hit his leather jacket, since frying him was not conducive to securing his assistance.

The zap was still enough to buck him off me, allowing me to roll out from under him.

"Don't mess with Lady Shock and Awe," I warned.

Rohan pulled on the jacket, examining it. "Fuck a duck, you're giving yourself superhero names already?" He rubbed the small scorch mark on his upper sleeve, then scowled.

"Your predilection for fowl aside," I flicked a spark of electricity at him. "I have a question."

"Good for you." He stood up, brushing off his ass.

Yeah, I looked. Yeah, he caught me. Yeah, I shrugged.

I pushed to my feet. "A nice butt won't get you out of answering, Emo Snowflake."

"Don't call me that."

"It's not your superhero name? Never mind." I patted his cheek. "I'll find you something."

"Lucky me." Rohan motioned for me to follow him out of the moonlight and into the shadows. "What's the question?"

I twirled a finger indicating the perimeter of my yard. "I know there are wards. You're here guarding me. So why was it weird when I asked to go home? What did Ari refuse to tell me?"

"You can stay here tonight but tomorrow you move into the chapter house." He placed his hand over my mouth to keep me from protesting. "It's the safest place for you to be. Especially if Asmodeus learns it was you."

When, not if.

I pulled his hand off, resisting the urge to suck one of his fingers into my mouth. "Okay." Was it getting hotter out here? I pushed my hoodie sleeves up.

He tensed. "That's it? No fight?"

"You have a fabulous impression of my intelligence. I'll explain this once so remember it. I'm not stupid. I'm also not endangering my family." I wound a curl around my finger, all casual. "Hey, I was just thinking. I know you checked actors on Samson's film, but what about the rest of the crew?"

Rohan rubbed the back of his hand across his chin. He hadn't shaved since yesterday, and the dark stubble along his jaw combined with the steely glint of his eyes was insanely hot, giving him a dangerous air. Correction. More dangerous.

"Drio checked producers, directors, all other above-the-line positions on King's last few films against the database maintained by intelligence," Rohan said. "No hits."

Damn. "There's a database?"

I guess I said it a little too fervently because Rohan held up his hand. "Stand down, Lolita. You don't get to troll for famous people we suspect."

Someday. When I was allowed to do more than just train and prove I should be allowed to continue breathing.

Now that I'd been out here a while in my pajamas, my skin was beginning to get goosebumps. I tugged my sleeves back down, zipping my hoodie up against the cool night air. "What about Samson's make-up artist?" I tapped my finger against my lip. "Obviously Samson is glamoured up and I get that if he is a demon, he's far more powerful than Josh, but when Josh got… excited, he flickered. Actors spend a lot of time with their make-up artists and maybe he'd want someone trustworthy around him in case he exposed himself."

Rohan was already texting a note to Drio to check it out.

"Seeing as I'm so useful–"

"Potentially," he said.

"How about a little quid pro quo?" I figured I'd work up to specific details. "I'm thinking that the downfall of a major demon would be just the thing to get the Brotherhood to listen to me."

Rohan slid his phone back into his pocket. "Don't even think of going out to look for one. You wouldn't know where to begin and you can't take one on."

"Rohan..." He waited while I debated how much of my Ari worries to share. "My brother isn't doing well. I'm scared he may not recover from this." My voice shook. "I know he's still an initiate and if I have some leverage that gets the Brotherhood to check and confirm it–"

"They'll induct him right away, and Ari will have his magic to keep him safe," Rohan finished.

"Yeah." I shot him my best beseeching look.

He sighed. "I feel for you and Ari both, but you need to be patient. It hasn't even been a week. Rushing into situations you're not yet ready for gets you dead."

And not rushing things might lose me my brother.

Shivering as much from cold as disappointment, I hooked my chin into the neck of the hoodie, folding the cuffs over my hands.

"You barely have anything on under there." Despite Rohan's contemptuous tone, when he poked at my sleeve, his hands lingered a second too long.

"Maybe the demons aren't the only ones who want bragging rights of bagging the first non-dick-swinging Rasha." I tugged away, irritated.

Rohan's nostrils flared. "Fuck you the first for thinking I kiss and tell," he said. "And fuck you the second if you think I need bragging rights when it comes to sex. You're not that much of a novelty." The angry growl in his voice convinced me that his motives were the normal "have sex because sex with an attractive girl would be great" variety and not anything involving notches on belts.

This game I could play.

I placed my hand on my hoodie's zipper. "You want me to flash you?" My half-smile was accompanied by my best "sideways eye slide looking up through half-open lashes" maneuver.

A car's headlights swept over us.

Rohan pushed me deeper into the shadows. "Don't do me any favors."

I slid the hoodie zipper down, waiting to see if he'd stop me.

He didn't. Instead, he frowned as he inspected tonight's cotton sleepwear offering. "Yesterday's was cuter." He motioned around my cleavage. "It had that purple lace."

I glanced up at my window, realizing how far into the room I could see from here. "You perved on me last night? Some guard you are."

He didn't even have the good grace to look ashamed. "Bring more of those when you move."

"Because this is all about you."

Rohan bopped the end of my nose with his index finger. "See? Was that so hard to admit?"

Grumbling, secretly pleased, definitely annoyed with myself for figuring out how many cute, electricity-proof outfits I owned, I zipped up my sweater and headed inside.

11

What an ass.

And *what* an ass. I grasped the top of the chair in my bedroom against the full body swoon making me wonky. My body was on fire after that little encounter. Not in a Rasha way. I throbbed in a simmering coil of need, the feel of every steely inch of him imprinted on my skin.

I switched off my overhead light, pretending I was just getting ready to go to sleep, and enjoying the delicious sense of anticipation. Rohan might be infuriating in real life but he was prime source material for personal fantasy usage.

After latching my window and drawing my blinds tight, I settled myself on my bed. Letting myself get comfortable by taking a few steady inhales and exhales before I slid my hand under my shirt to skim my palms across my breasts.

Rohan's intense gold irises danced in my memory. My tits grew heavier and heavier in my hands and I tweaked my nipples, biting the inside of my cheek to keep from crying out at the zing that shot through me.

My other hand crept into my shorts, as I mentally lingered on all of Rohan's fine attributes, starting at the bottom and working my way up. The clench of his gluts as he'd jumped out the window that first night demanded multiple replayings.

I imagined what it would be like to start at his toes and lick my way up his body, lingering in the hollows behind his knees, nipping the hard muscle along his inner thigh, saving the image of taking him in my mouth–for now. My fingers met with wetness as I ran my index finger up and down along my opening. I wanted him bad, those hands holding me down. I wanted him to ask me to flash him in my backyard and I wanted to do it. My hips rolled.

Fumbling over my head with my other hand for my pillow, I stuffed it over my face to muffle the quiet moans I was beginning to make. Cuntessa de Spluge pulsed, demanding some "me time" so I obliged, ghosting my finger over my clit in the slowest of small circular motions.

I couldn't remember the last time I'd been so turned on. Or liked a guy so much. No, craved a guy. That's all it was.

Part of me yearned to tease this sensation out for as long as possible but patience was not my strong suit. I yanked my shorts all the way down and shoved the fingers of my other hand inside, pretending they were Rohan's. Praying my gasp was muted by the pillow in my mouth. Everything about him would be big and rough. His stubble against my nipples, his callused hands pushing deep within me, sending me over the edge. I bit my bottom lip, a heavy sigh shuddering through me.

Champagne bubbles danced through my body, my ab muscles tightening at the growing pull spiraling deeper and wider inside me. I rode my hand harder, not able to take it slow. My thighs shook; my breath came in irregular pants. Tipping my head back, I muffled my cries against my pillow. Tiny waves rippled out from my core, growing bigger and more intense.

Just as that final vibrating quake should have hurled me over the edge into fabulous free fall, an image of his smug grin at being my masturbatory material popped up on my internal screen.

There was a flash of blue. A burning sizzle lit Cuntessa up in high-voltage agony. I screamed into the pillow in the way one does when one has fucking electrocuted her clit, doubling over into the fetal position. I was hyperventilating, swearing in breathy gasps.

I guess no one else was upstairs to hear my shriek of pain because thankfully nobody came to check on me. Tears streamed down my cheeks. This was so unfair. My body could be literally coated in electricity and it didn't hurt but accidentally give myself one bad touch and I almost passed out. Shouldn't I be immune from myself? One more stupid detail to master.

Eventually, the pain knifing through me subsided enough for me to catch my breath. I flung the pillow covering my head across the room then probed Cuntessa gently with a gasped wince. I offered my profuse apologies to her but could practically hear her snottily informing me that this was the last straw. Mentally slapping me with a restraining order until such time as her pleasure could be guaranteed without useless dicks or lightning strikes.

Damn you, Rohan Mitra.

Damn you, Rasha.

And damn you, destiny.

With pain and sexual frustration vying for control of my body, I rolled into a tight ball. Stupid me fixating on the worst choice in men imaginable. Rohan wasn't hot stuff and he didn't have me under his sway.

On the plus side, now that he was out of my system, I was free to focus on what mattered–Ari. My mind was crystal clear, even if the occasional tear still leaked from my eyes.

A rather brilliant thought occurred to me as I lay sprawled on the covers, blinking through the hurt. Not every demon was equal on the evil hierarchy, and while lots were big bads, many more were mostly bottom feeders. Like the araculum. Still capable of doing damage, sure, but trading on intel rather than brute force and malevolence to stay alive.

If Rasha were the cops of the demon world, then there were bound to be some snitches amongst the criminals. All I had to do was find one and have him pass a message up the food chain to Asmodeus that I was the one who'd killed Josh and his sister.

I was moving into the chapter house anyway, and by the time Asmodeus showed up, I'd be living safely behind the wards and the guys could help me take him out. Even Rohan wouldn't be able to be mad at my outside-the-box thinking then, and he'd be honor-bound to help me. Of course if he wasn't, then he sucked, but with a big win like that, I'd be useful enough to force contact with the Executive, protocol be damned.

I drummed my fingers against my mattress. The good little Rasha thing to do would be to go tell my babysitter about this idea, except in this case, it was better to seek forgiveness than permission. I toyed with the primer and my stack of notes. Based on my admittedly limited understanding, curupira fell into a kind of mid-level bad zone. I'd dealt with the one I'd met quite effectively. How hard could it be to deal with a snitch?

Hmmm. Tiptoeing to the window, I cracked my blinds just enough to peer out, considering my odds. No sign of Rohan, but he still had to be prowling around. Keeping well away from the window in case my shadow gave me away, I slipped into a little all-black number–low slung jeans and a fitted, scoop neck top–perfect for cat burglary and escaping a house undetected. The final touch? Stuffing my hair under a black knit cap. Okay, perching it jauntily on my hair but it really completed the look.

Rohan was probably watching my window for signs of life, so I crept out of my room in a low crouch which wouldn't be visible from the ground. Once in the hallway, I exhaled, and strolled to Ari's bedroom.

I rapped on his door before easing it open.

Ari sat on his bed against his wooden headboard, still-dressed, his legs stretched out on his brown comforter with its graphic blocky design. Surrealist prints like Dali's *Persistence of Memory* with its melting clocks, Magritte's painting of a pipe with "Ceci, n'est pas une pipe." in script underneath it, and Gonsalves' row of ships that seemed to turn into an arched bridge, framed his walls.

"Whatcha doing?"

He looked up guiltily from texting, fumbling his phone. "Nothing."

"Or," I amended, skipping toward him, "*who* are you doing?"

He placed the phone face down on the bedside table, leaving it free for me to scoop up. "Have you no respect for personal property?" he sputtered.

I didn't bother responding to that ridiculous question, busy swiping the screen to get to the goods. I scrolled past a couple of flirty texts from whomever Ari had labeled as "Do Not Engage." Then jackpot. "Your 'nothing' has an awfully familiar nipple ring," I said, studying the well-defined naked chest in the photo that he'd been sent. "Thought you were mad at him?"

"I am. Which in his head means dial up the charm to get me to fall back in line." Ari snatched the phone away with, what was for him, a pretty good glower, stuffing it under the pillow behind his back. "What do you want?" His expression was infused with all the pain and long-suffering stemming from having a bratty younger sibling.

Younger by twelve minutes, but I did my best to be exemplary in the annoying department.

I perched on the end of his bed, suppressing my urge to rip out his hospital corners. "While I could pester you with questions that you really don't want to answer, I will skip that part because I am such a good sister."

His eyes narrowed. "You want something else."

I pointed a finger at him. "Bingo. Here's the thing." I cleared my throat trying to figure out how to ask my question while technically keeping my Rasha oath of secrecy.

"Nava." That was his impatient "talk or leave" voice.

"Know of any demon informants?"

Arms propped behind his head, he leaned back against the headboard, studying me. "What are you trying to find out that you don't want Rohan to know?"

"Just learning all aspects of this brave new world."

The gears turning in Ari's head were practically audible as he pinned me in his steady gaze. He tried to figure out what I was thinking, and I sat there pretending it didn't matter either way. It was our thing.

"Don't get mixed up in their mission. I know you and starfucking–"

"Hey!"

"Gossip," he amended.

"Don't say it like a euphemism," I muttered.

"But this is serious. They've been amassing info on Samson for ages. You charge in and you'll screw things up."

Startled, I raised my eyes to his. "Wait. You know?"

"No shit."

"Kane is such a blabbermouth."

Ari's frowned. "Why do you assume I heard it from Kane?"

I spread my hands wide. "Who else would you have heard it from? How'd you get past the Mafia cone of silence?" I gasped. "Did you eavesdrop? Because only Rasha can know this stuff."

My brother flushed in what definitely was "Nava Red." He kicked my foot. "Are you fucking kidding me? You've been Rasha for the approximate life of a fruit fly and you think you're already going to know details I didn't after being around the Brotherhood my entire life?"

I bit my lip. "I don't think they live that long. The fruit–"

The mattress bounced as Ari lunged for me.

I jumped to my feet with a yelp. "I'm sorry. Jeez. I didn't know they were bandying about that information to all and–" I snapped my mouth shut at the look on his face.

"Let's try this again." I plastered on my sweetest smile.

He pointed at the door.

I straightened, wanting to present my idea with as much confidence as possible. On second thought, offering myself up as bait for Asmodeus might not secure me Ari's assistance, or worse, get my brother insisting on helping. Plan B–lie about my reasons. "Rohan and Drio have to go about this officially." I wrinkled my nose. "Somewhat officially. They have to pursue leads and all that bullshit."

"Actually investigate."

"Whatever." I picked up the cologne on his dresser and sniffed it. "Unofficial channels can make things happen so much faster. If there is a snitch, he'd be in a good position to put us on to the hard evidence we need to prove King's demon status and take this bastard down." I cracked my knuckles. "I'll make the snitch an offer he can't refuse."

"No." At least he didn't laugh. He also confirmed there was a snitch, which strengthened my resolve.

I crawled back onto the bed with my best pleading look.

Ari pulled his phone out from beneath the pillow and snuck another look at it. "Rohan had Xiaoli check that possibility out before he was reassigned to Istanbul. The redcap didn't know anything."

"Aha! Being such a devoted student, I know that a redcap is a goblin and that goblins are notorious trickster demons. Perhaps this snitch pulled one over on ol' Xiaoli. See how equipped I am to deal with him?"

A flash of amusement crossed his face. "Left off your studying at 'G,' did you?"

I pressed on. "How hard can it be to intimidate a goblin? Aren't they short old men?

"You're thinking of gnomes."

"Red hats, beards, it's all of a type."

"Goblin beards are optional. Also, gnomes don't exist and if they did, they wouldn't bathe their hats in the blood of their victims," Ari said. "Or have razor sharp teeth."

"But they share pointy ears."

His gaze drifted back to his phone. "What's your point?"

I grabbed the damn thing, trapping the phone under my leg. "Maybe Xiaoli's incentive wasn't strong enough."

"Death and torture. Pretty reliable." With a quick fake-out, he stole the phone back but didn't look at it.

"You boys," I scoffed, flapping a hand at him. "Always going for the stick. How about trying a carrot now and then?"

"Such as?"

I ran a hand along my body.

Ari's head shake was pure bafflement. "What is it with you and demon sex?"

"I'm not sleeping with him." I smacked Ari's arm. "But if he gets to be the first demon to meet the female Rasha and live...?" A nod and a wink.

Resounding silence.

"Come on," I begged. "You said it yourself. You grew up around Demon Club. You have to know who the snitch is."

Ari tugged off his socks, firing them into the corner of the room. "I don't know who he is. Just what he is."

I scooted away from his gross bare feet. "A promising start. Besides, I bet he's not all that dangerous as demons go, right? Introduce me."

"Why are you so desperate to be a part of this? Are you trying to impress Rohan?"

"No." Well, not like that. I wasn't ready to tell Ari about my plan to restore him to his rightful path because he might be angry enough to tell me to butt out and forget it. I settled for giving him a half-truth. "I want to up my stock."

Ari waited long enough before answering that I thought my idea was dead in the water. "Rohan isn't going to let you leave," he said.

I clapped my hands in delight. "Of course he isn't. Which is why you need to sneak me out. Then you can return to your regularly scheduled sexting. Or is this angry, make-up sext?"

Given the choice of helping me, the Rasha, or dishing with me, the sister, it was a no-brainer that Ari would pick the former.

The sneak out was a success. I gave a loud whoop, zipping down the street in Dad's Prius, though a cooler ride would have been nice. Hybrid electrics didn't exactly scream badass but blasting "Bad Girls" by M.I.A. went a long way to set the correct ambience.

Where would a scuzzy demon informant hang out? Or rather, the person who knew the scuzzy demon informant, since Ari could only get me to a go-between. Would I have to navigate a low-rent bar filled with sketchy clientele? A drug den at the end of a shadowy alleyway?

Or the brick bungalow I pulled up to? The front grass had been replaced with raked gravel which gleamed in the moonlight, while a giant fig tree off to one side provided the only greenery. A quick double check of the address confirmed this was the right place so I crunched my way along the dark flagstone path and up the stairs.

I rapped twice, remembering Ari's warning that this guy was human and I wasn't allowed to zap the info out of him. Still, that left a lot of leeway.

An old man with a pronounced Adam's apple, his pants and argyle sweater hanging loose off his lanky frame, answered the door. He took a long drag from the ashy cigarette in his hand, exhaling slowly with a bushy raised eyebrow.

"I'm looking for the goblin," I said.

"Stellar verbal skills, kid." He stretched an arm out to tap off some ash. Onto my shoes.

I kicked the side of my runners against the stones, trying to shake them clean while putting all my "don't mess with me 'tude" into the glower I shot his way.

"Let me guess. Bad cop?" He sucked back another hit and waved me inside.

Old Dude led me through the tiny entryway and into his living room. Every inch was covered in UFO paraphernalia. Yellowing news clippings detailing sightings papered the walls. The ceiling was plastered in UFO photos of varied graininess.

I let out a low whistle.

Years of cigarette smoke had baked into every particle of the place and was rapidly baking into me. I didn't want to spend any longer here than I had to. I lay a hand across my mouth and chin as if deep in thought, but really trying to make a filter so I wouldn't gag.

A wooden bookcase held models of different types of spaceships and figurines of alien races. I scanned them, noting the careful detail. "You made these."

"Give the girl a gold star." His sarcasm grated on my nerves but I needed the snitch's location.

"I've always wondered about alien life," I said politely.

He snorted, scratching at his stubble with a nicotine-stained finger. "Because you're stupid? They don't exist." He glanced wistfully around the room.

"Demons exist. Why can't aliens? Maybe they're just waiting to show themselves."

He exhaled a stream of smoke at me. "False hope'll kill ya."

I fanned the second-hand death out of my face. "Then why have all this?" I motioned to all his ufology stuff in confusion. "The models alone must have cost a fortune."

"African nations have smaller GDPs than I spent on these fuckers." His jaw hardened. "Two doctorates and I still got it so wrong." He ground his cigarette out in a mug with Scully and Mulder's faces on it and the phrase "I want to believe" written in blocky print underneath.

O-*kay*, bitter. "Goblin," I prompted.

The old man blinked as if he'd forgotten my presence. "You allergic to small talk? Sit down already." He dropped into a worn recliner with several burn marks on the shiny arms. "Did you bring payment?"

My face fell. "Payment?"

"A token of gratitude for my information. It's a give and take economy here, missy."

I lit up my left hand, holding its snapping crackling glory out with a cruel grin. "One zap or two?"

The unlit cigarette he'd just picked up tumbled to the carpet. "Rasha?"

"Give the man a gold star."

"How?" He reached over to pick it up, popping it in the corner of his mouth.

"Shit happens," I said. "Now, the clock is ticking. I'm not up to snuff on all the Rasha rules and regulations, plus this is an unsupervised visit, which means I have no trouble finding out firsthand how much damage I can do to you."

He lit the cigarette. "Do your worst," he rasped. "I never planned on living this long anyway."

"Figured the mothership would get you long before this, huh?"

He sucked down a lungful of death, pursing his lips and making three lopsided smoke rings. "Aren't Rasha supposed to be menacing badasses?"

I shot a couple of sparks at him. "I'm a menacing badass."

He leaned back in his recliner with a smirk. "You don't have the literal or figurative balls to hurt an old man, and since you didn't bring the appropriate bribe, we're done."

I stood there seething because he was right. I couldn't hurt him. But if I didn't, and word got out that I was soft, it'd mean a rep as easy prey.

Easier prey.

"Tell me what you want and I'll get it for you." If the Vancouver chapter dealt with this guy even semi-regularly, there had to be some kind of contingency fund for the bribe. Though I shuddered at the paperwork involved. And explaining how I'd found him. Could I bribe Ms. Clara to keep this visit from Rohan?

The old man rose out of his seat, heading for the front door at a good clip. "Out you go..." He paused, half-turning back to me. "What's your name, anyway?"

"Nava," I sighed.

He choked on his cigarette. "Nava?" He stabbed a finger at me. "What's your last name?"

"Katz," I replied, totally confused.

He burst out laughing.

"Old man, you're pissing me off."

A few more guffaws and he got himself under control. He tore a corner off a detailed sketch of an alien, grabbing a stubby pencil and scrawling something across the drawing. "The goblin should be here for another half hour."

I took the paper. "What about the cost?"

"This one's on the house."

"Why?"

He reached his knobby fingers out as if to pluck the paper away. I got the hint and fled.

I plugged the address he'd given me into the car's GPS, finding it on a two-block long street in one of the skeezier areas of town. I pulled into the tiny, weed-choked parking lot, gazing up at the sputtering neon sign for Motel Shangri-Lola, having had no idea this place existed.

Motel Shangri-Lola was a low slung building painted a faded green. More a memory of green than actual paint. Lola wasn't some former grand dame of a motel fallen on hard times, no, she'd been brought into existence a hard-livin' fungirl. An impression made more vivid by the row of outward-leaning scraggly pines extending from either side of the building, like legs drunkenly falling open.

I slammed the car door, strode up the sidewalk, flung open the lobby door, and gasped. My eyes watered at the overpowering stench of tuna fish. I threw my sleeve up over my nose until I'd climbed the worn stairs to the second floor. Sniffing and finding the air tolerable, if not fresh, I dropped my arm, searching the room numbers for 207.

It was a thick brown door like all the others in the hallway. I pressed my ear against it, but couldn't hear anything, so grasping the knob and finding it unlocked, I opened it, hoping to surprise the demon.

A dim table lamp provided the sole lighting in the room but it was strategically placed to show off the velvet painting of "Shangri-Lola" herself, a large-breasted wonder in shades of blue. On the table under it sat a digital recording device, capturing the sounds from the room adjacent to this one. Specifically the slow but steady pounding of the headboard against the wall and some man's rumbled, "Yeah, baby. Use that cat tongue."

I didn't realize he'd meant it literally until I heard his partner answer in some kind of demon language. Seems the snitch was a goblin P.I. on the case of some human/demon bow chica wow wow. Gathering evidence of a little interspecies adultery?

Speaking of the snitch... On the far side of *this* room, lay some short chick in shadow. She rested atop a garbage bag spread on top of the faded bed-spread, staring up at the ceiling, one black, knee-high boot tapping against the lumpy double mattress.

I hadn't expected a female goblin. I stepped closer trying to spot her pointy red cap and long white beard, or just her facial features, when I got distract-ed by the guy in the next room orgasming with a final hard pound against the wall and a lusty shout.

There was silence for a minute and then the sound of wet snuffling. I grimaced.

"One minute you're enjoying your tawdry affair in a bed solidified with the sweat of a thousand asses, the next you're laying in a demon wet spot with the niggling suspicion that your kink is a bit too out of hand," said the woman here with me.

I froze, knowing that voice anywhere. "Leo?"

My high school best friend bolted up, allowing me to see her face, and the familiar fall of red hair that spilled over one shoulder. She blinked her brown eyes twice, her small silver eyebrow ring glinting as it caught the light. "Nava? What the shit are you doing here?"

"What are *you* doing here?" My brain failed to compute her presence.

She motioned toward the neighboring room with the sex noises. "I was on a job. P.I. work."

Huh? But the old dude had sent me here because– "You're the goblin?" My heart stuttered. That wasn't possible. This was my Leonie in her trademark black stockings, cut-off shorts, and funky T-shirt worn underneath a cool velvet long-sleeved shirt, accessorized with all her silver jewelry.

Leo scrambled off the bed, looking around frantically. "Is Ari here?"

Ari?! A growl tore from my throat and I slammed my crackling hand right into her chest, knocking her back.

"Psycho!" Leo threw a chair at me.

It winged me in the gut.

"Fuuuhhhck." I ran after her but she'd raced into the bathroom and slammed the door. "You used me for my brother?" I jiggled the knob but it didn't turn so I tried ramming it with my shoulder. Still nothing. Lola had surprisingly good bones.

I pounded on the door. "Come out here and face me, you demon coward."

"Who said I was a demon?"

"Nice try."

She pounded on the door back at me. "Stop pounding!"

My hand was getting red. I considered blasting the door open but didn't want to risk sending all of Lola up in flame. That didn't stop me threatening to do it if Leo didn't open up.

"You pyro cow!" she screeched.

"Practice for what I'll do to your manipulative goblin ass as soon as you unlock this door." I kicked the wood.

"I can stay in here all night," she tossed out in a self-righteous tone.

I pulled a chair up close, straddling it backwards. "As if. You can't go two hours without food."

"I didn't use you for Ari. I didn't even know you existed at first."

"Because that makes it so much better." My heart pounded in my ears. Our entire friendship was a lie.

It wasn't that she'd hidden her goblin status from me, or that as a demon, she'd infiltrated my family to spy on my brother, though those ranked close seconds on things I was pissed about. The thing that hurt the most, that knotted my guts and strung my chest tight, was that our friendship hadn't even been real, just another means to an end in the ongoing demon-Rasha war.

I don't know how long we sat there in silence, me white-knuckling the top of the chair. Long enough for Cat Tongue to hit round two with his bed partner in the next room. Long enough for my hurt to harden into rage.

Long enough for Leo to say, miserably, "I'm hungry."

"Then come out," I answered in my sweetest voice.

There was a pause before she spoke. "How are you Rasha anyway? Your balls finally drop and you realized your pathetic rack was really flabby manboobs?"

I kicked the door, relishing her yelp. "I prefer Fallen Angel. My hot badassery could no longer go unrecognized."

Her snort sounded like an asthmatic donkey. Hearing it again, I almost laughed. Almost. "You can't kill me," she said. "Goblin or not, I'm still the one who leant you my favorite shirt for your first date with Stefan and held your hair when you puked your guts out later because he was such a dickhole."

She totally had. "Had you actually been my friend during that time, those points would count in your favor," I snottily replied.

The door flew open. Leonie hopped out, a tiny ball of fury, and winged a roll of toilet paper at me. "There may have been a few facts I left out about my personal history but I was totally your friend. *You* dumped me. *You* stopped calling me." She crossed her arms, her chin jutting out.

That was kind of true, too. "You were spying on my brother." I stroked my chin. "No wonder you always had to pluck your chin hairs. I thought you were part goat, but it was just your goblin heritage."

Leo covered her chin. "Take it back. You know I'm sensitive about that."

I bleated at her.

She smacked me. That's when it descended into the worst of catfights.

It was official. I sucked as a demon hunter.

12

Half an hour later, Leo sported a split lip and my scalp was raw from the hair that she'd pulled out, but we'd exhausted our pent-up resentments and called an uneasy truce. We made our way to our favorite diner, the only conversation in the car being Leo's comment that my dad's taste in music still sucked balls.

The Chesterton had gone hipster in the year and a half or so since we'd last been here. Gone were the abundance of spidery ferns and the mini jukeboxes at each booth. Now, a DJ spun electronica in one corner, while an open kitchen showcased the tattooed staff making hand-scratch food and baked goods. At least I didn't have to suffer through the misery of a communal table. A blessing upon the crippling cost of gut-job renos that kept this place from complete desecration.

I studied the collection of kitschy salt and pepper shakers on shelves running the length of one wall, searching for a safe topic of conversation because I wasn't sure how to dive back into the shark-infested waters of our hemorrhaging friendship.

"Leonie? Nava? Ohmigod!"

We both winced at the squeal from the cash register. "Back Rub" Bailey was our high school's most popular everything, with a tendency to get touchy-feely when she got drunk. Bailey was also the sweetest person who ever lived. I think she bottle-fed endangered baby seals in her spare time. Leo and I were just such cynical twats that she grated on us.

But we pasted bright smiles on our faces and gave the requisite hugs.

"What are you guys up to?" she asked.

"Crim major," Leo said.

"Got some things on the go," I replied.

That earned me a pity smile. "That's great."

I nodded gamely. "What about you?"

"I'm dancing with Ballet BC now!"

My smile wavered. Bailey was a bunhead and as determined to make it with her dance career as I'd been. "I'm happy for you." I wasn't petty enough to be catty since it was ballet. Had she been a tapper, shanking may have been involved.

Leo shot me a sideways glance before asking, "Still dating Suki?"

A brilliant smile lit up Bailey's face. She thrust out her hand. "Engaged!"

Leo squinted at the small diamond. "Hmm. Princess cut, nice girth. I grade—"

"H grade," Bailey corrected.

Leo shot her an appraising look. "Half carat. Payment plan?"

Bailey blinked. I could have enlightened her about the whole goblin thing and their gem fetish, but it was just clicking for me why Leo had always made us swing by the jewelry stores at the mall when we were teens to check out the most jewel-encrusted old lady designs.

"Um, cash," Bailey said. "Those interest charges will sneak up on you."

"Find you in a dark alley and try to break your kneecaps," Leo said, nodding sagely.

Bailey's mouth fell open in a horrified "O."

I cut in, leaning my elbow on Leo's shoulder. She tried to jostle me off, but at five-foot-two, her shoulders were perfect resting height, and there my elbow remained. "You picked a winner, Bailey," I said. "We're happy for you."

The hostess motioned to us that our table was ready, so we said our good-byes.

"You think her and Suki have figured out how to make out like normal people yet?" I asked, sliding into the booth across from Leo.

Leo put in her drink order then leaned toward my face in slow motion, her mouth open wide. "Kiss me," she said in a weird distorted voice.

"Yeah, baby," I answered, equally slowly and messed up. Our mouths came closer and we snapped our teeth at each other a few times. Then my anger trumped our jokey solidarity and I dropped the mocking impression, sitting back with a rigid spine.

That set Leo off. "'*We're happy for you.*' Gawd, you *are* Rasha. Earnest bitch."

I slapped my menu down on the green and white marbled arborite tabletop. "All right. You've got one chance to stop me from dusting you after I eat. Asmodeus, what do you know?" I figured the Rasha code of silence didn't apply to demons. Well, not this one.

"Not much beyond he's big time." Leo didn't look up from her menu, but she also didn't scratch the inside of her right wrist so she was telling the truth.

"Can you get a message to him?"

The waitress arrived with Leo's Coke and my water, asking for our orders–pulled pork poutine for me because, bad Jew, and a mushroom burger that I know Leo got so that I wouldn't want a bite. Fungus was a medical condition to clear up with ointment, not food.

Leo took a dainty sip of her Coke. "Are you going to apologize?"

"Why? So you can and it's all better? It doesn't work that way," I said. "You came into my life, into *Ari's* life with the intent to cause harm. It's an unforgivable offense. Plus, you know. Demon. Which, what? Are you glamoured up right now?"

Leo violently crunched a piece of ice. "I'm a half-goblin. From the French fling that led to my existence. Mom still doesn't know and I don't have another form I revert to. So no. No glamour required."

"You're a PD?"

"Yeah, I'm Pissed. Definitely." Leo ripped off a chunk of her burger. "Screw you. I'm not practice."

My best friend from high school was a halfie, a practice demon, though the moment I'd seen Leo's expression, I'd regretted saying it. "I'm sorry about that but it doesn't change the fact that you're a goblin."

"You're a lot of things, Nava," she said, "but I never thought you were prejudiced."

"I'm Rasha. You're evil spawn. It's natural order, not racism." I traced a line through the condensation in my water glass with intense fascination.

"Good luck navigating the demon world with that attitude."

"What's there to navigate?" I toyed with the salt shaker, tilting the salt back and forth between my hands. "Kill. That's it. It's pretty black and white."

Leo plucked the shaker out of my hands, dumped some salt in her palm, and licked it. "Nice try. Also, you're wrong. It's all shades of gray. That's your problem, Nee. You've never seen that. None of the Rasha do."

I slammed my hand against the table. "You lost all rights to that nickname."

She held up her hands, more warding me off than calming me.

The waitress deposited our food without picking up on the tension.

We ate in silence for a bit.

I stirred a fry around in the gravy. "What do you mean that none of the Rasha see the gray? Is that relevant to Asmodeus?"

"Could be. Even a villain is a hero in his own story." Leo pulled the pickle off her burger, popping it in her mouth.

I balled up my napkin, frustrated with the lack of concrete information. "The why doesn't matter. Just the what. So tell me, *bestie*, what's Asmodeus up to?"

Leo gave good glare. "It's not like there's a newsletter where the members list their current nefarious plots."

"So much for your stealthy P.I. skills." There was more bite in my voice than I'd intended.

Leonie hit the ketchup bottle with a hard thwack. "Back off. It pays my bills and tuition. Not all of us have Mommy and Daddy footing the bill for our prolonged adolescence."

"If I was still dancing, my scholarship would have taken care of it."

"Nee-Nava, come on. I'm sorry." She raked her hands through her bone-straight hair. "That was super bitchy. You're just not giving me a break here."

"Why should I?" Aside from the fact that I miss you.

"Because I didn't infiltrate your family, okay?" Her cheeks flushed as red as her hair. "Yeah, I did use you for Ari. I was massively in love with him."

"With all the sweet longing that only a thirteen-year-old can have," I mocked. I'd had no clue. That rankled too. "Get a message to Asmodeus. Tell him I'm the one he's looking for and that he can find me at the chapter house. Can you do that?" I wished I could let go of my resentment and just trust her again. Have us pick up where we left off like nothing had changed between us.

But everything had, and given the equal parts anger and hurt in her voice when she snapped, "Enable your death wish, Rasha? Why, I'd like nothing better." Leo wasn't ready to let bygones be bygones either. "Are you sure about this?" she asked a few minutes later.

I speared a cheese curd. "Do you want to be friends with me again?"

She grimaced and took a big bite of mushroom burger, glowering at me until she swallowed. "No, but still. Asmodeus is bad news. And when you upset a demon–"

"Bad things happen, yada yada." I made a talking mouth noise with my hand. "Believe me, I've gotten the spiel."

Just to be certain, Leo went into graphic detail about what he might do to me in payback, using two forks, half a hamburger bun, and the desecration of my poutine to illustrate. "You still want me to pass on this message?"

"No, but yes. It's Ari."

She sighed. "It's Ari."

"And speaking of my darling twin, if you want back in my good graces, you'll also let me read your teen diary."

Leo had been a freak about me never even touching the glittery thing.

She gave this incredibly demony half-growl. Amazing I'd never figured it out before. Then she sighed. "If I bring it over, are we friends again?" She said it like she didn't care, but she was leaving gauges in her remaining burger.

Even if it was Leo and me, it was still demon and Rasha. Talk about complicated. Rohan would never agree to help me with Ari if he found out. Being considered a demon-lover wasn't going to win me any friends–of the human or devil spawn variety. In fact, I'd probably just signed my own death warrant with the Brotherhood.

I snagged one of her fries since she'd rendered my poutine inedible. "Dummy. Your diary better be PG where my brother is concerned."

"Please. I know what you consider PG. I read your fanfic." She handed me the vinegar before I could ask for it.

I grinned for the first time since I'd found her again, remembering the whopper of a bombshell I had yet to drop on her about the inclusion of a certain Rohan Mitra in my life.

Leo narrowed her eyes at me. "I know that look. It preceded my broken arm, three double dates I'd pay to have surgically removed from my memories, and a ride home in a cop car. Forget it. I want an annulment."

I blew her a kiss. "Too late, baby. We're friends." Or would be eventually, I hoped.

I had a lot to think about on my drive home after I dropped Leo off at her apartment. Yes, I'd nearly killed our friendship when I'd been at my lowest, but that had been my screw up. The universe had given me a second chance and no matter how hard repairing it would be, I'd regret it forever if I didn't try.

However, it would take some massive finagling to keep Demon Club from finding out about her. *I* could threaten to kill Leo but no one else could. Xiaoli had known about her for sure, but I doubted any of the new guys did, since they'd have confronted her already if they had. That left Kane. I'd have to find out what he knew.

I floored the gas pedal to catch a yellow light.

These past few days had been a trip, and not a particularly pleasurable one. Would they have treated Ari the same way had our positions been reversed? No, I'd be willing to bet good money that had some dude suddenly found himself one of the Fallen Angels, he'd have been welcomed with open arms. Also hookers, blow, and a giant circle jerk. Not patted on the head, and placed under armed guard, while his fate was decided upon.

My near heart attack today had proven one thing to me. At the end of the day, the only one who could save me *was* me. So I'd play their games. I'd train. I'd fight. I'd study. I may have been a fuck up but I was also a survivor. Whether the Brotherhood liked it or not, I was going to survive them too.

And get my twin fighting beside me where he belonged. That idea just got cooler and cooler.

The car in front of me braked, so I did too, caught in a momentary snarl of traffic headed into downtown to party, the other cars filled with laughing people enjoying life. Good attitude.

With both demons and certain Rasha gunning for me, who knew what tomorrow held? This was my life and, ultimately, I was the one who had to figure out how to live–and live with–this new version of it.

So when Rohan ambushed me at the curb after I'd parked, planning to menace me into submission or apology or something, all I did was grin at him. My talk with Leo hadn't been all Asmodeus-focused. I'd also gotten a tidbit of Samson info from her since I needed something to show for my excursion. Telling Rohan that I'd outed myself to Asmodeus was not going to happen. I'd mention it after the demon was dead.

While Leo hadn't been able to tell me what type of demon Samson was or even that there was any actual confirmation of his evil status since he was that sneaky, she did tell me that she'd heard he had spent time in France. I passed the information on now.

Given how Rohan flattened his lips, he didn't expect that. His expression as I told him what I learned was priceless, cycling through suspicion, disbelief, a momentary flash of impressed approval–which I savored–before veering back to suspicion.

"Let me get this straight," he said. "You managed to find a demon informant who happened to have this knowledge and was willing to give it to you, when Xiaoli could get nothing?"

I nodded.

"You got the intel how?" He smirked at me.

"Not like that, you pig."

"I want to talk to him."

"No!"

"No?" Rohan's voice was a deadly calm. He braced his hand against the car roof, trapping me.

Oy vey. I was walking a serious subordination line here but I couldn't let him get to Leo. "This informant could prove a valuable resource. He trusts me. You guys go storming in and scare him and that'll be the end of it. It can't hurt to check out what I've said. If it turns out to be a crock of shit, then we know not to trust the goblin."

I crossed my fingers behind my back, keeping my gaze steady until he gave a sharp nod. "I had one other thought," I said.

"Give me a minute to brace myself."

"Since Mommy and Daddy demon probably didn't name their bundle of joy Samson, there has to be a reason he chose it. Does the obvious biblical connection get us anywhere?"

Rohan raised an eyebrow. "Us? Did I miss the memo where you were assigned to this mission?"

"Wouldn't you rather have me occupied in a productive manner?"

He looked doubtful at that, but answered me. "We checked out that possibility ages ago. Nothing correlates. But you're thinking along the right lines," he added begrudgingly. "However, you're done fact-finding for tonight. Fact-finding entirely where Samson is concerned. He's dangerous and I don't want him getting even an inkling that you're looking into him."

"Aw. You care." I ducked out from under his arm.

"Yeah. About you blowing all my hard work. Got it?"

"Got it." I headed up the front walk. "See? Going upstairs now."

He stood there, watching me. "No more sneaking out."

"Promise."

I'd tested my limits with Rohan and thus the Brotherhood. Any more unauthorized dealings on my part would undermine my plan and possibly lead to my "retirement" by Demon Club. No, I was smart enough to quit while I was ahead.

There would be no more sneaking out tonight.

This time, when I left the house again about twenty minutes later, I did it pretty blatantly. No way was I jumping out windows in my black three-inch stilettos with the hot pink soles–my one pop of color, save for my equally hot pink lips. Despite the warm weather we'd been having, this early in March it was still a bit too cold to go jacketless, but a coat would have ruined my overall effect and besides, the peaked nipple look really accessorized the outfit.

I sashayed down my front stairs, making a silent bet as to whether I'd make it to the taxi idling at the curb before Rohan found me or if I'd have to go find him first.

His hand clamped on mine before I was halfway down the walk, spinning me around. "Where do you think you're–"

He choked like he'd swallowed his tongue. Highly gratifying.

I pinched his cheek like a maiden aunt. "We're going out."

Not only had I almost died today, I'd also made some very good progress. A treat was in order and a cookie wasn't going to cut it. Balls, babes, and booze it was.

It took a moment for Rohan to register that I'd spoken since he was too busy staring at the silky scrap of black fabric I called a dress. "You should be in bed," he said.

I leaned in close, my orangey perfume teasing the air around us. "Mmm, I should. The question is, with who?"

The taxi driver honked.

"My chariot awaits." I tugged my arm free. "I expect demons will be after me soon and I'm not going to be shut up like a nun for the rest of my life. Now," I strode toward the cab, forcing Rohan to follow me. "I'm off to play pool and get exceedingly drunk." I opened the back door and slid in. "Coming?"

He squatted down out of view of the cabbie and flicked out one of his finger blades. "I could make you stay."

I crossed my bare legs, tantalizingly slow. "Do your worst."

He flicked out another blade.

"In or out?" the pudgy cabbie asked.

Grumbling, Rohan shoved me over, got into the cab, and slammed the door shut.

I laughed. "Neon Paradise," I told the driver. It was my favorite club boasting reasonable-ish priced drinks, pool tables, a low douchebag to normal guy ratio, and good music.

The cabbie grunted in confirmation.

Other than the Bhangra music on the stereo, the ride was pretty quiet. My smile widened with each block away from home. This was the best part of going out, when infinite possibility stretched out before me.

The cab hit the lit up Granville strip in Vancouver's downtown entertainment district, the streets teeming with people in a free-flow of life and music.

I paid the fare, then got out, trusting Rohan to follow.

A quick shake to my mane of curls, then clutch in hand, I waltzed past the people stuck in line, strutting right up to Max, the huge bouncer and keeper of the velvet rope. The red glow of the sign cast a soft filter over us.

"Looking extra fine tonight, Nava," he said, unhooking the rope for me to pass.

"You charmer, Max. I brought a friend. That okay?"

Rohan stood behind me, scowling.

"He's not as pretty but we'll let it go." He winked at me. "Have a good time." The bouncer peered at Rohan. "Do I know you?"

"No." Rohan grabbed my hand.

I barely had time to toss Max a little wave over my shoulder before Rohan dragged me into the club's all-black foyer, the floor vibrating with the pounding bass coming from deeper inside.

I tried to pay for Rohan's admission. "My treat," I said, pushing his wallet away.

He knocked my hand out of the way and handed the cashier a couple of twenties. She practically fell out of her little black dress in her haste to take the money and make skin contact with him.

"That's very sweet, but I forced you down here," I said.

"Don't I know it," he replied.

"So I pay."

"No, I pay."

I shrugged, holding out my hand for the black-light stamp that would allow me to be re-admitted. "Then the first round is on me."

Rohan made a noncommittal sound as we stepped into the club proper, already busy scanning the room. I did too, trying to see the large space as he did. Pleated curtains framed by multi-colored spot-lights illuminated cozy booths along one side. An enormous dance floor separated the seating area from the curved bar and pool tables that ran along the far wall.

A techno remix of a disco classic had the dancers going wild. My foot tapped to the music, my brain automatically finding "one" in the beat as my jumping off point to move to this rhythm. You could take the girl out of dance...

"How long do you plan on being reckless?" Rohan asked, his eyes not leaving the crowd.

"Putting a time frame on it defeats the purpose. Tell me something." I centered myself in his field of vision so he was forced to look at me. "When did you quit going out? Right after you became Rasha? Or was it a gradual slide into boring?" I rested my hand on his bicep, sending a clear message to the statuesque brunette honing in on him.

She sailed past like this had been her direction regardless, though not without a dismissive sniff my way.

Rohan was oblivious. "That's different."

"Why? Because you're male?"

"Because I'm trained."

"Does training keep you from being killed?"

A muscle jumped in his cheek. "It helps."

"But it doesn't prevent it. You said it yourself. You don't expect there to be enough of you to bury. This gig doesn't come with guarantees, Rohan. I know I'm the big shiny prize, but can you honestly say that hasn't been each of you at one time or another?"

From the tight frustration on his face, I'd made my point.

"I'll give this my all," I said, flipping my dark hair off my shoulder. "Prove my worth so that the demons are scared shitless of me and the Brotherhood can't bear to do without me." I jabbed him in the chest. "But I won't give up who I am in the process. Those evil buggers are going to come after me until I die. Don't force me to stop living in the meantime."

He rubbed his hand roughly through his hair.

I curled my fingers into my palms, imagining playing with those silky strands. Toying with them to my heart's content. Toying with *him* in all the most delicious ways.

"I'm supposed to take care of you," he said.

"You're supposed to guard me," I corrected. "I have to take care of myself. But if you really want to be useful?" I pointed to the pool tables across the way. "Rack 'em."

With that I went off to get shots, enjoying all the blatant looks from hot boys. One way or another, I was going to scratch the itchy edge inside me, tomorrow be damned. Which in this crazy new reality was a distinct possibility.

13

From the glowers I got when I arrived at the pool table with our shots, it appeared Rohan had forced a group of frat boys to wrap up their game. While they were too wussy to say anything to him directly, it didn't stop a few hissed "pushy bitch" comments flung my way.

My bodyguard had made himself positively cozy, draping his leather jacket over a tall stool, leaving him in a tailored, short-sleeved charcoal shirt that emphasized his athletic build.

Drinks in hand, I let myself enjoy the vision of him racking for Eight-ball.

He removed the triangle with a deft hand, then seeing me with the drinks, eyed the clear liquid. "No whipped cream?"

"I prefer my shots not remind me of STIs. These are G Bombs." I said, holding one out to him. "Cinnamon schnapps and vodka."

He didn't take the glass.

"Sorry. I didn't even think to ask. Are you an AA member?"

"Hardly."

"You were a rock star. Addictions are within the realm of possibility." I waggled the shot glass at him again.

"I'm on the clock."

I left the drinks on a nearby high round table, licking sticky spicy cinnamon schnapps off my fingers before choosing a cue stick off the wall rack. "Right. Babysitting duty. We'll play for it. Loser drinks."

He tested out some cues as well. "I'll try to contain my excitement."

Rohan offered to let me go first but I wanted to see his form on his break shot, so I waved him over to the table. He bent over, cue held steady, preferring to hit the head ball from slightly off to the left. The racked balls broke with a satisfying crack. He even managed to sink the three-ball, but his five got tangled up in a nasty cluster.

"Not bad." I eyed the table for my best move.

"By all means, do better." He slid past me, his ass deliberately brushing against my hip.

Amateur. I wasn't that easily distracted, though feel free to rub up against me any time. Gripping the cue with a confident hold an earthquake couldn't shake, I sank three balls in rapid succession. I straightened up and smiled. "Better, like that?"

Rohan scratched at his chest. "I was going easy on you, but if that's how you want to play it…"

I picked up the chalk. "It is."

He leaned over the table. "Buckle up, baby."

I learned something very interesting in the next little while. Rohan was exceedingly competitive. There was no banter, no joking around. You'd have thought humanity's survival depended on the outcome of the game, he was so laser-focused.

In the end, though, I sank the eight-ball first. I picked up both shots and made him take one. "L'chaim." I clinked my glass to his and shot the drink back, shivering at the sharp burn of booze hitting my throat, warming a path down to my stomach.

"Rack 'em."

Rohan placed his empty glass next to mine. "What happened to 'loser drinks?'" he asked, as we moved around the pool table removing balls from the pockets.

"I didn't say winner couldn't drink." I rolled balls over to him, hips shaking to the up tempo dance music.

A few people drifted over to watch the next game. I ended up with a small group of interchangeable hipster fanboys–thankfully beardless–alternating between cheering me on with poorly disguised innuendo and offering tips. Neither of which impressed me.

Rohan's posse, on the other hand, consisted of a trio of chicks named after designers, sporting streaked blonde hair and prodigious breasts. Armani, Chanel, and Prada were either incestuous triplets or friends with benefits who didn't like each other. I wasn't sure how to deconstruct their alternate sniping and groping.

About halfway through the game, the girls started buying Rohan drinks. Sure, them, he'd take booze from. I hoped he'd become a sloppy drunk. No such luck. If anything, his playing got better.

"You guys learn to fight wasted, don't you?" I muttered after he slammed back yet another tequila then pocketed the eight-ball with an impressive stroke that won him game two.

He gave me a wide smile and handed me my loser shot.

I fired it back. Good thing I could hold my liquor. I couldn't afford a loss in motor skills.

"Let make this interesting," Rohan said. "If I win..."

Cuntessa de Spluge woke up, having a vested interest in hearing the rest of that sentence.

"You go home," he finished.

Back to seniors' hours. "All right," I said, "but if I win, we stick around for dancing."

The DJ was winding the crowd higher with a little Usher. How fun would it be to be out there with Rohan? I made a face. "Unless you can't dance." I beckoned him closer. "If you have no rhythm, tell me now."

"My rhythm is bang on," he drawled in my ear.

Cuntessa pulsed.

The two posses took our escalation into betting territory as the green light to place bets with each other. Given the shrieking giggles of the girls, it wasn't hard to guess what was at stake. The trouble was that they now ganged up on poor Rohan and me, deciding that a shot of their choosing (and buying) had to be drunk for each ball missed.

Rohan readily agreed to this. I did too. I could hold my booze and was determined to crush him.

It was on.

I lost track of everything around me. My world narrowed down to the felt, the cue ball, and the occasional fresh cool glass pressed into my hand. Which started happening more and more often as that one drink too many tilted my pool playing abilities into potential epic failure territory. My stomach protested the boozy onslaught.

"Spit or swallow?" Rohan murmured to me, near the end of the final game. We were neck and neck for balls sunk.

I sputtered the water I'd been gulping down. "Beg pardon?"

He nodded at the triplets. "Spit or swallow? What are your boys in for tonight?"

I didn't even need to glance at the girls to answer that one. "Neither. Those girls are not putting their mouths on it."

Rohan gaped at me like door number three wasn't even a reality in his world.

I laughed and patted his shoulder. "Such a sheltered life you've led, Snowflake."

Rohan shot the girls another perplexed glance. They flashed their cleavage while staying primly out of groping reach, resulting in more than one of the hipsters pulling a "trying to adjust myself" shifting side-to-side move in response.

"How can they ask a guy to go down on them if they won't do the same?" he asked.

Cuntessa throbbed at his implied readiness to boldly go where many men would not.

"They don't," I said. "No guy is putting his mouth on it either."

"They're missing out on a whole realm of excellent," Rohan said.

"God, yes," I said, louder and tipsier than I intended.

We grinned at each other in perfect harmony but the conversation had me regretting my choice of bet. Wanting to explore that particular realm of excellent with him. Still. I'd used dancing as foreplay on more than one occasion.

Despite all the drinking, victory was almost mine but I got cocky, using a bit too much force on my final shot. The eight-ball hit the back of the pocket and bounced back.

Cuntessa gave a disgusted grunt.

"It's almost no fun winning this way," Rohan said, not hesitating to sink the ball. He pumped his fist in victory but there was no answering gush of approval from his posse. Come to think of it, no grumbling from mine, either.

We were yesterday's news. The group had already paired off into dry hump partners. One of the pairs had gotten especially frisky. The guy's shirt was pushed halfway up while his partner's tipsy maulings had caused his jeans to slip dangerously low on his ass.

I grabbed my clutch then nudged Rohan, motioning toward the two with a jerk of my chin, notably dude's pale butt. "He could be arrested for possession of that much crack."

Rohan pressed his head close to mine. "'Never back down.'" He read the tattoo written in graphic print at the base of the guy's spine. "Dude," he said with a mournful shake of his head. Booze exaggerated his word into pure Southern Cali drawl.

"Factoring in the placement, those words cover so many possibilities," I said. "Everything from empowerment to grim determination in the face of prison showers. Wonder which it is?"

Rohan smothered a laugh against my hair. It shimmied down to my toes, which curled under to contain the sparkly lightness. He took my slight sway of motion for our cue to leave. "Since I trounced you," he said, handing his stick over to a woman waiting for the table, "it's time for all good little girls to go to bed. You, too."

"To think that wit was wasted in the music industry."

Rohan scooped up his jacket with one hand, placing his other on the small of my back to lead me away from the table.

I skirted the edge of the dance floor with its strobing lights, the alcohol in my system warming me as much as weaving through the press of bodies. Colors were more saturated. Time and my body moved more languidly. The music slithered up from the floor, pulsing into my skin. I stepped toward the other dancers, wanting to join them. To lose myself.

Rohan kept me on course, steering me to the exit with a steady hand.

I had to concentrate what he was babbling on about to me because words took a bit longer to penetrate. Oooh. Penetrate.

The cool night was a welcome relief. I swayed to the throb of the still-audible bass, watching Rohan grow more and more frustrated trying to flag down a cab.

"Give it up. It's practically impossible on a weekend," I said. "We'll have a better chance a few blocks away."

"So many things wrong with this city," he muttered.

"Follow me," I trilled, pushing through the crowd.

The night had turned unseasonably muggy, the air heavy with that metallic smell promising rain. A born and bred Vancouverite, rain didn't phase me.

Dodging through the late night crowd, we'd just hit the mouth of an alleyway when we heard a hissed, "Wanna blow your mind?" I would have sailed past but Rohan clasped my wrist to stop me. The dealer stepped into view. Your run-of-the-mill slime bucket, he wore a skull and hearts T-shirt under a jean jacket. A crescent-shaped birthmark edged his left cheek.

The dealer jerked his chin at Rohan. "Interested, man?"

Rohan hooked an arm around my neck. "My girlfriend might be. She likes to live on the edge." *Girlfriend?* Under his breath he said, "Like taking off on her own when ordered otherwise." He pushed me forward. "Show her what you've got."

Slime Bucket's eyes glittered. "Devil's candy. A rush like nothing else."

Evil and unsubtle, a winning combo. I barely refrained from rolling my eyes. "Let's talk." I walked forward.

Thinking he had a customer, the dealer accompanied me into the shadowy alley reeking of urine, Rohan trailing us. The demon led us in through an open door to a small back room with a couple of couches. A naked bulb in a hideous ceramic table lamp cast a dim light, but it was enough to see the young man sprawled out on a couch, pressed close to a willowy, blue-haired female bearing an identical crescent birthmark as the dealer.

What really squicked me out was that the man was sucking on the female's thumb, his face lost in orgiastic delight, even as clumps of his hair fell to the stained concrete. With every moan the guy let out, Blue Hair's skin seemed to plump with an extra layer of collagen, her hair shine and thicken, and the crow's feet by her eyes and lines by her lips vanish.

My head swam from whatever bliss drug she was secreting. I clutched the top of a chair to keep from sinking onto that sofa with them and joining in. Rohan, on the other hand, slouched against the doorframe with his hands jammed in his pockets. Not an ounce of tension in him.

The dealer noted the affect the place was having on me. "Go on," he murmured into my ear as he pried one of my hands off of the chair, "live a little."

"Just say no." I gripped the chair harder and blasted the demon back against the wall with mega-current shot from my eyes.

Oh my God, I had a literal death glare! It was official: I was a badass.

Blue Hair flicked the fingers of her free hand at me, prismic drops of her evil sweat flying through the air to land on me like a gentle spring rain. Well, a gentle spring rain that exploded light into trippy colors and amped oxygen into a liquid happiness rush.

My knees buckled and I swayed toward her with a moan.

Rohan slammed the dealer up against the wall, stabbing him through the right palm with a finger blade. With a pop, the dealer dissolved into an oily puddle.

Blue Hair rose up, the man clutching at her leg, his mouth working uselessly, sucking nothing. Fury blazed in her eyes as she snatched her victim up in her arms and blurred past us into the night.

Rohan pulled me into the alley after her but she was gone. I sucked in a head-clearing breath.

"Remember that helplessness the next time you plan on taking off alone," Rohan said.

"I accessed my power."

"Yeah, but you still needed back up."

"Still need babysitting. Got it."

"Hey." He ran his hand along my back, the tension in it lessoning at his touch. "I didn't mean it like that."

I nodded. "So? Why aren't we hauling ass after them?"

Rohan leaned back against the alley wall. "Did you see how far gone he was? Those scum pimp a hallucinatory secretion that induces bliss while they drain the victim's life away. That guy has maybe fifteen minutes left in him tops. And even if we did rush in, save him?" He glowered at the empty room. "Addicts always go back."

I hoped dude's death was painless. Then I blasted a dumpster into a brick wall hard enough to crack it.

Rohan placed a hand on my shoulder. "We don't always win."

Not wanting to go home on that note, I strode into a small urban park, headed for a narrow stream flowing along a concrete channel. It cascaded into a circular pool inset in the ground before gurgling up from a fountain in its center.

Four brick archways flanked the fountain—one at each corner. I picked one at random, sinking onto the bench underneath the overflowing foliage, which provided a thick leafy canopy. I stretched out my legs, looking up at the stars and focusing on their beauty so I wouldn't lose myself to the ugliness.

Traffic in the background provided a soothing white noise.

I hoped that man had had a full life, short as it was.

"Don't get comfortable," Rohan said.

"Too late." I dug around in my clutch. "Aha." I pulled out my tiny black pot pipe and lit up, holding the smoke in past the initial burn in my lungs.

Rohan plucked the pipe from my fingers and took a deep drag. I was so shocked that I sputtered out all my smoke. I waved a hand in front of my face as he patted me on the back with one hand.

"Thought you were on duty," I said, reclaiming the pipe and dragging on it again.

Rohan exhaled in a steady breath. "I've fought more wrecked than this."

I offered him the pipe again but he shook his head. I placed it and the lighter on the bench beside me. "How rock star did you get at the height of things?"

He folded his hands on his stomach, looking up at the few stars visible through the light pollution. "Pretty much every cliché you'd imagine."

That conjured up images of writhing, barely clad bodies that I was either too stoned or not stoned enough to handle. "Why'd you quit?"

He was quiet for a long time. I wasn't sure if I'd pushed one too many times for an answer, or if he was zoned out. "Fame isn't as cool from the inside."

I flicked my eyes sideways at him, feeling every fraction of an inch that my eyeballs moved. So I did it again because shifting them in my head from side to side was a weirdly wonderful sensation.

It got me thinking about pinball, which morphed into the image of poor Rohan being batted around by giant flippers of fame. "It's like you were a pinball." I flicked my left hand like a pinball flipper. "Bam. Paparazzi." I flicked my right. "Bam. Managers."

"Bing! Full tilt. Fans," Rohan chimed in.

"Exactly." I wiggled my toes. What other profound insights might moving various body parts bring?

Rohan reached up to pluck a low hanging leaf, rubbing it between his fingers. "The need to keep racking up points, to stay in the game becomes addictive. But the machine isn't sentimental. If you fall down the hole out of play, it's got another ball ready to take your place. It did a number on me and I fucked up." His eyes grew distant and haunted as he added softly, "Big time."

Before I could ask what he meant, he reached inside his inner jacket pocket and removed a small, disc-like container. Twisting the clear plastic cover, he shook out a few candy-colored rice grains and popped them in his mouth. "Coated fennel seeds. Want some?"

A burst of licorice hit my tongue when I crunched into them. I held out my hand for a few more.

Thunder rumbled in the distance.

Above me, a massive dark raincloud menaced. That wet electric smell had gotten sharper. It was still muggy though, and I was stoned and comfortable under the canopy of leaves so I didn't bother moving.

I glanced at Rohan who still seemed lost in painful memories. I decided not to probe. "You sound remarkably well-adjusted now." I brushed the wreckage of the leaf he'd shredded off of his thigh. "Or not."

Rohan gave a wry laugh. "This is definitely the well-adjusted version. You should have seen me even a year ago."

"Fucking everything that moved?" I asked, cursing myself for putting images into my very visual brain.

"More like fighting."

"Hence your impressive kill record."

"What about you?" he asked.

I laughed, shaking my head.

"What?"

I repositioned myself, sitting sideways on the bench, my legs tucked up alongside me. "You get this is surreal, right? Sitting here getting stoned with Rohan Mitra while he asks about me?"

He preened. "Your teen fantasy made real. You're overwhelmed."

I shoved his shoulder. He didn't budge, but when he nudged me back, I jostled sideways. Such strength. Bet he could pin me down.

"There's not much to tell." I curled my fingers under the bench to grip it.

Rohan extended the blades on his right hand, bringing them up to eye-level with a waggle. "Ve hav vays of making you talk," he said in a horrible German accent. The blades disappeared. "I know you didn't spring fully formed. You'd have been nicer." He jabbed my side. "Tell me. Ari was the initiate, you were the what?"

I rubbed my arms.

Rohan shrugged off his jacket and draped it over my shoulder, shaking his head at me when I tried to protest.

Feebly.

What can I say? The thing was soft as butter and smelled like him.

"I was going to dance," I said.

"Like around a pole?" I shot him the finger at the giggle that escaped him.

"Like Heather Cornell, Chloe Arnold, Dormeshia Sumbry-Edwards, Lady Di Walker, you asshole. None of whom are Shirley Temple and all of whom are amazing tap dancers."

He held up his hands. "Sorry. So that was your dream?"

I brushed my cheek against the collar, pretending to be scratching my jaw with my shoulder, snuggling into his residual warmth, and letting myself be enveloped in a Rohan cocoon. "Yeah. When I was about three I saw this old Ginger Rogers and Fred Astaire tap number. After that I insisted my dad fix my shoes to 'make those noises,' so he taped pennies to my slippers." I smiled at the memory. "I refused to take them off. They enrolled me in my first class that fall."

"What was the highlight?" I checked to see if he was humoring me but he seemed genuinely interested.

"The summer before grade eleven, I got accepted into a special program where I studied with master tappers and then performed at Lincoln Center. That was pretty fucking mind-blowing. Not sold out concert stadiums though," I said, with a wry grin.

"I never played Lincoln Center. I'm impressed. So, what happened?"

I shrugged, not able to get into it right now. Damn stoner confessions never went anywhere good.

Rohan didn't press me. "Do you miss dancing?"

"Like breathing," I said in a thick voice.

He slung an arm around my shoulder and curled me into him. Nooked into his arm like that, I felt protected. Snug.

Home.

Bad stoner thought. I disengaged from his hold. It was stupid but I missed the warmth of it. The protectiveness. "Do you miss it?"

"Fame? Not even a bit."

"Singing. Your band." I cocked my head to look at him. "Do they know you're Rasha?"

"Zack does. The other three were dicks. We're not in contact anymore."

"And the singing?" No answer.

He'd been a rock superstar and I didn't understand how someone walked away from living the dream. Especially when I'd have given everything for it. "You can't tell *me* of all people that you don't miss something you cared so much about for such a long time."

He shrugged.

"What about the music itself?" I said. "You say the rest of your band are jerks but you guys were together for a few years. There must have something good about the collaboration."

Rohan raised an eyebrow. "Still dwelling on the wrong members of the band, are you?"

"You never know. I might want to revisit my fanfic." I nudged his leg. "Come on. I'm talking shop with the great Rohan Mitra and you're not gonna tell me?"

He reached over me to pick up the pipe and lighter, sparking up with a flick of his thumb. I waited as he inhaled, watching him leaning forward, his elbows on his knees. He held the smoke in for so long, it had to be a stonewalling tactic. Finally, he exhaled, a long column of smoke that dissolved into the late night mist.

"The writing, the jamming, was one of the best parts." He gazed up at me through his lashes. "I mean performing is always tops, you know that."

I nodded sagely.

"But sitting down with the guys and realizing I could put all the shitty things I was feeling, all the dreams I never thought I'd share with anyone, into words that I wanted to belt out to the world in this incredible music? Having my lyrics come alive for my audience?" He laughed, but it sounded too soft, deflated.

"Sing for me," I blurted out.

"More teen fantasy?" he teased. "I don't think you can handle intimate and interactive."

"Try me." I swear I was still talking about his singing. Not my fault that that his lids lowered a fraction over his eyes with a look of simmering desire.

I swallowed, desperately trying to get saliva into my very dry mouth.

Honestly, I didn't expect him to start. I sure as hell wasn't prepared for it to be his first number one hit "Toccata and Fugue." The song jolted me back to being thirteen, to the first time I'd heard it.

It was a hot summer night. Leonie and I were slumped in the backseat of her older cousin's beat-up Jetta that to us seemed like the greatest car in the world because it was owned by a teenager, not a parent. I remember resting my hand out the window and the hot wind rushing through my splayed fingers as we drove back from the beach. Our hair was a wet tangle of salty strands and the faint scent of coconut clung to our skin.

Leo was pissing off her cousin, dusting the sand from her bare feet onto the backseat carpet. Then this song came on the stereo and a guy's raspy voice singing a stream of consciousness love song overrode the bickering in the car.

That voice unnerved and excited me, igniting this wildness that at that tender age, I didn't know how to handle and couldn't name. I'd strained against the seatbelt to push my face and shoulders up to the night air, like the breeze could make the restlessness subside. I don't think I breathed until the song was over.

I caught myself holding my breath the same way now. Rohan's voice called that same wildness to the surface of my skin, dancing over me. His eyes never left mine as he sang the chorus of the girl with the lightning eyes and the boy with demons in his soul.

My stomach plummeted. What the holy fuck were the chances of universe convergence that would make me, him, and those lyrics end up in the same place? It freaked me right out. I'd just learned of one destiny in the past couple days and him singing this song right here, right now, was calling into prophecy something that I wanted no part of.

I'd give freely of my body. My heart was off-limits. Especially to a guy like him. Seriously. I'd take the demons.

Thankfully, I wasn't the only one unnerved. Rohan broke off midway through the second verse, looking like walls were closing in on him. He cleared his throat a couple of times as I stuffed my feet into my shoes, and grabbed my clutch.

"Good thing my eyes are bluish-gray," I joked. "We should get–" I didn't even bother to finish. Just up and bolted along the sidewalk, ready to push anyone out of my way who tried to get between me, a taxi, and home.

I spied the steady "on" light of a cab, waiting at a traffic light a couple of blocks away, and sped up, cutting through the playground to hit the street in time to flag it down.

The ground shook as I passed the swings. I grabbed onto a chain, trying to keep my footing as a massive being winked into existence with a rumble of thunder. Nothing like a demon arrival to sober a girl up.

14

Rohan yanked me away from the swing set, shoving me behind him and blocking my body with his.

"I got your message, Rasha," the demon growled. "So delighted to see who killed my children."

Asmodeus. Oh, shit. Leo wasn't supposed to have been this efficient. He wasn't supposed to have found me until I was safely behind the chapter house wards. At least I had Rohan.

"Message?" Given the cold, flat fury on his face, Snowflake would happily feed me to the demon himself.

I rose onto tiptoe to see over Rohan's shoulder. His body was taught with tension, which was unsurprising since Asmodeus was built somewhere between a tank and a small mountain range and boasted three heads: a bull, a ram, and an ogre. His chest was covered in hardened scales. *Gulp.*

"Kill now, talk later," I muttered.

"If there's anything left of you when I'm done," Rohan murmured back.

Blades snicked out to outline Rohan's entire body, running up from his left ankle, along the outer edge of his leg and arm, over his head and down the other side. Plus the short wicked steel extending from his fingertips. His front and back were still vulnerable but he was pretty fucking intimidating glinting in the moonlight.

Asmodeus sauntered forward, as if giving us puny humans time to marvel. I couldn't see this creature inspiring anyone to lustful thought and deed because he was a ghastly fucker. Prime candidate for needing a glamour. Though it was interesting to see who his spawn took after, in a *huh, would you look at that?* way.

I tossed my purse and Rohan's jacket on a bench with trembling hands, visualized throwing my power switch to on, and stepped out from behind Rohan. "Good of you to reply in person."

Asmodeus stopped, not ten feet away, showing the first glimmer of interest since his arrival. Little clouds of dust swirled around his rooster feet. Then he laughed. At least, his ogre head did. "A female Rasha."

Oooh. Now the lust part made sense. Three boring words spoken in a dark, seductive voice and I'd gone sopping wet. Cuntessa was frantically dog paddling. I flicked my eyes to Rohan's bulge. This was indeed an equal opportunity demon.

Rohan glared at me but I took it as a bonding moment.

"Where's his sweet spot?" I asked, speaking low into Rohan's ear.

"No idea." Officially fucked now. "Watch him fight," Rohan said. "See if he shields any part of himself. That could be a clue."

Asmodeus prowled toward us. For each one of Asmodeus' steps, Rohan forced me back two. I barely registered what he was doing, my attention fully focused on the demon.

Asmodeus reached the swing set, but instead of batting the structure out of his way or sidestepping it, he ripped the thick metal chain right off the frame, tossing the entire swing aside onto the wood chip-covered ground. The disinterest with which he so casually desecrated a piece of kid's playground equipment drove home that nothing was sacred where demons were concerned. They would show up anywhere, go after anyone.

Right now, he was after me. I jumped back another step without any prompting from my bodyguard.

"I could be persuaded to keep you as a plaything," Asmodeus said. "I like new toys."

"Yeah, but there'd be this whole hook-up with your son between us. Best not." I could barely hear myself speak over the crackle of my magic and the pounding of my heart.

Reminding him of his son—and by extension, my role in his demise—was not the smartest move. A cruel smile spread across all three faces simultaneously. "It wasn't up for debate," Ogre head informed me, reaching one fleshy hand out.

Rohan sprang into action, diving to the ground in a roll. With a sharp flick of his neck, he used the blade along the top of his head to slash the tendons of Asmodeus' rooster feet.

Black fluid gooshed out as the entire left side of Asmodeus' body sagged like a landslide, but he didn't die.

Rohan sprang to his feet, then rushed the demon again.

Asmodeus held up a hand, looking almost bored.

Rohan stopped inches from the demon, lips parted, giving breathy gasps, like he was stuck on the verge of an orgasm.

"Bring me the girl," Asmodeus ordered. His eyes glowed as he caressed Rohan's neck with his warty index finger.

Rohan rubbed up against him like a cat. It was the new gold medal standard of creepy. Physical danger from demons was one thing, but I found the psychological threat of being compelled via voice command even more disturbing. Rohan marching toward me with jerky steps, uselessly fighting the demand, unnerved me more.

I sprinted for the section of playground designed for older kids, crossing a small, arched bridge that traversed a blue river painted on the concrete, and swung myself up to the top of a plastic climbing structure. Grabbing the safety rail, I fired a forked blast of electricity at Rohan from my index finger. One day, I'd master this technique from all my fingers simultaneously and have a handy little arsenal going.

It knocked into his right side with a sizzle, but didn't deter him. Rohan came puppet-like, closer and closer, Asmodeus trailing, limping behind him—almost like a bored parent.

Frantic, I scanned the area for some kind of projectile, but these stupid modern playgrounds were made for safety and all the plastic was nailed down tight. Next option. With a running jump, I leapt onto the fireman's pole. In my head, I was super stripper personified as I swung my way down–legs out, core taut–around the pole to kick Rohan. To be fair, I was aiming for his chest, but my sweaty hands slid, knocking me off-balance.

The thud as my foot collided with Rohan's skull jarred me hard enough to rattle my teeth, so no surprise that it was enough to snap him out of his demon-induced spell.

"Wanna not do his job for him?" Rohan bitched, knocking me to the ground as Asmodeus' twisted ram's horn slashed the air where my head had been.

"That's nothing like thank-you." I scrambled to my feet.

"You got that, did you?"

We backed into the grassy field. "You want her?" Rohan asked the demon. "You gotta go through me." I shivered at the menace in his voice.

Asmodeus charged, fiendishly pointy horns thrust front and center.

Rohan grabbed the closest horn before it could do any damage, using momentum to swing himself around. He was amazing to watch, all lethal elegance as he struck the demon with short, fierce blows. He swung his leg around in a brutal roundhouse kick, the blade along his thigh jamming into the neck of the ram's head, lodging there. With a quick jerk of his hip, Rohan popped his leg free, slashing the ram neck in the process.

Viscous goop gushed out in an arc as that head flopped forward onto the demon's chest.

My jaw dropped. "Whoa." I defied anyone to say that move wasn't hot.

Rohan smirked at my reaction.

I narrowed my eyes. No way did he get to have all the fun.

Rohan jumped into my path to block me. "Hey, Dark Menace," he said, "stay back."

I'd sidestepped him before the words finished leaving his mouth, intent on my target. I was still terrified, but then again, becoming blasé around demons would be at my peril. Watching Rohan use his entire body fighting Asmodeus had inspired me so I tried pulsing electric blasts in waves off my body. It was too clunky, depleting, and I didn't yet have the range so I switched it up, flinging lightning balls at Asmodeus, rapid fire like a pitching machine set to eleven.

Rohan grabbed my non-pitching arm, but I shook him off.

Asmodeus lit up as my blue voltage covered him, his flesh smoking. "Is that all you can do?" His laughter boomed, echoing off the trees around us. The demon wasn't shielding shit. He was fearless, taking everything we threw at him without batting an eye.

Rohan swore and jumped back in the fray.

Thunder ripped across the sky, crashing over us. My heart jumped into my throat, and as the skies opened up, my power went into overdrive as if in response to nature's call. The rush was insane. My body tingled, like the explosion of energy inside me needed a way out through my skin. I reached for the electric moisture blanketing me. The rain ran over me in velvet rivulets, dancing over the magic pouring out through every pore.

Everything took on a surreal, dreamy quality– even Asmodeus, swinging back and forth dodging our dual-sided assault. Despite his injuries, he fended us off pretty well, looking almost amused by the entire encounter. Demons were such dicks.

Asmodeus feinted left to avoid Rohan and snatched me up by the back of the neck. That fucking hurt. The sweet release of my magic cutting off mid-stream hurt more. Like having a giant shit suddenly reverse course. My entire body convulsed in wave upon wave of needle-like stabbings.

"Motherfucking, limp-dicked, piece-of-shit," I raged at Asmodeus.

"The first two contradict each other," he said with infuriating condescension. "Watch it, puppy. Keep snapping and you'll get nipped by much larger teeth."

Rohan leapt for me, but Asmodeus backhanded him with a hard crack, winging him halfway across the park to wallop against the post of another brick archway. Rohan crumpled to the ground.

Asmodeus' strength, his compulsion abilities were demonic power on a terrifying scale and I was in his grasp, powerless and unable to stop my shallow panting.

He stroked my cheek, my red-hot agony morphing to a molten heat that consumed me, and lifted me up so that I was eye-level with him. I squirmed, driven by a deep-seated compulsion to do anything he asked of me if he'd satisfy the knife's edge I teetered on. My lips parted in silent plea.

The demon tilted his bull and ogre heads, studying me. All four eyes widened, as if surprised. His bull nostrils flared with a soft snort, he tightened his grip, and the world swung sideways with sudden sharp violence.

Dizzy, unable to summon my magic, I screwed my eyes shut, praying he didn't toy with me too long before I died. Missing the good old days when the loss of a purple bra was the sum total of my worries.

"You want... so much." He touched my face. "Peel back the false layers and embrace your deepest, darkest desires."

Syrup slithered through my bones. *Yes.*

I opened my eyes.

A monster had me. A nightmarish image with too many heads and a horrific mashup body, smirking as I struggled in his grasp. "Help me! Heeeeellllllp!"

A dark-haired man charged us, arms raised. His fingers ended in blades, glinting in the moonlight.

I screamed again.

"Nava!" the man cried out. He skidded to a stop before us. How did he know my name?

I screwed my eyes shut, whimpering, stuck between a nightmare and another nightmare. Wind whooshed against my legs and I was dropped onto the ground.

I cracked an eye to find the man battling the monster. Not on the same team, then?

"Use your magic!" the man barked at me.

I stared at the crazy stranger. Then I did what any sane person would do and ran screaming into the night.

Behind me, I heard the man swear, and the monster laugh.

The stranger caught up with me in the middle of the road. I glanced over my shoulder but the monster was gone.

"Let me go." I tried to tug free.

"I can't." The man's face was tight with frustration. He no longer had blades. Had I imagined them? Imagined everything of the past few minutes? Trying to remember events leading up the monster's appearance left me clutching my head in agony.

The stranger ignored my distress, hauling me back toward the park. I doubted he'd saved me just to kill me on his own terms but a girl could never be too careful. Another man had scared me recently. This one? I didn't think so, but I couldn't remember.

Running had gotten me nowhere and there was no one else around to help. I really needed some time to process what the fuck had just happened. Preferably at chez Katz because if my knocking knees gave out here, I suspected I might just curl up in the fetal position and be done.

"I'm super grateful for your assistance, but how about we call it a night and go our separate ways?" My feet slid in a puddle of something that didn't match the clear rain water falling around me. I leapt onto the grass.

"I'd love nothing better, Nava," the stranger snapped. "Seeing as how you're a royal pain in my ass."

"Excuse me?!" I planted my hands on my hips. "I have no clue how you know my name but you obviously haven't spent any time around me because I'm a delight."

The bastard actually laughed.

I punched him in the chest hard enough to illicit a satisfying "oomph." Cool. That one kickboxing class I'd taken last year had really paid off.

He grabbed my wrist. "You can do better than that, Rasha."

Rasha? And what was with his tone of voice? Like a taunt? A challenge? No, an order. Big surprise this jerk bossed people around. I tried to break free but he simply stood there, my arm caught in his grasp, one eyebrow cocked arrogantly at me.

That look pushed a major button. Something shifted inside me, like a switch being thrown on. Electricity burst from my palms, causing Rohan to jerk back. My memory was now working just fine. "Asshole," I snarled, lowering my hands.

"There she is." He smiled and I was undone at the tenderness in it.

Our chests heaved in identical rhythms. We were both dirty, our filth ranging in color from demon innard black to demon innard red with a soupçon of purple bruising as an accent. The rain had soaked our clothes and plastered our hair to our heads.

I checked the park but Asmodeus was really gone. The question was, why?

15

"I didn't kill him," Rohan said. "I don't know why he left and I'm certain it wasn't because of anything we did because the two of us on our own had no hope against him. We haven't seen the last of him." He pinched the bridge of his nose. "You used the snitch, didn't you?"

"To be fair, I figured I'd be safely behind the Demon Club wards before he got the message. Before he got to me." I shivered. "What if Asmodeus was right, and all I want is to forget any of this ever happened? I thought I'd been dealing, but..." I blew out my cheeks.

Rohan tipped my chin up, forcing me to meet his eyes. "You are dealing. Brilliantly." He tucked a dripping strand behind my ear.

My chest constricting at this new layer of intensity to an already brain-exploding night, I grasped his hand, intending to brush him off, but found myself leaning into him.

He tilted his head, looking at me oddly. "Your eyes," he said, in a strangled voice. "I can still see lightning in them."

Panic clawed at my throat. I opened my mouth to protest the lightning girl label but the sky above lit up with a brilliant flash that let me see the truth of his words in the reflection of his eyes.

And the heat simmering in their depths. Ironically, that calmed me down. Lust didn't frighten me. Quite the opposite.

Rohan curled his fingers around my waist, ducking his head toward mine.

I slammed my hand over his mouth. "No kissing."

That activity had been kiboshed over a year ago after a spectacularly disappointing session with one Elvis Persig. His fishy-lipped nibbling of my face had felt too much like the time I'd stuck my feet in one of those tanks for squirming, toothless carp to eat my dead skin. Except without the exfoliating benefit.

I loved kissing. Or rather, loved the idea of it as this precious gesture to be shared between two people in love. I just wasn't sure that love existed. Case in point, my ex, Cole, who was supposed to be there for me when I'd learned I had to stop dancing. The one who'd fucked off instead, leaving me to break down alone. Relationships had become hookups. While I'd kept the kissing–at first–these hookups weren't about tenderness and intimacy.

Easier to let kissing stop being part of the equation.

Rohan shot me a look of disbelief.

I gently cupped his crotch, feeling a cheap thrill at his hard-on. "This isn't romance, baby. It's lust, pure and simple."

"It may be pure but there's nothing simple about it, Lolita. In fact," he traced a finger down my cleavage, "it's rather complicated." He leaned in toward me again and I put a hand on his chest to stop him.

"I'm not dreaming about happily-ever-afters and I'm not your girl with the lightning eyes." I practically sneered that last bit at him.

It took a second for him to believe me. Trust me, I saw the moment that he did because a dark savagery crossed his face. I skittered back, my back hitting a wide tree trunk but Rohan didn't move. He clearly wanted me, so what was the hold up? His eyes were intent on mine, looking for something.

Ah.

"Not backing up because I'm afraid, baby." I winked, throwing a glance at the tree behind me. Though, okay, I did experience a moment of panic about the possibility of another misfire and Cuntessa once more being reduced to a charred nubbin. I wasn't sure her and I could get past it happening twice.

But where Rohan was concerned? No, I'd backed up to get some much needed distance at the lust triggered by the look on his face. My need for him had reached supernova levels. The potential big bang worth any risk. I licked my lips, crooking a finger at him. "Do you need an engraved invitation, Snowflake?"

"Fuck," he ground out, prowling toward me.

My toes curled at the hot look in his eyes that dipped and lingered on the hollow of my neck, only to be replaced by his lips there as he gathered my hair in his fist and tugged it to one side.

His tongue, hot on my cool skin, swirled in tempo with the beats of my heart, now hammering Indy-car fast under the onslaught of his mouth on my collarbone. "Sugar," he murmured.

"Body scrub." I tilted my neck to give him better access, but with a sharp jerk, Rohan spun me around, pressing me against the rough bark. He slammed my hands over my head, gripping them lightly but firmly in one hand. I scrabbled for a hold, my eyes falling on the words "Party like it's 1999" scratched into the trunk, just past the tip of my nose. Rain cascaded down around us like a steamy waterfall, but the leaves made a dry, cozy bubble above us.

Rohan raked his nails up my spine.

I shivered, totally in thrall as he pressed the length of his body against me. Trapped between the tree and him—a near-stranger, and dangerous at that—heat spread like wildfire deep in my core. Flamed high. The unpredictability of it brought out an interesting little kink I had, though it wasn't a case of any guy would do.

My head fell back against his chest and my breathing deepened. A slow legato. How could it sound so languid when my entire being was coiled tight in a dark smolder?

The traffic quieted. We'd hit a lull at this time of night before the bars emptied out, but in this deserted downtown park with a silent city around us, it was easy to believe we were the only two alive.

I closed my eyes, all the better to lose myself to sensation. The scrape of bark against my cheek, his breath gusting my neck, the rough tip of his finger skimming the thin fabric along my hip. Every nerve ending flared to life under his touch. Sweat pooled between my trembling thighs.

Rohan blew a lock of my hair off my neck, ducking his head to nip at my ear.

I twisted my head around, my breath punched out of me at his eyes sparking darkly with need. I tilted my hips back, pressing into his hard-on to get some form of contact.

He hissed, jerking his body away from me.

I arched back, trying to follow him but he kept me in place with a palm between my shoulder blades. My newly-released hands fell limp at my sides. At least now I could touch him, too.

I reached behind Rohan to curve my hand around his hip as he wormed my skirt up from behind to slide his hand between my legs. He gave a satisfied chuckle at how wet I already was. I didn't care. Smirk away, just keep stroking. I closed my thighs around his hand, rocking my hips back and forth.

Rohan moaned into my ear and my belly fluttered.

"Tell me what you want." The rough rasp of his voice scraped over my too-tight skin, kicking my torment up into new stratospheres.

Cuntessa de Spluge swooned. I imagined her screaming like a teenybopper. With my hands still behind me, I roughly caressed his ass. "You. Now."

"That can be arranged."

A whisper of wind hit high on my thigh as my bikini briefs floated to the ground in a scrap of lace. Fuck me, he'd cut them off with one of his finger blades. My knees wobbled. Cool air cascaded over my very flushed nether regions.

Rohan knocked his knee between my legs, nudging them wider. Then he crooked a bladeless finger inside me, rotating it as he thrust it in and out.

I rose onto tiptoes, my stilettos not providing enough height on their own to let him hit *my* sweet spot deep inside. My legs shook and my feet barely touched the ground. Every cell hummed in greedy delight.

"Rohan." The gasp of his name was almost a plea. I was coming undone in his hands.

"Say my name like that again." His voice was hard. Not a problem, since his name was the only thing I was capable of saying right now. I complied.

He swore and leaned away from me. I was about to voice a complaint but then a rip of foil cut through the silence.

"What a Boy Scout," I teased. It came out a bit needier than I'd intended.

"Always prepared," he agreed.

I wished I was facing him to see him roll the sheath over his cock, to see him touching himself, hard and ready and knowing that at least right now, I was the one who'd inspired that reaction, but Rohan kept me in place.

He pushed into me from behind with a hard thrust that stole the breath from my lungs.

Arching back to rest against the hard planes of his chest, I opened my legs wider.

"Is this what you want?" he growled. "Rough and messy where anyone could see us?"

A bolt of lust ripped through me at the image. I grinned over my shoulder at him.

Rohan pulled out long enough to spin me around to face him. The smirk on his face was at odds with his frosty gaze. He gripped my upper arms, once more slamming inside me. I trailed my finger along the hard plane of his stomach. His abs clenched under my touch, resulting in so many delicious contoured ripples that I did it again.

Every thrust knocked me back into the tree, the pitted bark shredding my poor dress and scratching my skin. "Harder."

Rohan's jaw tensed at my command, holding himself in check. He emanated pure, brutal energy, and he was seriously and obviously pissed off.

I caressed his cheek, but he jerked his head to fling my hand off. I shrugged off my unreasonable sting of hurt. I'd set the rules. "No one is forcing you to play with the unclean, Snowflake."

"No, that's on me," he snarled, slowing, teasingly pulling out before thrusting once more inside me. Unleashing himself on me. There was no other way to describe it. He was without an ounce of mercy.

If this was supposed to be some kind of punishment, then I'd happily take double helpings.

Rohan threaded his fingers with mine, using his blades to anchor our two hands to the trunk. An interlacing of dusky brown and pale white skin. He rose up onto his toes, his fucking changing angle and gaining force. The expression on his face was primal.

I clutched at his shirt with my free hand so I didn't try something stupid like tenderly stroke away his anger. These intense coils rippling inside were a new feeling for me. I hooked a leg around his waist, rocking mindlessly against him. My entire body arched in unfettered pleasure.

My hand snuck down to give some love to Cuntessa but he swatted that away too, replacing it with one very capable finger. Go power plays. I happily let him take charge.

My grip on him tightened. I'd have closed my eyes but there was a dare in the hard line of his jaw and in the glint of his eyes that had me hold his gaze in challenge. This wasn't slow and it wasn't gentle. Our fuck was a hard storm. An all-consuming vortex. My hair tangled in sweaty strands; my dress rode higher and higher up my hips. I had to force air into my lungs.

Still I couldn't get enough.

It had been a while since I'd orgasmed from men I'd slept with. Those college guys with their misguided mood music and fumbling chivalrous "No, you come first" that became an obligation I faked my way out of. Mild levels of happy tingle generally constituted a win for me. But here? In this park, with this arrogant boy and his waves of unbridled hostility?

I bucked violently, coming harder than I ever had. Shattering and uncertain that I'd ever be put back together properly again.

The irony? His stunned look and the fierceness of his convulsion made me think he'd experienced the same thing.

The girl with the lightning eyes and the boy with demons in his soul.

Shivers burst across my skin like a mirror shuddering into a thousand pieces. Everything went dark and silent and then the hum of the city rushed back into stereo surround, snapping the bubble of us. Just as I realized I'd fallen against him, one of his arms holding me up and holding me close like the gentlest band of steel, he pulled out. I almost pitched forward at the lack of contact.

Rohan stepped away to strip off the condom and tuck himself back into his pants. He was mere feet away but might as well have been miles.

I tugged down my dress with a wriggle, stuffing the remnants of my underwear into the trash, and struggling to understand how something so tawdry felt anything but.

Disoriented, fluttery, I didn't know if my dizziness stemmed from euphoria or something else I couldn't name. I pinched my cheeks, grateful for the biting pain.

We straightened out our clothes, both so careful not to look at each other. Generally, I was a pro at the après. At bantery fun time that took any weirdness out of the situation and made it clear that I had no expectations. But this? This was awkward beyond all salvaging.

I tried to take a deep breath but I swear my lungs had filled with cold water and it came out as a stuttery hitch. In theory I'd just experienced my dream encounter. So how come I wanted to puke?

"Let's get you home," Rohan said in a flat voice.

Mercifully, I flagged down a taxi as soon as we left the park. The driver didn't even look up when we got into the back seat which was good, since he may have refused us entry had he seen our damp, demon gunkified selves. Apparently reeking of sex didn't matter.

There was no talking on the ride back. I kept sneaking glances over at Rohan but he stared straight ahead into the darkness of the backseat, the occasional slither of passing streetlight over his face letting me know that he wasn't any happier.

I gnawed on the inside of my cheek, my dress drying from soaked through to a more-disgusting clamminess.

No sooner had the taxi pulled up to my front curb than I shoved some money at the driver and bolted inside the house. Thankfully, my family was asleep and I was spared questions and more screaming at the sight of me. I pressed a hand to my cheeks, feeling their warm flush. Probably coming down with a fever. I had to get out of my wet clothes but first I made myself some Neo Citran–perfect for cold symptoms and knocking me out so I couldn't lay there thinking all night.

By the time I got out of my shower, the warm lemony liquid was already kicking in, leaving me groggy. Grateful for the miracles of modern over-the-counter medicine, I crashed. Hard.

16

I woke up Friday morning to the hangover god smashing me in the head with his evil hammer. Groaning, I pressed a hand to my temple, regretting the last four shots.

Wishing I regretted the entire evening.

My mouth tasted of dirt. I scraped my tongue with my teeth but to no avail. That particular flavor was gonna require hella mouthwash to kill.

Ari rapped on my door. "Want some help packing?"

I closed my eyes briefly. Moving day. "Yeah. Give me ten minutes, okay?"

"I'll grab containers," he said, his footfalls getting fainter.

I flung off the covers and stumbled into the bathroom for my morning pee. Awesome. My period had arrived and it was so heavy my vag looked like a *CSI* outtake. The brutal squeezing cramps along my thighs were no great delight either.

Forget looking pretty. Today's fashion highlight? Another pair of black sweats and a faded red Harry

Potter tee with "I solemnly swear I am up to no good" spelled out in spiky black letters.

Bedding got stripped and hauled down to the washing machine. I wanted my own sheets with me at Demon Clubhouse.

I popped a couple of much-needed Midol, knowing I'd be fine in twenty minutes when they kicked in. Too bad Rohan found me *fifteen* minutes later, still in pain and taking a stitch ripper to my bras to savagely yank out all the metal underwire. "Not one word," I said, as I pitched another lacy number into a large Rubbermaid container.

"I'm just the help," he said. "What do you want packed up first?"

I exhaled. There'd be no rehashing of last night. Cuntessa shot me the metaphorical finger at the fact that there would probably be no round two either.

"I only need my clothes and my laptop." Between it and my phone I'd have my music, and digital copies of any books and photos I cared about. Damn it. My phone had been confiscated while they waited for my new encrypted model, with my laptop to follow today.

Rohan hesitated. "You're sure that's all you want? Who knows how long you'll be living there."

I didn't know what else he expected me to have. "I'm good." I pointed at a pile on my bed. "Start with those, please."

Ari jogged into the room. "Need more containers?" He stopped as he saw Rohan. "Hey." My brother puffed up as he stepped closer. "I'm Ari. And you are...?"

To his credit, Rohan stuck out his hand for Ari to shake. "Rohan."

Ari shook it. "You're watching Nava."

Rohan tilted his head. "That a problem?"

Ari draped an arm over my shoulder. "Not if you keep my sister safe."

"That's my job," Rohan said in an even tone. "I'm very good at my job."

They stood there, eyeing each other.

I made an "ugh" sound and stepped away from my brother. "Did you put a Rubbermaid in the laundry room for the sheets?" I asked him.

"Yeah. I'll bring them over once they're dry." Ari picked up the first full Rubbermaid. "I'll take this out to the car."

"Put it in mine," Rohan said. "No point in two cars going."

Ari nodded and headed out.

It didn't take long to pack the rest of my stuff. I snapped a hair elastic around my wrist in case I needed to tie my hair back later, then exited the bathroom with my container of make-up, bath products, and hair stuff and dumped it on the bed, looking around my room for anything I'd missed.

"I guess that's it." Five medium Rubbermaids. The sum total of my adult life. I wasn't sure if it was depressing or liberating, so I didn't dwell. I reached for the container with my bathroom items, jerking back at a sharp slicing pain in my middle finger as I caught it on a ragged edge of the lid. Holding my bleeding finger upright, I used my other hand to pull the lid off, rummaging for my Band-Aids. I held out the box to Rohan. "Could you put one on me please?"

He applied the Band-Aid.

Then he kissed my finger. A pointed and deliberate touch of his lips to my skin that went on for several beats too long. He stared at me with those sumptuously lashed eyes, his lips soft and warm.

A giddy bubble danced around in my belly. I snatched my hand back.

Rohan tossed the Band-Aid box into the Rubbermaid, the look on his face daring me to say something.

I bit back a sigh. "Do we need to talk about this?" Much as I didn't want to share my deeply held beliefs around the whole kissing thing, I also didn't want–couldn't afford–weirdness with him.

"We don't need to do anything." His amber eyes were clouded with anger.

I tried to convince myself that not all of it was directed at me but I wasn't that deluded.

"Look, about last night–"

He fit the lid back on the container and hefted it up. "Nope." He popped the "p" for emphasis. "Changed my mind. There is something you need to do."

I smoothed down the edge of the Band-Aid. "Yes?"

"Not talk."

"Ever?"

"Is that an option?" he asked.

I held up my middle finger. "Thanks for the bandage."

He stomped off, grabbing a second container along the way.

"I see," Ari said as he entered, listening to Rohan pound down the stairs.

"No, you really don't." I sank down onto my bed.

He sat down beside me, ticking off items on his fingers. "You had sex, your dysfunctional kissing issues surfaced, and now you're both messed up over it."

"Oh. Guess you do. Except I am neither dysfunctional nor messed up about anything. Everything went according to plan."

We both flinched at the sound of a trunk being slammed much too hard.

Ari's eyes darted over to window. "Yup. It went swimmingly. You get that he's feeling used, right?"

I slapped a hand over my mouth in mock shock. "A man feeling used after a sexual encounter? Oh my

God, whatever will we do?" I dropped my hand. "He knew the score. No one forced him."

I sounded a bit pissy but I couldn't believe I had to defend myself. A man had no-strings attached sex, he got high-fived. I did the same, even with the no-kissing, and the entire male gender posse'd up around poor, fragile Snowflake? Screw that.

Ari stood up, stacking the last two containers on top of each other before picking them up. "You're playing with fire."

"I'm not playing with anything. The fire was ignited, blazed, and doused last night. End of story."

He shook his head at me and carried my stuff out.

I pushed thoughts of Rohan out of my mind. I was leaving home. A lump formed in my throat. Going downstairs into the kitchen, I found my mom making my favorite breakfast of waffles and extra-crispy bacon. There was enough for a small army, along with a heaping platter of cut strawberries. She motioned at the coffee pot. "I could warm the milk," she said.

"That would be great." Part of me wanted to rush into her arms but another perverse part of me refused to give her the satisfaction of needing her. I'd learned my lesson with that bullshit vulnerability.

"By the way," Mom said, jerking her spatula toward the counter, "you got a letter."

A letter that she'd already opened. I scanned the contents. It was from the University of British

Columbia asking me to contact them about the status of my enrollment.

"I can let Admissions know you're going back," she said.

"Kinda busy with Rasha stuff right now. Might have to hold off for a while longer."

"Being Rasha never kept Ari from his studies."

"Well, Ari was an initiate and he'd had his entire life to adjust to his schedule. Maybe I could have a *whole week* to deal with it before you get on my case about throwing school into the mix," I snapped.

"Don't take that tone with me." Mom turned away to refill the waffle platter.

I balled the paper up in my fist, tossing it into the trash. Though I made sure she didn't see me do it.

To say the meal was strained was a massive understatement. I kept my eyes on my plate. Mom kept hers on her waffles. There was no talking. No bothering to find out how I was doing with moving out.

Dad ambled in trailing citrusy *4711* cologne, a ratty sandal held up in one hand. "Shana, did you already pack the other one?" My parents were leaving for a two-week Caribbean cruise today, originally booked as a celebration post Ari-induction. Not sure what they saw it as now. Funereal?

Mom pointed her spatula at him. "We discussed this."

Dad clutched the sandal to his chest, a mournful expression on his face. "But they're so comfortable."

"I've packed the black ones." She held out her hand for the sandal, but he ignored her to grab a plate and get himself some breakfast, the sandal stuffed defiantly in his waistband.

This Rockwellesque picture was how Rohan and Ari found us.

I met Ari's eyes, miming shooting myself in the temple. He squeezed my shoulder in sympathy as he brushed by to take a seat next to me.

"Eat," Mom said to Rohan, thrusting a plate at him.

He took it, but didn't move to fill it up. "No harm will come to Nava," he said.

"I'm more worried about you boys," Dad joked.

My grip tightened on my fork.

Rohan shot me an uncertain look.

Ari shoved the maple syrup at me. "Eat," he ordered. He tugged on his earlobe, our private twin code for "Relax. I've got your back."

I'm sure it was a delicious breakfast but I barely managed to choke down three bites. "Better hit the road," I said about five minutes later.

My mom glanced at the clock on the stove. "Oh. Yes. I need to finish packing." She came up behind me and kissed the top of my head. "We'll talk soon."

Not if I could help it. I gave her the "I'm wearing my happy face" smile that I'd perfected to get my parents off my back. "Have a great vacation."

Dad walked me to the front door. There was a moment there when I thought he might say something but he just hugged me. "It'll be fine," he assured me.

Again with the "it," not the "you."

"Yup. Have fun, Dad. Drink a mojito for me."

That left Ari as my sole escort to the car, which was perfect. He scooped me up into a giant hug. "Kick demon ass." His voice was shaky. This would be the first time we'd be away from each other for a prolonged period of time.

I grabbed on to him harder.

"We have to go," Rohan said in a gentle voice.

"I'll see you later," Ari said, stepping back. I think his eyes were wet but it was hard to tell through the blurriness of my own.

"And often?"

"And often," he promised.

When he let go of my hand, I stared down at the empty space like I was leaving a limb behind. I'm sure the separation from my twin was healthy. I couldn't give a shit. This sucked. But I dealt, opening the door to Rohan's two-door vintage muscle car with its midnight blue finish and white racing stripe.

The interior had clearly never seen a fast food wrapper. Even the mats were pristine. I relaxed, wondering why I felt so comfortable until I realized that it smelled like Rohan in here.

I rolled down the window.

Rohan fished a pair of sunglasses from his shirt pocket, pushing them up the bridge of his nose before sticking the key into the ignition. Hand on key, he hesitated, shifting slightly toward me.

I got extremely fascinated by my seatbelt. "Nice car."

He gave an insulted snort, stroking the wheel. "This is a fully restored '67 Shelby. First thing I bought when the band hit it big. Drove it up here from L.A." With a twist of the key, he started the engine, roaring away from the curb with a sharp left that flung me against the passenger door. His hands rested almost carelessly on the wheel.

I tried very hard not to remember the feel of them on me, but that left my eyes trailing down his work-of-art body to his muscled thighs tensing as he shifted gears.

My mouth went dry.

The middle-aged dad in the minivan next to us glanced over, longing at the total picture of hot girl, hot guy, and hot car written so clearly on his face that I took pity on him and winked cheekily.

He grinned back, swerving toward us before regaining control of his vehicle.

Rohan sped ahead. "Wrecking havoc with traffic, Lolita?"

I reached for the power button to put on some tunes but Rohan swatted my hand away.

"I control the music," he said.

"Fallen angel with domination issues. Shocker."

"Takes one to know one," he replied.

"It *is* a nice car," I said, ignoring his childish retort.

"Best ride I ever had," Rohan said with a sly smile my way.

"You mean best wank." I kicked off my flip flops. "It couldn't be more of a jerk-off machine if you'd painted balls on the back tires."

Rohan gave an amused snort. Ready or not, I was on my way.

17

We carted my things up to my new room in a couple of trips. The bedroom was serviceable, if somewhat masculine. Tolerable queen mattress, wood furniture on the heavy side. This crazy print of two people against a stormy sea sat atop the dresser, propped against the wall. The person on the left was merely a strip of face and neck, as if torn off the person on the right, whose missing strip revealed weird cables and balls. It was the kind of thing Ari would have dug, if not my style. At least the view to the backyard was nice.

The best part was the small ensuite bathroom. I would not have wanted to share with the boys and learn firsthand who missed the toilet seat when he peed.

Rohan took my laptop to give to Ms. Clara.

"Be sure to bring back a receipt," I mocked.

He spread his hands in a "what are you going to do" way. "The Brotherhood is incredibly anal."

"Well," I deadpanned, "anal *is* the new black."

He blinked slowly at me with a fascinated gleam in his eyes. I stumbled back a step, my knees hitting the mattress, but he simply held up the laptop. "Anything you don't want people to see?" he asked.

I checked the heel of my shoe, as if that had been responsible for my lost footing, forgetting I wore flip flops. "You sound positively hopeful."

"Just don't want you to be embarrassed." He paused in the doorway. "More embarrassed."

I grabbed the closest thing handy, which happened to be a boot, and flung it at him. He rocked back on his heels, shaking with laughter, not even flinching as my footwear missed decapitating him by mere millimeters.

"Leave," I ordered.

"Baruch wants you in the Vault," he called back, my computer tucked under one arm.

I popped another Midol and hustled my ass downstairs.

"Yo, Tree Trunk. I'm–" I came to an abrupt stop at the sight of Drio waiting for me in sweats torn off at the knee and a white long-sleeved tee with perfectly placed holes that I swear he paid extra for. The overall effect was mouthwatering. Damn, these boys were annoyingly hot.

"Where's Baruch?" I asked. My previous encounter with Drio had burned up my fear quota, leaving me irritated at his presence.

"You're with me today."

I crossed my arms. "Why?"

Drio cracked a smile at my suspicious tone as he pulled the door shut. "Because I scare you," he said in a stereotypical vamp accent.

"Was that supposed to be a Count Dracula impression? Because you sounded more like Count Chocula."

His brow creased in confusion. I opened my mouth to explain the difference. "No. I don't care enough," he said, crossing the room.

I was about to ask if I should follow but I got distracted by his pants sliding down his hip and the tantalizing glimpse of olive skin revealed. He caught them before things got interesting and tugged them up. Too bad. My dislike of him did not override my voyeuristic tendencies.

Though I hustled to catch up when I saw the vein in his forehead throb at my dawdling.

"Heard you ran into some trouble last night." He flipped a small panel mounted to the wall open, revealing a flat black pad. "Good work pissing Asmodeus off, since it's not like we have enough to do with Samson."

I pulled off the elastic band I wore on my wrist and tied my hair up into a messy ponytail, choosing to ignore his sarcasm. "Here's a question. Last night, Asmodeus compelled me. How do I fight back against—"

I gasped finding Drio with his hands around my neck. He wasn't hurting me, but I hadn't even seen him move. One second he was ten feet away, the next he was behind me.

"Against surprises?" he asked.

I screwed my eyes shut, my heart hammering. "Don't flambé me."

Drio dropped his hands.

I cracked open one eye to see him bring his thumb to the fingers of his right hand, shaking it in what even I recognized as an Italian gesture of frustration. "What are you talking about?" he asked.

"Your fire powers."

He massaged his right temple. "What fire powers?"

I straightened my T-shirt with a sharp tug. "You know, your anger issues that manifest in some kind of elemental flame deal."

His eyes narrowed. "My anger issues? Because I'm Italian, I must be a hothead? Got any other ethnic profiling?"

"Please. You being Italian has zip to do with it. You raging at me since day one on the other hand?" I spread my hands wide, encouraging him to make the tiny jump from A to B. My empirical evidence presented, I rocked back on my heels.

Drio glanced skyward with a pained look, as if seeking divine patience. Then he waved his hands at me. "No flames. Though I'd be happy to find some matches. My power?" He zipped across the room and back in a blink.

"Super speed?"

"Technically, I flash step. I'm not zipping across the city."

"Oh."

"Don't sound so disappointed."

I wasn't disappointed; more confused about how this ability fit in to Ari's theories about personality flaws and power manifestation. I'd have asked but the look on Drio's face made it clear that he was not in a sharing mood. "How do you kill demons then? Flash stepping is hardly attack magic."

Drio looked insulted at the question. "It's still the same inherent Rasha magic. If a bystander stabs a demon in their kill spot, the demon wouldn't die. But when a Rasha zaps that place, touches it directly, or funnels his magic through a weapon to hit that same spot?" He brushed his hands together in an "all done" gesture. "My magic works fine. I don't need fire powers."

"Fine. You weren't going to immolate me. My mistake. What was your point?"

"I lost it in all your…" He made the international symbol for "blah blah blah" with one hand. "For the record, I don't agree with you being here. But Rohan said you deserved it since the make-up artist was your idea and you did pretty well last night. Even if your one-on-one leaves something to be desired."

Had Rohan said something *not* in conjunction with the fight to Drio? I shook it off with a "Let's do this."

"We wouldn't even have to do this if Rohan wasn't so damn stubborn," Drio said.

"Stubborn?" I jabbed his side when he didn't answer. "About what? The difference of opinion between him and the Brotherhood on how to proceed with the mission?"

Drio did a double take. "He told you that?" I didn't even have to fudge the truth about not knowing specific details because Drio was in a mood to rant.

"It's a no-brainer," he said. "Forrest Chang, the director of *Hard Knock Strife* is a huge Fugue State Five fan. He contacted Rohan to do the theme song."

Interesting.

"That doesn't mean Rohan would have the chance to buddy up with Samson."

"Invite King to sing as a cameo. Get in close to the bastard that way. We've tried everyone else in his inner circle. No go." Frustration tightened the corners of his eyes. "It would be so easy for Rohan to get to know Samson. Who'd question a rock star hanging around a bunch of actors?" He pinched his lips together. "But he refuses to step back into that role."

"I think he's afraid of what he could slip back into becoming." Given what Rohan had told me, the scars ran deep, evidenced by the fact that he refused to take on something that would move this assignment forward.

Drio slapped his palm flat against the center of the pad mounted on the wall. "You two have gotten chatty. Why don't you talk some sense into him?" A red light scanned him as he studied me.

If I managed that, the Executive would adore me. Desperate as I was to get Ari confirmed, I couldn't use Rohan like this. It was a million kinds of wrong. "Let's pursue the make-up artist avenue first," I said.

Part of the wall slid away, revealing a smaller room within the larger Vault, its floors and walls made of iron. Drio motioned me through the concealed door. Ignoring my tiny frisson of fear, I stepped inside, the wall sealing shut behind us.

A beautiful Korean woman sat in the middle of the space, duct-taped to a thick iron chair bolted to the floor. Her eyes bugged out, darting around as she strained against the tape covering her mouth and binding her feet and hands to the arms and legs of the chair.

She turned a pleading look on me.

"Oh my God!" I took a step forward to help her but Drio knocked me back with a sigh.

Flashing over to her side, he did some Vulcan neck pinch thing and she transformed into a sleek white fox with multiple tails. Mostly transformed. Her hands, feet, and face–all the bits touching the tape, stayed human. The overall effect was somewhat disconcerting.

"Nine," he said, seeing me count her tails.

I inched closer. "What is she?"

"King's make-up artist, Evelyn. Also a kumiho. A master illusionist usually plying her tricks to seduce men."

"But this one puts hers to use on King?"

"That's the theory."

"How did you know she was a demon?"

He tugged me forward, shoving my face inches away from her neck. "Smell."

This close to her, I accessed my magic just in case, a low level hum under my fingertips, but despite her growling and thrashing, she was bound fast. I sniffed, blinking at the faint smell of strawberries.

"It's her natural scent," Drio said. "She can't disguise it."

I walked around Evelyn, who was struggling against her bindings. "How did you get close enough to smell her?"

"My natural charm."

I poked at a binding. "Duct tape? That holds them?"

He shrugged. "Specially threaded with iron and salt fibers."

"What are you going to do with her?"

His smile bloomed, both terrifying and sexy. "Have some fun."

Evelyn's tails thumped in syncopated agitation against the floor.

I glanced at the demon. "Do I need to worry about sexual misconduct?"

Drio shot me a disgusted look. "I don't do that," he replied in a hard voice. "Even to demons." Just regular torture then.

"This isn't about using her to get close," I said.

"No. She's going to share what she knows about King." He pushed up his sleeves.

The demon's eyes flashed red.

Time to go. I had no desire to watch his methods of fact finding.

"Pussy," he snickered, pressing his hand against the scanner mounted inside the small room to open the iron door on this side.

"You ate your siblings in the womb, didn't you?" I said, pausing in the doorway.

Drio licked his lips with relish.

Riiiight.

I stepped into the Vault, the wall sliding shut between us. On my way upstairs, I ran into Baruch, coming out of Ms. Clara's office, clad in black nylon workout pants and a tank top.

Wonder if they're tearaway. Bet Ms. Clara knows.

"Not interested in seeing Drio work?" he asked.

"I'm skipping today's session of 'Creative Sadism with Batshit Crazy.'" I jogged up to my room, finding a note from Rohan ordering me to the library for study time. First, I allotted myself a few minutes to shower off that unpleasant encounter and root through my still-packed clothing for skinny jeans and my navy tunic embroidered with a brilliant dragonfly. Rohan didn't make an appearance in the library, though he'd set out some books on the long table for me to dive into.

I tried to study. I took notes and everything, in between glances toward the hallway at every footfall and voice. It's not that I care if Rohan shows up, I told myself, as I read a particularly gruesome passage about the damage a se'irim could do, it's just that he should be showing a bit more responsibility in overseeing my studying. What if I have a question about a demon that needs answering?

The hundreds of books surrounding me mocked me in response.

Adopting a less formal study position, away from the table and onto a couch, didn't help me focus. Nor did twisting myself upside down, my head hanging to the floor.

Screw it.

Corralling a laptop I found in a cherrywood cabinet, I logged on, seeing what I could find on Samson King, wanting something that would help Drio. Samson's bio before he hit big–which happened with his first role–was pretty sparse. That gelled if he was a demon, since it would be fake. Out of curiosity, I checked the meaning of his name. I was always curious if a person's name meaning correlated to them. Like Nava meant "beautiful" so bulls-eye, Mom and Dad.

Samson meant "sun." I leaned back against my chair. Sun King. Hang on. Leo had mentioned that King had spent time in France. During a trip with my family to France a few years ago, I'd learned that Louis XIV had called himself the Sun King. He'd been a live large, divine-right conferring narcissist and maybe Samson had modeled himself on this guy. Or, actually picked up few tips from him, since many demons had long life spans.

I drummed my fingers on the tabletop, waiting for the page to load in order to get verification for what I was thinking. Here it was. The original Sun King had been a ruthless bastard whose rule had established France as one of the pre-eminent powers in the world. I leaned back in my chair, fingers steepled together. Since it appeared *this* sun king had similar aspirations, maybe this tie to Louis would reveal what type of demon Samson was, or offer more specificity on the master plan.

I leapt out of my seat, sprinting down to the Vault, then back up the stairs with a frustrated growl, since I didn't have access yet to open the door. Kane did though, and I dragged him with me, insisting that he had to get me to Drio now.

He let me in to the Vault and I pounded on the wall concealing the iron room until the angriest of all Rasha answered. Purple goo was smeared across Drio's temple, and his hair was matted with sweat.

Not wanting Evelyn to hear, I whispered my theory into Drio's ear.

The tight expression on his face sent my stomach plummeting into my toes, doubt at my brilliance slithering through me. Then he gave a sharp nod, his eyes glinting dangerously, and returned inside, the wall whooshing shut behind him.

"Nee?" Ari called out from upstairs.

I sped up so fast to meet him that I practically got lift off, throwing myself into his arms. Hugging him and the overflowing pile of bedding he carried.

"This way," I sang, tugging him up the stairs to my room. "Guess what?" I nattered on about Evelyn and my Samson realizations. "Dump the bedding on the mattress," I said.

He stood in the doorway, stock still, clutching the linens.

"What?" I glanced around in confusion.

"Your room."

"Uh-huh." I tugged him forward. "You're not going to get cooties, bro."

He flung the sheets down. "This was supposed to be *my* room. You got my room."

"I did?" I screwed up my face in puzzlement. He'd never mentioned he'd be moving in.

Ari jerked his chin at the painting. "Magritte. That didn't tip you off?"

I flinched at the anger threading his voice. Examining the art hadn't been a top priority in my short time here. Not sure what I could say to make it better, I opted to go with the tried and true. "Sorry."

"No, you're not."

I blinked at him.

"You're enjoying this. Your training." He waved a hand at me. "Your little realizations."

"My little...?" I unclenched my fists. "I am sorry, Ari. But you know what? I can only apologize so many times. None of this is my fault. I'm doing my best here." I picked up the fitted sheet, shaking it out to unroll it.

He snorted.

"What's that supposed to mean?"

"Doing your best?" he sneered. "You're loving this. You're happy."

I popped the corner of the sheet onto the mattress with a violent snap. "God knows we can't have that. There's only one Katz twin allowed that emotion."

"Hey, don't put your fuck-ups on me," he retorted.

"Then don't put other people's on me!"

A muscle ticked in his jaw. "Enjoy your room." He stalked out.

"Oh, I will!" I threw my pillow against the far wall with a scream. I stomped across the room to retrieve it for scream two, glancing out the window. Ari and Kane were having some kind of intense conversation at the front of the house. At least Kane had put a shirt on. It rode up as he gestured with sharp, angry jabs.

Ari was really going for the gold in pissing people off because while Kane was still speaking, my brother slammed into the Prius and drove off. Kane punched one of the front porch pillars.

Feel your pain, dude. I could clock my passive-aggressive brother for walking out before we'd finished our fight. I threw everything out of my containers looking for my damn phone to call Ari's cell and hash this out once and for all, before I remembered that Ms. Clara still had it. Great. No phone, and now my room looked like a hurricane had torn through it.

The frenzy left me exhausted. Heaving a sigh, I bent down to pick up the pillow, my head jerking up at a shout from outside.

Rohan sprinted up the driveway, favoring one ankle, his shirt torn. No, not just his shirt. His arm was a twisted mass of glistening, ripped open flesh that I could see from the third story.

The pillow tumbled out of my hand to the floor.

I threw the window open to find out what had happened.

The noise made Rohan look up at me. I don't know if it was my twin sense or something about his stricken expression clear to me even three floors up as his eyes met mine but I knew.

Something horrible had happened to Ari.

18

I flew down the front stairs, fear fish-hooking into me. "What–"

Baruch and Drio, huddled around Rohan, looked up at the sound of my voice. The ensuing gap allowed me a close up look at the inside of Rohan's right arm. I clapped a hand over my mouth, swallowing hard against the taste of bile. Someone was keening and I had the sneaking suspicion it was me.

Baruch ripped his shirt off, making a tourniquet to staunch the bleeding.

"Kane!" Rohan failed to look perturbed at the sight of his tendons spilling out of his skin but he was mightily annoyed at me swaying on my feet.

Kane leapt off the bottom front stair, his arms coming around me. "Inside."

"Where's Ari?"

Rohan's expression softened. "Demons got him. Right outside the gate."

Outside the wards. "Asmodeus?"

He shook his head. "They were trying to get past the wards. I think it was just bad timing on his part and opportunity on theirs."

"They think they snatched a Rasha?" Kane asked.

Rohan's shrug turned into more of a flinch as Baruch tightened the tourniquet.

"If even one of you had bothered to help me convince the Brotherhood to confirm Ari's initiate status..." My voice shook. There was a good chance that he'd have been inducted by now. That he'd have magic at his disposal.

Rohan limped his way up the stairs, waving off Baruch's offer of assistance.

"If the ritual didn't work, he has no status," Drio said.

"I hate you."

"Va bene. One thing going right in my day."

I lunged for Drio, but Kane strong-armed me inside the house and into a den.

I vibrated so hard that any more delays in getting me info and I might have combusted. It's not that I was unsympathetic to Rohan's giant gaping gash, it's just that Rasha had extra-spiffy healing powers and he seemed calm enough as Baruch tossed the bloody wadded up shirt onto a table, replacing it with a fluffy towel that he must have picked up as they came inside.

"Where's my brother?" I demanded, brushing off Kane's attempt to seat me.

"I don't know," Rohan said. "And I didn't follow because I was busy killing the massive fucker that'd been left on clean up." It was obvious Rohan had to work to keep his voice steady.

Drio entered with a sewing kit and a bottle of vodka.

My butt crashed down onto the chair. Except it wasn't the chair, it was the coffee table, and my tailbone caught the corner. "Fuck!" The bite of pain in my lower back helped keep me from plummeting into full-on hysteria.

Drio had passed the bottle to Rohan, who'd taken a swig, but one look at me and Rohan handed me the booze.

I took a swig or three as well before Drio took it away.

With a deep inhale, Rohan nodded at Baruch, who removed the towel. It had soaked up so much blood that it made a wet splat when he dropped it on the table next to the bloody shirt.

That was Drio's cue to pour the alcohol over the gash.

Rohan convulsed, the breath audibly leaving his lungs.

Baruch pinched the flesh to keep the two edges more or less together as Drio opened the lid on the sewing kit. He threaded the needle.

If I hadn't needed my stupid sheets, Ari would never have been here in the first place. We would never have fought.

He would never have been taken.

I dug the nails of my right arm into my left wrist, welcoming the pain. Welcoming the distraction from my worst nightmare that my brother was in danger. I'd known this was a possibility when Ari joined the Brotherhood as a full hunter, but for it to have played out now in light of what had happened seemed like a needlessly cruel twist of fate.

Drio patted Rohan's cheek gently, piercing Rohan's flesh with the needle, the thread trailing off of it like the end of a comet.

I tore my eyes away.

"Who?" Kane's voice was so low, it was practically a growl. His arms were crossed and his jaw was clenched so hard it could probably cut glass.

"Sakacha and dremla." Rohan winced as Drio sewed up the last few stitches.

I squeezed my hands between my knees, shoulders tense, waiting to hear more, breathing through the antiseptic tang permeating the room.

"Together?" Baruch barked. "Those two are not known for playing with others."

"I don't care what the hell they're known for!" I stamped my foot on the ground. "I want to know who they are and what they did with Ari!" My voice was a panicky screech but for fuck's sake, talk to me like I was a child because I didn't know all the ins and outs here.

Rohan gingerly flexed his arm. "Sakacha are pain demons. Physical pain. Dremla are soul leeches."

"And?"

"I. Don't. Know." His breath rushed out in a hiss.

"Not good enough," I snapped, swiping at my eyes with my hand. "Is he alive?" I could barely choke the words out through my tight throat and I dreaded the answer but I had to know.

Rohan's bleak look conveyed his utter lack of knowledge. "There were five of them. They attacked his car as soon as it left the grounds and pulled him out. I ran over to help but..." He shook his head. "One of them dragged him out of the car, threw him over his back, and bolted."

Kane rubbed his forehead with his fist. "They're on foot."

"But they're fast," Baruch said. "Who knows where they've gotten by now?"

"So I track." Drio cut the thread with a small pair of scissors, tying the loose ends in a small knot.

"Take Baruch," Rohan said.

Baruch was already in the hallway headed for the front door.

"I want to go with Drio," I said.

"You can't. You'll just get in his way." Kane slung an arm over my shoulder. "Why don't you go move your dad's car?"

It wasn't up for debate.

Grabbing my Ryan Tedder sunglasses off the table in the foyer for courage, I jogged down the drive to the abandoned car, parked sideways right outside the gate.

I sidestepped the wreckage of Ari's phone, smashed on the concrete. Even if Ari had still had his special Demon Club phone, Rohan wouldn't have gotten to the scene any faster, but this broken piece of crap was a reminder of how helpless my brother was.

I pounded my fist on the hood.

The incessant chiming of the open driver's side door taunted me. *Gone. Gone. Gone.*

A bloody streak ran from the shredded seat belt along the frame of the driver's side door. I clamped my lips together, very glad my parents had left town and I didn't have to tell them what had happened to their son.

Miserable, I got into the car, Ari's blood literally on my hands as I drew the seat belt across my chest. The engine sputtered when I pushed the ignition button, but caught. My fingers tightened on the wheel, resentment burning hot and deep at being relegated to valet.

A one, a two, you know what to do.

I *did* know what to do. Let the boys pursue their leads, I'd pursue mine. I had to find Leo and get her demon insider knowledge. No one was going to sideline me when it came to Ari's safety. Saving him was the one thing I could do right now.

I'm coming for you, Ace, I vowed. Stay strong.

With a glance up the drive to make sure no one was watching, I backed the car out onto the street. The world sped by in a violent blur as I drove like a madwoman to Leo's place, streaks of traffic and barely-dodged pedestrians set to a cacophonic soundtrack of honking horns. Flicking on my signal, I made the final right turn onto Leo's street. As usual, there was no parking, so I zipped into the alley to double park.

A black SUV T-boned me, spinning the car.

The air bags deployed. One second they weren't there, the next *PHOWOMP*, the bags had exploded out of the front and side of the Prius, blowing my head back with a jarring snap of my neck.

I came to with my ears ringing, and three very cute paramedics crouching beside me. "Hello, boys," I slurred. My arm burned like a son-of-a-bitch, covered in the world's worst case of rug burn. Wrong day to wear short sleeves.

They held up the same three fingers in sync. "How many fingers do you see?" The three spoke in unison really well.

I squinted at them. "Are you guys identical triplets?" I closed my eyes because it was somewhat disorienting every time they moved. Also, my face throbbed.

"You've got a concussion. Do you know your name?"

"Nava. Katz."

"Do you remember what happened?"

Closing my eyes didn't make the world any less spinny-ride, so I opened them again. "I was hit."

Triplet melted down to a duo, his faces furrowed in concern. "Do you know why there's blood on the seatbelt? It doesn't appear to be yours."

That's when everything came rushing back to me. "Ari," I gasped, struggling up out of my seat.

"You need to stay put." Hands grabbed at me. One set since he'd finally snapped into focus. "I'm going to cut you out because the release mechanism got mangled in the crash." He jogged over to his car.

Adrenaline rode me like a little bitch, but struggle as I might the belt had me trapped tight. A quick glance in the rearview mirror showed bruising around my nose and left eye. I probed the puffy skin with a pained hiss. The fine white powder from the deployment that coated me didn't add much to the overall effect, and only half of my beloved sunglasses now sat on my head. The other half was nowhere to be seen.

Neither was the hit-and-run black SUV.

I had to get out of here. There was no way to get past the airbags to try the ignition button and, given the crumpled frame and odd way the door hung open, I doubted the car would start anyway.

Dad was going to lose his shit.

I opted to try and zap my way loose from the seatbelt, since the paramedic was taking too long to get whatever tool he needed. I was so focused on the best way to free myself that I failed to realize he'd returned with what appeared to be a very thin, orange, post-modern stapler-shaped thing.

I shut my magic down with a lame, "It's not what you think."

He frowned at the tool. "The seatbelt cutter?"

No way he hadn't seen my magic. Ignoring the impossible? Dodging that bullet worked for me except something about the way he watched me–his smile a little too bright, his gaze a bit too intense–made the back of my neck prickle.

Paramedic man squatted down, sawing through the belt with one sharp slice.

I pitched sideways. The world swung around me, my hand shooting out to grab the warped doorframe for balance. Out of the corner of my eye, I caught sight of the paramedic. Underneath his image, he was rippling.

A hot, bright burst of panic bloomed in my chest. I slammed my hand into his shoulder.

For a brief second, he transformed from shaggy cuteness to a silvery-blue serpent with an overly large mouth and needle teeth, made entirely of water. My electricity dissipated harmlessly over the surface of him. A weak cloud of steam rose off of the serpent, but that was it. His only reaction was to ask if I needed help standing up.

I doubled over, hyperventilating–not entirely an act–to buy me time.

"Come on. I'll get you to the ambulance." He tugged on my elbow, trying to pull me to my feet.

An icy certainty that I couldn't let him put me in there slithered up my spine. I flashed back on the guy sucking that demon's thumb, unwilling to contemplate what this one might do to me. But if my magic was useless on him, how was I going to get away?

Another tug. "Get checked out and I'll help you find your brother."

My head snapped up at his words. At his encouraging nod, the picture of compassion. Except I'd never said Ari was my brother. The mention of my twin triggered the memory of Ari's concentrated salt-coated blade that had been tossed in the car door pocket. In one fell swoop, I thrust it upward into the demon paramedic's jugular.

His eyes widened and his glamour fell away, leaving his watery serpent self with the knife sliding downstream to his toes.

I jumped to my feet, dizzy, and tense, waiting for the clatter of the knife on the ground. Waiting for his nasty retaliation.

Instead, he puffed up, solidifying into a Jell-O-like state, the knife buried inside him.

I'm not sure which of us was more shocked.

The demon tried to move but the salt content made him unwieldy. He wobbled from side-to-side, exactly how I'd expect a giant gelatin cube to walk.

"Bloating sucks," I said, shooting a fairly decent forked lightning bolt from my eyes, which was so fucking cool. Thanks to his super salt content, he now conducted electricity just fine. His body wobbled back against the attack.

The demon curled into his left side. He had to be protecting his sweet spot. Excellent. That left a lot of him to work on.

"Where's my brother?"

Silence.

Electricity crackling off of my finger, I ran the tip along his wrist, slicing through him like butter. His hand dropped to the ground with a meaty splat. His face tightened but he stayed mum.

The demon snapped at me with his spiky teeth but I sidestepped him, one magic-charged hand held up. "I can do this all day. Ari. Why was he taken?"

The demon edged away from me.

"Who are you afraid of?" I forced myself to voice my deepest fear. "Asmodeus?"

His imperceptible flinch was my answer. All guilt, all terror, I shoved down into a well-buried box to torture myself with later. Then I killed the uncooperative bastard.

The demon convulsed, contorting around himself until he became smaller and smaller and then nothing at all. All that was left of him was a few drops of water splattered on the ground and Ari's knife.

I didn't stick around to gloat, bolting for Leo's place, since I had no phone to call her with. Luckily, she lived around the corner. Hand pressed to my sides, lactic acid burning its way through my muscles, I leaned on Leo's intercom, holding the wall for balance, and praying she was home.

"Hello?"

"Let me in!" I scanned the area for any out-of-place twitch or suspicious person.

It seemed like an eternity before the door buzzed open. I cracked it enough to slide inside then shut it tight, wrenching on it a couple of times to make sure it had locked behind me. With one last look around the lobby, I stumbled into the elevator, hit three, and crashed on my ass to the floor.

I managed to shove my foot into the open door when it reached Leo's floor, but couldn't get up on my own, mostly because everything spun so violently, I wasn't sure which way *was* up.

Leo ran over to me, hooking her arms under my pits. "Your face," she gasped.

"Demons took Ari."

I let her drag me inside. My adrenaline gave out, leaving my legs shaking, and my stomach doing dry heaves. I collapsed onto the round, red brocade chair by the window that she'd brought with her from her bedroom when she moved out. The stories this chair could tell.

"You need to go to the hospital."

"No time." I filled her in on what had happened.

"Shit, Nav, that was a kapasca demon. Psychopathic serpents. If he'd managed to haul you back to the water?" She shivered.

"How do I find Asmodeus?"

"I'm sorry." She shook her head. "No clue even where to begin."

"You got him a message."

"Not directly and no one is going to give up his hideout."

My hopes deflated, leaving me with a gut-level queasiness. I'd been positive Leo would know how to find him. I pressed a hand to my head.

"Got any Tylenol?" If she couldn't help, I had to patch myself up and find Rohan. My accelerated healing powers weren't accelerating fast enough. That, or my concussion was a lot worse than I thought.

"Not Tylenol," she said, handing me a tablet and a glass of water a moment later. "Paracetamol." She took the glass back from me, helping me to sit up.

I didn't question her having the meds on-hand. Leo was a bit of a hypochondriac.

She gave me the bottle in case I needed another pill later. "I'll put out feelers." It was a start.

"Can you drive me back to the chapter house first?" I asked.

She hesitated. "Why don't you just call them?"

"Because the stupid Fallen Angels never bothered to give me their cell numbers." I seethed. "I promise not to let anyone hurt you. Or find out you're a demonette."

"No worries." Leo grabbed her purse, patting it. "Custom made iron switchblade. Very effective. Even on Rasha." She smiled evilly. "Remember that." Then she grabbed her keychain from where she was using it as a bookmark in one of her crim texts.

I groaned at the distinctive logo, pressing a hand to my throbbing head as the sound sent a fresh wave of nausea through me. "Not the Vespa." Given the one second delay between my brain and my body, I'd fall off the damn thing.

"Mom's got my car. This is the fastest way unless you want to wait around for a taxi," she said. She tossed me a spare leather jacket that was too short in the arms and too tight in the boobs, but would keep me warm and protected from any road rash.

The ride back wasn't too bad, with only two stops for me to throw up–once in a box hedge, and the other right into the gutter like the classy kitten I was. We pulled up to the chapter house gate. Tossing her my helmet, I got off the bike to hit the buzzer next to the scanner panel.

"Yes?"

"Yum," Leo mouthed at me, at the sound of Drio's Italian accent.

I squeezed my right fist open and closed twice rapidly, our code for giant anal sphincter.

Her face fell.

"It's me, Drio. Let me in."

"Qui?"

"Nava. Quit screwing around. We don't have time."

"Bella, I assure you," he purred, "You and I have all the time in the world."

Leo shivered. "Could he just be one–" She opened and closed her fist once, indicating a partial anal sphincter personality. "I could deal with that level of douchery."

"Are you fucking kidding me?" The sentiment applied to the two of them.

There was a pause from the intercom, then Drio said, "I'll be out in a minute."

Leo parked the bike, while I leaned up against the gate in a pose I hoped conveyed nonchalance rather than assisted standing.

Drio finally arrived but didn't open the gate. Asshole could have flash stepped outside instead of making us wait. Though he did darken at the sight of me. "Who hurt you?" he asked, pointing at my face.

I rattled the bars which failed to rattle. "Let me in and I'll tell you."

"Tell me and I'll let you in."

Was he really going to do this now? "Where's Kane?" He'd let me in.

Drio braced a hand against the bar. "You're not his type, bella."

"What's your type?" Leo piped up.

He rounded on her with an interested gleam.

"Not the time," I hissed, smacking her across the top of the head. "I know who has Ari."

Drio straightened up, all flirtiness gone, and opened the gate. "You better come talk to Rohan."

I grabbed his wrist, bracing for the worst. "Did you find him?"

Drio glanced down at my hand on his arm. "You dare to wear the hamsa?" he growled in a low voice.

Dread sat in my gut like hot lead. Drio might not like me but he wouldn't joke about me being Rasha. "Don't you know who I am?"

"Problem?" Rohan asked in a silky voice, joining the party. He was not a happy camper.

Leo, however, was ecstatic for about the thirty seconds she fangasmed all over him once recognition kicked in.

Rohan bestowed a rock fuck grin on her and said, "Always pleased to meet a fan."

That did it. I let my magic out in full force.

Ordinarily, I'd have loved making the boys' jaws drop in shock at my amazing abilities, but the fact that my powers were news to them meant that *they had no clue who I was.*

I wrapped my arms around myself, a million worst-case scenarios of how this could have happened flashing through my head. Trembling, I started up the drive, needing more than ever to get my fellow Rasha onboard with saving Ari.

Rohan attempted to stop me but I burst into full crackle. "I will go psycho like you've never seen if you don't get yourself, Drio, Baruch, and Kane into the library this very second," I said.

That's when Rohan saw the ring. He grabbed my hand, barely flinching at the electricity scorching his skin. He tugged on it but of course, it didn't move. His hand clamped on my wrist, he dragged me up the driveway without another word.

"Wait for me!" Leo called out.

Reality slowed down into a slow motion "Noooooo." I yanked free of Rohan and sprinted for Leo before she could try to step over the ward and be repelled off of it, visions of Drio dusting my best friend dancing before my eyes.

"Rohan is highly overrated," Drio said. "Allow me." He took her arm, escorting her onto the premises, as I stumbled to a stop. Did he know she was a PD and was toying with us? Or had he inadvertently saved her?

Leo winced, her eyes widening in comprehension, but she regained her composure in an instant, flipping her hair as she assured Drio it would be her pleasure. Not that she had a choice. Drio may have sounded player personified, but the set of his shoulders assured me that neither Leo nor I were going anywhere until they had answers.

Brilliant. A goblin, a Rasha, and two amnesiacs walk into a house–I couldn't begin to imagine where this joke was going to end. Or at whose expense.

So long as it wasn't Ari's.

19

Rohan led me all the way around the house and in through the back door to the kitchen, presumably so I wouldn't see anything I shouldn't. I tried to explain that he was wasting valuable time, but he wasn't inclined to listen.

They really had no idea who I was. How was this even possible?

How could I be so easily erased?

The mean little voice inside my head scoffed. Not that hard, Nava. Other than to Ari, weren't you pretty much incidental to everyone anyway? And he wasn't exactly feeling the love either, was he?

Shut. Up.

Once they had us corralled in the middle of the room, Rohan leaning casually against the back door and Drio lounging in the doorway, blocking our escape, I was ordered to start talking.

"Baruch and Kane," I said. "Where are they?"

"Here. You are who?" Baruch barked at me, lumbering in past Drio. The color drained from Leo's face and she scooted back a few steps. Not surprising.

With their height difference, Tree Trunk could drop kick her across the yard. Or snap her in two.

I squeezed her hand. "Get Kane," I insisted. After me, he was the most invested in Ari's well-being.

"He's busy." Rohan's pose didn't change. "Now, who are you?"

"I'm Nava Katz." They guys exchanged a look at my last name. "Look, I know who took Ari."

"Why should we listen to you?" Drio asked.

"If you don't believe that I'm Rasha after seeing my power, maybe this," I pointed upstairs, "will help convince you."

"Power?" Baruch asked, but Drio had already allowed me to pass.

I led everyone up to my bedroom, showing them my stuff which was helpfully strewn across the room after my earlier phone search. "Rasha. I live here. See?"

"Lucky," Leo sighed. She snapped her mouth shut as all three guys conferred identical expressions of barely veiled annoyance on her.

Drio poked at a lacy blue demi-bra.

I smacked his hand away. "I've been here training with you guys for almost a week. The Brotherhood thought Ari was the initiate all this time but when Rabbi Abrams did the second ceremony, it turned out it was me."

They watched me blankly.

I straightened up with steel-spined determination. Remember me or not, all they needed to do was help me get my brother back. "Ari is my twin. You sent me to go pursue a lead," I said, fudging the truth, "and I was ambushed by a bad guy." Emphasis on the last two words.

"Nava is so hush-hush with her new job," Leo joked. "I'd tell you but I'd have to kill you." She broke into a snorting laugh.

I face-palmed.

"Thing is, you've seen her power," Rohan said. "What do you know about that?"

So tempting to slap the re-appearance of rock fuck grin off his face. And hello? How come that grin had never made an appearance with me?

Leo batted her eyelashes at him. "I'm very good at keeping my mouth shut."

An incredulous laugh that I didn't exactly turn into a cough escaped me.

That earned me the finger. Behind her back, so her new friends wouldn't see something so crass. "I wouldn't do anything to endanger my best friend," she said. "Even if she is astoundingly annoying."

Her words made me think of my twin, also astoundingly annoying at times. And the person I wanted most safe in the world. I'd managed to forget about Ace for a quarter of a second and I hated myself for it.

I massaged my temples. "Hold me accountable if she blabs, you know where I live."

Baruch waved a dismissive hand at my belongings. "This means nothing. There is no such thing as a female Rasha."

I appealed to Rohan in desperation. "Last night. We talked about your music. About how incredible it was to sit down with the rest of your band and put all your bad feelings, all your dreams into words for the world to hear. What it was like having your lyrics come alive. You've got to believe me. We're wasting time here."

"Wow," Leo murmured.

Rohan's expression shuttered.

"Ro doesn't talk about those days. With anyone," Drio said. "Nice try." He broke out the psychotic smile that tended to precede Torture Time and stepped closer.

My power didn't convince them. The fact of me living here didn't convince them. Recapping events of the past few days also a big fail. How could I prove I was telling the truth?

"Ari didn't have a twin." Perfect. Kane had shown up, sporting a fine scowl. "I was listening. Might want to do your homework before leading with an easily verifiable lie."

"I'm not–" I stumbled, realizing he'd used the past tense in talking about my brother. I lunged for him, grabbing his shirtfront. "What do you mean 'didn't?' I want to see his body."

He took pity at the desperation in my voice though he pried my fingers off him. "There wasn't enough of him left to see."

"Ari's not dead," I protested. I'd have known. There wasn't a doubt in my mind that Ari, while in danger, still lived. But for how much longer? I had to convince them.

I was about to remind Rohan of how we'd fought together when it hit me. The memory loss. "Asmodeus. He took Ari and he's the reason you can't remember."

"Impossible," Baruch said.

Somehow the demon had compelled the Rasha to forget me. The same way he'd managed to compel me to, well, forget myself. From Rohan's thoughtful expression, he was turning the idea over in his head. How was it possible for a demon to alter someone's memory? Because one, that was terrifying, and two, I was totally going to have words with Ms. Clara about my demon-punching contract not being more upfront about stuff like that.

I kicked Rohan in the head, intending to snap him out of the compulsion like I'd done in the park. It failed to work. He cursed, Drio and Kane tackled me, and I ended up facedown on the floor, sputtering about the demon through a mouthful of carpet.

What Asmodeus had done to me had merely been a taste, weak enough that my anger at Rohan's assholeness had snapped it. Well, these guys were furious and that wasn't snapping shit. Asmodeus had baked the memory loss into them.

"Lock them up," Rohan directed. "Then meet us in the library."

Drio seized Leo and I each by the arm.

Damn it! Why had I told Asmodeus to come after me?

"As your demon master isn't here right now," Drio murmured into my ear, "you'll have to contend with me." He shoved Leo and me out the door. "Resist me, access your power, I so much as feel your muscles tense, and I'll make things very unpleasant for you."

He frog-marched us down to the Vault.

"Drio," I reasoned, half twisting around to face him, despite the pain lancing up my arm, "how could I wear this hamsa if I wasn't Rasha? You think a demon would be able to wear the ring without repercussion? Isn't the simplest explanation the most logical? That I *am* a hunter and you're all suffering from some kind of demonic spell? I'm telling you, Asmodeus did this. You have to believe me."

He slowed for a second then wrenched my arm up higher. "The simplest explanation is a human obeying a demon," he countered. "Since female Rasha don't exist."

Trying to prove my hunter identity was pointless. I had history and misogyny working against me. I'd have to save Ari another way. Problem was, if everyone believed that Ari was dead, they'd no longer be looking for him.

I had to escape.

Leo broke into a coughing fit halfway down the stairs to the basement. While she looked like staying upright required her full concentration, I'd swear the coughing was fake.

"You okay?" My thoughts were occupied with how we were going to get out of this. Even if I lit up to attack, the chances of Drio zipping away before I could hurt him were high. Payback would not be pretty. I needed to catch him off-guard.

"No talking." Drio tightened his hold on us.

Leo glanced pointedly down at her bag, slung across her chest. It took me a minute to clue in. The switchblade.

I gave the tiniest shake of my head.

Drio locked us up in the room where the kumiho demon had been. There was no longer any trace to show she'd existed. That was creepy and didn't bear thinking about.

He left us there, sealing us in with only a dim bulb for light.

Leo sunk to the ground with a moan. I ran over to her but she held me off. "I'll puke if you touch me." She pressed a hand to her head, the skin at the corners of her eyes tight.

"It's the wards," I said. "I'm sorry. If Drio hadn't pulled you through and you'd been outed?" Unable to punch the solid iron wall for fear of breaking my fist, I gave a loud "fuuck!"

"Forget it. I should have remembered this place was warded." She gave me a faint grin through her pain. "Rohan distracted me."

"He does that."

"Why didn't we take Drio down?" Leo asked.

"He'd have gotten away before you had the knife out. Then we'd really have been screwed." I slid down the wall. "All I wanted was to keep Ari safe until I could give him back his destiny. I failed. Where's the gray area now, Leo?"

She was seated with her arms curled around her knees in a tight ball, as if trying to make the least contact with all the iron, taking deep, even breaths. "Your brother spent his life training to be a hero. Not an insurance agent. He was never going to be safe."

I leaned my head back against the wall, defeated. "But if he'd become a hunter he would have had magic. A fighting chance. He's helpless against them."

"And there will come a time, more than one I bet, that you face demons when you're helpless," she said. I already had with Asmodeus. "Whose fault will it be then? The *Brotherhood* screwed up with

Ari. Not you. Stop being so committed to your guilt over this."

"How do you do it?" I asked. "Live in the gray and still have such a strong sense of yourself? You're a good person and yet you still have to balance a demon heritage. No offense."

"None taken. I've known what I was since I was tiny. The goblin used to come visit me when I was small, telling me who I was, what to expect. What I could have if I embraced it. I didn't want it. I like being human. The trick has been figuring out how to use my goblin side to enhance my humanity. Just like you'll have to do as a hunter." She shrugged, her voice growing weaker. "It's a work in progress."

"I think you're amazing as is."

She swayed slightly and I caught her, propping her up with my hand on her back.

"Apparently this much iron and me don't get along," she whispered.

I wasn't ready to absolve myself, but I was more than ready to save my twin and, more immediately, my best friend. I took stock of our surroundings. No windows, a bare bulb, nothing in here other than that chair bolted to the floor. One door that required—

I could have kissed Drio, that "females can't be Rasha" nonbeliever, for putting us in here. Informing Leo I was letting go of her, I scrambled to my feet, blood pumping and pressed my ear to the door, straining to hear if he was gone, but the walls were soundproof.

"Here goes everything." I lay my hand against the scanner, hoping my access had gone through and that I still existed for Demon Club administration.

After the longest second in the world, the light turned green and the door opened, releasing us back into the Vault. We crept up to the ground floor office level. It was slow going because Leo was still shaky but we made it to the outside door without mishap. "Go." I whispered, one eye on Ms. Clara's office.

Leo shook her head.

Still keeping my voice low, I said, "I can be found here. You can't."

"Nee, I told you, you won't find Asmodeus."

"I don't have to. Do you need me to take you back across the wards?"

"No. I'll be okay leaving. It's entering that's the problem."

I hugged her. "I appreciate everything you did. Call me if you learn anything. Now get."

"Call if you need me," she whispered back, and left.

Soon as she'd safely made it across the yard to the trees, I inched my way up the stairs, holding the bannister so it would take most of my weight in case any of the treads were prone to creaking. I expected to be caught at any second, but no hand came down on my shoulder, allowing me to reach the library door, crouch down, and listen.

"I'm sorry about Ari," Rohan was saying.

I peeked through the crack between the open door and the frame to see Rohan lay a hand on Kane's shoulder. Yeah, *he* was the one who needed consoling.

"I'll confirm the demons' location. Then we do clean up." That was Drio. I didn't begrudge him his bloodthirsty tone, though I worried they'd be so focused on killing they'd fail to find Ari. Or worse, hurt him in the carnage.

"Meantime, I'm off to confront Montague." By the growl of Rohan's voice, this wasn't going to be a friendly meeting.

"Nothing he says can justify betraying fellow Rasha," Drio said. "Undoing our wards and letting Asmodeus in."

A *Rasha* had taken down the wards?

Baruch's blink of fury made my stomach plummet into my toes.

"Even though Ari wasn't Rasha..." Kane trailed off.

"He was still a Brother." Really, Baruch? Because he wasn't when I'd been pleading my case to get Ari's initiate status confirmed. Bogus death revisionist history.

Not that Ari was dead. Still, I'd had it with these guys.

"Ms. Clara tapped Montague's phone for GPS in-activity," Rohan said. "We've got his location."

I didn't stick around to hear more. Five minutes later, I was hiding on the floor of the cramped back-seat of Rohan's Shelby, curled tight into a ball and silent as a mouse, tagging along to go confront our rogue Rasha. Rohan leadfooted it to our destination, but despite being tossed around, I didn't make a sound.

I gave him some time after he cut the engine to get inside wherever we were before unfolding my stiff joints and scrambling out of the car. I was back in the Motel Shangri-Lola parking lot, site of my re-union with Leo last night. "Fuuuck!" I kicked at the car tire.

Rohan grabbed me by the waist. "How the hell did you get free?"

"I want first crack to see what he knows about Ari." I jerked free. "Room 205."

Rohan stepped around to face me, a dangerous flicker in his icy eyes. "You know this, how?"

I opened my mouth, then snapped it shut, not having a lie ready. If I said I'd met the snitch here, he'd demand to meet him. Her. I would too if I was Rohan. It was an awfully big coincidence on the face of things and I'd need to find out what led Leo to this case. But she was not the bad guy here.

Rohan pinned me against the hood, the warmth of the engine against my back at odds with the cool blade along his forearm pressed across my throat. "Explain."

I swallowed. "You wouldn't kill a fellow Rasha."

"If this alleged Rasha posed a larger threat to the Brotherhood? Try me." He looked a tad too willing for me to take him up on his offer.

"I met an informant here last night. A demon informant."

A muscle jumped in his jaw. "Call him."

I jutted out my chin. "No."

"I'm sorry?" Despite the barely suppressed fury in his voice, the blade wasn't hurting me.

Yet.

Though the stress of the situation had brought my headache back like the cast of *Stomp* had set up shop in my skull. Screwing up my face, I fumbled in my pocket for the pills, holding them blindly out to Rohan.

He took the bottle, releasing me to pop the cap.

I slumped over the hood, my fingertips pressed to my throat but there wasn't any bruising.

Rohan hooked an elbow under me to pull me up. He probed my black eye. "Where's the demon that did that to you?"

"Dead," I said viciously, jerking away from his touch. He'd been gentle but it still hurt.

"Good. He's involved with Katz's death how?" That question would have been brutal to hear spoken aloud if I wasn't sure that Ari lived.

"His abduction," I corrected.

Rohan tilted his head in acknowledgment. "His abduction."

"I'm not sure." I described the accident. "That's how I know it was Asmodeus. He's behind your memory loss, too." I pointed to the pills. "Can I have?"

"You shouldn't need these."

"Tell that to my head."

"How many have you taken already?" Rohan pressed a tablet into my palm.

"I'm a good time on over-the-counter-meds."

"Expired meds."

I held out my hand for the bottle. "Aren't expiry dates just a suggestion?"

"Surprisingly, no." Rohan handed back the bottle, tugging on my ring one more time like he couldn't believe I was actually Rasha. "Ari really is your twin?"

"I swear it with every fiber of my being." I infused my words with as much sincerity as I could and while Rohan studied me, as if weighing their truth, he nodded, convinced. About my sibling connection at least.

Though he shot me one more hard look before stalking off across the parking lot. Gravel crunched under his feet. He still had the slightest limp, courtesy of his earlier injury. "Why do I get the feeling you are all kinds of trouble?"

I scurried after him. "Beats me."

The front desk was unmanned, just like in my first visit, though I did hear a tinny TV set playing some soap opera in a room off back.

Rohan pushed me in front of him. "Lead the way."

Lola didn't reek of tuna fish this time, which was a good thing, but the many oddly colored stains on the cheap beige carpeting running the length of the hallways seemed more pronounced today. The walls were too closed in, the dingy green brocade wallpaper exuding wrongness, though maybe that was me projecting.

It was a good thing that housekeeping was so lax. And that magnetic key cards were an unknown technology in this dump, allowing Rohan to pick the lock. He shouldered open the door, both of us flinging our arms over our noses at the stench. Not from the body. There wasn't enough of Montague left on the bed to stink: several gnawed-on bones, a curled-up strip of skin hanging off the bed like a discarded towel, and a brownish red squishy that might have been part of an intestine. No, the foul stench came from the giant pile of demon cat piss on a wadded up section of bedding. The creature had soaked half the mattress through with its ungodly urination.

"Bhenchod!" That sounded like an excellent curse. I'd have to ask him about it later.

Rohan shoved me out into the hallway, slamming the door closed. "Jax demon. Toxic urine. It ate away the body. This is a relatively fresh kill."

"Ate him out, then ate him. Hope it was worth it."

Rohan grimaced. "Montague fucked that thing? What is it with people and demon sex?"

I shrugged. "Couldn't tell you. Though your subject and object are reversed. Montague being the fuckee and thus the object of the sentence."

He made a call. "Drio? I need a clean up." He filled him in as quickly as possible. "Now," he said in a voice far too sweet, his phone held out to me, "let's try this again."

20

"Leonie is my high school best friend." I slung an arm around her, the two of us huddled together on her sofa under her giant framed poster of Andy Warhol's large multi-colored flowers.

"Best friend *since* high school," she clarified. "On my end, I wasn't on a break."

I elbowed her side. Yeah, but she hadn't called me either so it's not like my existence mattered. No, I couldn't let this memory loss bullshit mess with my head.

"Best friends. With a demon." Rohan paced in front of us, every now and again stopping to shake his head like he couldn't believe the level of stupidity in this room. "Demons and Rasha can't be friends."

Finally. I let out a relieved sigh that he'd conceded I was Rasha.

I threaded my fingers through Leo's. "That's the problem with Rasha males. They see everything in black and white. It's a dangerous way to live."

Rohan was turning "Nava Red" so I quickly added, "Leo is only a half-goblin and I didn't know until last night she was even that. She's also given the Brotherhood a lot of good intel." I had no idea if that was true or not but I psychically willed Leo to confirm it.

She did. "I am a highly valuable informant."

"We'll see." He grabbed a kitchen chair, since Leo's funky open concept apartment was not all that big, and doing his backward straddle, sat down. "Tell me everything about how you got this case and I may let you live."

"You'll totally let her live," I said, squeezing Leo's hand for support. She'd gone a little pale.

"I haven't even decided if I'm going to let *you* live." He grinned at me. All teeth, the way a shark would while contemplating which part of your soft underbelly to rip into in the most painful death strike.

I shrank back into the sofa. "How'd you get the case, Leo?"

Apparently it had been a routine hire. The jax demon contacted Leo by email, the money wired to her account. She'd been given the time and the place of the meeting and told to record it.

"Why?" I asked.

Leo toyed with her long silver necklaces. "He didn't say, but meeting with a Rasha like that? He probably wanted proof of identity in case the hunter wasn't feeling cuddly post-coital."

"Shouldn't Montague have been more worried about the jax?" I said.

Leo shook her head. "It's rare that jax kill."

"He did in this case. On Asmodeus' orders?" I asked Rohan.

"That's my guess. Where's the recording now?" Rohan's hands hung loose and casual at his sides and even his voice sounded relaxed. Pure man candy. But he commanded the room like he was a conquering army of one, so assured of his right and might that all other lesser beings kneeled in his presence.

I fought the desire to present my throat to him like I was a werewolf and he was my alpha. Okay, yes, I read way too many shapeshifter romances.

Given Leo's fidgeting, her desire to obey warred with her determination to stand her ground. "That recording is confidential. I'm not handing it over to Demon Club."

Rohan smirked at her as if her little show of defiance was cute. He held up a finger. "One." A blade snicked out of the end, startlingly loud in our tense silence. "Two." A second finger and blade followed. There was no doubt in my mind he'd use them on her.

Leo muttered a bunch of expletives under her breath, but got up from the sofa, squeezing her right fist twice at me.

"Totally," I agreed in a low voice, after she'd handed her digital recorder over to him.

"That was for you," she said, "for having led him to my door."

Rohan held up the device. "We'll listen to it here. No one will be the wiser."

Leo blinked at him. "Oh. You're very–Well, thank you."

Ugh. Rock fuck grin alert. "I am very," he agreed.

"I know you are," she said, all injustice forgiven.

"For the love of fuck," I snapped, muscling in between them before they could keep verbally diddling each other, "hit play already."

The recording yielded nothing other than confirmation of Montague's identity and a lot of demon-human porn sounds.

Dusk was falling as Rohan and I headed back across the parking lot to the Shelby. The heavy gray clouds cast an ominous spell over the fading light. Darkness was going to be a step up.

"How do we break this compulsion and get your memories back?" I asked on our drive back.

"The surefire way? Kill Asmodeus."

At least that fit in with my plan to help Ari. I twisted my hair into a bun at the nape of my neck. "How do wards work?"

"The magic in the wards is the same magic that flows through a Rasha's veins," Rohan said in a clipped voice. "As is the blood used."

"So only Rasha can set wards?"

"Yeah. And only Rasha can undo them." Rohan clenched the steering wheel. "Montague let a demon enter a Rasha house." Rohan curled his lip. "Asmodeus had to be close enough for us to hear the memory loss command." The odometer needle inched higher and higher.

I sympathized with his anger, but I didn't want to die in a horrific traffic accident. "Speed limit," I yelped, my death grip on the seat easing up as he slowed the car down. "You think Asmodeus used the sakacha and dremla attack as cover to buy time for Montague to take down the wards? Allowing Asmodeus to get close enough to compel you into forgetting me?"

"Yes."

I rolled down the window, letting the breeze cascade over me. My concussion symptoms were gone and the burn on my arm was starting to fade. Too bad that my Rasha healing didn't cover wounds of the emotional variety, because the painful needles of ice piercing my heart since I'd found out about Ari's disappearance hadn't eased up any.

Rohan took a hand off the wheel to squeeze my shoulder. "We'll fix this."

"How did Asmodeus even know how to find Montague," I said, "if Montague snuck into town for this liaison?"

Rohan braked at a red light, drumming his fingers on the steering wheel. "Prince of Lust. He'd make it his business to know things like this."

I frowned. "I still don't get why he helped Asmodeus at all." How could he betray everything he stood for and help a demon? Even I wouldn't do that and I'd just been Rasha for a few days. Protecting Leo's identity wasn't the same thing. "You think he was compelled?"

"Probably threatened to take away his playmate," Rohan said darkly. The light turned green and we shot forward. "The jax demon. There's a secretion in its tongue that," he made the sound of a bomb going off with the accompanying hand motion. "Provides a very good time."

"What is wrong with you men? You'll strangle yourself, let demon cats lick you, all because you need a bigger bang."

"It's insanely addictive."

I threw him a look.

He threw me a look back. "So I've been told." He slowed the car at the chapter house gate.

"That's no excuse."

"It's not. And if Montague was still alive?" Rohan's finger blades popped out and he studied his hand in a scarily casual way. "I'd kill him myself for the betrayal."

The gate opened, allowing Rohan to swing into the long driveway.

"I made Ari bring my stupid sheets and then fought with him, stupidly forgetting that I'd told a demon out for revenge where I live." I buried my head in my hands. "I should have at least been guarding him."

Rohan braked in front of the house and cut the engine. "You'd have gotten yourself killed fighting the minions off." He flung open his car door. "As a new Rasha you couldn't have taken those demons on your own, so quit beating yourself up about it. Which brings us to last night." Rohan escorted me up the stairs. "Asmodeus learned about you and re-vamped his plan. That's probably why he left the fight."

"No point killing me when he still planned to toy with me."

Rohan paused at the front door. "Make you hurt the way he does. I think you're right and Ari is still alive. He's worth more to Asmodeus that way."

"Great." My mouth twisted. "My brother is being tortured because of me."

"Tortured isn't dead." A stricken expression flashed over his features. "You can come back from tortured."

"To live what kind of life?" I walked into the foyer, my shoulders hunched tight up around my ears.

"That'll depend on Ari." His clasped my wrist with a feather-light touch, his brows drawing together with an expression of uncertainty. "Last night. It's... blurry. I really spoke to you about my music?"

He sounded so hesitant. So unlike himself. "You really did," I said.

Rohan stalked off. I didn't understand the big deal and honestly, right now, I didn't care. I needed to find my twin.

We assembled in the library where Rohan caught Kane, Baruch, and Drio up on the situation, leaving out Leo's identity, for which I was grateful. And surprised. Though they were super pissed at me for going behind their back with the snitch to begin with.

Also, Drio bristled like he wanted to eye-for-an-eye *me* for getting away on his watch. I stuck close to Rohan because if Drio didn't remember me, he certainly didn't remember his reluctant promise to protect me.

"Pretty genius," Kane said. "At best, the memory loss complicated things for you immensely, at worst, we might have killed you ourselves."

"Still might," Drio said. "We only have her word about who she is."

"The ring and the power are proof," I said.

"We'll see if the Executive thinks so."

"No!" I grabbed Drio's arm as he stood. Baruch caught me with one hand and Drio with the other, pushing us back into our respective seats.

"Maspik." Given Baruch's growl I figured he was telling us to knock it off.

"Tell him not to tattle on me to Big Brother," I said.

"No one is tattling," Kane said.

Drio crossed his arms.

"We done?" Rohan leveled a hard gaze between the two of us. I nodded and Drio sat there stonily, which was the best case scenario.

"Do we know where the demons are holding Ari?" I asked.

Kane's expression gentled. "Ari isn't–"

"Yes," I snapped. "He is. My twin is alive and if it's all the same to you, I'd like to go find him." I jumped to my feet. "Can we do that?"

Baruch nodded. "We can, in fact."

Rohan's hand came down on my shoulder. "That anger? Hold on to it. Don't let it rule you. But let it fuel you."

Count on it.

"It would have to be Riverview." I peered through a copse of trees at the largely abandoned psychiatric hospital located about a half hour drive outside Vancouver.

The looming stone buildings with their iron-barred windows were creepy enough when seen in all the various TV shows that shot here. Onscreen didn't come close to capturing the eerie vibe while actually standing on the edge of the property under an ink-black sky with only the faintest trace of moonlight. Suddenly, that oppressive dusk seemed like the better option.

I'd requested one of those crazy bright flashlights that Scully and Mulder always seemed to have on hand. Instead I'd been clothed in lightweight, fibrous clothing like an armor covering me from neck to ankle that would help deflect demon claws and teeth and given a tight scratchy black cap to tuck my hair under. I resembled a giant black sock with boobs.

The four guys, on the other hand, looked like cool ninja assassins.

It was a good thing I only got the vaguest sense of the buildings. Too much of a close inspection would have played havoc with my already fraught nerves. I'd heard rumors of voices here at Riverview and that was without a demon presence.

Even knowing I was going in with the super mensches and my own magic abilities didn't stop me from jumping at every little sound and obsessively checking over my shoulder.

"Got an idea of what we'll be faced with when we get inside? Based on all the successful demon raids you've led?" I whispered, creeping behind Rohan in the shadows.

"Danger." At a sign from Drio that he was zipping ahead, Rohan put up his own hand to bring the rest of us to a stop.

"That vagueness doesn't inspire confidence."

He flashed me a wry smile. "I rock improvisation."

We waited in tense silence. I sort of wished the demons would hurry up and rush us because the anticipation was awful. At long last, Drio returned, pointing to a building on the west side of the property. "In there."

In another time and place, say on a sunny day in the Deep South, sipping sweet tea while rocking lazily on the front porch, our destination would have been a charming place to hang out. A long staircase led up to a row of two-story columns, supporting the wide balconies on each floor. Now, however, the once-white paint was streaked with black. Clumps of moss clung to the sides of the railings and ferns grew in wild abandonment over the windows.

I shivered, very glad to have Baruch at my back as we stepped inside because my inner things-that-go-bump-in-the-night-o-meter was vibrating hard enough to snap. A coat of silver paint, probably from a film shoot, had been applied, now peeling in huge scabby swathes. Or rather, flaked like something with massive nails had tried to scrabble its way out through the walls. There was junk everywhere, from plaster, wood, and pipes vomited out of the structure itself and strewn around like a bomb blast, to an abandoned shopping cart sitting in an otherwise empty room.

Drio kept zipping off ahead to scout. This time when he came back, he touched Rohan's shoulder to turn us into a large room, then, motioning for Kane to come with him, left.

Rohan, Baruch, and I picked our way over fallen ceiling tiles.

I looked up, then wished I hadn't because the ceiling was rife with gaping holes, perfect for some demon to drop down on us. Say, a seven-foot-high wooden snowman demon, exploding out in a shower of ruptured tiles.

I rocked sideways at the resounding crash of the demon hitting the floor.

The demon's head, the smallest segment, was a good foot and a half in diameter. His eyes took me a moment to find, since his skin was the consistency of weathered bark, but finally I saw the slowly blinking slits. He had no legs and stumpy T-Rex arms. It would have been comical except each of these tiny limbs ended in foot-long, blood-encrusted pincers. He slithered toward us with a scraping sound, each of his segments wobbling in different tempos.

"Sakacha," Baruch said. The pain demon.

This atrocity was one of the creatures that Asmodeus ordered to kidnap Ari? Before I could light up, Baruch stepped in front of me to battle it. The foresty showdown of Tree Trunk versus Segmented

Wood Block. Baruch ducked under the demon's snapping left pincer to pop up behind him and snap his head off. He broke off that heavy chunk of wood as easily as if he was breaking off a piece of a cracker.

Being headless didn't deter the demon. The saka-cha swiveled his head, now laying sideways on the ground, to watch the fight, turning his body accordingly in order to take Baruch on, like a remote control.

Rohan grabbed my arm.

My neck jolted sideways as he pulled me along. The reverberations of other thunks of wood followed us as we sped through the building, each hit managing to make the floor tremble no matter how far away we got.

I threw a worried glance over my shoulder as we ran, praying Baruch was all right.

"He's fine," Rohan said, as if I'd spoken, because he was a freak that way. "The kill spot is a knot in the center of the lower segment. Baruch has to take him apart to get to it."

"With his bare hands?"

A finger traced down my back. I swung around throwing a voltage-heavy right hook that would have made Baruch proud. But there was no one there. Though I swear I heard a laugh. If that had been Drio with some sick joke, I'd kill him.

I'd never been big on running, but I experienced a sudden deep love for flat-out sprinting. I vaulted down some stairs and skidded to a stop next to Rohan, my chest heaving. Oh. Whatever had touched me before hadn't been Drio. He was otherwise occupied.

Pillars dotted the large room in which we stood. The light coming through the warped window at one end threw slithery shadows that danced along the floor, turning Drio's battle with the half-dozen saka-cha demons present into an eerie ballet.

Kane was nowhere to be seen. I crossed my fingers that he was searching for Ari.

Drio used his flash stepping to dance and weave through their number, disappearing from beside one only to appear next to another. In the seconds it took for *that* sakacha to realize Drio was there, he'd used this small axe blade to slice a piece off it.

Where'd he been storing that thing?

Giant sakacha slivers flew to a soundtrack of axe whistling and wood scraping against the floor. Drio was doing an impressive job holding his own but he was still outnumbered and slicing them apart to get to their knots required time we didn't have.

Rohan pointed to a pillar. "Stay over there. You'll be safe."

I planted my hands on my hips. "Excuse me, Tarzan?"

"We'll find your brother faster if I don't have to worry about you. Don't underestimate these demons."

"What exactly are you going to do against those wood monsters? Carve your initials in them until they beg for mercy?" I pushed Rohan back with a sweeping arm. "Stand back." I struck the nearest demon with a bolt to his middle and like all dry wood, he burst into flame. His pee-wee arm sizzled away, sending his right pincer clattering to the ground.

My smug triumph lasted about ten seconds.

With a grinding noise, the sakacha demon transformed from wood to stone, dousing the flames and making his skin impenetrable.

Houston, we have a problem.

21

"Um…"

"Stone," Rohan said, pinching the bridge of his nose. "How they react to external threat."

"Like Drio's ax is party time for them?"

"It's iron. It renders them incapable of–" He jabbed a finger at the demon. "That."

Talk about stone-cold killer. Drio's ax now did nothing on the demon, who had, in his rage, seized Drio by the shoulder with his remaining pincer, grinding his long claws into Drio's flesh.

I flinched at the loud snap of Drio's shoulder breaking.

The blood drained from his face and he grit his teeth so hard that the tendons in his neck stood out in sharp relief. His agony must have been incredible but the freak didn't cry out. Using his good hand, Drio awkwardly attempted to jam the axe blade between his skin and the demon's pincer. Like a lever, using it to try and pry the pincers open.

The remaining sakacha converged on them but Rohan jumped into their midst, a human Ginsu knife of slicing and dicing.

Right, his blades were iron.

Three of the demons skittered back out of reach, but one suicidal fucker charged Rohan, the full force of his bulk nailing the Rasha in the small of his back. The jolt should have sent Rohan stumbling forward but the demon caught him by the scruff of his neck with a pincer.

A sly, satisfied smirk spread over the sakacha's face.

I wanted to help but I was scared I'd make things worse. How could I free Rohan if I couldn't use my power?

Didn't matter. Rohan freed himself by jerking away so hard that a chunk of flesh remained in the demon's grasp. Blood streamed down his back. My stomach heaved at the strong coppery stench filling the room.

Drio had yet to unseat his sakacha. One arm hung uselessly at the Rasha's side while the other couldn't get a proper angle to loosen the pincer from his broken shoulder. The demon wormed his claw into Drio's shoulder with an expression of sadistic glee.

A sheen of sweat dotted Drio's face and given his wavery movements, he hovered on the edge of consciousness. Of all the people on Team Rasha, you'd think I'd be most okay with losing him, but I didn't want him to die because I'd messed up.

Thankfully, at that moment, Baruch charged through the door and ripped the entire pincer arm off of the demon torturing Drio. The pincer itself went slack and fell off. Drio's arm hung at a nauseating angle from his broken shoulder, blood flowing from the gauges that the pincer had made. He ignored it to go help Rohan.

In the trauma of losing *his* arm, the sakacha reverted to his natural wood state. My firebomb had done enough damage that once the demon transformed back, he fell apart like cheap particle board.

Tree Trunk thrust his hand into the spongy mass, grabbed the knot–about the size and shape of a large lima bean–and crushed it under his foot.

All the remained of the demon was a pile of sawdust.

With Drio's help, Rohan was able to destroy the sakacha who'd injured him. Baruch seemed to be holding his own against the rest.

As I wasn't needed here, I raced deeper into the creepy building, past water-stained walls with their faint tang of mold, and under graffiti-tagged ceilings, on high alert for Ari.

Having imagined my twin beaten, bloody, and caged, I thought I'd prepared myself for the state in which I'd find him.

Imagining the scene was nothing like seeing it.

Ari was a pulpy mess, his flesh a rainbow of bruising. He sprawled on the filthy floor of a small room so obviously broken that the demons hadn't even bothered to chain him up.

Tears streamed from my eyes as I ran over to him and hooked my hands under his armpits to help him to his feet. "I've got you." My voice cracked.

My brother couldn't even support himself. I staggered under his weight until I managed to find my balance for the both of us. "I wondered when you'd get here." He stared at me blearily, his blinks too slow, his expression too dazed.

My heart stuttered. "Sorry to make you wait." Sorry about everything I ever did to hurt you, intentionally or not. There'd be plenty of time to apologize once we were away from here.

We shuffled to the doorway.

Ari cradled the arm not slung around my neck against his body, his wrist puffy. Blood-encrusted scars were gashed diagonally along his chest and he sported a hell of a black eye. Walking seemed to be a shambling challenge but he wasn't limping.

Shafts of weak moonlight lit our way along the quiet hallway. My scalp prickled. Where was everyone, Fallen Angels and demons both? Being allowed to wander around unchecked had to be part of a massive trap.

It took some time to backtrack but we made it to the large room where the sakacha battle had occurred. The floor was strewn with sawdust though the sakacha were all gone.

A horde of short, fuzzy, pink heart-shaped demons with enormous darkly lashed eyes and arms ending in fat white-gloved hands, things I swear I'd had in pillow form as a kid, greeted us. Sure they were cute, but I wasn't an idiot. They were still demons. If these were the dremla, they were soul leeches.

Careful not to jostle my brother who still clung to me for support, I fired up my left hand–the one farthest from him–with a nice, bright electrical ball.

The demons all burst out into short, nasty quills.

"I'm going to have to let you go now," I said in a low voice, my focus on the demons.

Ari's arm that was slung around my neck tight-ened to asphyxiating proportions. "I don't think so."

I feebly slapped at my brother with my right hand.

"Take whatever form you want, demon. I'll still kill you."

Huh? Was he talking to me? "Not funny," I man-aged to gasp.

Ari flipped his poison ring open and threw the contents at me.

I jerked sideways. My poor hair took the brunt of the maybe half teaspoon, but I still screamed, feeling like my scalp was on fire. A clump of charred hair fell to the ground, and my left ear lobe bubbled. My stomach heaved.

"I may not be Rasha," Ari hissed, "but I still trained as one. You hurt me, unholy spawn, I'll hurt you back."

"Unholy spawn" was not a nickname of mine. Ari didn't know who I was.

My blood ran cold.

"Ari," I said in a steady voice, "I'm your sister, Nava. Look at my ring. I'm Rasha."

He laughed mirthlessly. "Good try, but there's no such thing as a female Rasha. And I don't have a sister."

Asmodeus could make the rest of the world forget about me. But not Ari. The demon didn't get that win.

I dropped low, ducking under Ari's arm with a shocked yelp as he kicked me sideways, sending me partway across the room. I smacked the side of a pillar, all air knocked from my lungs. Of course, I had to make sure my darling twin didn't kill me first.

Ari crouched in fighter stance, fists up and a determined look in his eyes. "Make the dremla stand down or I swear I'll kill you. I know your weak spot."

Yeah, idiot. You.

The demons flanked me like an army. *My* army.

My eyes widened. "Oh no. Not mine." I fired at a couple of them.

"We are sorry to disappoint, my Queen," they said in musical voices. Faking, bunny-eyed spawn.

Before I could insist that I had no royalty status among the demonically-inclined, Ari rushed me. I was no match for my brother. The first few hits hurt but it was the punch to my eye that sent me over the top.

I slammed my hand into his chest, spreading my electricity in a fine web around his torso. Ari took deep gasping breaths, his entire body spasming. I kept the voltage low because I had no desire to heart attack him into me being an only child, but I had to make my point. "Who took the blame when you broke the dining room window with your homemade catapult, Ace?"

Still caught in my magic web, Ari raised a shaking hand and shot me the finger.

So much for using my words. I tugged at my non-poisoned earlobe once, in our "I've got your back," code.

His face creased in confusion. Then he tugged back, staring at his hand like he wasn't sure why he'd done that.

I stopped my magic, catching him as he sagged. "Let's get out of here."

Asmodeus stepped into the room, slow clapping, and totally healed from our fight the other night. There were no signs of any of the wounds that Rohan and I had inflicted on him. Not even the slash across his throat. "Good job, catching the prisoner for me,

Nava." Once again, only his ogre head spoke, though he refrained from getting all Lust Master on me.

"As if, you–"

I froze at the look of hatred on Ari's face. "Knew it," he whispered. With that he was ripped out of my arms by the demonic pillow horde and marched away, leaving a couple dremla behind to help Asmodeus.

I faced the demon, jaw tight. Killing his spawn was nothing compared to what I planned to do in retaliation for putting that look on Ari's face.

"So easily forgettable," Asmodeus said. He scratched at the fur on his bull's head, this encounter with me a minor irritant. Hot bovine stank wafted off him. "Your comrades, your own brother? None of them able to remember you."

"Drop their compelled memory loss and their love of me will rush right back in," I countered.

Asmodeus' thick ogre lips drew together in a distorted expression of pity. "Don't you realize how my compulsions function? I work with what people already want. I prefer to deal in lust, but I can affect any desire. I simply amp up that craving, maybe small, maybe buried deep down, but still burning hot and bright inside them. With the memory loss? All those people couldn't wait to forget you. Even you know you shouldn't be Rasha. That's why you wanted to forget the joke of you as a hunter. The joke of your entire existence."

His voice slithered through me, pulling down stone after stone in the wall of my self-confidence that I'd so carefully erected after my dreams went up with the snap of my Achilles. Exposing these bricks as hollow, plastic shells.

"No." I barely choked the word out through the thickness in my throat.

"The Rasha don't want you. Your brother doesn't either. It's your fault he didn't get to take his rightful place."

Shards of my heart cracked off. I clapped my hands over my ears, not wanting to hear the demon's insidious words. Not wanting him to see my hands shake. Not wanting to hear the truth my own experience borne out. The Rasha wanting to forget me I could live with. It sucked, especially from Rohan, but I got it.

Ari, though? Asmodeus killing me over and over again couldn't inflict as much hurt.

He laughed. The same laugh I'd heard in the supposedly empty hallway earlier when he'd also touched me. Creeped out, I skittered backwards.

"I was simply going to leave your brother's body for you to find. But erasing you as his sister altogether? Having him think you're one of us?" The demon hummed in glee. "You've been so entertaining in so many ways."

Head bowed, my hands slid down the side of my head, my palms skimming over my ear lobes. The ongoing searing on my left side was a distant second to my broken heart. I flashed on Ari giving me our secret "got your back" twin code. Asmodeus wanted me devastated. Wanted me to lay down and die. But he'd failed to realize one very important point: even if Ari did hate me right now, he needed me. I wouldn't stop having his back until I was dead.

I straightened up, beckoning the demon forward with my hand.

His three heads looked between each other in amusement. Bulls and rams should never look amused.

"My turn to be entertained. Gonna kill you now." Pushing past all my exhaustion and pain, I dug deep for my anger. Letting my hatred of Asmodeus not rule me, but absolutely fuel me. My magic coated me in a bright blue glow, lightning bolts slithering over my skin like animated tattoos.

"Cute," he said. "But you can't take me on your own and your friends are," he paused for effect, "busy."

I fired a lightning bolt into his side. He didn't get to walk away from doing this to my brother. To me. "Don't be such a coward, Asmodeus."

In the blink of an eye, he dropped what little civility he'd pretended to have. The monster that now faced me was primal, brutal, and very much a deadly prince of his realm. "As you wish." He leapt at me, kicking me in the head.

Light exploded in my brain. If I was going to see stars, it better damn well be from the other kind of hard pounding.

I staggered back only to be caught by the throat with one enormous hand.

The more he squeezed, the harder my power flared up. My vision flickered, white spots dancing before my eyes. Blood seeped from my temple, mingling with my sweat. My inner voltage fluctuated wildly and my heart pounded so hard, I was amazed I didn't crack my rib cage. I had to shut myself down, but since that would leave me powerless in a demon's grasp, I chose to let the needle on my inner meter break and allow my magic voltage to flood me.

Asmodeus roared as I flared bright, releasing me from his grip. Gulping air in heaving breaths, I fell on my butt, my hands sliding in a thick, viscous goop.

I scrambled to my feet, darting away and using every iota of mental strength I had to bring my power levels down. My magic didn't simply dissipate. The electricity bounced around my body before snaking out through the soles of my feet. It didn't hurt though, so that was a step up.

Asmodeus faced me, bits of his flesh blackened and smoking dropping to the ground with sickening thuds. A rat scurried out of the shadows, going to town on this all-it-could-eat demon buffet.

I dry-heaved.

Suddenly, the demon's side went limp.

"You might want to start wearing shoes," Rohan said to the demon. "Because those tendons of yours are baby-sensitive." He reached down and hauled me to my feet, raking an intrigued eye over me. "Magic ink. Nice."

Lightning bolts danced over my still-blue skin. "Took your time."

One of the dremla attached to Baruch like a barb, looking like it was trying to cuddle him to death. Baruch's skin rippled. His eyes rolled back, showing the whites, before he let out a war cry, grabbed the demon by its arms, and ripped it in two.

I expected to be showered in fluff but instead this maggot-like creature fell wriggling to the floor, so I stomped it to gory smithereens. The remaining dremla fled.

Asmodeus regrouped, lashing out.

Baruch tossed me a pair of red ear plugs.

I popped them in and the world fell silent. Which was weird since I should have heard the sounds of the brutal and bloody fight we were engaged in–or Asmodeus using his voice compulsion on us.

His ogre face grew redder and redder as he tried, his features more and more twisted with fury. Drio grinned his unholy grin and mockingly tapped his ears.

The fight raged on. Magic continued to pour out of me with no problem, though my poor meatsack stayed upright through sheer will alone.

Earlier, Baruch had assigned us each a battle zone. A part of Asmodeus' body to focus our attack on. Best case scenario, we'd notice him trying to protect the sweet spot. At the very least, we'd be weakening his body with strikes.

I'd been assigned the demon's back. I wounded him. I even bloodied him but not enough to do real damage. I was tiring far faster than Asmodeus was. True for all of us. With his broken shoulder, Drio looked about ten seconds away from passing out.

Asmodeus had gotten in enough licks in that our blood splattered the floor like a Jackson Pollock painting.

Then Rohan managed to slice off one of the hardened scales on the demon's chest. Asmodeus flinched. The tiniest movement but compared to his lack of reaction with the rest of our hits, fairly telling. As if we were Borg, connected by a hive mind, Baruch, Drio, Rohan, and I refocused all our magic on his chest. Drio and Rohan used their ax and blades respectively, Baruch weaved in to rip off scale edges in order to expose more vulnerable flesh, while I blasted any bit of skin uncovered.

That's when Kane, sporting a nasty cut across his temple, hobbled in with Ari. He gave me a sheepish grin, resting Ari carefully against a pillar. *Told you my brother wasn't dead.* Why wasn't Kane jumping into the fight? I did a full-body scan to check if his injuries were more extensive than I could see, but that wasn't it at all. He waited until we'd torn a wide strip of scales off Asmodeus' torso. Kane swaggered up behind him and then, his skin iridescent purple with poison, he hugged the demon.

Asmodeus convulsed.

Kane said something to me but when I shook my head at him, unable to hear, motioned for me to pull out the ear plugs. I did.

He bowed low, with a flourishing arm. "I left you the good part. Care to do the honors?"

Chest heaving, I caught my breath enough to answer. "Hell, yeah. Hey, Asmodeus."

The demon zeroed in on me, the poison rippling through his shriveling frame and tight pain etched across his three faces. His ram's head gave a wounded bleat as he unsuccessfully attempted to protect his right pec. The sweet spot.

I shot him the finger, a perfect forked bolt shooting off that digit to bullseye him. "See who's forgotten now, bitch," I crowed.

Asmodeus fell apart into puzzle pieces, all of him winking out of oblivion with a sucking noise.

It was over.

The lightning bolts disappeared from my skin as I powered down from blue to my usual Snow White pale, though I still reeked of electricity. Despite my bleeding, my bruising, my burned ear, and my bone-deep exhaustion, the knot in my stomach overrode everything else. "Tell me you remember me."

Drio eyed me with distaste. "Sì. I like you even less now." Keeping his shoulder more or less in place with his other hand, he strode out.

"One thing going right in my day," I called out after him.

Still all poisonous, Kane blew me a huge kiss with a "Hola, babyslay." He toed at the floor. "I'll get the sodium peroxide mix to scour off our blood. Don't want demons getting hold of it." Especially not if they used it to take down our wards.

Baruch gave me a proud eye blink.

"Awfully sweet of you, Tree Trunk," I said as they hurried off.

Rohan didn't say much one way or the other. He shot me an inscrutable look and left.

Then there were two.

"Hey, Ace." I slung my arm over his shoulder. Please let Ari remember he comes as a matched set.

"Hey, Nee." Yay! "Sorry for the whole trying to kill you thing."

"No problem." My grip on him tightened. "But do it again and I'll stab you in the tits."

He mussed my hair with more noogie than fondness. "Like you could."

"I so could."

Ari laughed then pressed his hand to his side. He looked like a human punching bag and needed to rest, as did I.

I grabbed him in a hug, practically squeezing the life out of him with my tears falling against his neck. He returned it, just as fiercely. Just as choked up. I wanted to ask if this meant we were okay or... not. But I wasn't that brave. I'd do it after I got his initiate status confirmed.

I disengaged with a sniff. "Come on," I said and my brother and I trekked out of the darkness and back into the moonlight.

Together.

22

By Sunday, we'd been moved to a new chapter house already fully operational. We could have re-warded the old place but once a ward had been taken down, subsequent wardings were never as strong as the original. Rather than risk vulnerability, the Brotherhood had opted to move us.

The new Demon Club was identical to our previous one, aside from being situated on more land. When I commented on the fact that the Brotherhood could have gone for something different, say a twenty-first century design, Rabbi Abrams answered, "Change is not always a good thing." With a pointed look at me.

Message received, Rabbi.

It was a week since I'd become Rasha, and while my life was totally different, it was also infuriatingly the same. Asmodeus going after Ari wasn't enough to shift the Brotherhood's position, nor was me helping take the demon down. When I'd broached the subject yet again with Rabbi Abrams, he'd simply informed me that killing demons was my job and that the Brotherhood wouldn't look kindly upon me using it as some sort of bargaining chip.

Rohan and Drio were equally frustrated, since even with Drio torturing Evelyn to the best of his ability, she hadn't cracked. Now she was dead and they were no closer to getting into Samson's inner circle. From the snatches I heard around Demon Club, the Executive was not happy.

Meantime, Ari had been sent with us to keep an eye on his recovery in the first crucial forty-eight hour period. Over the next few days, I spent most of my time draped in a chair beside his bed, watching him sleep. Well, watching him thrash under the covers.

While he healed, I did too. Not my physical self: that happened pretty quickly. No, I needed time to get over my hurt and anger that Ari had wanted to forget me. I wasn't a saint. I nursed my grudge and then I got over it.

It wasn't until the following Wednesday that Ari sat up, bitching that he wanted proper food not broth, and looking, on the outside at least, somewhat healed. I brought him chicken noodle soup, filled with chunky pieces of meat.

Ari sat up and took the bowl, eyeing me warily. "Are you going to mother me?"

I shook my head. "After everything that happened, do you still want to be Rasha?"

Ari swallowed a spoonful. "It's not possible. The ceremony didn't work. That means that they were wrong about me from the get-go. You were always the initiate, not me."

The inconsistency made no sense. Besides, he was a natural at this. All these years, he'd carried the quiet confidence of becoming Rasha in his bones. No mistake.

"Not my question."

Ari's shoulders set in a tense line as he answered. "Yes." His eyes glittered dangerously, a contrast to the purple bruising on his face.

"For revenge?"

"Does it matter?"

Absolutely, because that attitude would get him killed faster than any stupid hero impulse. I blinked away the tears threatening to pool in my eyes. "I just want you to be happy."

He relaxed against the headboard. "You can't orchestrate that for me. All you can do is be there."

Yeah, but he needed to be alive for me to be there for him. "Always."

After another couple of spoonfuls, he handed me back the bowl. "I'm going to crash again."

I headed downstairs into the kitchen where I found Rabbi Abrams taking a box of tea from the cupboard. I washed and dried the bowl, then wandered over to the large island in the middle of the room. Opening the box, I sniffed the loose black Darjeeling.

"How can I help you?" Rabbi Abrams leaned against the counter, a green ceramic mug in hand. His black suit smelled of lavender which was an improvement from moth balls.

I eased onto a high bar stool. "Explain something, Rabbi. Why did David call us Rasha? We're not wicked. We fight the wicked."

Rabbi Abrams put the mug down. "Rasha does mean wicked or guilty as sin. But its more literal meaning is one who departs from the path and is lost. This was David's reminder to his hunters how close they are to darkness. How easy it would become for them to truly be Rasha in every way."

I'd had no idea.

All of my fellow Fallen Angels, at least the ones that I'd met, were battling their own demons. Even Ari. "Begs the question if maybe out of all the descendants of the original group of Rasha, those of us who actually become hunters happen to be that much closer to the darkness to begin with."

The rabbi regarded me shrewdly. "Could be, Navela. Could be."

"About Ari?"

He sighed. "I performed the rites. He is not Rasha. We were wrong about him." To be fair, he sounded pained saying it.

I slumped in defeat. "He's going to hunt demons, magic power or not. And we both know how that ends." I grasped the rabbi's hands in mine. "Please."

The kettle let out a shrill whistle. Waves of impatience rolled off me as he poured the steaming water into his mug and filled a tea ball, dropping it in the boiling liquid to steep. "There may be another way to check," he admitted.

"Then–"

He held up a hand. "It is not usually sanctioned by the Brotherhood. In fact, in our entire history, I've only heard of it being allowed once."

"Help me. I'll do anything. Fight more actively or not at all. Whatever they want. Whatever it takes."

Rabbi Abrams got out the honey and a spoon. "Drio learned nothing from Evelyn and everything else we've tried to determine if Samson is a demon has been a dead end. We have one avenue left open to us. Get Rohan to do the theme song and I'll confirm Ari's status."

"Rohan doesn't want to do this."

"He's all we have. Do it and I give you my word." He lay the tea ball on a small saucer, spooning honey into his mug. "I too very much want Ari to be Rasha."

My stomach twisted, but it seemed I had no other choice. "Done."

Ari found me a few hours later, sitting motionless on the edge of my bed, an unfolded pile of laundry next to me. "You okay?" he asked.

I forced a wan smile. "Yeah. What's up?"

"Drive me home? Kane does any more disinterested hovering and I'll kill him."

"Hovering, huh?"

"I'm not up to his game-playing." Ari was disinclined to say any more. He looked around my room, wistfully. "I think it's time for me to go."

Much as I wanted to force him to stay here until he was completely healed, I understood. And honestly, I was glad of the excuse to get away. He came with me downstairs to tell Ms. Clara we were leaving.

She greeted us with a smile. "Feeling better?" She tapped her head.

"Depends," my brother replied. "Unfortunately, I now remember I have a sister."

I licked my finger and stuffed it in his ear. He shoved me away.

"Before you leave," she pulled a new phone out of her desk and tossed it over to me. "I'll have your new laptop put back in your room. Remember, this goes with you everywhere."

I gotta admit, I had a pang or two as I picked up the sleek technowonder. "You're not going to be able to find my iPhone anymore," I said to Ari, with a mournful shake of my head.

He smiled. "You forbade me."

"Like you believed me."

Ari took the phone away and smashed it against the desk.

I clutched at his arm. Ms. Clara was going to murder him. "He didn't mean it," I yelped, blocking him from bodily harm.

Ms. Clara laughed.

Ari waved the phone at me, intact and not even dented. "Indestructible. You'll save a bundle on replacements." He dropped the phone in my hand.

I ran a finger over the spot on her desk that he'd whacked to make sure it wasn't dented either, because no way did I want Ms. Clara angry. But, like the rest of her office, it was in perfect, orderly condition.

We said goodbye, then headed out to Dad's Prius, sitting gleaming in the sunlight, scratch-free. Demon Club had restored it to showroom pristine condition.

"Dad's totally gonna know," I said. Ari and I had been driving the car for a couple of years. Pristine had been blown off its list of adjectives in the first two weeks.

We exchanged mischievous grins. He picked up a rock and I got out my key and we proceeded to nick and scratch the thing back to its former state. Five minutes later, we surveyed our handiwork with pride. Much better.

The house was empty when we pulled up, since Mom and Dad weren't due back from their cruise for more than a week. Party animals that we were, Ari went straight to bed and after triple checking that he didn't need anything, I went into my room. Funny how small it seemed. I trailed a finger over my stuff, restless, bored, but not wanting to leave Ari alone until he woke up. I could have watched TV, but daytime programming blew at the best of times. Besides, I was too distracted.

How was I going to convince Rohan to step back into the spotlight and do the theme song? It wasn't my place to force him back into something that had deeply scarred him. He might have stopped singing because he no longer enjoyed it. I'd never gotten an answer out of him one way or the other. On the other hand, if I didn't convince him? Then Ari's chances of becoming Rasha were well and truly dead. As dead as *he* might be if he started hunting.

Absently, I stopped in front of my tap shoes, picking them up to wipe the dust off with my sleeve. Once they were in my hands though? I itched to put them on, something I hadn't done in over two years.

There'd been no dancing in moderation since my dream had come crashing down. My heart couldn't take it. The only way for me to cope had been to go cold turkey. Slam that door forever and padlock it tight. I couldn't handle having something that had been my entire life be relegated to a hobby.

The taste of copper brought me to my senses and I released my poor bottom lip from my teeth, shocked at how strong my urge to slip the shoes on was. Maybe I'd grieved enough. Still, I hesitated, running a hand over my calf. Did my Rasha healing mean I wouldn't relapse into the pain of my dance injury?

I'd do anything to be able to dance on a regular basis again but, for many reasons including my new-found destiny, the ship had sailed on my dreams of dancing professionally. I'd resigned myself to it, believing I couldn't dance anymore. But now?

I wasn't ready to think about the long-term ramifications–or lack thereof.

The ringing metal as I clacked the taps together decided it. Dancing had always helped clear my mind, focus me. Hopefully, it'd provide much needed answers now.

I slipped downstairs, shoes in hand. Flipping on the light in the basement, I felt a nostalgic pang seeing the special wooden tap floor that had been installed in the corner of our rec room so that I could practice. While the floor was worn with black scuff marks from my metal taps, it was clean and polished. Mom may not have been a fan but she wasn't going to let anything get dirty on her watch.

After checking the soles for loose screws and finding the taps tight, I put my shoes on. My feet instantly molded to the worn contouring. I let out a sigh I didn't know had so badly needed to be exhaled.

I grabbed a homemade CD from the tower that had been relegated to the basement about five years ago, starting with a slow swing version of "Caravan" to warm up. Flaps, shuffles, paddle rolls–nothing fancy. I let my body fall into the muscle memory of balance and movement. A small smile crept across my face hearing how clean my moves still sounded.

Next up was the Verve remix of "Sing Sing Sing." I threw myself into it, choosing to improvise to the melody line, playing my own variation of the tune through my feet. A twinge in my left Achilles tendon–literally my own Achilles heel where my dance career had been concerned–had me slow down, testing my foot for further signs of pain.

Tap involved most of my weight being on my toes, with heel stomps aggravating my tendency to swollen tendons. But the pain really was just a twinge. I was good to keep dancing.

It was as if a dam inside me broke. I needed to go hard. To pound the rhythm. Pound out my roller coaster of emotions and stress. I threw on "How You Like Me Now" by The Heavy, craving that driving beat to quell the edge inside me. One-footed wings, syncopated pullbacks, over-the-tops–I pulled out all my moves in addition to the flurry of basic steps rendered at breakneck speed.

Fuck, how I'd missed this.

Barely winded, soaring on adrenaline and happiness, I thumbed through the other CDs in search of what to play next, my hand stilling over the copy of Fugue State Five's first album that Leo had forced on me all those years ago. I smiled when I saw her "Listen to it or I'll kill you, dummy!!!!" written in gold marker on the CD.

Pressing play, I counted down the end of the eight-beat opening of "Toccata and Fugue." In contrast to the raspy growl of Rohan's voice, my steps were lightness themselves. The floatiest soft shoe to counterpoint all the emo feels pouring out of the song.

I'd never danced to this before, but it was the perfect fit. I lost myself in the joy of taking this beautiful piece of music and putting my own stamp on it. While Rohan singing to me in the park had freaked me out, now the song soothed me. My feet twined with his voice to create something altogether new.

I matched the crescendoed ending of the song with a series of turns that propelled me across the floor, my hip bumping into the wall because I ran out of room. I laughed at my spatial miscalculation, the sound ringing clear in the silence.

Then I saw Rohan's face. He stood stock still in the doorway, staring at me like I was an alien. I wrapped my arms around my chest, my gaze sliding away from his. People could be extremely judgmental about tap's place in the dance pantheon. Weirdo might have been offended by my dancing to his song.

"I always thought tap dance was like—"

"Shirley Temple," I interjected dryly. "So, you've said." I crossed the room, cutting off his next song with a push of the button. "What are you doing here?"

I bent over to untie my shoe but he stopped me, stepping forward with one hand up.

"Don't. I mean, don't let me interrupt. I just wanted to tell you I'm leaving. I have to go back to L.A."

A rush of panicky adrenaline speared through me. I clacked over to him, my shoelace trailing on the floor. "You can't go."

"Why not? I haven't been back to my apartment in weeks and Mom wants to take me for pizza at Highland Park Bowl." Rohan pushed me back a couple of steps. "You're all pale. What, don't want to be without your main babysitter?"

Apparently his memory return had come with the return of his anger over our hook-up.

Discussing the theme song right now would only add fuel to that particular fire. I knelt down to take off my shoe. "Have a good trip."

He didn't say good-bye.

I leaned on Leo's buzzer, muttering a steady stream of curses.

She let me in, waiting bleary-eyed in her doorway. My friend appeared crazed: no jewelry, greasy snarled hair, a coffee stain on her denim miniskirt.

"What happened to you?" I asked.

"Huge exam."

"You want me to leave?"

She grabbed my arm, pulling me inside. "No! It's my Ethics course and–"

"Having none, it pains you to understand the concept?" I tossed my bag on her couch, flopping down on the lumpy cushions.

"Something like that." She padded into her kitchen in heavy wool socks with enormous holes in the toes and heels. "Coffee?" She sniffed the pot and recoiled. "Diet coke?"

"Sure, if you have rum. Hold the coke."

Leo took two mismatched mugs out of her cupboard and reaching up on tiptoe, grabbed the bottle of booze sitting on top of her fridge. A generous sloshing of rum into each one and she joined me on the couch. "Ari is doing okay?" she asked. I'd called her once he'd been rescued.

I nodded.

"You're persona grata now?"

Again, a nod. I took a very large slug of rum.

She pursed her lips. "That leaves a guy. Ooh, don't want to let your precious Fallen Angels know you were slutting around?"

I couldn't help myself. I smiled.

Her mouth fell open. "Which one?"

I smiled wider.

Leo launched herself at me, smacking my chest. "Liar!" she howled, her disbelief clear. "Where?"

I held my cup up, out of splash danger. "You know the park by the theater on Seymour?"

"Yeah."

I waggled my eyebrows at her.

Her mouth fell open. "You strumpet."

"Jealous?" I smirked between sips.

"D'uh." She leaned in, a manic gleam in her eyes. "Give me details."

Bless Leo's heart, she embraced her best friend role, listening to me dish and not complaining when I couldn't decide whether I wanted to rant about Rohan or rave about how good he was.

"Yup, better than ever before. I heard you the first four times," she said.

I'd been talking a while, mostly ranting at this point, and Leo had gone back to her homework. She sat at her kitchen table, books spread around her, while I munched salt and vinegar chips on the couch I'd commandeered.

Leo's purple diary lay beside me, a little beat up but still astoundingly glittery. She'd gone to her mom's and dug it out of storage. I'd read a few of the initial goopy entries which had been enough to make me believe her about being in love with Ari.

That and all the hearts with their initials doodled over the pages.

"What's the big deal about kissing anyway?" I asked.

She raised an eyebrow at me.

I pointed a chip at her. "It's not the same for guys. It certainly shouldn't matter to Rohan. You know how many girls he must have slept with?" I bit savagely into it.

"You think he's slept with any guys?" she asked.

We both got lost in that image for a moment.

I shook my head. "Don't distract me. I'm ranting about sexual inequality and power dynamics here. The issue is not that he couldn't kiss me. It's about control."

"Boys like him do enjoy control," she said, pencil in her teeth as she marked up her book with a yellow highlighter. "This should not be a surprise."

"Great." I tipped the bag into my mouth, determined to get every last drop of salt and fat. "He's all pissy because I was the one calling the shots." I got lost in the memory of ordering him to go harder, and shivered.

Leo spat out the pencil. "Come on my couch and you're buying me a new one. Scotchgard does not protect against psychological staining."

"Maybe I should have asked him for permission. Guys like that." I pitched my voice an octave higher. "Ooh, Daddy, please may I?"

"That etiquette is especially appreciated when a man thrusts his dick in your face," Leo agreed.

I buried my face in my hands. "I loathe him. But he was so good. I want seconds. Thirds. Thirtieths."

"Sixty-ninths," Leo quipped.

I looked up. "Oh yes. Most definitely sixty-ninths." I sighed. "This is bad. I think I might be addicted to him."

"Eh," she shrugged. "Breathing is an addiction. But once you've stopped for an hour, it's reasonably easy to quit forever. So how hard could this be to kick?"

"And to think I never figured out you were a demon before." I licked my fingers clean.

"It's because you're so self-obsessed."

"Probably." I checked the clock. Time to head back. "'K, babe," I walked over to where she hunched at the table studying, intending to hug her, then decided I didn't want to touch her until she'd showered. "Schmugs."

Leo shook her head at me. I hadn't used our special shortened goodbye of "hugs, schmugs" since we became friends again. "Last time you schumgged me," she said, "I didn't hear from you for over a year. You suck, and I have no idea why I accepted you back into my inner circle."

"Because I am your inner circle. Besides, who else is going to get you up close and personal to your teenage masturbatory fantasy?"

Leo blushed.

"Eww. Rubbing one out to thoughts of Rohan Mitra is strictly verboten from this point forward. Besides, don't you have that Madison chick on speed dial?"

Leo gave a dreamy smile. "Ooh, yeah. She does know how to work her tongue. But that doesn't preclude my fondness for boy parts. Hook me up with his friends."

"Schmug me and I'll consider it."

I spent the rest of the week so bored out of my mind that I even adhered to Rohan's stupid schedule. At least it passed the time, since there was nothing else to do right now other than train and study.

Rohan was still in L.A. and even if I figured out the best way to approach him, I wasn't doing it over the phone. Drio wouldn't let me help with investigating Samson. Kane was working a security contract– turns out he was a coder who did a lot of surveillance software development for both the Brotherhood in-house and David Security clients, and Baruch was using the time not spent with me to inventory our equipment and weapons. My brother had decided to go back to class and told me to quit calling and checking up on him.

I'd tried hanging out with Ms. Clara but ten minutes in her office poking at her stuff and she'd threatened to break out the whip. So I was actually excited the following Tuesday when Baruch got me for a conference call with some Executive Rabbis at HQ in Jerusalem wanting a debrief on Asmodeus. Might as well suss out the Powers That Be on their feelings for me.

Of the three men on the other end, Rabbi Simon had been grudgingly complimentary on my performance, Rabbi Ben Moses hadn't said much at all, and the head of the Executive, Rabbi Mandelbaum, a sneering chauvinist who sounded surprisingly young, was clearly never going to be Team Nava, even if I killed every demon in existence single-handedly.

I'd bet money that he was one of the Jewish men who said his morning prayer thanking God for not making him a woman with great sincerity and mean-spirited glee.

It was a no brainer, then when asked if I had any questions for them, to pipe up, "How come you don't bring some female rabbis into the fold?"

Baruch shook his head at me, though his eyes danced in amusement.

Rabbi Mandelbaum, showing great restraint by not declaring outright that that would happen over his dead body, explained that female rabbis weren't really rabbis.

"Pretty sure they are," I said. "You know, on account of having the rabbinical title. It's not something you can send away for on a matchbook. Or wait, can you, Rabbi Mandelbaum?" I asked in breathy sweetness.

Baruch kicked my leg.

The sexist jerk on the other end of the conference call then switched tactics, saying that the few rabbis that worked for the Brotherhood were all descendants of previous rabbis who'd been part of the organization.

"Exactly." I wanted to reach through the phone and throttle him. "You missed me as a potential Rasha. How many other women, rabbis and potentials both, have the Brotherhood missed? All those traditions weren't rules. They were assumptions. Wrong assumptions. Plus, the name needs to go. Brotherhood is no longer applicable. I'm thinking–"

Baruch leaned across the table to cut off my access to the speakerphone, wrapping up the conversation–in Hebrew. Once disconnected, he steepled his fingers together. "Tell me, are you trying to get on their bad side?"

"Nope. It comes naturally."

"Nava." His tone was pure warning.

"Lady Shock and Awe, Tree Trunk," I said brightly. "It's the only way I know how to live." Damn it! Ari had been right.

23

I gave up on the urban fantasy novel that had seemed so engaging a couple weeks ago, tossing my phone on the bed. Fictional supernatural beings failed to hold the same allure given my new career. Chances are Drio and Baruch would go home soon, leaving me with Kane, who was great. But how weird was it going to be living here with just the two of us? What if he was reassigned? How small was my world going to become? Who would train me? Sure, Rabbi Abrams would arrange for someone but I was attached to my Tree Trunk.

This mattress was too hot. I kicked off my covers. Giving in to my loneliness-induced insomnia, I got up to get some water. Everyone was asleep, but I tiptoed down the stairs anyway wearing my black sleeveless nightgown that hit mid-thigh.

An ajar door threw a slash of light into the hallway on the main floor. I veered away from my original destination of the kitchen and toward the door, because it was Rohan's bedroom and I was curious.

I knocked.

"Yeah?" Rohan pulled his sweater up over his head, leaving him in a black button up shirt whose fit left very little to the imagination.

I had a very active imagination.

"You're back." I tore my eyes away from him to take in the space.

The rest of us had rooms together upstairs, all in varying shades of beige, which I planned to paint soon. His room, however, already featured dark green walls with gorgeous black and white framed photography and warm wood furniture all bathed in the soft light of his bedside lamp.

"What's the deal?" I asked. "Me, the local, is in the institution special and you, the transient, gets VIP treatment? What'd you bribe Ms. Clara with?"

One corner of his mouth quirked up. "We have an arrangement." He lifted a small roller board suitcase off the bed, stashing it in his closet, allowing me a glimpse of his clothing arranged just shy of color-coded.

"What kind of arrangement?" Okay, that came out sulkier than I'd intended but gawd, they'd be pretty if they hooked-up.

He threw me a look that was far too shrewd.

Seconds and now, please. I stepped into his room, shutting the door behind me. Then in a move I hoped looked sexy, pulled my nightgown over my head, pitching it to the floor.

Silence, though Rohan did rake a very slow gaze over me.

I leaned back against the door, my palms flat, pushing my rush of nerves into the cool wood and calculating how fast I could grab my nightgown in case I'd made a horrible mistake. "Tell me if I'm being presumptuous."

"About me wanting to fuck you?" He closed his eyes briefly, his "yeah, right" coming out on a rush of pent-up breath.

Cuntessa woke up with a vengeance.

Pushing Rohan onto the bed, I straddled him, rubbing over his very hard cock straining against his pants.

Rohan gripped my hip, gently moving me off of him.

Here it came. His reasons why this was a bad idea and not going to happen. Instead, he leaned over to snap off the light. Moonlight streamed in through his blinds.

Mental fist pump!

"This time, we do this my way." Rohan kneeled at my feet.

"Works for me." I spread my legs but he ignored my invitation to get in and get going.

Cuntessa was not his destination. He took my arm, placing a kiss to the inside of my wrist, massaging his way up the skin with a combination of kisses and his fingertips.

I watched him, a frown puckering my brow. No one had ever paid attention to my arms before. Guys tended to dive in to the sexytime body parts of tits and pussy. Not that that was necessarily successful but if I couldn't will myself into a happy ending with those, what was the point of spending time on an arm?

Rohan acted like those parts didn't exist. He lay me back on his bed, sucking my big toe into his mouth.

I jerked off the bed.

"Should I stop?"

"No." I tried to explain my hesitation. "I'm not sure this is doing anything for me."

Rohan leaned in to lick my clit with a long, slow stroke. "Is this what you want?"

In response, I opened my legs wider, leaning back on my elbows.

He closed my legs. "Tough. Like I said. My way."

"Or not at all?"

Smirking, he squatted back on the balls of his feet.

Bah. I waved a hand at him. "Have at it." My tone made it clear that I didn't think he'd be all that successful doing this his way.

"Turn off your brain."

"What?"

He stared at me, impassively.

I crossed one leg over the other. "Women think about stuff to help them get off."

"Not with me."

Head tilted, I raised my right eyebrow. "Wanna bet?"

"You are not seriously going to fight me about getting you off so hard you can't see straight just to make a point, are you?"

I opened my mouth and then snapped it shut, because, yes, I had been about to do that.

Moron. Cuntessa despaired.

"Shut off everything except the sensation of being in my hands."

"What if your way isn't working for me?"

"I stop. Or," he brushed a hand along my hip, "I have rope." He waggled his eyebrows at me.

I burst out laughing. "Yeah, right, Mr. Grey."

He pretended to look affronted. "Are you mocking me?"

"Incessantly, though if you are a billionaire I'll temper my snark to the occasional gibe." I lay back against his mattress signaling my agreement to do this his way. But I was still tense, dreading orgasmic failure with Rohan. I bunched the pillowy softness of his blanket in my fists.

"I dunno, Nava." Rohan said, in a voice smooth as honey. "I think you're bent that way."

"Come at me with a rope, buster, and find out." Though the idea of tying him up held great appeal.

"Turn." He twirled a finger around and I flipped obediently onto my stomach, my left cheek pressed to his covers, figuring he was going to give me a massage to put me at ease.

Nope. He trailed his finger over my body. That's it. Again and again. He dipped into the hollow of my knee, gliding up along the inside of my thigh only to veer away toward my hip.

At first I found it ridiculous. But after a bit, his caress soothed me, my spine softening, my pliant self sinking deeper in the mattress. He lifted the hair off my back to expose my shoulder blades, writing my name on my back, my body shivering in delight and a small smile tugging my lips. A whisper of a caress, a leisurely stroke along my spine–I craved that single point of contact, his feather-light touch, never knowing where he'd abruptly leave off, only to commence stroking me somewhere else.

Relaxation thrummed into arousal. My skin pulsed a split second behind his touch, my entire body sparking in desire, igniting a long, smoldering burn.

"More," I breathed, wanting anything, even him kissing my arm again.

His hand stilled. "I told you," he said, in a maddeningly calm voice, "my way."

"I have to keep silent?"

He chuckled, the sound spiking my nipples into hard peaks. "You don't like something, you want me to stop? Speak up. You try to direct the action? Game over."

I growled, hating his bossiness, and myself for wanting this enough to put up with it. "This better be worth it, Snowflake."

He raked a nail up my spine.

No. Not a nail. A blade.

I moaned.

The tip of his blade ghosted in long, lazy circles over my body. "What do you feel?"

"It's like sensory phosphorescence trailing in the wake of your touch."

"Cool." He sounded like such an eager little kid that I had to smile.

Rohan rolled me over, continuing his slow exploration, tracing his blade reverently over my left breast, his breath blowing warm gusts over my flushed skin. The focus on his face was absolute. His eyes were molten pools lingering hungrily on my body.

Hypersensitive from his playing, I was wound tight, vibrating with a corked fizziness that was almost too much and not nearly enough. I clamped my mouth shut so I couldn't beg for more.

The feeling of him sucking my tit into his mouth was as intense and amazing as the best orgasm any other guy had ever given me. I clutched his hair, feeling his ragged breathing against my skin. The press of his shirt buttons into my breastbone as I arched against him caused a twinge that did nothing to distract from my pleasure but did remind me he had way too many clothes on. I fumbled at the buttons.

He helped me undress him, shrugging out of his shirt.

"Pants, please."

He lifted his head, his pupils dilated. "I'm busy."

"Multitask." I snapped my fingers at him, figuring that he was too into this to follow through on his "game over" threat at my command.

Rohan rolled his eyes but pretty much ripped his pants and boxers off in record time, leaving him naked and magnificent. "May I return to what I was doing?"

"You may."

He stretched out along side of me, his skin hot against mine.

The air was cool on my back and I wriggled against him, wanting more of his warmth. More of his everything.

He pressed his hand between my shoulder blades, keeping me close as he swirled his tongue along my nipple. My tits grew full and heavy. I placed his palm underneath one to fondle it.

Even during sex, Rohan possessed a graceful elegance, a precision. He veered between an economy of movement that was obscene in its effectiveness on me and a drawn-out languidness that left sensations sinking so deep inside that sparks literally shot off my skin.

One singed his eyebrow. Rohan jerked away.

I blushed beet red.

He gathered me in his arms, turning me to spoon me. "The dangers of lightning girls," he murmured.

How would I ever explain that to any other guy? Was I only going to be able to sleep with Rasha from now on?

Rohan sighed, nudging at my jiggling leg. "Quit thinking." He reached between my legs.

Cuntessa pulsed in a steady slow throb. His stroking was an exquisite torture.

"Fuck, you're wet," he said.

"That's on you."

"Yup," he said in a voice 150% smug.

Our bodies were curved tight around each other. His stubble rasped my skin as he sucked my shoulder. I reached back to stroke his cock, loving its hot, hard fullness. Giddy with anticipation of having him inside me.

Our hips rocked. Rohan hooked his leg over mine to open me wider, a second finger plunging inside me.

"I don't want to come without you inside me," I gasped.

"Tough. Because I need to taste you."

Hello, lucky sixty-nine.

He started with a slow tease of my clit, either forgetting or totally remembering that his dick now hovered over my mouth and two could play that game. I licked the head of his cock, tasting those first salty drops on my tongue. A pioneer in the land of Rohan, I surveyed the length and girth of him with my lips. Not yet taking him into my mouth, simply enjoying a leisurely exploration.

Rohan groaned. There was a squirt of lube and then his finger rimmed my ass.

"Wrong hole." I twisted, all squirmy.

"Or very right if you're up for it."

He pressed some spot at my opening and my stomach clenched in a delicious swoon. Oh. If I could get more of that feeling, I was open to reconsidering my "no buttholes here" stance. Plus, his dirty side was incredibly hot. What the hell. I pushed back against him in answer.

He inched his finger into me.

I gasped, my muscles clenching tight around him.

"Good?" he asked.

"Uh, I don't know?"

Rohan see-sawed his finger in and out.

I practically came right there. A wanton moan ripped from my throat.

He laughed. "You're *so* bent, Lolita."

I deep-throated the smirk out of his voice. Rohan's dick hardened further, jumping to a new level of swollen arousal.

Miracle of miracles, for once in my life my brain shut down. Got to hand it to the guy, it was more fun when I stopped thinking. I was lost in the increasing tempo of his tongue and fingers at play on me, and focused on returning that same level of pleasure to him.

I fumbled on the bed for the bottle of lube he'd tossed there, squirting some into my hand and getting my finger well-oiled up for some play of my own.

Rohan mumbled a whole bunch of words in a language I didn't understand when I slid *my* finger into his ass, but his hips pumped with more urgency so I kept going, almost as heated by my own actions as his.

Behind my eyelids, I saw white. My muscles tightened, my body flushing hotter and hotter. I rocked against his fingers in an ever-spiraling circle of wild abandon, until I shattered.

Every other orgasm prior to this was relegated to a boring black and white, but this was glorious Technicolor. 3D IMAX. And I came not once, but twice! The incredibility of achieving that Holy Grail made me forget everything else–like my name and his cock in my mouth.

Didn't matter though because the second I stopped orgasming, Rohan started, half-arched on the bed above me, biting my hip as he came. He fell back against the bed, his head by my thighs, turning to press a soft kiss against my flesh. "That was round one."

24

Round two? People had those outside of movies? Yowza.

I eyed my nightgown because round one's conclusion was when I should have been getting dressed, but it was way on the other side of the room, and Rohan was lazily stroking my arm, his eyes the color of melted honey, and really how much of a hardship could round two be?

I nestled into the mattress. Even Rohan needed some re-up time so I curled in close, being the one to do nothing more than run my hands over his body.

Gawd, what a beautiful body it was. As the interwebs had shown me–time and time again–plenty of guys were ripped and chiseled. That was their endgame. Rohan was a fighter. He was functionally fit, all sinewy grace. His body had a purpose and while it was obvious in the hard planes of muscle, his tapered torso, and long leanness that he took great care of it, he also displayed an ease and lack of ego in his own skin that I found refreshing.

He had nothing to prove.

Rohan's body wasn't a temple, it was a finely honed weapon. Though that didn't stop me from worshipping it now. I nudged him to turn over, noting the silver scar from his sakacha encounter at the base of his neck. A gorgeous black script was tattooed between his shoulder blades. "Hindi?" I guessed, tracing the letters.

"Yeah. It says 'Kshatriya.' It's the warrior caste."

"It's beautiful." I trailed my hands down his back, rubbing at a patch on the base of his spine that was a bit darker than the rest of his skin.

His gluts tensed. Ooh. Pretty.

I rubbed the spot again, then gave in to my urge and bit his ass cheek.

Rohan yelped, flipping himself flat on his back. "Teeth. Not a kink of mine."

I propped myself up on one elbow, batting my eyelashes at him. "I'm betting that's a very short list, Mr. Mitra."

He grabbed my hips, pulling me across him, while giving my ass a swat. I squealed in laughter which ended in a smothered yelp as his mouth got close to mine.

He froze. "Right," he muttered.

I bit my lip, then wriggled onto my side to face him, running my hands over his body in long strokes. "How was L.A.?" As a distraction technique, my question was only moderately successful. It didn't dissipate the tension that had come over Rohan at the kiss thing, but he did answer and let me keep touching him.

"Got to see my parents, so that was good." The affection in his voice triggered a stab of longing for something I'd never had. "As for the mission? Supposed to be a quick and easy kill. Instead?" He scratched his stubbled chin. "Too much mishegoss."

"You know Yiddish?" I couldn't believe he'd used the slang term for craziness.

"Just the good words. Jewish grandmother."

"Can you imagine if demons spoke Yiddish? Oblivion would be filled with the kvetching of the damned."

Rohan giggled.

I bopped the tip of his nose with my index finger. "Aww. Cute."

He scowled at me, more embarrassed than angry given the way he ducked his head. "I am a former rock god and current Rasha. Not cute."

"So cute." I twisted my body around, reversing my head and feet placement, happy to find him charged again.

Rohan switched on the bedside light, raising his head off the pillow to better take in the sight of his cock filling my mouth.

I raised my eyebrows at him, all the while sucking on the ridge of his penis.

He groaned but didn't stop watching. If anything, his gaze grew more intense.

"Dirty boy, wanting to watch," I said.

He threw his arm behind his head and threw me an unrepentant grin. "Dirty girl," he countered, "liking it."

I couldn't argue.

Rohan caught my leg up by his head, sliding his lips along my calf. "I want to play, too."

"Nope." I angled my body away from him. "I want you in me. Now." Getting onto my knees, I reached into his bedside table drawer and plucked out a condom. It could only mean one thing, since he wouldn't have brought other women to Demon Club. "Look who was hoping I'd stop by?"

"Don't be cocky." He parroted back my earlier words to him. "It's insufferable."

"But I pull it off so well." I tossed the package at him.

He tossed it back. "Put it on me." His command was issued in a husky rumble.

Blood rushed from my brain in a dizzying surge. I ripped the foil packet open with my teeth and rolled the condom over him, so frantic to ease the pressure inside me that I didn't do my usual tease. In fact, I screwed up the direction, cursing when I put the condom on backward, essentially short-sheeting his dick.

Rohan rectified the situation with ease. And great haste.

Knowing from previous encounters that this was another place where guys took the opportunity to kiss, I scooted to the edge of the bed still on my knees, my forehead bowed to the bed.

He didn't argue, coming to stand behind me. "Open your knees wider."

I complied and then, finally, he pushed achingly slowly inside me. My eyes rolled into the back of my head at the delicious prolonging. "That feels... yesssss."

Rohan pressed a kiss between my shoulder blades. He rocked back and forth for a second, his hands braced on my hips.

I pushed back against him and that was it. Any thoughts of taking it slow were out of the question. I luxuriated in the feel of him, pounding into me, hard and fast. The top blanket bunched under my calves, our movements making a jumbled mess out of his sheets, every thrust causing my sensitive nipples to brush against the bed. My eyes were wide, my mouth hung open slack, and my fists balled the blanket on either side of my head. Pleasure snaked through me.

I stroked Cuntessa, feeling another orgasm starting to build.

"Not yet," Rohan commanded. He pulled out of me and I whimpered. I'd have begged at this point for more. He rolled onto his back, setting me on top, cowgirl-style.

I groaned as every inch of him slid fully and completely inside me. "I'm at your mercy," I said in a thick voice.

My words kicked him into overdrive. He caressed my breasts, placing one hand on my hips to help bounce me up and down.

I fluttered a look at him from beneath my lashes.

He looked amused so I raised an eyebrow. "Shimmy and bounce," he said. "Very accomplished, Lolita."

"I am a woman of many talents," I replied, staring down at him through eyes half-lidded in lust. I ran my free hand over his heated skin, tightening my knees on either side of his legs, and rocking in tiny rhythmic motions.

"Wide-eyed, breathy, a little off-balance, the look works for you."

Using just enough force to blur the line between pleasure and pain, I raked my nails down his front, marveling at the fullness of him inside me. My lids fluttered closed, startling open again when he released my hand, placing it on my clit.

"I want to watch you," he said. The gravely timbre of it sent shivers of delight spearing through me.

I flushed. This was a whole other level of intimacy.

"Please." Sitting half-curled up, Rohan laced his fingers with mine, squeezing tight.

Who was I to refuse? Our gazes locked, I stroked myself as he continued his forceful thrusts, my other hand held fast in his. The familiar pressure grew and grew. Rohan's free hand moved to my breasts, fondling, kneading.

"You feel so good inside me," I said, the last word coming out as a groan.

I'd had good sex before, my disappointing experiences of the past few months notwithstanding. This was something else entirely. It was more than Rohan knowing what I wanted, or what I needed. He played my body like it was his favorite guitar. Each roll of the hips was a chord progression, every slide of his skin on mine a slow strum. He coaxed a song from my blood and spun lyrics with every fevered caress.

Rohan threw back his head as his orgasm ripped through him.

The vibrations inside me pushed me over the top. My screams were loud enough to wake the dead. Totally spent and deliciously satisfied, I fell across his body, our sweat causing me to slide a bit. We lay there panting a moment. I for one, was mind-whacked.

Rohan held up his hand for a high-five.

Laughing, I returned it.

The room stank of sex. Was he always this vigorous? I shut my thoughts down before I could get weird about the idea of Rohan and other girls. I had no claims on him.

I rolled onto my back, stretching like a cat to enjoy the delicious aftershocks rolling through my body. "Is there a round three?" I looked over at Rohan, his cheeks flushed and his hair sticking up in spiky bedhead and my heart did a little flip.

My throat tightened.

Rohan didn't notice. "You're trying to kill me."

I forced myself to relax. "Not before I get my fill of orgasms from you."

"Humans don't live that long, sweetheart."

I poked him in the side and he squirmed. "You're ticklish?!" I clapped my hands in glee.

He grabbed my wrists, pinning them above my head. "Don't even think it."

I smiled my best feline smile, very much liking our positioning.

"Definitely trying to kill me." He nudged his knee between my legs. "You're a good dancer."

That was the last thing I expected him to say. "I told you, a woman of many talents. You need to re-member these things about me, Snowflake."

"And you glow," he said, one hand playing with my hair.

I glanced down at myself.

"Not the magic. When you dance. When I saw you that day?" His eyes went distant. "I remember that look from when I used to perform."

"You could have it again. Do the theme song."

He stiffened, his expression turning to ice. "Is that what this was about?"

"No!" I sounded horrified.

His expression softened. A little. "Then what?"

I screwed up my face. "Rabbi Abrams said if you agreed, he'd find a way to check if Ari is still an initiate."

Rohan laughed bitterly. "Right."

"Wrong." I pushed him down against the mattress, leaning in. "You want to know why I don't tap anymore?"

He frowned at my abrupt topic change. "Why?"

"Remember, I told you about playing Lincoln Center?" Off his nod, I continued, "Out of that, during my junior year, I was invited to audition for a professional tap troupe." I adopted a snooty tone. "New York City, don't you know." I flipped onto my back, staring at the ceiling. "But I got dumb. I pushed myself too hard, got a snapped Achilles, surgery, and physio instead of the bright lights of Broadway."

I ran a hand up my left calf, phantom pain ghosting under my fingers.

"So you missed the audition."

"No. I did all my physical therapy in time to get cleared a week before. I nailed the audition, and I was all set to go."

He propped himself up on his elbow. "Then why didn't you?"

"Because I ruptured it again during spring competitions. There was no way I could join the troupe after grad–I'd just be in and out of hospitals, tearing myself apart."

"I'm sorry."

I shrugged. "They said I could defer until I'd completed rehab, but by that time, my university acceptance letters came in." I wrinkled my nose trying to keep the wetness in my eyes from turning into actual tears. "Let's just say, healing took longer than anticipated. I think my parents were happy for the excuse to steer me back into their comfort zone of academia. Having a tapper for a kid doesn't buy much cred at faculty parties."

"That sucks." His arms came around me. He had very sexy arms.

"Not dancing was like cutting out a piece of my heart." I met his eyes. "I know you feel the same way about singing."

Resounding silence.

"You wanted to know about my heart tattoo?" He lifted his arm up to look it at.

Now it was my turn to adjust to the topic switch. "Who was she?"

He didn't answer so I ran my heel up his leg.

Rohan flinched at the roughness of my heel. "What are you, part dragon?"

"Answer."

"Contrary to your belief that I'm both the world's biggest horn dog and a hopeless romantic whose heart was shattered, this?" He tapped the tattoo. "Has nothing to do with some girl I was in love with."

No? Excellent. Wait, I didn't actually care. "A guy?"

He shot me a wry look. "Not that either." He lay his arm across me, studying the tattoo. "It's a reminder. For my weaker moments when I crave the spotlight again."

"Nothing wrong with the spotlight." I placed his hand on my hair to play with it. His fingers toyed with my strands, massaging tiny circles against my scalp. The effect was almost hypnotic.

"I was young and stupid," he said. "I thought I could put my soul out there with my lyrics and be loved. Turns out people are cruel. The more famous you are, the more the knives come out. Conversely, the more your sense of self gets inflated and you get cruel. *I* got cruel." Rohan gave me a self-deprecating grin. "Imagine that."

That explained his magic turning him into a giant human blade, a reminder to guard his emotional well-being and his lingering regret over the person he became once famous. It made me and my electric powers look positively cuddly.

"That's not the full story though, is it?"

He cleared his throat. "I mentioned in the park that I'd fucked up?" His expression grew tight, but at my nod, he continued. "I had a cousin, Asha."

My stomach twisted at his use of the past tense.

"A year older than me," he said. "Asha was like my sister." His face lit up at the memory of her. "Amazing, hilarious. She was worth a billion of me. And when she needed me most?" He practically spat the next words. "When I could have helped her the most as Rasha? My head was so up my own ass from my rock star trip that I was convinced I knew best. Fuck everyone who didn't agree with me. I let her down."

His silence after that statement was loaded.

"She died?"

Rohan laughed bitterly. "That's the kind way of putting it. There wasn't enough left of her to bury." He echoed the words Kane had mistakenly said earlier to me about Ari. If Rohan had loved his cousin half as much as I loved my brother, his grief and guilt must have been immeasurable.

I eyed the heart tattoo. Still was. "That's why you stopped singing, wasn't it? As a punishment."

"Criticism? From you?" He tensed.

"Hardly," I said.

He relaxed a fraction, but I remained pensive. Bad enough that he'd tattooed this heart on his arm to be slashed–symbolically broken–time and time again, in penance. Destroying his dream on top of that was truly heartbreaking.

More than his agreement to the song, I wanted him to understand.

"My entire life, Ari was the bright shiny twin with a future and a destiny and I wasn't. I had a dream, but it never qualified me for bright shiny status. Except then *I* was Rasha and he wasn't and..."

"You felt guilty."

"Beyond anything."

I sat up, holding the sheet against my chest. "You know why I forgot I was Rasha? Not because I didn't want it. Because I was starting to like it. Coming home that night when I first found Leo, I'd been thinking I had something to offer this gig. That maybe, for the first time since all my life plans had crashed and burned, I'd found something I could excel at again. Except I didn't believe that I had any right to it. Any right to be bright and shiny. And the really fucked up thing? I never considered if maybe that label, that expectation, had weighed Ari down all these years, just as much as lack of expectation had me."

I lost my fight with the tears, but before I could swipe at them, Rohan gently brushed his thumb along my skin to wipe them away.

"Despite what happened, Rohan? You're denying an essential part of yourself. I'm not saying go all rock star again, but you can't stop singing and making music. It's who you are just as much as being Rasha." I cupped his jaw. "Even if you don't do this song, please think about what I've said. You don't need to live with that deep-seated unhappiness. You don't need to live with that guilt. You have the right to decide how you want to live. You have the right to be happy."

Rohan didn't say anything, just held my gaze. Every particle between us was charged with this intense intimacy and, in that moment, I almost broke my rule and kissed him.

Our mutual tensing hit at the same instant.

I dropped my hand. "What are we doing here?"

He sighed. "Fuck if I know."

"Right." I sat up and retrieved my nightgown, pulling it over my head. "Thanks for the sex stuff."

"Any time."

I paused at the doorway. Normally sexytime did not require any clarification because normally I would not be seeing the dude again. However, with Rohan and I being in such close quarters, I figured the laying out of mutual expectations would be appropriate.

"Are you still mad?" I asked.

"About what? Using sex to get what you want, your issues with kissing, or the fact you apparently have never met a personal boundary you care to respect?"

I winced, toeing at a groove in his floor. "Yes."

"No, because I believe you weren't. No, because I'm almost impressed with your level of dysfunction–"

"Your issue shit doesn't smell like roses either," I shot back.

"It would if I had any."

I rolled my eyes at his ability to say that with a straight face.

"And no," he said, "it's annoying, but I'm not mad."

The tightness in my chest relaxed. "Last item. To ensure there is no slap down of a Sexual Harassment 101 course on our," I circled a finger between us, seeking a noun that wasn't *relationship*, "situation by the HR department."

"You mean our resident dominatrix?" Rohan asked.

"Stay professional, Snowflake."

He schooled his features into a serious expression, nodding for me to continue.

I repressed my grin at the amusement in his eyes. "To clarify," I said, ticking the items off on my fingers. "Our future dynamic includes training, dispatching unholy spawn, and doing the horizontal mambo at every opportunity, correct?"

"Except Saturdays," he said. "I rest on Shabbat." The Jewish Sabbath.

My face fell and Rohan laughed. "So easy on so many levels," he teased.

"So mind-blowing on so many levels," I corrected, and left.

25

Our talk didn't bring Rohan to an earth-shattering epiphany. It certainly didn't get me any closer to my goal of having Ari checked. All that happened was that Rohan avoided me the next day. I buried myself in more training, then headed up to my room, stopping in surprise as I entered.

My tap shoes were sitting on my bed. I reached a tentative finger out to touch them. Last time I'd seen them had been at my parents' place. Ari would have mentioned if he'd brought them over. Except he wouldn't have. As far as he was concerned, I'd shut that part of myself down. Only one person was aware that I'd danced again that one time.

I pressed my palms to my cheeks. Was this about me? About him? About us? Not that there was an us.

"Babyslay?" Kane stood in my doorway. "Rabbi Abrams wants to see you in his office."

Hope rising in my chest, I bolted downstairs, skidding to a stop as the rabbi's office door opened and my shell-shocked twin stumbled out.

"I'm still an initiate," Ari said.

Behind his desk. Rabbi Abrams paused his polishing of a gold bar engraved with symbols to throw me a thumbs up. With a whoop, I jumped up and down.

Ari wore the same dazed look all the way out to the car.

"You're happy, right?" I asked.

"Yeah. I just... need to process that it's for real." He sank into the driver's seat, shaking his head. "Listen, Rabbi Abrams wants us to keep this between the three of us for now. Something about figuring out why re-running my induction ceremony didn't work." He popped his seat belt in with a click.

"Okay, but that means no unting-hay emons-day on your end."

Ari started the car. I shut his door, doing my happy dance for the benefit of his rear view mirror until the car had veered out of sight down the drive.

I danced my way up the back stairs into the kitchen where I found Rohan sitting on the counter, texting. "Thankyouthankyouthankyou!" I threw my arms around him.

He jumped down, sliding his phone into his pocket. "I shouldn't have held up the mission like that."

My exuberance leaked out of me and I stepped back. I mean, yeah, it was a perfectly good reason to do the theme song but what about the tap shoes? Weren't they symbolic of well, something?

Before I could ask, Drio bounded into the room and grabbed Rohan in a bear hug, spinning him around.

"Dude. Put me down."

Drio squeezed him one more time then messed up Rohan's hair. "I could kiss you!"

I could watch that.

"We'll have the proof to take Samson down in no time." Drio did a quick one-two step. "Prague, here we come!"

"Why Prague?" I asked.

"The final part of the production is being shot there." Drio eyed me up and down, one hand braced on the counter. "Want to go?"

"Suuuure." I pointed to the stairs. "I'll pack my bags."

"I'm serious." He jerked his index finger up and down my body. "You're attractive enough."

I fluttered my hands in front of my face. "You think so?" I dropped the act. "Attractive enough for what?"

"Yes, Drio," Rohan said. "Whatever are you up to?"

Drio's hands gestured excitedly as the words tumbled out of him. "You doing the song opens up a bunch of new ways to plant more Rasha in the inner circle. As part of your entourage, I'll be vetted by his posse no problem." He jerked his thumb at me.

"And any 'friend,'" he used air quotes, "of the great Rohan Mitra's…"

"Hell no," Rohan growled.

I punched Drio. "I'm not whoring out for a demon."

"You don't have to fuck him," he said. "But you're his type. Be a tease. I don't care. The more people we have on him, the faster we take him down. Besides, you're a good Rasha," he added grudgingly.

Wow.

Still, any plan of Drio's to send me in and play nice with a demon needed to be examined inside and out for all the possible ways I could end up dead. I started with Baruch, dropping the comment casually in during a training session the next day. "Drio wants me to go to Prague undercover and get close to Samson for proof he's a demon. What do you think?"

I startled my trainer enough that I managed to land a right hook on his jaw. A first.

"Ben zona," Baruch swore. "No."

"It wasn't a yes or no question, Tree Trunk. I could help." I raised my fists back up to my face.

"You have no experience." He corrected my stance.

I laughed. "Getting guys? That's pretty much the most experience I have."

"Outing demons. You don't have to do this."

Oh, I knew that, but I figured that the Brotherhood would, too. Sure, Ari would be taken care of now but they were still undecided on me. I wanted to change that.

"Scale of one to ten," I asked later, "with one being me coming out unharmed and ten being my grisly remains found twenty years from now. Where do you put this job?"

"Fifty-seven," Kane said. We sat on the front porch, Kane keeping me company "for no reason" but really because Ari was coming over.

"You don't think I could do it?"

"I don't think I could do it and I've pulled straight boys with the best of them." Kane wagged a finger at me. "King is dangerous. And not in the fun way that makes you do that moaning sound that I find highly irritating to have to hear, child who has not processed that my room is directly over Rohan's."

I blushed.

Ari showed up, looking between me still totally embarrassed and Kane, legs splayed in his Adirondack chair. "Do I want to know?" he asked.

"Your sister is being very naughty."

"That would be a no, then."

"Also, she has a death wish." Kane got up. "Talk to her." He swatted me across the top of the head and went inside.

Ari sat down in the vacated chair and held out a gift bag.

"What's this?" I pulled out a giant box from the fancy-ass chocolatier I loved but could never really afford.

"Because you believed in me."

"Aww, Ace." I kissed his cheek.

He allowed one peck before he swatted me off. "What was Kane babbling about?"

"Prague." I explained the situation and why I wanted to do it.

"You're not ready."

"I'm Rasha." I lit up my hand. "I am not without resources." I flexed my fingers. "Ever since I became a hunter, I've been focused on doing this job to survive or prove a point that I wasn't a total fuck up. But I've missed having something to be passionate about and being Rasha might be it. You were right. I am happy. At least, I'm starting to be."

Ari was silent for a while. "Okay."

"Also, I–wait. Okay?"

He nodded. "You're right. You're Rasha. This wouldn't even be a discussion if you were a guy. And the passion for the gig? I get it."

"We are going to be the coolest super twins ever." I broke open the chocolates. While I chose mine by shape most likely to contain nuts, Ari carefully studied the legend. My first choice contained a macadamia so I nailed it. Next I went for a dark chocolate surprise. "So you don't think the Prague idea is a subtle murder plot by Drio?"

"No. Though once Samson's dead, you might want to watch your back. Sweet! Hedgehog."

"Wait!" I tried to grab the chocolate, but Ari stuffed it in his mouth before I could. "No fair. There was only one of those."

"You snooze, you loose," he said through a mouthful.

"So much for gratitude."

He looked at me like I was insane. "It was a hedgehog. You'd push me into traffic for one." I couldn't argue with that, though I did make sure and eat his second favorite flavor of Mexican hot chocolate truffle next.

Once I had Ari's support, blessing, and common sense take on the matter, I gave Drio my assent. He told me that he was waiting for official permission from the Brotherhood, but that he expected the call soon.

I hurried downstairs to Rohan's room, rapping softly on the door. "Hey, Snowflake." My plan was to keep things professional. He hadn't said word one to me about the tap shoes so I was taking that to mean it had simply been a kind gesture from a colleague.

Rohan stepped out from behind his half-open closet door, dressed in tight black jeans and a white T-shirt, his hair spiky and gelled. And, oh my, he was wearing eyeliner.

He grinned his rock fuck grin.

I clutched the doorframe in support as every bone in my legs dissolved into jelly. "I've decided to go to Prague." My voice came out in a squeak.

"I heard." He advanced on me, pure strut. The light caught the silver of his multiple rings on each hand.

I eeped and held onto the doorframe harder. "Maybe I'll run into you while I'm there."

I prayed that Prague was a big enough city that that absolutely would not happen, because with him dressed like this and in full rock god mode, I didn't stand a chance.

"I'm sticking close to have your back on this assignment." He skimmed his hand over my hip, the warmth of the black leather strap worn with a single fat silver bracelet on his right wrist brushing against my skin.

"Dressed like that?" I stammered. My heart beat a furious tempo at the clear and present danger of this incarnation of Rohan. I flapped a hand at him. "Surely, you don't have to go zero to a billion? Start small."

"I've been thinking a lot about how you missed dancing like breathing." His arrogance fell away, leaving a soft vulnerability that hit me harder than the rock god look. "It made me realize that I'd been holding my breath, too. That, after Asha, I hadn't thought I deserved music in my life." His gaze turned penetrating. "I hadn't admitted that to anyone. Not even myself until now. Until you."

I had to jump start my breathing. "Happy I could help," I squeaked. I tried to step away but he held me fast. Careful what you wish for, idiot. I swallowed, his raw charisma flooding my system.

"I'm meeting with Forrest about the song. And I wrangled an intro to King. Now I need more of an entourage than just Drio." He leaned in, his lips hovering over mine. "You were nominated and won as groupie."

"Mazel tov to me," I murmured, practically pulling the frame off the wall. My mouth was dry and my brain had gone wonky and stupid in the face of his pure male swagger. Oh, how misguided I'd been with my whole "players and their games" insight I'd had on Rohan.

I hadn't even begun to see his game because Rohan Mitra had been slumming in the junior league with me. Nope, I was screwed, and this time, I didn't think I'd get a say in how.

End of Book One

Thank you for reading!

D^{ear} fabulous reader,

    Thank you for giving me the gift of your time and I hope you've enjoyed the beginning of Nava's journey. These characters are definitely close to my heart (and my inability to say the loud part quiet). I promise you the rest of the series will be a wild ride.

    I've had so many people fall in love with Nava, Rohan, and the rest of the crew. It's great hearing your thoughts, so stay in touch.

    Now, I have a favor to ask. It's your reviews that help other readers to find my books. You, the reader, help make or break a book. So please, especially if you want more Nava and Rohan, spread the word. Leave an honest review of *The Unlikeable Demon Hunter* on Amazon, Goodreads, your blog, etc.

xo
Deborah

Nava explains awesome Yiddish and Hebrew words used in this series.

- Bar Mitzvah (Hebrew) - A boy's coming of age ceremony when he's thirteen. Moving, ritualistically important and, should the right guests be invited, an excellent way to build the foundation of one's university fund.
- Beseder (Hebrew) – Okay.
- Boker tov (Hebrew) – Good morning.
- Bubelah (Yiddish) – adding "elah" to something gives it that cute diminutive. Literally it means "little grandma" but is used as "sweetie" – generally with children. Yeah, I don't see the logic on that one either.
- Kvetching (Yiddish) – Complaining. But like seriously and chronically getting your whine on. Hand wringing optional.
- L'chaim (Hebrew) - Literally "to life." This is the Jewish "cheers" and really easy to slur after you've had a couple.
- Maspik (Hebrew) – Enough. Sounds way better growled at someone than the English equivalent.
- Mazel tov (Hebrew) – Congratulations. Can be shortened to "mazel mazel" which sounds super snarky and may leave the recipient in doubt as to how to take it.

- Mensch (Yiddish) – a person of integrity and honor. Technically it's gender neutral, though I see it applied way more often to men. Go figure.

- Mishegoss (Yiddish) - Craziness. Senseless behavior or activity. I thought this was my grandmother's nickname for me when I was little.

- Oy vey (Yiddish) – A very handy exclamation of dismay and grief conveying everything from "aw, man" to "kill me now."

- Shalom (Hebrew) – Peace. Used for "hello" and "good-bye."

- Sheket bevakasha (Hebrew) – Be quiet, please. A classroom/camp favorite, used to bring unruly children in line. The teacher sings "sheket" and everyone else sings "bevakasha, hey!" in response. As Pavlovian conditionings go, it's a keeper.

- Todah rabah (Hebrew) – Thank you very much. Important to know when expressing gratitude – and scoring points – with any (grouchy) Israelis in the Brotherhood of David.

Check out this sneak peek of book 2

THE UNLIKEABLE DEMON HUNTER: STING

"Shove it in already," I said through gritted teeth. My back was freezing from the damp, flaking basement concrete I lay against, while the two-foot-tall, rat-shaped demon pinning me down was doing shit for my front.

Rohan Mitra, rock star turned demon hunter, shook his tousled dark hair, his full lips puckering in obvious disgust. "I'm not putting my finger in there. You want it so badly, do it yourself."

I slammed an elbow into the underside of the vral's jaw, whiplashing her head sideways, intent on keeping the demon's double row of razor-sharp incisors out of my shoulder. One bite and I'd be paralyzed.

And lunch.

"Now you're going to get all pussy about sticking your finger places it doesn't belong?"

"I'll reconsider if she begs as nicely as you did, Nava."

The vral snapped her teeth at me, the sound a loud crack in my ear. Her dank, rotten-meat belch wafted over me.

I tried to plug my nose with my shoulder, my arm muscles straining with the exertion of holding her at bay. "Bite me, Mitra."

He sipped his latte, standing there immaculate and infuriating in a camel-colored trench coat more appropriate to a night at the theater than a demon raid. A raid it turned out that Rohan had no intention of participating in, deeming it "a training exercise for the newbie."

Overhead, a bulb sizzled and popped out, dimming the light and casting almost-romantic shadows over the warped structural beams and grotty walls.

Rohan had the gall to check his watch.

"Don't let me keep you from anything." I shot lightning bolts at the vral from my eyes and she jerked, her weight almost off me. Hand blasts were so level one. I rolled sideways, but the demon crashed back down on top of me. The two of us tumbled into the shadows.

"Then finish her," he said.

"I'm trying but I don't think she's into me that way."

Rohan took another sip. "Make her want it."

Continued grappling with the demon wasn't going to get me anywhere other than exhausted and then dead. Fine, mostly dead. Rohan wouldn't let me be unequivocally taken out.

I wove an electric net around the vral's body, temporarily paralyzing her with my magic so I could scramble free. My problem? The only way to permanently stop a demon involved hitting their weak spot. My other problem? There was a different spot for each demon. With vral, it was their left eye. As in the one that bulged jiggling out toward me from her socket, laden with pus. "If I blast her eyeball, demon goo will splooge everywhere."

"Always about the hard and messy," he chastised. "Gentle has its place, too, you know."

The vral, who I'd thought was still suffering the effects of the paralysis, lashed her tail around my arm. Surprise. What looked like smooth fur was actually dozens of tiny barbs. I wrenched free, my stomach heaving at the sight of my arm that now looked like raw hamburger. I blasted the demon in the chest, snapping at Rohan, "Have it at. Gently use one of your blades to puncture–Son-of-a-bitch!"

The vral convulsed under the sharp crackle of my power, locking onto me in a spasming hug, her claws shredding my sweater. Eight bleeding gashes were not my idea of body adornment.

The air stank of sizzling fur, which was still a step up from the stale B.O. and garbage juice that had seeped into the walls of this squatter's paradise.

"Stop acting from the flight part of your brain and go to the fight," Rohan said.

Thrashing on the floor, I squeezed my eyes shut against the blood and sweat dripping into them. The vral's claws remained burrowed into my back. "What do you think I'm doing?"

"Napping? Baruch trained you better than this."

Yeah, for three whole weeks. Muttering an anatomically impossible suggestion Rohan's way, I pulled out a self-defense move that Baruch had drilled into me. Before the demon's tremors could subside, I wrapped my right leg around her left foreleg to trap it, curling my right arm over the same side of her body in a tight overhook. My fingers dug deeper into her wiry, scorched fur, hitting something squishy that was matted into her side.

Please don't let that be leftover homeless person from her earlier meal.

I planted my left foot firmly on the floor, bridging up, my hips exploding into the air. The combination of that momentum, along with the pull/push dual action of my arms as I chopped my left hand into the demon allowed me to swing on top of her.

"That's a start," Rohan said.

Snarling, the vral bucked me off like a seasoned rodeo bull. I flew onto my ass, then scrambled to my feet, panting, my right foot buckling as I stumbled backwards over a piece of fallen ceiling tile.

Rohan tsked me. "We're Fallen Angels, not Falling Angels. Try to stay on your feet." In a display of rampant egotism, my fellow all-male hunters had dubbed themselves Fallen Angels. I'd graciously been extended the label.

"You're hilarious."

"I am rather," he replied in a put-on posh British accent that intoxicated me like a shot of liquid sex. He gestured to the trash-strewn floor. "Be aware of your surroundings," he directed, in his normal voice that was all smoky baritone and velvet Californian curls. "Garbage can be your downfall."

I flung a damp lock of curly dark brown hair out of my face.

The vral scrambled back onto all fours, shaking out her fur like she was waking from a nap. Then the man-eating little fucker lunged and sank her two rows of teeth into the toes of my boots.

Steel-toed, but still. These babies were new. Very expensive. Who knew it was such a challenge to find badass boots with reinforced steel, a chunky heel that was far more practical to run in than stilettos, and silver buckles running up the side? It was my consolation gift to myself for having my lovely life of partying, sex, and naps getting shot to hell with the recent discovery that I was the first female Rasha, or demon hunter. I'd been reluctantly inducted into the Brotherhood of David, a dick-swinging secret organization. Yeah, they weren't thrilled to have their first vag-sporter either.

The vral's eyes locked onto mine. She gave a chittered cackle, her teeth cracking deeper into the leather.

My old tap dance mantra popped into my head. A one, a two, you know what to do. Nothing to it but to do it. I blasted the vral's eyeball, shielding myself with a ceiling tile against the putrid pus arcing out of her like a Tarantino kill. The splatter guard worked well, with only a few drops of warm liquid hitting my cheek. It tingled but nothing got in my eyes or mouth so score one, Nava. Which tipped into score the second as the demon death throe'd down to a single nubbin of fur.

The faintest scuff of claws on metal was our only clue that another demon was present. It flew off an overhead pipe, claws outstretched and the fur on its back raised. A baby vral, much smaller in size, but still deadly.

Before I even had time to gasp, Rohan's hand shot up, one wicked sharp blade extended from his index finger, the movement pulling his coat tight around his astoundingly well-defined shoulders. His magic allowed him to do that party trick with all his fingers, not to mention extend a blade that ran the length of his body like an outline. One time I'd asked him why his clothes didn't get shredded each time he brought out his knives. Maybe I'd said it a little too dejectedly because he'd stopped instructing me on the proper way to punch a chupacabra in the face and raised an amused eyebrow as he said, "It's magic."

He didn't look up when he aimed now, didn't even stop sipping that stupid latte, yet he shish-kabobed the vral right through the neck. Since it wasn't the sweet spot, it wasn't a kill strike, but he still stopped the demon in its tracks.

"Admit it. You're the devil." I trained my eyes on the shadowy corner of this dump but didn't see any other movement.

"Nice to see I've risen in the hierarchy of Hell during our brief acquaintance." With a snap of his wrist, Rohan flicked the demon over to me.

Baby vral plopped at my feet with a wet splat, still quivering.

"Don't say I never give you anything," he said.

"I couldn't possibly accept. You caught it. You kill it."

Rohan waved a hand at me. "I insist."

I toed the baby vral. Hmm. I stood behind it, which meant its eyeballs faced Rohan. "I serve at the pleasure of my commanding officer." Barely hiding my snigger, I nailed its eyeball with a concentrated stream of electricity, killing the demon with a tad too much enthusiastic zeal.

Her entire body exploded. Pus, guts, and fur flew, dousing our immediate area like the splash zone after Shamu bellyflopping at SeaWorld. Her various bits then winked into oblivion like they were supposed to when a demon was offed, but the damage had been done.

Rohan remained pristine. He looked like a god and I looked like the aftermath of a Dumpster fire. A dank, gooey, Dumpster fire of demon pus. Awesome.

Acknowledgments

First and foremost, thank you to my two secret weapons without whom, this book would only have amused me. Alex Yuschik, I officially give you rock star editor status. You always understand what I'm trying to do and then push me to go farther and be better. Rudy Thauberger, my "nerd editor" extraordinaire, you are amazing and insightful and I look forward to many more nerd talks with you.

Big thanks to Dr. Marc Nantel for the magic chats, Ita Margalit for reading this and saying that she enjoyed it like a real book and not just written by her friend, and Bryn Donovan for her eyes on a very early draft.

To my romance peeps who populate my happy corner of the internet, all the good karma and your favorite things to you. You authors keep me sane, make me laugh, and generously share your wealth of knowledge and experience.

And last, but never ever least, thank you to my husband and daughter for not resorting to physical bodily harm when I'm zoned out at the computer yet again. I love you two crazy, ridiculous amounts.

Get a free download!

If you enjoyed this book, then how about a free short story of a Nava/Rohan demon adventure from Rohan's POV?

Demons and sexytimes, galore! (Book 1.5.)

Go to: http://www.deborahwilde.com/subscribe

Enjoy!

About The Author

I'm Deborah (pronounced deb-O-rah) and I write sexy, funny, urban fantasy.

I decided at an early age to live life like it was a movie, as befitted a three-syllable girl. Mine features exotic locales, an eclectic soundtrack, and a glittering cast–except for those two guys left on the cutting room floor. Secret supernatural societies may be involved.

They say you should write what you know, which is why I shamelessly plagiarize my life to write about witty, smart women who kick-ass, stand toe-to-toe against infuriating alphas, and execute any bad decisions in indomitable style.

Catch me at:
www.deborahwilde.com
Twitter: @wildeauthor
FB: www.facebook.com/DeborahWildeAuthor

"It takes a bad girl to fight evil. Go Wilde."

CPSIA information can be obtained
at www.ICGtesting.com
Printed in the USA
LVOW03s1826060418
572590LV00001B/21/P